PORTO BELLO
GOLD

Nautical Fiction
Published by McBooks Press

BY ALEXANDER KENT
Midshipman Bolitho
Stand into Danger
In Gallant Company
Sloop of War
To Glory We Steer
Command a King's Ship
Passage to Mutiny
With All Despatch
Form Line of Battle!
Enemy in Sight!

BY CAPTAIN FREDERICK MARRYAT
Frank Mildmay OR The Naval Officer
The King's Own
Mr Midshipman Easy
Newton Forster OR The Merchant Service

BY NICHOLAS NICASTRO
The Eighteenth Captain

BY W. CLARK RUSSELL
Wreck of the Grosvenor

BY RAFAEL SABATINI
Captain Blood

BY MICHAEL SCOTT
Tom Cringle's Log

BY A.D. HOWDEN SMITH
Porto Bello Gold

PORTO BELLO GOLD

by
A.D. Howden Smith

CLASSICS OF NAUTICAL FICTION SERIES

McBOOKS PRESS
ITHACA, NEW YORK

Published by McBooks Press 1999
Copyright © 1924 by Arthur D. Howden Smith
Copyright renewed © 1948 by Dorothy D. Smith
First published by Brentano's 1924

Book and cover design by Paperwork.
Cover painting by Howard Pyle.

Library of Congress Cataloging-in-Publication Data

Smith, Arthur D. Howden (Arthur Douglas Howden), 1887-1945.
    Porto Bello gold / by A.D. Howden Smith.
        p.   cm. — (Classics of nautical fiction)
    Prequel to: Treasure Island / Robert Louis Stevenson.
    ISBN 0-935526-57-9
    I. Stevenson, Robert Louis, 1850-1894. Treasure Island.
    II. Title. III. Series: Classics of nautical fiction series.
    PS3537.M278P6   1999
    813'.52—dc21

                                        99-14322
                                        CIP

Distributed to the book trade by
Login Trade, 1436 West Randolph, Chicago, IL 60607
800-626-4330.

Additional copies of this book may be ordered from any bookstore or directly from McBooks Press, 120 West State Street, Ithaca, NY 14850. Please include $3.00 postage and handling with mail orders. New York State residents must add 8% sales tax. All McBooks Press publications can also be ordered by calling toll-free 1-888-BOOKS11 (1-888-266-5711). Please call to request a free catalog.

Visit the McBooks Press website at http://www.McBooks.com.

Printed in the United States of America

9 8 7 6 5 4 3 2 1

TO R. L. S.

Oh, Tusitala, you who lie
"Under the wide and starry sky"
On that Samoan hill,
Think not this wretched, miswrought tale
Is meant to breast the thundering gale
Of your great art and skill—
As well the humble trading bark
Might sail to cloudland with the lark!
Be patient, sir, until
We meet on some far height of dreams
And I explain just why it seems
John Silver's with us still,
And all the raffish, ruffian crew
That you and young Jim Hawkins knew—
They burst Time's dungeon-grill!

Fenley Hunter, Esq.,
Flushing, N. Y.
Dear Fen:

You are responsible for some of the incidents in this roaring yarn, and for that and other reasons it should be inscribed to you—who, in your own person, lead a life as swaggeringly varied from the existence of office, home and country-club as any character I have created between these covers. If it detains you from the out-trail for a night or two, persuades you to sample the pleasures of the sheltered hearth, I shall be rewarded.

Yours,
King Arthur.
Babylon, N. Y.,
Feb. 9, 1924.

CHAPTER I

MY FATHER'S SECRET

I WAS IN the counting-room, talking with Peter Corlaer, the chief of our fur-traders—he was that very day come down-river from the Iroquois country—when the boy, Darby, ran in from the street.

"The Bristol packet is in, Master Robert," he cried. "And, oh, sir, the watermen do say there be a pirate ship off the Hook!"

I remember I laughed at the combination of awe and delight in his face. He was a raw, bog-trotting bit of a gossoon we had bought at the last landing of bonded folk, and he talked with a brogue that thickened whenever he grew excited.

"For the packet, I do not doubt you, Darby," I answered. "But you must show me the pirate."

Peter Corlaer chuckled in his quiet, rumbling way, his huge belly waggling before him beneath his buckskin hunting-shirt, for all the world like a monster mold of jelly.

"*Ja, ja,* show us der pirates," he jeered.

Darby flared up in a burst of Irish temper that matched his tangled red hair.

"I would I were a pirate and had you at my mercy, you butter-tub!" he raged. "I'll warrant you'd tread the plank!"

Peter gravely unsheathed his hunting-knife, seized Darby's flaming locks and despite his wriggles went through the motions of scalping him.

"If I tread der plank, first I take your hair, *ja,*" he commented.

"Not if I had my growth," snapped Darby.

"T'ree growths you must get to fight me, Darby," rejoined Peter placidly. "You better ask Mr. Ormerod dot he let you come with me into the Iroquois country. We make a forest-runner out of you—*ja!* Dot's better than a pirate."

Darby contemplated this, drawing a circle on the floor with the toe of one boot.

"No," he decided finally. "I'd rather be a pirate. I know nothing of your forest, but the sea—ah, that's the life for me! And sure, a pirate has more of traveling and adventure than a forest-runner, with none but red savages and wild beasts to combat. No, no, Master Peter, I am for the pirates, and I care not how soon it may be."

"It will be long, not soon, Darby," said I. "Have you done the errands my father set you?"

"Every one," answered he.

"Very well. Then get you into the store-room and sort over the pelts Peter fetched in. Even a pirate must work."

He flung off with a scowl as I turned to Peter.

"My father will wish to know the packet has arrived," I said. "Will you go with me to the Governor's? The Council must be on the point of breaking up, for they have been sitting since noon."

Peter heaved his enormous body erect. And I marveled, as always after a period of absence, at his proportions. To one who did not know him he seemed a butter-tub of a man, as Darby had called him—a mass of tallow, fat limbs, a pork-barrel of a trunk, a fat slab of a face upon which showed tiny, insignificant features grotesquely at variance with the rest of his bulk. His little eyes peered innocently between rolls of fat which all but masked them. His nose was a miniature dab, above a mouth a child might have owned.

But under his layers of blubber were concealed muscles of forged steel, and he was capable of the agility of a catamount. The man had not lived on the frontier who could face him bare-handed and escape.

"*Ja,*" he said simply. "We go."

He stood his musket in a corner and slipped off powder-horn and shot-pouch the while I donned hat and greatcoat, for the air was still chilly and there was a scum of snow on the ground. We passed out into Pearl Street and walked westward to Hanover Square, and there on the farther side of the Square I spied my father, with Governor Clinton and Lieutenant-Governor Colden.

And it made my heart warm to see how these and several other

gentlemen hung upon his words. There had been those who slan-
dered him during the uproar over the '45, for he was known to have
been a Jacobite in his youth; but his friends were more powerful than
his enemies, and I joy to think that he was not the least influential
of those of our leaders who held New York loyal to King George
when many were for casting in our fortunes with the Pretender.

He saw Peter and me as we approached and waved us to him, but
at the same moment there was a slight disturbance on the eastward
side of the Square, and another little group of men came into view
surrounding a grizzled, ruddy-cheeked old fellow, whose salt-stained
blue coat spoke as eloquently of the sea as did his rolling gait. I could
hear his hoarse, roaring voice clear across the Square—

"—ran him tops'ls down; —— my eyes, I did; and when I get to
port what do I find, but not a King's ship within—"

My father interrupted him:

"What's this, Captain Farraday? Do you speak of being chased? I
had thought we were at peace with the world."

Captain Farraday discarded the listeners who had attended him so
far and stumped across the Square, bellowing his answer in tones
which brought shopkeepers to their doors and women's heads from
upper windows.

"Chased? That I was, Master Ormerod, by as ——, scoundrelly a
pirate as flouts the King's majesty i' the—"

Here he perceived who accompanied my father. Off came his hat,
and he made an awkward bow.

"Your sarvent, your Excellency! My duty, Master Colden! But I have
no words to withdraw, for all I did not see who was near by to hear
me. Aye, there is more to be said, much more; and matters have come
to a pretty pass when the rascals come north to these ports."

Peter Corlaer and I joined the little group of merchants who were
with the Governor, and the other curious persons hovered as close
as they dared.

"But I find this hard to give credence to, captain," said Governor
Clinton pleasantly enough. "Pirates? In these latitudes? We have not
been bothered by such of late."

Captain Farraday wagged his head stubbornly.

"That's true enough, I grant your Excellency; and since the peace we have not been bothered by French privateers, neither. But the day'll come we fight the French again, and then the letters of marque will be scouring the Atlantic north and south. And by the same token, sir, I bid you remember the pirates are always with us, and clever devils they are, too; for if they find their trade falling off in one part they are away at once elsewhere. And the first you know of them is a score of missing ships and a mariner like myself lucky enough to give them the slip."

"You may be right," acknowledged the Governor. "Tell us more of your experience. Did you have sight of the ship which pursued you?"

"Sight? Marry, that I did; and uncomfortable close, your Excellency. She came up with a so'easter two days past, and at the first I made her out for a frigate by the top-hamper she carried."

"A frigate?" protested Master Colden. "So big as that?"

"Aye, sir, my master! And if I have any eye for a ship's lines and canvas she was none other than the *Royal James* that chased me three days together when I was home-bound from the West Indies in '43."

"That would be the vessel of the fellow known usually as Captain Rip-Rap," spoke up my father, and there was a quality in his voice which led me to regard him closely.

It was manifest that he labored in the grip of some strong emotion; but the only indication of this in his face was a slight rigidity of feature, and none of the others marked it. I was the more amazed because my father was a man of iron nerves, and also, though his earlier year had been starred with a series of extraordinary adventures, so far as I knew, he had had nothing to do with the sea.

"True for you, Master Ormerod," answered Captain Farraday; "and since Henry Morgan died there hath not lived a more complete rogue. One of my mates was taken by him off Jamaica ten years gone and cites him for a man of exquisite dress and manners that would befit a London macaroni, God save us! And moreover, is as arrant a Jacobite as ever was. Witness the name of his ship."

"I have heard he sails usually in company," remarked my father.

"He works with John Flint, who is no less of a rascal, albeit rougher, according to those unfortunates who have fallen in his path. Flint sails in the *Walrus,* a tall ship out of Plymouth that was on the Smyrna run before she fell into his hands. Betwixt them they are a pretty pair.

"Did you ever hear, gentles, how they sank the Portuguese line-ship off Madeira for naught but the pleasure o' destruction? Aye, so they did. They ha' the metal to hammer a brace of King's ships. But they are wary of such.

"Portuguese, Frenchies, Spaniards or Barbary corsairs they will assail, but they will not stop for a powder-blow with his Majesty's people. Why? I know not, save 'tis never for lack o' daring. Mayhap they know if they ever did my Lords of the Admiralty, that take small account of the sufferings of us poor merchantmen—always saving your Excellency's presence—would be stirred to loose a fleet of stout frigates against 'em."

Captain Farraday stopped perforce for breath, and Governor Clinton seized the opportunity to ask with a smile:

"Captain Rip-Rap did you call your pursuer? What manner of name is this?"

The merchantman shrugged his shoulders.

"Nobody knows, sir. But 'tis the only name he goes by. I ha' heard that years past—oh, it may be twenty or more—he stopped a home-bound Chesapeake packet, and when the master was haled aboard the first question he asked was 'did he have any rip-rap in his cargo?' For it seems he is singularly partial to that mixture of snuff. And now, I ha' been told, his own men give him this name, for even they do not know for certain that to which he was born.

"'Tis said he was a gentleman who suffered for his political con-victions, but that is as like to be a lie as the truth. All I know is that he chased me in past the Hook, though the *Anne* showed him a clean pair o' heels and had run him tops'ls down wi' sunrise this morning. And when I made the harbor, 'twas to find there was not a King's ship to send after him."

"Yes," nodded the Governor; "the *Thetis* frigate sailed for home with dispatches a week ago. But I will send express to Boston where Commodore Burrage lies and bid him get to sea without loss of time. I sympathize with your feelings, Master Farraday, and certes, 'tis beyond toleration that such scoundrels as Rip-Rap and Flint should be per-mitted to flout his Majesty's Government so openly. Doubt not, our good commodore will make them rue the day."

"But doubt it I must, your Excellency," returned Captain Farraday with sturdy independence. "An express to Boston, say you? Humph! That will require two days or three. Another day to put to sea. Two days, or it may be three, to beat south. Why, my masters, in a week's time Rip-Rap and Flint will have wrought whatever fiendish purpose they have in view and be off beyond reach."

"Mayhap, mayhap," said the Governor with a touch of impatience. "But 'tis the best I can do."

And with Lieutenant-Governor Colden and the rest he made to move off. Only my father lingered.

"You have letters for me, Captain Farraday?" he asked.

"Aye, indeed, sir—from Master Allen, your agent in London. I was on my way to deliver 'em. And a goodly store of strouds, axes, knives, beads, tools, flints and other tradegoods to your account."

"I will accept the letters at your hands, and even save you the trip to Pearl Street, captain," replied my father. "My son, Robert, here, will visit you aboardship in the morning and take measures to arrange for transshipping your cargo."

"I ha' no quarrel with such terms," rejoined Captain Farraday, fishing a silken-wrapped packet from his coat-tail pocket. "Here you are, Master Ormerod. And I'll be off to the George Tavern for a bite of shore food and a mug of mulled ale."

My father fidgeted the packet in his hands for a moment.

"You are certain 'twas Captain Rip-Rap who chased you?" he asked then.

"I'd swear to his foretops'ls," answered Farraday confidently. "Mark you, my master, when I first sighted him I made sure he was a King's ship, and I lay to until he was abeam. Then I saw he showed no colors—and moreover, there was that about him, which I'll own I can not put a name to, made me suspicious. So I hoisted colors. And still he showed none. I fired a gun, and wi' that he bore up for me, and I made off, wi' every sail set; aye, until the sticks groaned. For I knew he was up to no good purpose, and I made certain that he was Rip-Rap.

"As I said afore, he chased me once in '43, and Jenkins he took off Jamaica in the snow *Cynthia* out o' Southampton, when Flint was for drowning the lot o' them; but Rip-Rap, in his cold way, says there was no point to slaying without purpose, and they turned 'em loose in the longboat. And there's none left 'on the Account' that sail in a great ship fit to be a King's frigate, save it be Rip-Rap—Flint's *Walrus* is a tall ship and heavy armed, but hath not the sail-spread o' the *Royal James*. Jen-kins says *she* was a Frenchman, and 'tis to be admitted she hath the fine-run lines the Frenchies build."

My father was hard put to it to make head against this flow of talk, but at last he succeeded.

"It was my understanding," he said, "that Captain Rip-Rap disappeared from the West Indies during the late war."

Captain Farraday shrugged his shoulders.

"Like enough. There were too many cruisers o' both sides at large in those seas to suit him. But now he knows we ha' back the piping times of peace—and when nations are at peace your pirates reap their harvest. You may lay to that, Master Ormerod."

"'Tis not to be questioned," assented my father. "I give you thanks, captain. Pray call upon me at your leisure, and if I can be of any service to you I am at your command."

Captain Farraday stumped off toward the George, a tail of the curious at his heels, and I grinned to myself at thought of the strong drink they would offer him in return for his tale. There was no chance of his being sober inside the twenty-four hours.

My father nodded absently to Peter, who had stood throughout the entire conversation, his flat face sleepily imperturbable.

"I like it not," he muttered, as if to himself.

Peter gave him a quick look but said nothing.

"Is there anything wrong, father?" I asked.

He frowned at me, then stared off at the housetops in a way he had, almost as if he sought to peer beyond the future.

"No—yes—I do not know."

He broke off abruptly.

"Peter, I am glad you are here," he added.

"*Ja,*" said Peter vacantly.

"You have not looked at your letters yet," I reminded him.

"I have no occasion to," he retorted. "There is that which—But the street is no place for such conversation. Come home, my boy; come home."

We set off over the snowy ground, and the people we passed bowed or bobbed their heads to my father, for he was a great man in New York, as great as any after the Governor; but he walked now with his eyes upon the ground, immersed in thought. And once again as we turned into Pearl Street he muttered—

"Nay, I like it not."

Darby McGraw met us at the door, and from his wild gaze I knew him to be half-expecting to behold the pirates hotfoot at our heels.

"Have you performed your tasks, Darby?" questioned my father as the lad backed into the counting-room on the right of the entrance hall.

"Yes, master."

"Be off with you, then. I wish not to be disturbed."

"See can you find us late news of the pirates, Darby," I added as he slipped by.

He answered me with a merry scowl, but my father spun on his heel.

"What mean you by that, Robert?" says he.

I was nonplussed.

"Why, naught, sir. Darby is daft on pirates. He—"

Peter Corlaer shut the room-door upon the Irish boy and came toward us, moving with the swift stealth that was one of his most astonishing characteristics.

"*Ja*, he does not know," he said.

"What?" challenged my father.

"What you andt I know," returned the Dutchman calmly.

"So you know too, Peter?"

"*Ja*."

I could restrain my impatience no longer.

"What is this mystery?" I demanded. "I thought I knew all the secrets of the business; but sure, father, I never thought to hear that we were concerned as a firm with pirates!"

"We are not," my father answered curtly. "This is a matter of which you know nothing, Robert, because until now there has been no occasion for you to know of it."

He hesitated.

"Peter," he went on, "must we tell the boy?"

"He is not a boy; he is a man," said Peter.

I flashed my gratitude to the fat Dutchman in a smile, but he paid me no attention. My father, too, seemed to forget me. He strode up and down the counting-room, hands under the skirts of his coat, head bowed in thought. Tags of phrases escaped his lips:

"I had thought him dead—Strange, if he bobs up again—Here is a problem I had never thought to face—Mayhap I exaggerate—it cannot have significance for us—Certes, it must be accident—"

"*Neen*, he comes for a purpose," interrupted Peter.

My father stayed his walk in front of Peter by the fireplace wherein blazed a heap of elm logs.

"Who do you fancy this Captain Rip-Rap to be, Peter? Speak up! You were right when you said Robert is no longer a boy. If there is danger here, he deserves to know of it!"

"He is Murray," replied Corlaer, his squeaking voice an incongruous contrast with his immense bulk.

"Andrew Murray!" mused my father. "Aye, 'twould be he. I have suspected it all these years—held it for certainty. But I made sure when he failed to show himself after the last war that Providence had attended to him. It seems I was wrong."

"Whoever he is, this pirate can not do harm to us in New York," I made bold to say.

"Be not too sure, Robert," adjured my father. "He happens to be your great-uncle."

He reached up to the rack over the fireplace and selected a long clay pipe, which he stuffed with tobacco the while I was recovering from my astonishment.

"Your uncle?" I gasped then.

Corlaer hauled forward a couple of chairs, and we all sat in the circle of the firelight, my father on one side of me and Peter on the other. The evening was drawing on apace, and the room was aswarm with shadows a few feet from the hearth. My father stared long into the leaping heart of the flames before he answered me.

"No; your mother's," he said finally.

"But he was the great trader who conducted the contraband trade with Canada!" I cried. "I have heard of him. 'Twas he established the Doom Trail to enable him to supply the French fur-traders with goods to wean the far savages from us! You have told me of him yourself, as hath Master Colden. 'Twas he whom you and Corlaer and the Iroquois fought when you broke down the barriers of the Doom Trail and won back the fur-trade for our people. Why, 'twas then you—you—"

I knew the deep feeling my father still had for my long-dead mother, and I scrupled to stir his memories. He himself took the words from my lips.

"Yes, 'twas then I came to love your mother. She—she was not such as you would expect to find allied by any ties with so great a scoundrel. But she was his niece—past doubt, Robert. She was a Kerr of Fernieside; her mother had been Murray's sister. Kerr and Murray were out together in the '15; Kerr fell at Sheriffmuir. His widow died not long afterward, and Murray took poor waif Marjory.

"He did well by her—there's no denying that. But he always intended to use her to further his own designs. He had a cold eye for the future, with no thought except of his own advantage, and if I—But there's no need to go into that. You know, Robert, how Corlaer and the Seneca chief, Tawannears—he who is now the Guardian of the Western Door of the Long House—and I were able to smash the vast power Murray had built up on the frontier.

"We smashed him so utterly, discrediting him too withal, that he was obliged to flee the province; and even his friends, the French, would have none of him—at least, aboveboard. I have always fancied he still served their interests at large; for he is at bottom a most fanatical Jacobite, and eke sincere in a queer, twisted way. Aye, there is that about him which is difficult to understand, Robert. Himself, he hath no hesitation in believing he serves high purposes of state in all he does."

"But a pirate!" I exclaimed.

"Oh, that is nothing to him!"

"Not'ing," agreed Peter. "He was a pirate on der landt."

"Only a madman could lay claim to serving the State as a pirate," I objected.

"You speak with overconfidence," rebuked my father. "There are men alive today who can remember when Morgan and Davis and Dampier and many another brave fellow of the same kidney lived by piracy and served the King at one and the same time. Some of 'em were hung in the end, and Morgan died a knight. It can be done."

"How?"

"Consider, my boy! Murray—your great-uncle, mind you!—is a Jacobite. For our present Government be hath only hatred and contempt. Any means by which that Government was undermined would seem to him justifiable as aiding to bring about its downfall. Look to the fantastic humor of the man in naming his ship the *Royal James!*"

"If he be, indeed, the man you think he is," I returned, none too well pleased with the thought of having a pirate for a great-uncle. My father laughed kindly, and tapped me on the knee with his free hand.

"I know how you feel, dear lad," he said. "'Twas so identically your mother talked. Bless her heart! We were fresh married when the precious rascal sent us by one of his tarry-breeks that necklace which lies now in my strongbox—the loot of some Indian queen mayhap. Afterward—after she had died—when you were scarce breeched— he sent again; those silver plates upon the sideboard in the dining-room. Dishonestly come by, of course; but what was I to do? I could not cast them in the river, nor did I know how to return them to him. And after that again came a third messenger, this time with no more than a letter in which he condoled with me upon the loss of her whom we had both reverenced above all others!

"Then, I admit, I could have strangled him, for had he been successful in his plans he would have mated her with a Frenchman who was servant to the Foul Fiend. Yet in his way he cared for her, and he took much interest in all she did. By hook or crook he had word of us, however far he wandered. He knew when you were born. He knew when she died. And now that you have reached manhood he shows his sails outside Sandy Hook. I do not know what it means, Robert, but I like it not! I like it not!"

"But we are not at sea," I protested. "We are in New York. There are soldiers in Fort George. Commodore Burrage will be down from Boston anon. What can a pirate ship, what can two pirate ships, effect against us? Why, the city train-bands—"

"'Tis not force I dread," my father cut me off. "'Tis the infernal cleverness of a warped mind."

"*Ja,*" agreed Peter.

My father thrust the stem of his pipe toward him.

"You feel it, too, old friend?" he cried then.

"If Murray is here he means no goodt," the Dutchman answered ponderously. "No pirate comes nort' in der coldt weather for just fun. *Neen!* Here is too much danger; no places to run andt hide."

"Aye, you have the right of it," assented my father. "And there have been those who claimed New York town was not so innocent of pirates as might appear upon the surface. Murray and his like must sell the goods they steal, and to that end they require connections with traders here and elsewhere. In Governor Burnet's time we used to watch the Whale's Head Tavern and other like hang-outs of the more desperate sort, but I am bound to admit we caught no bigger game than an occasional mutineer or deserter. Yet I know there are merchants in the town none too particular in their dealings, and not every ship that makes port is as peaceful as she seems by any means."

"At the least, sir, we are on the alert," I said.

My father laughed, and Corlaer's ridiculous, simpering giggle echoed his grim mirth.

"An intelligent foe discounts so much upon launching his venture," my father answered. "Let us hope we have a modicum of luck to aid us. Whatever plan Murray hath in trend 'twill come to us unexpected and adroit in execution. But tush. There's the dinner-bell. A truce to foreboding!"

CHAPTER II

THE ONE-LEGGED MAN AND THE IRISH MAID

THE NEXT morning I was occupied for several hours in checking over the needs of our trading-stations with Peter Corlaer, so that it was the middle of the forenoon before I was able to leave the counting-room to go aboard Captain Farraday's ship and concert with her people the lightering of that portion of the cargo which was destined for our warehouse.

Darby McGraw eyed me so wistfully when I took my hat that I sent him to the kitchen to secure a bag of fresh-killed chickens and Winter greens, knowing such food would be welcome to sailors after a long voyage, and bade him carry it to the dock. He was as pleased as if he had been presented with his freedom, and skipped along whistling like a skylark.

We walked down Pearl Street to Broad Street, where the landing-basin indents the land; and I was passing on, with intent to secure a wherry from the foot of Whitehall Street to row me out to the Bristol packet, when Darby drew my attention to the soaring masts and tangled cordage of a great ship lying at anchor in the East River anchorage.

"'Tis a frigate, Master Robert!" he exclaimed.

There was no mistaking the rows of painted gun-ports and the solid bulwarks; and for a moment I fancied Commodore Burrage had anticipated our needs. Then the flag at her mizzen truck rippled out, and I beheld the red-and-gold banner of Spain.

"D'ye suppose he hath come after the pirate?" whispered Darby, all agog.

"Not he," I answered, laughing. "'Tis a Spaniard, and he and his kidney are not hungry for pirate gore, Darby."

"Whisht, but if he would only make to shoot off a cannon or two!" sighed Darby. "Or maybe hang a poor soul at the yardarm the while we watched. Oh, Master Robert, wouldn't it be grand?"

"Go to," said I, laughing again at the quaint fancies of the lad. "You are as bloodthirsty as any pirate that sails the Spanish Main."

"I'll warrant you I am," returned Darby sturdily. "I'd be a grand pirate, I would—and I'd make naught of frigates, be they Spaniard or King's ship; aye, or Frenchies. I'd take 'em all!"

"Certes, you would," I agreed. "But look, Darby! There's another strange vessel—beyond the frigate."

I pointed to a battered little brig with patched and dirty sails and a spatter of white showing in her black-painted hull where a round-shot had sent the splinters flying.

"And he hath seen the pirates, or I am amiss," I added. "His escape must have been exceeding narrow."

Darby's eyes waxed as large as a cat's in the dark.

"Whirra, whirra, do but look to the shot-hole in the side of him! 'Tis he will have made a noble prayer. And now will ye mock me for saying there are pirates abroad, Master Robert?"

"Not I, Darby. Yon fellow has been closer to death than I like to think of," I answered.

"Now there was as true a word as ever was heard spoke," proclaimed a pleasant voice behind me. "And shows most unaccountable understanding and humanitee, so it do, seeing as there's precious few landsmen as stop to figger out the chances a poor sailor must take and never a thankee from his owners nor aught but curses from his skipper, like as not. True as true, young gentleman. I makes you my duty, and says as how, seeing I was one of them vouchsafed a miraculous salvation, I hopes you'll permit me to offer my most humble thanks."

I swung around to scrutinize the owner of the voice and saw a handsome, open-faced man in the prime of life, big and strong of his body, but with only one leg. The other, the left, had been lopped off high up near the hip, and he supported himself upon a long crutch of very fine-carved hardwood—mahogany, I afterward discovered. This crutch he employed with all the dexterity of his missing limb. A thong from a hole under the armpiece was looped around his neck, so that when he chose to sit down his support could never fall out of his reach; and in its butt was set a sharp spur of steel to give it a grip upon rough ground or slippery decks.

While I looked at him and he was first speaking he hopped up beside me with a confidential air that was very flattering to a young man and impressed Darby even more than it did me.

"Are you from the brig yonder?" I asked curiously.

"Aye, aye, young gentleman, I am; and one of the miserable sinners as was saved by an inscrootable Providence as takes no account o' men's deserts, just or unjust, as the preachers' sayin' is. Out of Barbaders, I am, in the brig *Constant*. Name o' Silver, sir—John, says my sponsors in baptism.

"But my mates most generally calls me 'Barbecue' 'count o' my being held a monstrous fine cook. And there's a tale to that, young sir. Ah, yes! This weren't the first time I suffered at the hands o' them pirates that scourge and ravage the seas to the despite of poor, honest sailormen."

He lowered his voice.

"D'ye see this lopsided carcass of mine now? You do, says you. Yes, yes; there ain't no mistakin' a one-legged man. And how do you suppose I lost my left stick, eh? Can't say, says you—nor it ain't strange, seein' as we've never met afore this.

"Well, I'll tell ye, sir. You ha' a young face, and kind, and I can see you take an interest in an unfortunate sailorman's sorrows—aye, and this good lad wi' ye, too—from Ireland, ain't ye, my hearty? I knowed it, I knowed it!

"But what was I a-sayin'? Oh, yes, to be sure. I was tellin' ye of my lost leg—and glad I am it wasn't my flipper as went. 'Cause why, says you? 'Cause a man can set himself to makin' good a lost leg, which ain't no use for nothin' except walking.

"But a hand now? Figger it out, my master! No hand, and ye can't work, ye can't fight, ye can't scarcely eat. That's why I says I'm lucky."

The man attracted me by his originality, and I own frankly I would have pressed him for further information whether Darby had been with me or not; but 'twas Darby brought him back to the main point of interest.

"Did ye see the pirates?" panted the lad in excitement.

John Silver drew himself erect upon his crutch and frowned out at the shot-scarred brig.

"See 'em?" he repeated. "Well now, my lad, that depends. Aye, aye, it all depends.

"This last time, d'ye mean? No, I can't conscientiously say I seen 'em this time. In the matter o' my leg 'twas different—and the time Flint marooned me."

"You know Flint then?" I broke in upon him.

He shook his head.

"Know him? Oh, no, young gentleman; I don't know no bloody villains like that. I ha' seen 'em, yes—a sight too many of 'em as ye might say. And suffered most terrible at their hands; but I make no doubt the Lord is decided I ha' suffered my portion, seein' that this last time

He delivered me safe and sound out o' the scoundrels' hands."

"Was it off Sandy Hook they attacked you?" I inquired.

"Off Sandy Hook?" he repeated. "Maybe 'twas so, young gentleman. We took small reckoning o' where we were. Our one thought was to make port whole and safe."

"But I see they hulled you?" I pressed him.

"That?" he answered. "Oh, yes; but—May I make bold to ask, sir, ha' other vessels been chased off New York port, do you know?"

I pointed to where Captain Farraday's craft swung at her anchor a scant quarter-mile above the brig.

"That Bristol packet ran the notorious Captain Rip-Rap tops'ls down but yester-morning," I told him.

His brows knit together in a frown, apparently of thought.

"Captain Rip-Rap you says it was! Blister me, young gentleman, but that's dreadful news. Well, well, well! A fortunate escape as ever was. And 'tis good hearing that others was ekal lucky. But I dare say the King's ships will be after him by now?"

"No, there's none nearer than Boston," I answered.

"'Twill be a week at the least before we can hunt the scoundrels hence."

He wagged his head dolefully.

"Blister me, but that's ill news. Fortunate, indeed, I was to draw clear. He was after me till darkness and sheered off more in fear o' the sands than for aught else, I dare swear."

"So it was yesterday he chased you?" I asked.

"To be sure, young sir. Wasn't that what I told ye? Yesterday, about the noon glass, he came a-thunderin' up, and towards dusk he could bring his bow-chasers to bear, and was for droppin' a spar to hinder us. But we took his shot in the hull, as ye see, and got off safe in spite of all he could do."

One of the wherrymen was sculling toward us along the shore, and I waved to him to pull under the piling on which we stood.

"I must be off," I said. "I congratulate you, Master Silver, on your escape. Whatever dangers you may have encountered in the past, your good luck was with you yesterday."

He bobbed his head and pulled at his forelock.

"Thank'ee kindly, young gentleman. Here, sir, let me catch the painter. Right! Will ye ha' the basket on the thwart by ye? And this nice lad here, doesn't he go, too? No?

"Maybe then ye'd add a mite to your kindness and let me borry his time for a half-glass or so for to show me a couple o' landmarks I must make in the town. I wouldn't ask it of ye, sir, only as ye see, I'm half-crippled in a manner o' speakin', and this is a strange port to me, as plies usual to the West Injies."

"Use the lad by all means," I answered. "Darby, take Master Silver wherever he wishes to go."

Darby's freckled face gleamed at the prospect of more of the company of this one-legged sailorman, who talked so easily of pirate fights and flights.

"Oh, aye, Master Robert," says he. "I'll help him all I know."

"O' course he will," spoke up Silver. "I never seed a boy wit a kinder face. A kind face means a kind heart, I always says, young gentleman."

My wherryman was on the point of laying to his oars when a sudden thought caused me to check him.

"By the way, Master Silver," I called, "it occurs to me that perhaps Darby may be unable to serve you in all that you wish. Do you seek any one in especial?"

He hesitated for just the fraction of a minute.

"Why, not especially in particklar, sir," he answered at last. "I am for the Whale's Head Tavern, if ye happen to know o' such a place."

I nodded.

"'Tis in the East Ward close by. Darby can show you."

He shouted renewed thanks and stumped off agilely on his crutch, Darby strutting beside him with a comical pride.

Aboard the *Anne* I found all in confusion. Captain Farraday, as I had expected, had not returned since he landed the preceding afternoon and undoubtedly was sleeping off an accumulation of divers liquors in the George Tavern. The mate had gone ashore that morning to search for him, and would probably take advantage of the opportunity to emulate his skipper's example. Master Jenkins, who had missed drowning at the red hands of the redoubtable Rip-Rap and Flint, was in charge of the ship. He was a melancholy, sour-visaged East-countryman, who moved with a deliberation as pronounced as Peter Corlaer's, and inspecting the manifests with him was a tedious business. I accepted an invitation to share his midday meal, and the afternoon was gone when we concluded our work, agreed upon the time of arrival of the lighters on the morrow and returned to the deck.

My wherry had been dismissed long ago, and he bade the bosun muster a crew to row me ashore. Standing by the gangway, I commented idly upon the two ships which had come in since morning.

"The brig had a close go of it with your friend Rip-Rap," I remarked.

"Aye," returned Jenkins glumly. "'Tis passing queer a Barbadan should be fetching sugar and rum to New York. They leave that mostly to the Yankees."

"True," I admitted; "yet there's an exception to every rule."

A silvery whistle-blast sounded on the deck of the Spanish frigate up-stream.

"Too bad that's not one of ours now," I commented. "Rip-Rap should have a dose of his own medicine."

Master Jenkins expressed utter disapprobation without a wrinkle on his features.

"They Spaniards!" he snorted. "What are they a-doin' here anyway, I'd like to know?"

"He may have been blown north on his crossing," I hazarded.

Master Jenkins snorted a second time.

"He hasn't started a rope. Mischief they're up to. Never knowed it to fail."

"What kind of mischief?" I inquired.

He shrugged his shoulders.

"Not knowin', can't say. But no good ever came from they Spaniards, Master Ormerod, and ye may lay to that."

Before I could answer him the bosun reported the small boat all clear and lying at the ladder-foot, and I bade Master Jenkins a hasty good evening, for his stolid pessimism became mighty irksome upon close acquaintance.

As my boat straightened away from the Bristol packet's side a barge shot around the hull of the Spaniard and pulled after us, a dozen brawny fellows tugging at the oars. A single cloaked figure sat in the stern sheets beside the officer in command. The two boats made the Broad Street slip almost together, and I leaped ashore, tossed several coins to the sailors who had rowed me and started to walk off, bent upon reporting to my father, who, I knew, would be provoked by the length of time my errand had consumed. But I had not walked far when a man called after me from the wharf-head.

"*Señor!* Sirr-rr-rah!"

I turned to face the coxswain of the frigate's barge and a farrago of Spanish gibberish of which I understood not a word. And upon my saying as much, a second person stepped forward into the yellow glow of an oil lanthorn which hung from a bracket upon a warehouse wall hard by. 'Twas the cloaked figure of the barge, and instead of a midshipman or under-officer the scanty light revealed a young woman whose lissome grace was vibrant through the cumbersome folds of her wrap. A single ejaculation of sibilant Spanish, and the coxswain was hushed.

"Sir," said she then in English as good as my own, "can you direct me to the Whale's Head Tavern?"

I could bring forth no better than a stammer in answer. She was the second stranger that day to ask for the Whale's Head, which my father had remarked the previous evening for a noted resort of bad characters; and certes, she appeared to be the last sort of woman who might be expected to have anything to do with the kind of roistering wickedness which went on there. Also, I could not forbear asking myself how came so fair a maid aboard a Spanish frigate.

In the soft lanthorn-light she was anything but Spanish in her looks. Dark, yes, with hair that shone a misty-black, but her eyes were as blue as Darby McGraw's, and her nose had the least suspicion of a tilt to it. Her mouth was wide, with a kind of twist at the ends that quirked up oddly when she laughed and drooped with a sorrow fit to crack open your heart if she wept. And she was little more than a child in years, with a manifest innocence which went oddly with the question she had asked me.

A slim foot tapped impatiently upon the cobbles as I stared.

"Well, sir," she said coldly, "does it happen you do not know English better than Spanish?"

"N-no," I managed to get out. "But—but the truth is, the Whale's Head is no place for such as you, mistress."

Her eyes narrowed.

"I do not catch your meaning, perhaps," she answered. "It is my father I go to meet there."

"But he would never favor your coming there at this hour," I protested.

She permitted herself a trill of laughter.

"You speak as if you had full knowledge of his ways," she admitted. "But the nuns at St. Bridget's were telling me oft and oft how I was going out into the wicked world, and sorra a look at wickedness have I had yet. So I decided this evening I should have some savor of adventure to make up for being cooped all these weeks in that horrid, dirty old ship; and I made Don Pablo, who was officer of the deck, call away a boat for me—and he wringing his hands and pleading would I bring about his ruin."

I laughed, myself, at the wonderful spontaneity of her mood. Faith, I could imagine how the young dons aboard the frigate philandered themselves sick over her.

"But that has naught to do with your going to the Whale's Head tonight," I reminded her. "Indeed, you should never think of it."

"I will be the judge of that," she retorted, instantly haughty. "And if my father is there I can come to no harm."

"If he is," I said. "I doubt you have mistaken his ordinary."

"No, no," she said decidedly. "I heard him speaking with them of it. But it may be you are right, sir, and I will not be so ungrateful as to flout a kindly stranger's well-meant advice. Juan can go into the tavern when we come to it, and I will bide outside. But somewhere I must walk, for my feet are all dancey with the sway of the sea, and we shall be away again with the tide in the morning. This is the last dry land I shall tread in many a week."

"If you will allow me, I'll put you on your way for the Whale's Head," I offered. "I must walk in that direction."

"Sure, sir, it is a great favor you offer," she answered. "I can not but thank you."

And she gave an order in Spanish which fetched the under-officer she called Juan and one of his men out from the shadows. They fell in behind us as we walked off along the line of the warehouses.

"You are upon a long voyage?" I ventured.

"You may well say so," she cried. "From here to the Floridas, and after that on to the Havana and the cities of the Main."

"You will soon have no need to regret a lack of adventures," I said. "There are few men, let alone maids, who fare so far afield."

"Ah, sir, that is what I like to think upon! I was near mad with delight when my father came to the convent and took me from the sisters. Until the ship's decks were under my feet I could not believe it was true that I was really free."

"But you are never Spanish!" I said. "I ask not in idle curiosity, though—"

Her laughter was like a chime of bells.

"Sure, they say I am as Irish as the pigs in the Wicklow hills where I was born."

And all of a sudden she was grave again.

"I am not knowing your politics, sir, but there's maybe no harm in just telling you my father was of those who opposed the Hanoverian and fought for King James and Bonnie Charlie. And because his own King can not employ him, he serves Spain."

"It is not pleasant for an Englishman to think of all the brave gentlemen must serve foreign monarchs," I acknowledged. "But I hope you will be happy in the Indies, mistress."

"Oh, we shall not be staying there long," she answered blithely. "My father is an engineer officer, and he must inspect the fortifications on the Main and elsewhere. We shall be returning to Spain within the year. But look, sir! Is not that sign intended to be a whale's head?"

"Yes," I said. "This is the tavern."

One look at its flaring windows and the cut-throat gentry who swaggered in and out of the low door convinced my companion that I had not misrepresented the character of the place. She drew back to the curb, and the corners of her mouth drooped sadly.

"Glory, what an ill hole!" she murmured. "Now for why would the *padre* come hither? Business, says he; but—"

And she shook her head with a vague doubting emphasis.

"I would not seem to be thrusting myself upon you, mistress," I said, "yet I am fearful your Spaniards can not make themselves understood. Will it please you that I inquire within for your father?"

She considered, catching a corner of her lip betwixt white teeth. "Troth, sir," she answered finally, "I see not how I can avoid going the deeper in debt to you."

There was a moment's pause.

"And how shall I—"

"Ay de mi!" she exclaimed with a bubble of laughter. "How stupid of me to be forgetting I am just a maid off the sea to you. Ask for Colonel O'Donnell, sir, and tell him his daughter waits without."

And as I started toward the door she added gayly:

"It is not every girl could step upon a strange shore and find a *cavalier* waiting to aid her. But what would Mother Seraphina say to such brazenness? Ah, I can see her now! 'The blessed saints preserve us, Moira! Have ye no manners or modesty into yourself at all? A hundred Aves and the Stations of the Cross twice before you sup.'"

Her voice was still ringing in my ears as I shouldered a drunken sailor from my path, lowered my head to pass under the lintel of the tavern's entrance and so gained the hazy blue atmosphere of the taproom, cluttered with tables, foul with smoke and stale alelees, abuzz with rough voices bawling oaths and sea-songs.

It was the chorus of one of these songs which first distracted my thoughts from the Irish girl outside—a wild, roaring lilt of blood and ribaldry:

"Fifteen men on the Dead Man's Chest—
  Yo-ho-ho, and a bottle of rum!
Drink and the devil had done for the rest—
  Yo-ho-ho, and a bottle of rum!"

I looked to the corner whence it came, and discovered the one-legged sailor, John Silver, thumping the time with a pewter mug on the table-top as he led the group around him, foremost amongst whom, after himself, was Darby McGraw, flaming red mop standing out like a buccaneer ensign, shrill voice carrying above the thundering basses of his companions—as villainous a crew, to outward seeming, as I had ever looked upon. I noted especially a pasty, tallowy-faced man, whose shifty eyes were masked by a skrim of greasy black hair, and a big, lusty, mahogany-brown fellow with a tarry pigtail, who evidently found as much satisfaction in the song as poor, fuddled Darby.

Silver saw me almost as soon as I spotted him, and with a quick word to the others, got to his feet and stumped across the room, dragging Darby after him by the arm. His large, good-humored features were wreathed in a smile tinged with mortification.

"So you come after him, Master Ormerod, did you?" he shouted to make himself heard in the confusion. "And ashamed o' myself I oughter be, says you, and with reason, too. But I'm not one to lead a likely lad astray, and all Darby's had was good, ripe ale and two earsful o' sea-gossip as'll give him things to dream o' for nights to come. I shouldn't oughter o' let him come back, sir, but when he stuck that red mop o' his in the door an hour past I hadn't the heart to send him away. He's come to no harm, so you won't hold it against him for a extry mug or two of ale; will you, sir?"

"I did not come after him," I answered; "but as I am here he had best return home with me. Where did you get my name, Silver?"

He pulled his forelock knowingly.

"Why, from Darby, o' course, sir—not that anybody on the water-front couldn't ha' told me, seein' what a kind-hearted, friendly young gentleman you are. But asking your pardon for the liberty, sir, can I serve you in any way?"

"I don't think so," I told him. "I am seeking a Colonel O'Donnell."

I fancied a flicker of surprise stirred the bluff friendliness mirrored in his face. He stared around the room.

"Never heard o' the gentleman, sir, which ain't surprizin', seein' I was never here before this morning, myself; but I ran into some old shipmates of mine as gave me the run o' the place, and it may be I can find out for you from one o' them. Just you wait here a shake, Master Ormerod, and I'll see what I can do."

This seemed the wisest course, inasmuch as it was apparent there was nobody in the taproom of the quality of Colonel O'Donnell, so I nodded assent; and as Silver stumped away, threading a nimble passage in and out of the crowded tables, I asked Darby what he had been doing. Somewhat to my astonishment, the boy lapsed into sullenness and answered in monosyllables. Only once he revealed a flare of interest, when I remarked:

"That was a sufficiently devilish song you were singing, Darby."

"That it was!" he exclaimed. "Whisht, whiles singing it ye can *feel* the blood a-dripping from your cutlasss."

"And who were the others singing with you?"

The sullen look covered his face like a curtain.

"Oh, just shipmates."

"Of yours?"

"No, of Master Silver's."

"What are their names?"

"I know not."

"Oh, come now, Darby!"

"Well, the one he calls Bill Bones and the other Black Dog—but there's no meaning in nature in that last."

Silver had disappeared through a door at the rear in company with one of the drawers, and now he came swinging in again on his crutch, ahead of a tall, lantern-jawed man in a rich dress of black-and-silver, whose gold-hilted sword proclaimed the gentleman. This man Silver ushered to me with a crudely hearty courtesy.

"Here's luck, Master Ormerod," he called when he was within earshot. "My friend had heard tell the colonel was above-stairs. This here's the young gentleman I spoke of, your honor. My duty to ye both, sirs, and always pleased to serve."

And off he swung on his crutch again to be received with acclamations by his cronies in the corner.

The lantern-jawed man gave me a keen glance, almost a suspicious glance, I should have said. He had a nervous manner, and there was a kind of restless glow in his eyes.

"Well, sir?" he said. "I understand you desired speech with me?"

"If you are Colonel O'Donnell—"

He nodded curtly.

"—I am to tell you that your daughter awaits you outside," I concluded.

He was genuinely startled,

"My daughter? But who are you, sir, who act as her guardian?"

I was nettled, and did not hesitate to show it.

"She asked me the way hither when she came ashore," I retorted, "and, deeming it scarce probable that you would care to have her enter the taproom, I even offered my services to fetch you forth to her."

I saw now his resemblance to her, for the corners of his mouth twitched down in the same way her's had. And he muttered something like a curse in Spanish.

"It seems I am beholden to you, sir," he answered stiffly. "She is a child, and vastly ignorant of the world, and I must be both father and mother to her."

I bowed and stood aside to make room for him to pass out.

"Master Ormerod, the seaman called you, did he not?" continued O'Donnell. "Perhaps, sir, you will permit an older man to compliment you upon an honorable deportment."

A slightly pompous tone invaded his speech.

"I am not unfamiliar with the chief centers of our Old World society, Master Ormerod, and I have the honor to hold the office of chamberlain to a monarch, who, though he may not be named upon English soil, will some day recover the estate a usurper has deprived him of. I need say no more, I am sure."

"I understand, sir," I replied. "And may I suggest that Mistress O'Donnell is awaiting you?"

He brushed by me with a click of impatience, and Darby and I followed him to the street, Darby thrilled anew by the sight of his luxurious habit, the five-pound ruffles that covered his wrists and the worked hilt of his sword. As we all three emerged, Mistress O'Donnell darted up to her father and caught at the lapels of his coat.

"Ah, *padre,*" she cried in a brogue that clotted and slurred her words, "You'll not be holding it against me because I wearied of the ship and would feel the earth crumbling underfoot, and me so lonely for lack of you I was near to weeping the while I sat in my cabin with naught to do but read my Hours!"

He wilted, as must any man have done, flinging his arm around her with a gesture that verged on the theatrical.

"Tush, tush, Moira," he rebuked her gently; "'twas unbecoming in you, and in Spanish lands such conduct would lead to trouble. See that you do it not a second time. I will give you in charge of Juan; and, having had your taste of freedom, you must return aboard, for I have matters yet requiring my attention. Ah, yes, and you must thank this gentleman properly for his gallantry. Master Ormerod, my dear! His father is a great merchant of this town."

Mistress O'Donnell swept me a willowy curtsey, and as I bowed acknowledgment I wondered where he had secured such exact information about me. He had seemed totally ignorant of who I was when we met.

"Sure, I'll not be after trying to thank you," says my lady to me with a twinkle in her eye. "For I couldn't find the words would express my gratitude. But for you, 'tis an awful fool I'd have made of myself this quarter-hour past."

Colonel O'Donnell hemmed reprovingly.

"Let it be a lesson to you, my girl. My thanks to you again, Master Ormerod. My compliments to your father, if it please you. Good night, sir."

I understood that he wished to be rid of me, and accepted the cue.

"Good night, sir," I replied. "And a fair voyage to you, mistress. If I can be of further service, pray command me."

"No, Master Ormerod, here our paths diverge," she answered softly, and placed her hand upon her father's arm.

A moment later I was hurrying north and west, Darby McGraw chattering beside me, for the lady's bright beauty seemed to have scoured the sulkiness from his spirits.

"Ah, there was the lovely, gracious maid for ye, Master Robert!" he cried. "Did ye hark to the song in her voice? And did ye see the blue in her eyes, like lake-water with green fields all around and the sun shining faint? She's the breath of the Ould Sod; and oh, whirra, it's never more I'll see it, for they say I'm to be a pirate."

"You talk nonsense," I returned harshly.

"Nonsense?" he repeated. "It's a grand word, nonsense, Master Robert. But whisht, now, ye'll say a good word for me with the old master, won't ye?"

I told him I would, mostly to stop the clacking of his tongue; and he skipped high like a colt that has just had its first meal of oats.

"She put the comether on ye, that elegant young maid," he continued. "She had a way with her, she did. Aye, for her I'd give over being a pirate."

"We'll never see her again, Darby," I said. "She'll be beyond the Caribbees a few weeks hence, and we plodding at our tasks here in New York."

He gave me a shrewd glance.

"Indeed, and it's a wiser man than the Pope can see beyond the weeks, Master Robert," says he.

CHAPTER III

A CALLER IN THE NIGHT

WE SAT late at dinner that night, for my father must needs have me repeat at length the tale of my experiences during the day, revealing a perturbation unusual in him, although Peter Corlaer ate on with placid solemnity, scarce a flicker of interest in his little eyes that were almost buried behind their ramparts of flesh.

"I have heard of this Colonel O'Donnell," said my father when I had made an end. "He was in Scotland with Prince Charles—one of the Irish crew who bogged a promising venture, if what men say be true. I marvel at his temerity in landing here, for there must be a price upon his head in England. Doubtless he was consorting with some of our Jacobite sympathizers at the Whale's Head—a fitting place for such an intrigue!

"The captain of the frigate called upon the Governor this morning, so Master Colden told me, with a cock-and-bull story of a mistake in his reckoning that took him north of his course. I smell the taint of a Jacobite plot! Your gloomy friend Jenkins had the right of it. Never trust a Spaniard when he comes with pretense of friendship."

"Mistress O'Donnell said they were for the Floridas," I protested. "Sure, they are not far out of their course."

My father smiled for the first time.

"The little maid would have no knowledge of her father's purpose. And if she did—No, no, lad, I had my share of plotting in my youth. Our Jacobites are a pernicious lot."

"Yet you, yourself, were one of them," I pointed out, a thought maliciously.

His face darkened.

"True, and I learned by experience. Set that to my credit, Bob. Britain is greater than any king or any family. 'Tis the country, not the man, must be considered. And Britain fares better under Hanoverian George than she ever did under a Stuart Charles or James."

I was still unconvinced.

"But certes, sir, 'tis in no sense strange for the Spaniards to dispatch an engineer to inspect their fortifications this side the Atlantic."

"An Irish engineer officer?"

My father smiled again.

"'Tis to be wondered at. But there! In such a devious business we might not hope to reach the truth, nor am I greatly concerned thereat. Most Jacobite plots are ill-planned sallies by desperate, misguided men. No, boy, what irks me most is the tidings you had of the one-legged sailor. Silver, you called him? Yes, I like it not to hear the pirates are outside our harbor. It hath the look of daring beyond the ordinary. If Murray—"

The door behind me opened, and I saw my father's jaw drop. Peter, at my right hand, let his eyelids blink, then went on quietly cracking nuts between his huge fingers.

"Did I hear you call me, Ormerod?"

The voice from the doorway had a chill, level quality that was as resonant as the tolling of a bell.

"'If Murray'—I *thought* I heard my name?"

I screwed around in my chair. There in the doorway stood the most remarkable figure I had ever seen. A large man, straight as an arrow despite the years that had planted crow's feet so thickly about his eyes, his square shoulders showed to advantage the exquisite tailoring of the black velvet coat he wore. His small-clothes were of a fine yellow damasked silk, and his stockings of silk to match. Diamonds flashed from the buckles of his shoes, his fob, his fingers and the hilt of his dress-sword. A great ruby glowed in the Mechlin jabot that cascaded from his throat. Over his arm hung a cloak, and under his elbow was tucked a hat cocked in the latest mode.

But it was the memory of his face that abided with you. The

features were all big and strongly carved; the nose was a jutting beak above a tight-lipped mouth and a jaw that was brutally square; the eyes were a vivid black, flecked with tawny lights. His hair was of a pure, silvery whiteness and drawn back, clubbed and tied with a black ribbon. His cheeks and brows were furrowed by a maze of wrinkles, yet the flesh seemed as firm as mine. In every way he suggested breeding, gentility, wealth; but there was a combined effect of sinister power and predatory will, a hint of ruthless egotism which took no account of any interests save his own.

He acknowledged my prolonged stare with a slight bow, mildly derisive.

"Your son, Ormerod?" he continued. "My grandnephew? Robert, I think, you named him, for the redoubtable Master Juggins of London, who aided you to start life anew after you had contrived to wreck yourself upon the rocks of a foresworn Jacobite career."

My father rose slowly to his feet.

"Yes, he is my son, Murray. It is neither his fault nor mine that he is also your grandnephew. As to his name, Robert Juggins was a better man than you or I, and you can not inspire my son against me by hinting at hidden chapters of my early life. He knows that I was deluded into serving the Stuarts, and lived to learn that country comes before king. We were talking of that before you entered."

The man in the doorway nodded his head.

"I seem to remember that became a topic of some interest to you—after the Jacobites hounded you from France and the Hanoverians drove you from England. Ah, well, I can commend a philosophical adaptability in face of adversity. 'Tis a trait I have had occasion to practise, myself."

He let the door swing to, and stepped behind me to the left side of the table, where there was a vacant chair.

"I would not seem discourteous," he remarked suavely. "I note another old friend, Ormerod—or perhaps I should say an old enemy. Permit me to observe, Corlaer, that you wear well with the years—as well as myself, indeed."

Peter squeezed a hickory-nut between his forefinger and thumb and looked up vacantly into Murray's face.

"*Ja,*" he said.

"Lest you should be tempted by some misapprehension," pursued Murray, "I may inform you that I have every reason to suppose myself safe from any measures you might take against me. I know well the dangerous swiftness of wit Peter conceals beneath that flat face of his, and I should not like to see him hurt—"

"*Ja*, you bet," giggled the Dutchman.

"I assure you such is the fact," answered Murray. "I hope to do what I have come here for tonight without injuring anybody, and if you gentlemen will listen to me quietly for a few moments I am confident that the issue will be harmless for all of us."

He cast his cloak and hat upon a chair by the fire, and put his hand upon the vacant one betwixt my father and me.

"May I?" he asked.

My father, still standing, said nothing; and Murray, with a shrug, accepted the silence for consent, sank gracefully into the seat and drew a golden snuff-box, studded with brilliants, from a pocket.

"With your permission," he said, springing the cover.

A fragrant whiff of snuff-tobacco tickled my senses as he offered it generally.

"'Tis excellent stuff," he remarked. "Ripe Rip-Rap. What? None of you? Ah, then—"

He dusted a pinch under his nostrils, inhaled and daintily used his handkerchief, a lace-edged morsel such as women carry.

My father leaned forward across the table, a blaze of hatred in his face.

"'Tis true, then!"

Murray regarded him in some surprize.

"True? My dear sir, I assured you 'twas Rip-Rap."

My father turned to Peter and me.

"After I told you—about this man, Robert—I hoped that I was wrong—that I had done him an injustice. But now he has convicted himself out of his own lips."

Murray gently deposited the snuffbox upon the table in front of him.

"Ah," he murmured. "I see! You were referring to my nickname, or, shall we say, *nomme de geurre?*"

My father laughed bitterly.

"*Nomme de guerre!* Name of a pirate! But let us have it, fair and openly, Andrew Murray. Are you Captain Rip-Rap?"

"I suppose most people would agree with your description," replied Murray; "although personally I prefer the word buccaneer. It is susceptible to so much wider use, and there is about it a suggestion of—However, we are not interested here tonight in the more abstruse branches of etymology. I am the person popularly known on the high seas as Captain Rip-Rap, and I fancy I might have logical grounds for arguing that if any disgrace adheres to me by that admission, 'twas you, Ormerod, who drove me to the practise of what you call piracy."

"'Tis like you to take that tone," said my father. "I drove you from the practise of what amounted to piracy on the land. There is no difference in the way you earn your livelihood today, Murray. You were an outlaw, and you are an outlaw."

"I fear you are incapable of doing me justice," sighed Murray. "You should know that I have always labored to serve higher ends than the mere sordid pursuit of money, such as has possessed you and those like you."

He wagged his head sadly.

"I had hoped better of you, Ormerod. You are of good blood, man. 'Sdeath, do you never think on what you lose by playing the small colonial merchant here?"

"I think better of the estate I won unaided, with my bare hands and wits, than of the manor I lost in England through youthful folly," rejoined my father. "But I never thought to hear a pirate prate of the blessings of birth. Phaugh!"

Murray's face purpled, and a Scots burr crept into his speech.

"No man challenges my birth," he shouted. "I am of better blood than you. I trace my lineage to James V. I quarter my arms with the Douglases, the Homes, the Morays, the Keiths, the Hepburns, aye, and with the oldest clans beyond the Highland Line!"

"I have heard so before," commented my father dryly.

Murray breathed deeply, obviously fighting for self-control.

"Let it pass!" he exclaimed with a magnificent gesture. "What doth it signify? I am what I am, sir—and the day comes when I shall stand as high as the highest."

He drew himself up very erect in his chair, but my father answered with the same dry scorn:

"That too I have heard before. Once, I mind, you expected to be a duke by exploiting ill-gotten gains with Jacobite intrigue. Aye, you would have ruined your country, sold her to the French like enough, all for a peerage. Now, I suppose, you would do it again."

"What would you?"

Murray flicked a pinch of snuff into his nostrils.

"The luck was against me, although you, yourself, and silent Peter there, know how close to success I came."

"*Ja,*" squeaked Peter, still busy crushing nuts and slowly crunching their meats.

"I have had the Devil's own luck," Murray went on, heedless of the Dutchman. "In the '45 I was half the world away, for there were too many cruisers abroad in the Caribbees for my comfort. Before I could get back the Prince had played and lost. A shame! With me—"

"With you he would have been sold to Government for the thirty thousand pounds reward that Cumberland offered," said my father.

Murray looked hurt.

"I have been accused of much," he replied; "but never of disloyalty to King James or his sons."

"True," assented my father; "you could never earn anything by it. Your opportunities all came from the other direction."

"Your words are unjust, sir," said Murray with a hauteur he had not shown previously. "Indeed, if matters fall out, as I anticipate, I shall soon give proof which can not be ignored of my devotion to the Good Cause. I am preparing a combination which—"

He swung around suddenly upon me.

"But I am forgetting my main purpose!" he cried. "Stand up, grand-nephew, and let me have a look at you."

I would not have heeded him, but my father said quickly:

"Do as he asks you, Robert. I'd not have him think you are crooked in the legs."

So I stood.

"A likely build," he remarked warmly. "You favor your father, I see—save in the face, it may be. There you are your mother, my maid

Marjory. Ah, sweet chit, would she were with us now! A sad loss; a sad loss, lad!"

The expression which came to my father's face was terrible in its intensity of passion. He leaned closer to Murray, white to the cheek-bones, his nostrils pinched in.

"Murray," he said, "make an end of such talk! As you value your life, mention her not again. I know not what cards you hold up your sleeve here, but if we all die in the next moment I will slay you as you sit if you profane her memory with your foul tongue."

Murray stared up at him coolly and took a pinch of snuff.

"Ah, well, you were always prejudiced," he answered. "I—But it serves no purpose to reopen old wounds. I am of one mind with you there. Yet tell me this: Have you poisoned the boy's mind against me?"

My father dropped back into his seat with a sour grimace.

"Poisoned his mind?" he repeated. "I told him no more recently than yesterday who and what you were. You brought that upon yourself by pursuing your rascally trade in these seas. Until then the boy did not so much as know that you existed—as his relative."

My great-uncle—I was gradually beginning to think of him as such—pondered this news, head on one side, peering from my father to me and back again.

"I see, I see," he murmured. "Humph! I fear his mind hath been corrupted. But I am not surprized. No, no! I prepared for this."

"For what?" demanded my father.

Murray leaned abruptly across the table.

"I will be frank with you, Ormerod—and with Nephew Robert here. I am somewhat in difficulties—"

"If 'tis money—" began my father.

My great-uncle's gesture was sufficient check to this.

"I am not in difficulties for money, although I am like to be in difficulties shortly in connection with an embarrassing quantity of it. In fine, sir, I am upon the point of launching the coup of my career, one which will entail consequences of a stupendous character, and in the end, I venture to predict, echo in throne-rooms and chancelleries. Aye, kingdoms shall—"

He broke off.

"It is not necessary that I should go into that. Suffice it for the present if I say that I am in the position of a man who has partially tamed an unwieldy band of wild animals. My own ship I can rely upon up to a certain point, but I have associated with me—"

"That would be Flint?" interjected my father.

"I am flattered by the knowledge of my affairs which you display," replied my great-uncle with one of his courtly inclinations. "Yes; I had occasion, when I first went to sea, for a competent navigator. Flint served me in that capacity until I became independent, and I then fitted him out with his own ship. We have cruised in company since. I am not betraying a professional secret when I add that he is a man whose undoubted force of personality is offset by a certain turbulence and crudeness of wit which make him difficult to handle— increasingly difficult to handle, I may say. I foresee trouble with him in the future in connection with the coup to which I have already refered."

"And is it your idea," inquired my father sarcastically, "that we should undertake to assassinate this man for you—out of the kindness of our hearts, as it were, and to stimulate the practise of piracy?"

Murray shook his head, wholly undisturbed.

"I never remove a man I can use," he answered. "Flint is still useful. No, I require a young man to stand at my elbow and assist me in curbing unruly spirits. I promise a great future for such."

"Command of his own pirate craft, no doubt?" pressed my father.

"That would be an offer to draw most stout youths," returned my great-uncle. "Bah, what is piracy, that you and your kind prate against it, Ormerod? Is it any worse in character than four-fifths of the business practised in this world? What are you and those like you but men who seek to deprive others of their lawful gains that you may add to your stores what the others possessed? I take from the wealthy, who can afford to lose, what they have dishonestly got, more often than not, and much of what I win I contribute to the Cause to which you gave your first loyalty."

"An admirable code of ethics," observed my father.

"'Tis as good as any I have discovered," agreed Murray smoothly. "You called me an outlaw a few minutes past. I can not deny it. I am an outlaw because I worked in my own way to reëstablish my lawful king. You, who once served that king in exile, turned against him and ruined me, made an outlaw of me. Well, I do what I may; and since Morgan's day no man has played the game so successfully, as any seaman would tell you."

"I'll vouch for that," said my father. "But come to the point. What will you have? That I should apprentice Robert to you to be indentured a good, honest, trusty and skilful pirate?"

"Even so."

My father sat back in his chair.

"I'll not," he said.

Murray treated himself to a pinch of snuff.

"What does our young man himself say?" he asked.

"I say that you offer me no inducement," I answered as shortly as I could.

"'Odslife," he swore. "No inducement? My dear nephew, I offer you an open, bracing life—for a brief space; a share in a brave venture; an opportunity to rehabilitate your family, to rise to place, title and honor."

"On a pirate's deck?" I jeered.

"From a pirate's quarterdeck," he corrected me gravely. "I am on my last cruise. The *Royal James* is to vindicate her name. Aye, in years to come she will be regarded as a shrine of loyalty and devotion, and to have sailed with Andrew Murray in her— Why, sir, who remembers today of Robin Hood aught but that he was true to King Richard in adversity?"

The man's surety was amazing.

"This passes all reason," said my father wearily. "You must be insane."

"Not at all," retorted my great-uncle. "I am the leading practitioner of my profession. Winter, Davis, Roberts, Bellamy, all the more noted— ah—pirates of recent years, were small fry compared to me. You would find it difficult to credit me did I inform you of my takings—"

"Blood-money!" roared my father. "Thieves' money!"

"Ah, that unfortunate point of view of yours again," protested Murray. "I tell you, Ormerod, you stand in the boy's way."

"He is not a boy, but a man," snapped my father. "And able to judge his own course."

"So be it."

My great-uncle turned to me once more.

"It appears this decision is left betwixt us two, Nephew Robert," he said. "So I must inform you that I am determined to have your aid in any event—by force, if you will not accompany me reasonably."

There was a snap as a Brazil-nut split apart in Peter's grip. Murray waved an airy hand in his direction.

"'Tis true that you are the most powerful man I ever met, Corlaer," he remarked; "yet I urge you not to attempt violence. I have sufficient men in the house to overpower you, and I should not hesitate to slay Ormerod or you at need. The boy is the only one of you three whose life hath value to me."

"He means it, Peter," said my father. "Keep your hands down."

"*Ja,*" squeaked Peter.

"You were ever a wise man, Ormerod," resumed my great-uncle. "I venture to congratulate you upon the soundness of your judgment. Now for you, Nephew Robert. Come with me you shall, but I prefer that you come willingly. Therefore I lay before you these inducements: Firstly, we sail upon a venture which hath a color of State business, although a strict legalist would denounce it piratical—you see, I endeavor to deal honestly by you after my fashion; secondly, no harm is intended to you; thirdly, the rewards of our project will be singularly rich; fourthly, I design to exploit the advantages which shall accrue to me solely for your benefit—you, Robert, are my heir, and if I have need of you in the execution of my coup, nonetheless I shall be able to repay you for whatever you do in my behalf a hundred-fold, both materially and otherwise. I am, after all, your nearest kin after your father, and I say in all humility my assistance is not to be despised."

From his manner you would have reckoned he was offering me the governorship of a province, at the least; and the undeniable charm of the man invested his words with a glamour which was augmented by the virility of his person—and this notwithstanding my fast-rising hatred of him.

"I won't go willingly," I answered. "Even did your arguments tempt me, I should resent your threat of compulsion."

"Admirably spoken," he applauded. "Egad, I perceive you have the proper spirit. You are exactly the lad I require."

I rose, whipped to wrath by the insolence of his assurance.

"I am the lad you'll not get," I shouted. "Call in your bravos, and I'll tear their throats out for you."

"Gently, gently," he remonstrated. "My bravos, as you term them, are not lambs, Nephew Robert, and I must warn you that the killings would not be all on the one side. If you value your father, stand fast."

And he drew from a waistcoat pocket a silver whistle, which he placed to his lips. A thin blast piped through the room, and a dozen hairy seadogs surged in from hall and kitchen. Raps on the two windows indicated that others mounted guard outside.

Peter Corlaer's little pig-eyes swept the invaders with a single glance, but he did not suspend for a second his steady crushing and munching of nuts. My father's face was a mask of mingled rage and fear—not fear for himself, but for me. He stared at the savage figures, the bared cutlasses, the ready pistols, almost with unbelief in the reality of his vision. And certes 'twas a weird spectacle in that orderly house in the town we of the province looked upon as the most advanced in the colonies—and became to me the more weird as I glimpsed next the hall door a grim mahogany face and a hangman look beneath a skrim of black hair, and behind the two a familiar carroty head.

"Ho, there, Darby!" I called out. "What are you doing in such company? Did you know those men for pirates when you drank with them at the Whale's Head?"

"Sure, they ha' taken me into their crew," he answered brazenly.

"Have you turned pirate, Darby?" says my father, seeing him for the first time.

"Oh, aye," said Darby with a swagger. "I'm as cruel wicked as any."

"And 'twas you let them into the house and betrayed your master!" returned my father sadly. "I had not expected this of you, Darby. Have we not been kind to you?"

Darby wiggled uncomfortably.

"Oh, aye; main kind, Master Ormerod," he admitted. "But they would ha' had ye, whether or no. Sure, they're a grand, tricksy crew. And anyway, ye see, I was born to be a pirate. My troth, I was!"

Murray laughed pleasantly.

"'Tis a valiant youth, and should go far," he observed. "Moreover, he speaks the truth when he says we should have won our way in to you without his aid. The accommodation was convenient, but by no means essential.

"Where is Silver, Master Bones?" he added.

The man with the mahogany face touched his hat.

"John was seeing to it the sarvants was all secure, sir," he answered. "Here he is now."

A gap appeared in the ranks by the kitchen door, and the one-legged man I had met on the water-front that morning stumped in on his long crutch, as cheerfully serene as any honest householder.

"Was you askin' for me, captain?" he said. "We just finished up behind there—all gagged and roped, Bristol-fashion, safe for a day, sir."

And to me—

"My duty, Master Ormerod, and I hopes we'll know each other better soon."

"I find we shall need a cart, John," said my great-uncle.

"Rambunctious, is he?" answered Silver with a wink. "Well, we has it all ready, and the tarpaulin over it, right here in the garding under the blessed apple-trees. 'Tis only a step to the boats, to be sure."

My father turned very pale.

"You—you—My God, Murray, you can't kidnap the boy this way! Think! There are troops in Fort George. Once the hue and cry is raised you'll be—"

"But it will not be raised," replied Murray calmly. "I regret it, but we shall be obliged to tie up you and Peter so that you will be incapacitated until some kind friend happens to call on the morrow. By that time we shall be at sea."

"You are mad!" cried my father. "Every frigate on the station will be after you."

My great-uncle chuckled mildly.

"That is an old sensation. I have known it for twenty-odd years."

I snatched up the chair upon which I had been sitting and brandished it over his head.

"Call off these scoundrels of yours or I'll batter out your brains," I snarled.

"John," he said, ignoring me, "you will be so kind as to pistol the elder Master Ormerod if his son launches a blow at me."

"Aye, aye, sir," answered Silver.

And he leveled a weapon at my father. I knew, without looking behind me, that Peter and I were covered by other men. It was Peter who spoke first.

"Put down der chair, Bob," he ordered quietly.

The man called Black Dog cast the noose of a rope over his head and jerked his arms close to his side.

"*Neen, neen,*" objected Peter, and with no visible effort he snapped the hempen strands.

A gasp went up from the room, and there was a hasty retreat from his neighborhood.

"Pistol that man, if you must," called Murray; "but use your cutlasses, if possible."

"*Neen,*" said Peter again. "We don't fight."

"We might as well be killed now as let them carry off Bob," said my father with a sob in his voice.

"*Neen,*" said Peter a third time. "Deadt, you stay deadt. Perhaps Bob gets away from them some time. Better he be with Murray than he be deadt."

"Intelligently logical," commented Murray. "I commend the sentiment to you, Nephew Robert."

Peter's little eyes glinted toward him.

"I go with Bob," he said.

"No, no," denied Murray quickly. "You were not invited, friend Peter."

"If I don't go, Robert don't go," replied Peter. "Andt you don't go. Perhaps I don't kill you, but if there is shooting you don't get away. *Ja!*"

Murray contemplated this speech.

"Your proposition then," he said, "is that you insist upon sharing my nephew's new career or else will endeavor to secure the deaths of all of us, including his and your own?"

"*Ja!*" answered Peter.

"You may come," decided my great-uncle. "Your muscles should prove useful. John, I fancy we shall require triple bonds on this prisoner."

"Aye, aye, sir," assented Silver. "We ha' plenty o' stout manila. One o' you lads run back and get those coils I left by the stove. That's the proper spirit, Darby. Always willin'. You'll make a rare hand, you will. And how about makin' fast that gentleman as is goin' to stay behind, captain?"

Murray looked at my father, and from him to me.

"Have you reconciled yourselves to what I may justly style the inevitable?" he inquired suavely.

My father collapsed into his chair with a groan.

"If you will not suffer the boy to be hurt!" he exclaimed.

"My word of honor to that," returned my great-uncle very seriously. "His comfort and safety rank ahead of my own, Ormerod, for I anticipate that he is to achieve all those triumphs which fate denied me. 'Tis true I hope to sample them briefly, but—" and for the first time a shadow clouded his face—"I am, as you doubtless know, in my sixty-fourth year, and a fickle Providence, regarding the divinity of which I am inclined to share the skepticism of the French philosophers, is scarce likely to indulge me in a very prolonged extension of life's span. Nor indeed would I have it otherwise. I feel no inclination for the senility of extreme age."

My father eyed him with unaffected puzzlement.

"You are a strange man, Murray. I would I might understand you."

"You can not, so why concern yourself? Well, time passes. We must be off. Do you submit?"

My father bent his head.

"Yes—for his sake, —— you! Robert, no violence. We are in a coil we can not escape for the present; but rest assured I will do everything I can to secure your release."

My great-uncle motioned Silver forward.

"Make Master Ormerod as comfortable as possible, John," he instructed. "Yes, tie him in his chair. By the way, Ormerod, touching your last observation, I would remind you that every shot fired at my ship will be as likely to strike Robert as another. Accept my advice, and leave well enough alone. Within a year, possibly—two, at most— the boy will be safe and advanced in fortune beyond your wildest dreams."

"Let me have him back as he is—'tis all I ask," groaned my father.

Murray took snuff.

"A highly correct attitude, sir," he remarked. "Have you more to say?

Very well, John; you may affix the gag. No, not that gunnysacking.
Here is a silken kerchief will do. And now, friend Peter, we turn to
you—and you, Nephew Robert. I would these precautions were unnecessary. Let us trust your inclinations will become more friendly toward
me upon closer acquaintance."

CHAPTER IV

AN INKLING OF THE PLOT

MY POOR father's face, with the tears standing in his eyes, was the
last object I saw in the wan light of the guttering candles. The next
moment my captors lugged me into the darkness of the garden and
pushed me upon a hand-cart such as was used to fetch up the frailer
kinds of merchandise from the docks. Peter's immense body already
occupied most of the cart's cramped space, and I was squeezed precariously between him and the near side, the which Silver perceiving he prodded Peter into a more restricted compass and then spread
a tarpaulin over both of us.

"There ye are, my gentlemen," he said cheerfully. "Safe as a round
of beef and a side o' pork, says you—and you says right. Ah, captain,
we're ready here whenever you are, sir."

"Proceed then, John," answered my great-uncle's voice.

"You remember the way? The Green Lane,[1] 'tis called. Four men
should be sufficient to accompany you. I will go on by another street
with the rest of our party."

"Don't ye worry yourself, captain," returned Silver.

Footsteps thudded away on the gravel, and I heard the scratching
of the one-legged man's crutch as he stumped in front of us and the
cart jolted forward. They evidently went out the back way into a little alley, where their exit was least likely to be observed, and paused
while Silver reconnoitred the Green Lane from its cover.

---

1. *Maiden Lane*

"Not a sail in sight," he said presently. "Dash my buttons what a night! Precious dark it is, and I'm main glad we didn't fetch Pew along, with his bleared deadlights to hold us back. Come along, Black Dog. Yarely, my hearties! If this breeze keeps up—"

We emerged into the Green Lane, heading toward the East River, and a thrill tickled my spine as I heard the chanting tones of old Diggory Leigh, our ward watchman.

"Ten o'clock of a clear, dark night, and the wind in the nor'west. And all's well!"

"Easy, all!" whispered Silver's voice. "Push on, ye swabs; push on! But hold your gab. I'll do the talking."

The steel piece on the butt of his crutch tinkled on the cobbles as he stumped ahead of the cart.

"Ho there, shipmate," he hailed cordially. "And does you do this the whole, livelong night?"

Diggory's lanthorn-stave jingled on the ground.

"I do," he returned in pompous tones. "What keeps you abroad so late? Y'are seafaring men, I judge."

"Now I calls that clever," protested Silver with unconcealed admiration. "You sees us in the dark, and straight off you says, 'seafaring men.' I can see you're a vigilant watchman, shipmate. I'd hate to be a neefarious fellow in your town. Blow my scuttle-butt, I would!"

Diggory's appreciation of this tribute was mirrored in his voice.

"'Tis essential that our citizens be protected," he answered. "Yet there are those who have accused me of sleeping on watch."

"Skulkers, they be—low-lived skulkers as ever was," Silver assured him. "I know how you feel. Here we've been a-workin' since sunup, a-shiftin' cargo and stowin' it aboard, and I'll lay you a piece of eight the captain never so much as sarves out a extry noggin o' rum."

Diggory's stave jingled again as he sloped it over his shoulder.

"The wisest men are not always those in authority, friend," he said. "Ye might think, from the way some of the Corporation talk, 'twas they bar the night-walkers and wastrels from the city's streets! Bah!"

And his wailing voice receded into Pearl Street.

"What are you night-walkers and wastrels a-sniggerin' about?" demanded Silver of his following. "George Merry, I'll lay into you with my crutch. Put some heft behind this here blessed cart. Ain't ye ashamed o' yourselves, a-laughin' at a brave, hard-workin' watchman as keeps wicked pirates from liftin' your goods?"

A few hundred feet farther on we rattled off the cobbles on to the planked surface of a wharf.

"That you, John?" growled a voice.

"Aye, aye, Bill. Where's the captain?"

"Gone off in the jollyboat. That 'ere Spanish Irisher is a-waitin' him aboard."

I heard Silver curse under his breath.

"What was you sayin', John?" asked the other man.

"What I was sayin' don't signify, but what I was thinkin' was that there's a deal o' mystery in this business," answered Silver with an edge to his tone. "But there! Why should I consarn myself as am no more'n quartermaster o' the old *Walrus?* You're Flint's mate, Bill, and if it don't tickle your dignity to risk your neck without knowin' what the stake is, why should I complain?"

The other man, whom I now identified as the very brown-faced fellow who had been sitting with Darby in the Whale's Head, replied with a string of oaths.

"———!" he wound up. "Flint hisself don't know much more'n you and me."

"He'll take a lot for a sizzlin', gut-cuttin' fire-eater," rejoined Silver. "I'm ——— if I'd eat the humble-pie as is his reg'lar diet. Look at what we been through already! First off we leaves a safe hangout and a rich cruisin'-ground by Madagascar. Then we barges off from an ekally safe lay on the Main. And his bloomin' lordship, not trustin' his own crew, calls a fo'c'sle council aboard the *Walrus* and asks for volunteers to go with him into New York!"

"No, no," struck in Bones—I could tell him by his voice, which was of a peculiarly hectoring, rasping timbre. "'Twas Flint would have him take *Walrus* men along, not trustin' what he was up to. I heard what was said, John, for Flint had me into the cabin at the end.

"'If you won't say no more, Murray, you won't,' says he. 'I know you well enough for that. And as for your ——— political combinations they mean nothin' to me 'nless there's money in 'em for my pocket. But I say flatly I won't trust you by your lone in New York; no, nor with only men of your own choosin'. How do I know you maybe won't sell me for your pardon?'"

Silver pulled the tarpaulin from over our heads.

"If Flint said that 'twas the best speech he ever made," he returned. "All I knows is that Murray came on deck before us all and says as how he has a mission of danger to perform and he knowed there was no daredevils like the old *Walrus* hands, and would a score volunteer?

"'For what do we volunteer, captain, if I may make so bold?' says I.

"'A fair question merits a fair answer, John,' says he. 'And I'll say to all you lads I'm planning a cruise as'll make the fortune of the last one o' you and set us in such a position that those as desires to go ashore and enjoy their ease in comfort can look to receiving free pardons.'"

"'Ah, yes, sir,' says I; 'but what might be the nature o' this cruise, and why does we go into New York, where there's sojers, and maybe King's ships?'

"'The sojers won't hurt you, John,' says he, 'and if there's King's ships we'll try again. We are goin' in for me to meet one man for a talk under cover, and while I'm a-meetin' of him we'll crimp a likely youth I have my eye upon.'

"And that was all I had out o' him, Bill. I volunteered for blind curiosity, hopin' for to discover what he was up to, and I'm free to say I've had my trouble for my pains."

"You're no worse off'n the rest o' us," growled Bones. "Belay that guff, and get these carcases aboardship. If we miss the ebb there'll be —— to pay. He's no friend o' mine, Murray; but he's kept me in rum and 'backy and spendin'-money since I joined up with him."

"Give Flint some o' the credit, Bill," objected Silver.

"I give him plenty," snarled Bones. "He's a rare fighter, Flint is. But he never had Murray's head to plan—and he knows that as well as me. Aye, for I've heard him say it.

"'Curse me if I like to bob and prance for the old hellion, Bill,' says he; 'but he has the skill o' the Fiend at our lay. He's lasted twice as long as me or any other.'"

"Skill is right," admitted Silver. "D'ye mind, when we was overhaulin' the brig, he ran up alongside the *Walrus* wi' his speakin'-trumpet out and hailed?

"'Ahoy, *Walrus!*' says he. 'Don't touch her spars or riggin'. Give her a couple o' round shot across her decks. We've got to get rid of her crew, anyway.'"

He chuckled enviously.

"But this isn't gettin' us all back to the *Walrus*, Bill," he added. "Here, George Merry, can't you and your mates handle the big fellow? Two to his head and two to his feet—and drop him easy or he'll stove in the boat. Now, my gentleman—" this to me—"we'll pass you down, too. You must pull a strong oar with the captain for him to be so anxious to get you offshore hale and whole. It'll be place and rank for you, messmate, or a chance to swim wi' the sharks.

"Where's the red-headed little Irisher, Bill?"

"I sent him off with the captain," replied Bones. "Down wi' you, John. We'll cast off."

From where I now lay, propped up in the bow with my head resting on Peter's huge stomach, I could see the wharf a few feet above and the vague figures of the pirates and behind them the shadowy outline of the warehouses and an occasional dim light. Silver—I knew him by his height and a certain hunching of the shoulder under which he rested his crutch—turned away as Bones addressed him.

"What of the cart?" he asked.

"That's easy," returned Bones.

And he gave it a shove that sent it splashing into the water off the wharf's end.

"No incriminatin' evidence or what the lawyer sharks calls clues," remarked Silver. "A good job well done, Bill, if you asks me."

He lowered himself to a seat upon the stringpiece of the wharf, dropped the butt of his crutch to the forward thwart, felt about with his one leg and came to rest in front of Peter and me. The crutch he allowed to slip to the bottom of the boat, and in its place he took an oar. Bill Bones found a seat in the stern sheets.

"All clear," muttered Bill. "Give way." The oars fended off from the wharf, and the boat crept out into the stream, where it felt the full strength of the tide, just beginning to turn. The bow bounced up as the first wave hit it, and Peter, beneath me, emitted a dismal groan through his gag. Silver, bending diligently to his oar, looked over his shoulder.

"You *would* come, messmate," he said. "'Tis nobody's fault but your own."

Peter gave a convulsive wiggle which almost knocked me out of the boat.

"Here, here," admonished Silver. "That's no way to act. D'ye want to drown us all?"

Another groan from Peter, and he lay still.

"Look sharp," called Bones. "The brig's just ahead."

A riding-light gleamed high above us in the velvet gloom. I heard the faint *slap-slap-slap* of water against an anchored hull. Other lights appeared, the square pattern of stern windows, a great lanthorn hung in the waist. A gruff hail reached us.

"Boat ahoy!"

"Bones comin' aboard."

"Aye, aye, Bill."

As we rounded under her counter a couple of ropes rattled down to us, and I heard the creaking of tackle and hoist. We ground against the dripping black hull, and one of the oarsmen seized the rungs of a ladder which dribbled in the waves.

"Make fast the young 'un first," rasped Bones as he went up the wooden rungs monkey-fashion.

"Aye, aye, Bill," answered Silver, and I became conscious that the one-legged man and another were knotting a loose rope beneath my arm-pits. "All right, above there," called Silver presently.

And to me as the block began to whine:

"Watch out for your head, my master. Up you go! All the sensations as come to a poor, honest pirate as is hung in chains at Execution Dock."

The rope tautened; the unseen block whined louder; and I rose involuntarily from my position across Peter's belly. My feet were jerked from a thwart, and I kicked the air. The grunts of men hauling in unison floated from the brig's deck, and as I rose faster I commenced to swing like a pendulum.

And now I understood Silver's warning as to my head, for I came into violent collision with the brig's hull and by mere luck escaped with a bruised shoulder instead of a broken skull. I would have cried out, I think, but the gag restrained me; and inside of a minute I was dangling over the bulwarks, feet kicking frantically for standing room. A man caught me by one arm and drew me inboard, shouting the while to "slacken away!" and so I came down again with a bump that was like to crack my knee-caps, deposited as so much cargo upon the pitchy deck.

Dazed by treatment I had never sustained before, I stood heedless as the ropes were unfastened beneath my arm-pits, my bonds slipped off and the gag extracted from my aching jaws. I was just beginning to take in the aspect of my surroundings when Corlaer's cask of a body topped the bulwarks, swung with ludicrous unconcern for an instant as I dare say mine had done and then lurched in and crashed to the deck. The Dutchman was purple in the face, with white spots dotting the congested area of his cheeks, and gasping for breath. His stomach heaved tumultuously as the gag was removed.

"What ails you, Peter?" I cried.

"Der water," he moaned. "It makes me sick."

And sick he was—violently.

I helped him to the side as a whistle trilled.

"Capstan men for'ard," shouted a voice.

"What d'ye say?" called Bill Bones. "Who ordered the anchor up? The longboat's still alongside."

"Captain's orders," rumbled the answer from the darkness. "Said to cat the anchor, Bill, and get sail on her. We'm to start so soon as the Spanisher goes off—his boat's under the sta'b'd gangway."

Bones ripped off an admirable stream of oaths.

"Might ha' told me," he complained. "Slack aft the longboat, a pair o' you. Is the jollyboat hove up? Aloft, topmen! Clear the braces. John, you'd better take the helm. I s'pose his lordship'll come up to con us out when he gets good and ready, seein' he's the only one o' us as knows his way about this blasted harbor!"

"Aye, aye, Bill."

Silver stumped out of the shadow for'ard into the glare of the big lanthorn that swung from a lower yard of the mainmast over the waist.

"But what about our pris'ners?" Silver asked.

Mr. Bones cast an uneasy glance at us.

"I can't have that there bloomin' volcano a-muckin' up the decks, let alone cabin or fo'c'sle. Leave 'em be, John. They can't do no harm, and any man as goes into that water tonight will freeze before he makes the shore."

"Spoke most accurate," Silver agreed in his cheerful way.

The rascal had a manner which contrived to invest whatever he said to you—to any one—with the implication that you were the most intelligent person he had ever had to do with and that it was an honor to obey and serve you.

He disappeared aft now, and Bones with him. I heard the latter continuing to shout orders; and there was a constant bustle of men running back and forth over the decks, a clattering of ropes and shrieking of falls and blocks. For'ard sounded an ordered trampling of feet and a chorus of rough voices bellowing the wild sea-song I had heard in the Whale's Head Tavern:

> "Fifteen men on the Dead Man's Chest—
> Yo-ho-ho, and a bottle of rum!
> Drink and the devil had done for the rest—
> Yo-ho-ho, and a bottle of rum!"

Corlaer, weak as a rag, sank in a heap of buckskin in a dark corner by the bulwarks.

"*Neen, neen,*" he answered when I would have helped him. "Not'ings, Bob. I get better by and by. Der salt water—it is always so with me."

"I'll get you some rum," I said firmly.

And, rising, I was on the point of seeking the nearest man to ask where a drink might be obtained when footsteps clicked on the deck behind me.

"They are a dangerous company," said a voice with an unmistakable brogue to it.

"What would you?" returned my great-uncle.

I could imagine the graceful shrug which went with the words.

"We could not employ his Majesty's people in such a business. And all things considered, my fellows can handle it far better and more expeditiously."

They passed through the rays of the lanthorn which swung from the mainyard. Aye, the first speaker was Colonel O'Donnell. The little Irish maid! His daughter. My father had been right in his suspicions.

But what could be the tie of interest between a colonel in the Army of the King of Spain and an outlaw who had defied the whole structure of civilization? A Jacobite plot? It seemed preposterous!

"'Tis my daughter I was thinking of," explained O'Donnell as they reached the starboard gangway close by where I stood over Peter's prostrate form.

"Ah!"

My great-uncle went through his courtly formula of taking snuff, and I watched him, fascinated.

"Your forebodings do you credit, *chevalier.* But you have no cause for concern. For reasons which I need not go into I have with me here men from the crew of my associate. On board the *Royal James* I think I may promise you and your daughter all the deference you might receive upon a King's ship. I will go so far as to say that I have taken steps to secure you additional protection. My great-nephew— and heir—of whom I have spoken to you, sails with me, a fine youth who shall yet make his mark in the world."

"But a woman on a pirate ship!" protested O'Donnell anew.

"My dear sir, Rule Four of the Code of Articles under which our company is governed—does it surprize you that we have our own laws?—forbids the taking and keeping of women as spoil aboard our ships. We have had experience in the past of the evils which flow in the wake of a struggle for women's favors."

"Shall you not flout your own rule if my daughter comes aboard?" pressed the Irishman.

"She will not come as a prisoner, but as a guest," returned Murray blandly. "After all, colonel, the *Royal James* is my ship—and in that respect differs from most outlaw craft which are held by the entire crew as a community. No, no; you need not concern yourself."

"I like it not, I say!" persisted O'Donnell. "Why did you bid me bring her? You were hot for her coming so soon as you heard I had a daughter."

"Would you have left her by her lone in a strange country?" answered my great-uncle impatiently. "Tut, man, be sensible. Who would suspect a man who had his daughter with him? 'Tis true this enterprise is fraught with danger, but no maid can go through life without sniffing peril. We will guard her as we shall the treasure."

"I'll hold you to that," rapped O'Donnell as he climbed over the bulwarks and felt for the ladder. "I am not proud of myself when I think of her innocence. Holy saints, what a coil! Well, well, no matter. I must be going, for the night wanes."

"Yes," assented Murray. "And stir your frigate's captain to a swift passage."

The Irishman nodded.

"If necessary we'll pass by the Havana. Luckily Porto Bello is the *intendente*'s chief worry. You'll hover, then, off Mona Passage?"

"Aye, from the south tip of Hispaniola to the north of Porto Rico, save it storms, when we'll run for shelter in the Bay of Samana, where the old buccaneers were wont to lie. Diego can find us. He has done it before. Just give him ample time."

"So soon as the *Santissima Trinidad* has her orders Diego shall know."

He started to descend and then climbed back.

"She has heavy metal, Murray. Are you certain—"

My great-uncle laughed.

"Be at ease upon that point, *chevalier.* We could take two Spaniards of the *Santissima Trinidad*'s metal. I fear I must bid you good evening, though. Hark!"

The bell of the Spanish frigate rang out eight times.

"Midnight!" exclaimed O'Donnell. "Can you be gone by dawn?"

"My dear sir," returned my uncle lightly, "this brig will never be seen again—anywhere—by anybody."

O'Donnell shivered.

"Good night," he said abruptly, and his head vanished behind the bulwarks.

I heard the rattle of oars, a low order in Spanish, the steady splash and spatter of rowers as the boat pulled away. My great-uncle watched it for a moment, then turned toward where I stood.

"Well, Nephew Robert, what did you make of us?" he inquired.

I contrived to keep my voice level, for I would not give him the satisfaction of supposing he had startled me.

"That you are engaged in deeper villainy even than my father feared."

"You have a narrow-minded view of life," he remarked. "However, 'tis a defect can be remedied by experience. By the way, do not jump to conclusions from what you overheard. You shall have the whole tale anon, but until you possess a more intimate knowledge of the situation you are better off in ignorance."

"I am no pirate, nor shall I be."

"Why make hasty statements, Robert?"

A hail came from Bones for'ard.

"Anchor a-cat, captain!"

"Very good, Master Bones," replied my great-uncle. "You may trip, and we will make all sail, if you please."

"Aye, aye, captain."

Peter groaned dolefully at the fateful words, and Murray stepped closer.

"What is that beside you, Robert?" he asked quickly. "Did our good friend Peter come to harm?"

"The water's motion sickens him."

"Ah! Strange how the strongest men succumb to it. We will have him carried below. I should have told you before this that I design to make you both as comfortable as possible. You berth aft with me. On the brig I can offer you very limited hospitality, but on the *Royal James* you shall have the comforts of an admiral."

"I want no comforts," I answered coldly. "Any comforts you may offer me would be a mockery. My very being here is a discomfort most in- sufferable."

He stiffened.

"'Sdeath, sirrah! Bear in mind that I am your elder in years and deserving of respect for my relationship."

"To me you are a singularly bloody pirate, and that is all."

"The injustice of youth!" he commented evenly. "I was the uncle and tender guardian of the mother you never knew, Robert."

"I share my father's feelings upon that point," I cried, and raised my hand in a threatening gesture.

He did not stir.

"Your conversion will be quite as difficult as I had foreseen," he said. "No, you would gain naught by striking me. Impartially I may recommend you to adopt an attitude which will secure you the maximum of liberty and opportunity. Of what avail for you to force yourself into confinement?"

"Sir," I returned, "be convinced of this: The day you attack a defenseless ship I will slay as many of you as I can and contentedly die."

It has a sound of theatricalism now, but I meant it at the time.

"I purpose nothing of that sort for you," answered my great-uncle. "And while I am tempted to argue you out of a position founded upon a false ethical basis, I shall content myself with the observation that you would do well to hold your temper in leash until you find a need for its employment."

He glanced overside.

"I see we are under way. I must ask you to excuse me for the present, Robert. I am constrained to serve as pilot."

He raised his little silver whistle, and its shrill call fetched several of the crew aft.

"Aye, aye, captain." It was Bones. "What's your wish, sir?"

"Have this poor fellow—" Murray gestured toward Corlaer's recumbent form—"carried to one of the staterooms. Use him gently. Bid the Irish boy—what's his name? Oh, Darby!—bid Darby tend him and fetch him what he requires.

"This gentleman, here—" he indicated me—"is my greatnephew, Master Bones. It may be he will succeed me in command of the *Royal James* some day, although he is not with us of his own wish as yet. He is to have complete freedom except he undertake to achieve aught to our disadvantage. Pass the word to the men, if you please."

"That's a queer lay," growled Bones. "Is he friend or enemy, captain?"

"An intelligent question," replied my great-uncle. "We may call him an enemy who is to be treated as nearly as possible as a friend."

"Blasted if I see any sense in it," affirmed Bones. "But whatever you says, captain."

"Exactly," said my great-uncle.

And to me he added:

"Oblige yourself, Robert. There is a berth waiting for you, or you may remain on deck and take a lesson in seamanship."

I cast my eye astern at the lights of New York, so low, so scattered, already so far away.

"I'll go below and do what I may for Peter," I decided.

"As you choose," responded my extraordinary relative, and walked aft.

"Stir your stumps, ye lousy swabs," roared Bones to his men. "Hitch on to this here land-whale. —— my lights and gizzard if I ever see such a monstrous heap o' human flesh! We'd ougther take him to the South Seas and sell him to the canneybals. That's all he's good for. Come on, young gentleman, you may be the captain's nevvy or by-blow or whatever 'twas he called ye, but everybody works on this ship. Lend a hand."

I obeyed him in silence, while he and the others cursed and blas-phemed with a fluency defying description. What a company! Except in Murray's presence they owned no discipline, accepted no restraint. Palpably they hated as well as feared him, and I found myself won-dering how secure a hold he had upon their passions. Let them once cast off the spell of his magnetism and superior wickedness, and they would become so many irresponsible agents of lust and destruction.

I shuddered and was glad of the hooded cabin-lamp as we stowed Peter's limp body into the constricted space of a bunk; gladder still when they tramped away and left me alone with the Dutchman.

Through a porthole the lights of New York winked farewell to me. I was as frightened as a child by himself for the first time in the dark.

CHAPTER V

ABOARD THE BRIG

I WOKE with a ray of sunshine streaming across my face through the thick, greenish glass of a deadlight and an odd feeling of con-tentment. Mice were cheeping in the paneling at my elbow; the tim-bers and planking of the hull were groaning and snorting; there was a soothing *swissh-ssh* of divided waters; and the brig herself was swaying easily in a following sea.

Corlaer was sleeping the sleep of utter exhaustion, and I was at pains not to disturb him as I slipped to the floor, opened the door and entered the main cabin. This was deserted save for the boy Darby, who was curled up on the seat under the stern windows, peering out at the brig's creamy wake. He heard the door close after me and swiveled round at once, landing lightly on his feet as if he had been to sea for years.

"Och, Master Bob," says he, "I thought ye'd never wake up. Ah, it's the grand, grand day. And do ye smell the brine in the air? It makes the toes of your two feet dance, whether ye will or no—troth, it does."

'Twas impossible to nourish resentment against the boy for his betrayal of us. He was as naturally lawless and unmoral as a young wolf, but I could not resist a jeer at his recent transformation.

"And how does it seem to be a pirate, Darby?"

"Oh, fine! Sure, I always knew I wasn't intended for a bond-boy to run errands and carry bales. Ah, it's the grand life, Master Bob! They tell me himself—" he jerked his thumb toward the door of a state-room opposite that in which Peter and I were berthed—"is own uncle to ye, and some day, if ye choose, ye can be as great as him. Faith, and I know what my choice would be!"

"Is it your idea that pirates never work?" I inquired.

His face fell a trifle.

"Och, there's work everywhere ye go, bad 'cess to it! It's, 'Darby, lend a hand here!' Or, 'Darby, catch hold o' this rope!' Or, 'Darby, fetch me a pannikin o' rum!' Darby this and Darby that the night long."

His face lightened again.

"But I'm to have my own cutlass and two pistols for my belt, and they say I'm good luck."

"Good luck? How's that?"

"Sure, it's my hair, I think. Flint—him that this crew sail with by usual—he has a liking for a red-headed lad. Such as meself brings him luck, so they swear, and Long John—"

"Who?"

"Long John—Master Silver, to be sure—him with the one leg we talked to by the shore yesterday—he says I'll go far with Flint."

I had to laugh at my own bemusement at the picture Darby's remark called up. Yesterday morning at this hour I had been laboring industriously in the counting-room in Pearl Street. And how much had happened since then! I harked back to my setting-forth for the Bristol packet, the casual conversation with the one-legged mariner—how skilfully he had pumped me and annexed Darby to his plot!—the encounter with the Irish maid—

With this I curbed my recollections. Thought of Moira O'Donnell was unpleasant, for I could not rid my mind of the suspicion that she must be bound up in some way in the schemes her father worked at in coöperation with my great-uncle.

But there! I found relief in this reflection. Certes, her father could be no worse than my relative; and here was I, innocent of any art or part in Murray's devious ploys, yet tossed into the grip of their mechanism as ruthlessly as if my life depended upon his success. And perhaps it did. What more natural, then, than that she was equally innocent? Aye, from the conversation betwixt the two conspirators I had overheard the night before it appeared that she *was* innocent, probably in greater ignorance of her father's plans than I, else how explain O'Donnell's concern upon discovering the character of the men with whom she was to be thrown in contact?

And this aroused a further recollection. What was it the lass had said as we parted?

"Here our paths diverge."

She would not have said that had she known all, for there had been no necessity for the lie. Doubt not, she was in entire ignorance of the black evil these two plotted! I was glad with a great burst of exultation which must have shown itself in my face, for Darby exclaimed:

"There was a good fairy flicked a wing over you, Master Bob! Glory, but ye had the happy thought. Will ye throw in with us and be a pirate chief? Troth, there'd be no better."

"Not I, Darby; but I will have a bite to eat, if such there be aboard a pirate craft."

"Lashin's of everything in nature," rejoined Darby briskly. "Sit to the table yon, and I'll fetch it from the galley."

The table was set and ready, not with coarse crockery and steel forks, knives and spoons, but with dainty china, heavy silverware and fine napery, too. I commented on this when Darby returned, balancing smoking dishes and a jug of hot chocolate upon a tray.

"'Tis the way himself—" his thumb indicated the starboard stateroom door—"will live. The best of everything he'll have, and on his own ship nigger slaves to serve him, and they in liveries like grand gentlemen have. Whisht!"

His voice sank to a whisper.

"He's a terrible unchancy fellow, yon, Master Bob. Not for all the gold onzas Long John do be always talkin' of would I ha' *him* for uncle! No, no! I'll sail with Flint, rather. The eye to him—and the soft voice and quiet ways! And him as swift to cut your throat or walk ye down the plank as Flint; aye, and swifter! I ha' the creepies on my back whiles I look at him.

"Flint, now, he's main different, Long John says. He'll swig rum wi' any man, and if he wants your life ye'll be in no doubt of that same; and he curses better'n Bill Bones."

"You seem to have experienced no trouble in becoming intimate with your new companions, Darby," I remarked.

"It's me head does it," returned Darby, unabashed. "As I told ye, it brings good luck."

"Not to me," I retorted with a grin.

"And don't ye be too sure," he flashed. "We'll maybe sail a long ways together; and I'm your friend, Master Bob, for ye were never one to let me be put upon in the counting-room."

"Humph," said I. "That is to be seen. Where is 'himself,' as you call him?"

"Asleep in his berth. Troth, he was up until dawn conning the brig through the harbor shoals."

"Are we outside?"

"Sure, we're by and beyond what they call Sandy Hook. There's only the wide ocean in front."

"I'm for the deck then," I answered. "Keep an ear on Master Corlaer, Darby. If he craves food fetch him some of this chocolate."

"Leave him to me," said Darby confidently. "He's another I like fine. Wasn't it him brought me the Injun scalp and the knife wi' blood on it? Oh, ye must both turn pirate! We'd make a grand crew, just the three of us."

The companionway was empty, and I met nobody until I had climbed to the deck. The brig was running free before a smart nor'west breeze, and there was just enough of a sea to toss an occasional shower of spray over the bows. The wind was booming in the hollow of the sails, and the cordage sang like a great harp. Sea-birds were circling the mast tops and skimming the waves with occasional raucous cries. And over all the sun cast a warm, golden radiance that held a magic spell.

I understood now the contentment with which I had wakened, although indeed 'twas passing strange that I so readily adapted myself to the sea and its ways, seeing that all my life I had never been beyond the waters of the inner harbor. Yet 'tis the fact I had no discomfort or misgiving and even acquired instinctively the sailor's tricks of standing and walking, as was commented upon by no less an authority than John Silver.

The deck was deserted for'ard. One man was lashed in the main cross-trees, sweeping the entire circuit of the horizon with a spyglass. Aft there were only Silver and another fellow at the wheel. The one-legged man waved to me with his crutch from his seat on the cabin skylight.

"Come and talk with Long John, Master Ormerod," he called. "Where did ye find them sea-legs o' yourn? You walk like a blasted admiral, no less."

"I found them below," I answered, for the life of me unable to resist the scoundrel's ingratiating manner. "Where are the rest of your company?"

He laughed and winked at the man at the wheel, an awful-looking creature, so heavy of shoulder as to appear deformed, with a green shade over deeply sunken eyes that were all pitted around with tiny blue scars.

"Ha, ha! Our young gentleman says to himself, says he: 'Only two on deck, one on 'em wi' a single leg, t'other all but blind. And here's me as is young and sturdy.' A clean field, says you, Master Ormerod; but you're failin' to reckon on John's crutch, which same can be a very nasty weapon at need; and if Pew's eyes don't see far he can shoot by ear as well as most o' us by sight."

I shook my head.

"Rascals as thorough as you, Silver, would never leave an opportunity like that. 'Tis true I have had no sea-service, but I have fought with the savages upon our northern frontier.

"I'll not move until I see a clear path before me."

He laughed uproarously at this.

"Now that 'ere's a good joke on me! Might ha' knowed you wasn't as open as your face. You'll learn fast, you will, Master Ormerod. I'll lay four spade-guineas to that. Bear over just a p'int, Ezra, matey. Aye, so!"

"Is that foretops'l drawin' full, John?" asked the man with the green eye-shade in a voice that was singularly soft.

Silver squinted aloft.

"She'll do," he decided.

"Would you mind telling me how a blind man can steer?" I inquired.

The man with the green eye-shade chuckled in a way to chill your blood, so sardonic, so overpoweringly evil was the caliber of the mirth it suggested.

"A poor, blind man has to earn his bread and 'backy somehow, young sir," he answered unctuously.

"Don't go to makin' up your mind Pew can't see everything, Master Ormerod," said Silver, shifting his crutch. "I'd hate to have him decide to take a shot at me. Steer? Well now, what's needed in steerin'? A strong arm, says you, and you says true. Also and likewise, an ear for canvas. Lastly and leastwise, an eye for the course.

"Any man can read a compass, young gentleman; but not every sailorman can feel how his ship takes the wind and meet his rudder quick when she wants meetin'. Pew can. Give him some one like me to play eyes for him, and he'll steer as straight a course as a packet-boat wi' a bonus on the voyage."

"Are there many cripples in your crew?" I asked curiously.

"Cripples?" repeated Silver. "It all depends on what you might mean. There's cripples and cripples. Me and Pew now, we got ours in the same broadside. 'Twas a Injyman wi' a fighting master, and she stood to us, board and board."

He slapped the stump of his thigh.

"An eighteen-pounder did that. *Whoof!* Off she went. Pew, he was rammin' home a charge and leaned out through the port and caught the flash of a carronade. 'Tain't good for the eyes, nowise; but as I was a-sayin', don't you ever go for to believe Pew can't see. He's sur-prizin', he is.

"But we was talkin' of cripples. Yes, there's cripples and cripples. Some on 'em ye pays their screw—"

"Their what?" I interrupted.

"Their screw, the what d'ye call it—insurance money. So much we get from the prize money extry for the hurt. Pew, he got a thousand pounds, which same he blowed in three nights in St. Pierre. D'ye mind, Ezra? I got eight hundred pounds for my leg—and fair enough, if you asks me."

"And that eight hundred pounds I'll gamble you ha' stowed away in a safe hole, John," said Pew with a gentleness which gave the words a peculiarly sinister significance.

Silver nodded almost complacently.

"What I gets, I keeps. I'm none o' your free spenders, rich today, poor tomorrow. Some day I'll be retirin' from piratin', and then I'll aim to ride in my own coach and sit in Parleyment."

"You'll have to sail your own ship first, John," said Pew, and the remark was fraught with implications that made me turn cold at the pit of my stomach.

It was as if you could see the trail of bloodshed and suffering Silver would blaze to possess that ship and to exploit her to advantage.

"And why not?" returned Silver vigorously. "We'll name no names, Ezra, but captains can't live for ever. Some is aged and some soaks theirselves in rum. You never know! You never know!"

"There's Bill Bones, as has ideas on the subjeck," remarked Pew.

And he contrived to make me feel the horror of a long-drawn-out feud and rivalry.

"Yes, there's Bill," ruminated Silver. "Flint's mate, is Bill. Flint's best pal, is Bill. Flint's confeydantey, some says, is Bill. Well, well! But we was talkin' o' cripples and how a blind man can steer, which is a long way off from Bill, who isn't neither crippled nor blind, and maybe has hopes, so he has, when he remembers that."

Pew laughed so coldly, with such demoniac inhumanity, that I experienced a sudden fellow-feeling for Master Bones, distasteful as I had found him—also, a pronounced desire to change the subject.

The bare proximity to such whole-souled, heartless cruelty was unpleasant.

"Do you commonly indulge in exploits like yesterday's, Silver?" I asked.

He cocked his head on one side.

"Exploits? Yesterday? Meanin' the disposition of yourself? We-ell, no, sir; not reg'larly, I'd say, Ezra."

"Not by a capful o' onzas," agreed Pew.

"I'm no man for makin' trouble," continued Silver, "but there's them as might say the captain was a mite rash."

"Why don't you call him by his name?"

Silver gave me an odd look.

"There's some names as is better off unmentioned in conversation," he said. "We'll call him the captain, wi' your kind leave and permission, sir."

"Call him what you please," I answered; "but I should think it was insanity for men with your reputations to venture into New York. Why, the second mate of that Bristol packet had seen Captain Murray, and would have known him."

"Ah!" said Silver, grinning. "But he didn't see the captain, which is more to the point, my master; nor he wouldn't have had the chance to see him in any case. 'Cause why? 'Cause the captain come ashore most careful in the dusk wi' his cloak around his face and three stout hearties to fend off inquisitive strangers."

"But the rest of you—"

"Now, Master Ormerod, what honest sailorman a-tremblin' for his life is goin' to remember faces out o' a crew o' pirates he sees on a shot-up deck? All he thinks of, says you, is a lot of villains as has likely slaughtered his messmates and looted his ship, and quite right. Why, I've been stood treat in Kingston by a skipper I'd stripped two months past—but that was afore I lost my leg, which bein' in other seas ain't as yet a mark of identification on me in these parts."

"And did you take this ship designedly to carry you into New York?"

"You might say truthfully she was the best fitted for it of several," he acknowledged. "Blow my other stick off if she was good for anything else."

"Not forty pounds in her," mumbled Pew, twiddling the wheel-spokes.

"Her crew—"

Silver raised his eyebrows and gave me a slow wink.

"Poor unfortunates! 'Twas one time we couldn't take chances."

Pew's chuckle trickled icily from under the eye-shade which cast a green blur over his whole lower face.

"I suppose there is a hell for such as you," I said, trying to keep my voice steady.

"Some says there is and some says there isn't," answered Silver reasonably. "No use to worry, says I."

I was so wrought up that I think I must have come to blows with them but for a fortunate diversion. Bones and several other men emerged from the fo'c'sle hatch, yawning and stretching their arms, evidently having just arisen from sleep. At the same moment Peter Corlaer climbed from the cabin companionway, lurched for a moment, on his feet and then staggered precariously toward the bulwarks. I started for'ard to aid him, and Bones ran aft with a loud yell.

"Don't ye spoil my decks, ye fat cow!" he shouted.

Poor Peter, regardless of both of us, seized a stay and clung to it abjectly, quite helpless. Bones reached him first and gave him a shove which sent him plunging into the scuppers head first.

"Get up," snarled Bones, and dealt him a vicious kick with a heavy sea-boot.

Peter groaned, and I caught Bones by the arm.

"——— you for a coward!" I shouted. "Captain Murray bade you use us gently. Is this how you obey?"

He snatched free of me and yanked out a knife.

"Obey, ye lousy lubber!" he howled. "I'm Flint's mate, and I'll show ye who can say obey to me. Get back there or I'll cut your heart out and eat it afore ye."

I looked about me for a weapon, anxious to give him a lesson; but there was not a sign of anything handy, and I backed away cautiously from the menace of his knife. He had been drinking through the night on top of liberal potations during the previous day, and the effect was to render him quite insensible to any rule now that his passions were aroused. Silver shouted to him to let us be, as did one or two others;

but his only answer was a string of the curses in which he was so proficient, and he continued to circle after me.

For myself I was not greatly frightened, for, as it chanced, knife-fighting was an art in which I was somewhat expert, thanks to instruction from my father's Indian friends; but I was concerned lest the scoundrel make a dart at Peter and slay the Dutchman as he lay inert. Judge of my amazement then when Peter swayed to his feet, holding on to the bulwarks to pull himself erect. His face was white, but he abandoned his support without hesitation and advanced, crooked-legged, across the deck toward us.

"I take him, Bob," he said.

I jumped between him and Bones in time to stop the pirate's rush, dodging a knife-thrust by the width of my coatsleeve.

"Keep away, Peter," I panted. "I can handle him. You can't. You'll—"

"I take him," repeated Corlaer.

He reached out his hand, grasped my shoulder and spun me from his path as easily as if I had been a child. And I did not attempt to return to his side, for I had felt the strength in his arm and knew that I had no cause to question his ability to take care of himself against any man, however armed.

Bones stared at him for a moment with a mixture of rage and sur-prize.

"D'ye *want* your —— throat cut?" he sneered. "Here, turn your head and I'll take an ear instead. There's naught in slaying a cow like you."

Peter said nothing, simply stood there before him weaponless, arms slightly bent, legs crooked at the knees. The Dutchman's little eyes, almost buried from sight in his face, glittered with a steely menace.

"Let him be, Bill," called Silver again—was I wrong in fancying his tone unduly officious, provocative?

"I'm —— if I do," rasped Bones. "If he wants it, he'll get it."

He sprang at Peter with knife upraised, aiming to slash his throat; but Peter moved with lightning speed to counter him. One immense arm, thick as a tree-bough, shot out and imprisoned the wrist of the knife-hand; a twist, and the knife pinged on the deck. The other arm captured a thigh, and Bones was reared above Peter's head.

Peter gave him a preliminary shake as if to prove to him how completely he was in his power and started to walk back to the lee bulwark. Bones shrieked like the lost soul he was, certain that Peter intended to cast him into the sea; but half-way across the deck Peter came to a loose halyard. He lowered Bones carelessly, tucked him under one arm and proceeded to reeve a landsman's slip-noose. We all watched him with utter fascination, and it is an indication of the pirates' code in such affairs that none of them intervened. But Peter was not to hang Master Bones.

"Your object is no doubt praiseworthy, Peter," remarked my great-uncle from the cabin companionway behind us, "but I fear I must request you to let the man go. He is of some value to a friend of mine."

Peter regarded Murray curiously.

"He knifes Robert and me—*ja*," answered the Dutchman.

"He will not do it again," Murray assured him. "Master Bones!"

Peter regretfully unhitched the noose from Bones' neck and administered a shove which sent him reeling across the deck, to carom into the butt of the mizzenmast, recoiling with the loss of a broken tooth and ending up in a battered heap at Murray's feet. My great-uncle regarded the fellow with obvious displeasure.

"Stand up, Master Bones," he said.

Bones stumbled to his feet, bleeding from several cuts and scratches. He was very plainly frightened at what lay ahead of him.

"Master Bones," resumed my great-uncle, "you are for the present under my command, and I happen to have somewhat old-fashioned theories as regards discipline and the carrying out of orders. You have recently disobeyed an order of mine."

"Sure, I didn't—"

"Master Bones," my uncle went on without raising his voice, "did you ever know a man named Fotherill—Jack, I believe, was the given name?"

Bones nodded, unable to speak.

"And what did I order done to him, Master Bones?"

Bones moistened his lips.

"Keel-hauled, he was."

"Correct," agreed my great-uncle. "Keel-hauled. A most expressive phrase, Robert," he added to me. "Technically, I should explain, it involves drawing a man under the keel of a vessel. It has—shall we say?—unpleasant consequences."

He turned to Bones.

"No man disobeys an order of mine more than once, Master Bones. That is all. You may go for'ard."

The man started to slouch off, wiping the blood from his cheek with his coat sleeve; but Peter stepped in front of him.

The Dutchman took an oaken belaying-pin from the rack around the mizzenmast, held it out toward Bones and the others and calmly broke it in two with his bare hands and tossed the fragments overside.

"Admirable!" exclaimed my great-uncle. "What words could hope to express so much as that gesture? And it intrigues me to note that Corlaer has a distinct taste for the dramatic. I trust that you are recovering from the seasickness, friend Peter?"

"I get well, *ja*," answered Peter.

"Then perhaps you will come below and join me at breakfast?"

Peter looked unhappy—he loved his food, did Peter.

"Neen," he said simply. "If I eat, I get sick."

"You have my sympathy," replied my great-uncle with unfailing courtesy. "I advise a modest diet for a day or two, with an occasional dram   of liquor to warm the stomach, and then I prophesy you will become   as good a sailor as any of us. You, Robert, I perceive to have made yourself instantly at home upon the strange element. That is excellent. You shall yet prove a credit to me. Do you feel sufficiently stimulated by your new experiences to partake of a second meal so early in the day?"

"I have just been hearing what became of the lawful crew of this vessel," I answered. "It left me no appetite for food."

"Regrettable," he returned sadly. "Life is a hard business, Robert, as you have yet to learn. Mercy is as often as not a mistaken policy, a vice as much as a virtue. Silver, has the lookout sighted any vessel?"

"Not a sail since we cleared Sandy Hook, sir," the one-legged man answered briskly.

"Very good. Keep on this course and call me at once should a sail show in any quarter." And he descended with proper dignity to his breakfast.

CHAPTER VI

TALL SHIPS AND LAWLESS MEN

THERE WAS a noticeable tightening of discipline after my great-uncle's admonition to Bones, and Peter and I were let severely alone, except by Silver, who, I think, found satisfaction in annoying the mate by the effusiveness of his cordiality to us. A second lookout was sent into the foretop, and the watch on deck were continually on the alert. But nothing untoward happened that day. The brig held on her course to the southeast, and the sea surrounded us with the immensity of its restless waters. One moment the land was a faint, hazy streak in the distance; the next it was gone.

My great-uncle paced the deck with measured strides throughout the afternoon, his head bent upon his chest, not a word for anybody. He ignored me as thoroughly as the members of the crew, who treated Silver and Bones with offhand familiarity, but scurried from his path if he came near them and were quick to bob their heads and tug at forelocks. When night came he supervised the hoisting of two lanthorns, red and green, one above the other, to the main truck; and he ate very little of the excellent meal which Silver cooked in the galley and Darby served us in the cabin. Nor, contrary to his usual mood as I had read it, was he inclined for conversation.

He returned immediately to the deck, leaving Peter and me to an exchange of casual remarks with the Irish boy before we went early to our stateroom, full sleepy with the heavy sea-air. Peter was almost himself again, although he dared eat but little and suffered qualms when the brig rolled much from the perpendicular. He was asleep as soon as he lay down, but I drowsed lightly for some hours, and all that time I could hear overhead the *tap-tap-tap* of footfalls in even cadence as my great-uncle strode from the stern railing to the cabin companionway and back again.

Yet when I went on deck in the morning it was to discover Murray already there, dressed with his customary immaculate precision, his face fresh and unfatigued. He stood astraddle close by the wheel, hands clasped behind him, his gaze fixed upon the tossing waters ahead. The wind had backed around several points during the night, so that we were making more difficult weather of it; and the easy, gliding motion of the previous day had been changed to a choppy roll.

Peter was not communicative; and as I was in no mood for Silver's hypocrisy or Darby's wild talk I strode up to my great-uncle.

"You seem perturbed," I said.

"I am," he returned frankly. "I have two problems upon my mind."

"Unfortunately, I see no signs of pursuit," I answered.

He smiled.

"Nor will you, Nephew Robert. No, my problems are connected with the difficult task of attaining an imaginary spot in this trackless waste and puzzlement as to whether I have correctly estimated an equation of human values. You are not, perhaps, mathematical? Ah, too bad! There is no mental exercise so restful and diverting to the mind as algebra. But figures lack the warm interest of human equations. As, for instance, the exact degree of trust to be imposed in untrustworthy persons."

"Sail ho!" shouted the lookout in the main crosstrees.

Murray's calm face flushed with sudden emotion, and he took a step forward.

"Where does she lie?" he trumpeted through his clasped hands.

"Maybe one, two points to larboard, sir."

"Can you make her out?"

"Only tops'ls, sir; big 'uns."

"Let me know as soon as you make her," said Murray, and turned back to me.

But almost at once the other lookout in the foretop sang out—

"Second sail to larboard, sir, comin' up arter t'other chap!"

Murray rubbed his hands together with every evidence of satisfaction.

"Ah!" he exclaimed. "It appears that my estimation of the safe degree of trust to be imposed in the given situation was within the bounds of accuracy."

"I don't understand you."

"No? In plain English let us say then that my own vessel and consort are meeting me according to plan."

"The sea is wide. How can you be sure 'tis they?"

"I can not. Yet the balance of probability is in my favor."

"Why do you speak of trust?" I challenged. "Can not you trust your own people?"

"I trust nobody farther than I must," he retorted.

And without another word he produced a patent folding spyglass from his pocket and clapped it to his eye. Silver, who had been an interested witness to the scene from his aerie atop of the cabin skylight, hopped across the deck to my great-uncle's side.

"Beggin' your pardon, captain," he said. "But I'd make oath that tops'l is the canvas you took out o' the Mogul's ship off Pondicherry. Mind it, sir? 'Twas uncommon bleached and looked whiter'n our cloth."

Murray handed him the glass.

"Stap me, Silver, but I believe you are right," he returned. "What a hawk's eye you must have! Here, see what you can make of it with this."

Long John peered through the glass, steadying his crutch against the butt of the mizzen.

"Aye, 'tis—"

"*R'yal James* to leeward!" hailed the foretop.

And the main crosstrees echoed, not to be outdone—

"*Walrus* comin' up astarn o' her!"

"'Tis they, never a doubt," assented Silver as he lowered the glass. "Diggin' into it they are, too, and a lusty show o' canvas to both o' them. If you was to ask me now, captain, I'd say Flint isn't willing to plow your wake."

If there was a hint of an indicated threat in this remark Murray ignored it.

"Master Martin knows his ship," he answered, "as doth Captain Flint his. You lads are forever pondering why certain men rise to command. There lies the answer, Silver. 'Tis knowledge of how to handle your ship; aye, and to fight her, and to plan at need how not to fight her."

Silver knuckled his forehead, handing back the glass.

"Sure, sir, they all says a good captain is born and never made, and

we be main fortunate as has two that can't be beat or took or har-
ried from their ways."

My great-uncle indulged in a pinch of snuff, a mildly cynical smile
upon his handsome features.

"I thank you," he acknowledged. "And now I would have the men
tumble up their gear from below and make ready the boats. I shall
also leave it to you, Silver, to lay the powder-train. How much have
you?"

"Three casks, sir."

"Excellent. But allow us ample time to get free."

"Why do you give your orders to Silver and not to Bones?" I inquired
curiously after the one-legged man had gone for'ard.

My great-uncle lowered his glass with a benevolent smile.

"I rejoice to perceive that you have an observant tendency," he
commented. "Why do I single out Silver for orders? Ah! The reasons
are quite obvious. To begin with, he is gifted with a personality which
enables him to secure the accomplishment of tasks; but perhaps as
important as that consideration is the parallel fact that it lies to my
interest to develop the seed of dissension in the *Walrus'* crew. The
future contains infinite possibilities. Who knows what trifling factor
may influence the dictates of fate?"

"They must be a strange crowd aboard the *Walrus,*" I said.

"They are," assented my great-uncle. "In piracy, Robert, as in politics and business, he wins who plays the opposing factions against
each other. I am, you may say, in a minority of one among some hundreds of headstrong, wilful, intemperate men. United, they would
crush me like a fly on the wall. Divided, and kept divided, they are
so many instruments for the fulfilling of my desires."

"How if I handed on your precept to them?" I gibed.

"They would not believe you. Their vanity would prohibit it. And
even though they did, I would divide them upon the very point you
raised."

The amazing ingenuity and fertility of resource of this heartless
old rogue who was my relative began to compel me to a reluctant
admiration of him. Perhaps some trace of this was revealed in my
face, for his own eyes brightened and he dropped one hand lightly
upon my coat sleeve.

"We shall yet come to an understanding, Robert. All is not so black as is painted. But my design is to induct you into the scope of my plans at one sitting, seeing that in such a manner I can most clearly present to you my reasons for requiring your assistance and the importance of the stake I play for."

"I know not of the blackness," I answered; "but I require no clearer understanding. Here on these decks have been murder and robbery, and in your ranks, if I mistake not, breed treachery and hate. 'Tis a sorry outlook. I would gladly be gone from it."

His face fell a little.

"Tut," he said. "We disposed of that before. Wait until we are aboard the *Royal James,* Robert. Then you will realize what I offer you."

"I have heard much of it already," I agreed dryly.

"Anon you shall hear all," he answered. "Let us get Flint across-table from us in the *James'* state cabin with a beaker of rum at his elbow. Then you shall hear me talk."

Bones came up to speak to him; and I rejoined Peter, who was glumly watching the unlashing of the small boats and the rigging of the falls by which they were slung overside.

"Now I get more sick again," he grunted.

"Cheer up," I told him. "You shall soon have a more substantial craft beneath you."

And I pointed to the two strange ships which had risen over the horizon line until the towering piles of their bellying sails were clearly visible. Like us, they rather quartered the wind; but they were of far heavier build, and they seemed to crash through seas that we were tossed over. While we watched, their upper works came into view, and I descried a long band of painted gunports on the leader's starboard side.

"She's a thirty-six, no less!" I exclaimed. "Can she be Murray's ship?"

"Whatefer she is, I be sick," rejoined Peter unhappily.

Silver stumped up to where we leaned upon the larboard bulwarks.

"Sightly, ain't they?" he said. "Nothin' like a fine ship wi' canvas drawin' for a picture, is there?"

His face shone with what, I am persuaded, was entirely honest emotion.

"They are big as frigates," I answered. "How did your company come by such craft?"

He chuckled.

"I ha' heard tell the captain had the *James* from the Frenchies in some funny way. A Injyman she was—the *Esperance*. But Flint and a few o' us took the *Walrus* with our own hands on the Smyrna v'yage. She's better nor she was then, but she can't sail wi' the *James* yet."

"Is she as heavy armed as the *James?*" I asked, for the leading ship partly blanketed her from our view.

"Pierced the same, she is, Master Ormerod, and both has eighteen-pounder carronades below, but where the *Walrus* carries long twelves on the main deck, the *James* has long eighteens."

As Murray nodded dismissal to Bones, Silver left us and hopped up to him.

"All set and ready below, captain," he announced.

My great-uncle cast his eye at the approaching ships, now so near that we could make out quite distinctly the contour of their hulls, painted yellow, with a white band delimiting the ports, man-o'-war fashion. The *James* was already beginning to take in some of her top canvas.

"Very good, Silver," he answered. "Master Bones! You bring the ship to and put over the boats."

There was a great flapping and banging as the brig rounded to, and with much yo-ho-hoing the boats were lowered into the water.

"You will go off first, Master Bones," ordered Murray. "Kindly present my compliments to Captain Flint and say that I should like to have a word with him aboard the *James* at his early convenience."

Bones sullenly touched his cap and led better than half the crew into one of the two longboats the brig had carried. Murray nodded to Silver as they cast off.

"Start your train," he said shortly. "Nephew Robert, I wish you and Peter to go into the second boat. At once, please!"

"Plenty o' time, captain," said Silver with a grin. "You can lay to it I'm a-goin' to give myself a chance to hop up from below."

The suspicion of a smile dawned in my great-uncle's eyes.

"It is barely possible that your disability is a factor in my arrangements," he answered.

Peter and I climbed clumsily down the ladder of cleats nailed to the brig's hull and dropped into the bobbing longboat. Peter groaned as we crawled over the thwarts.

"Like der waves is my stomach—oop—andt down. Now I be sick, *ja!*"

And he was.

Presently Murray descended the brig's side with an agility which put me to shame and took his seat in the stern sheets. Darby swarmed down like a monkey and ensconced himself beside us in the bow. Silver was slung over in the bight of a rope, and the last of the crew tumbled after him, one upon the other's heels. Oars were thrust out, and we pulled rapidly toward the *Royal James*, wallowing in the trough of the sea, a quarter-mile away. The *Walrus*, foaming up under a cloud of canvas, was almost as near, and on our weather board.

Darby crouched at my knees, drinking in the spectacle.

"Oh, the tall ships, Master Bob! Look to the water dripping from their bows, and the lordly way they stand up like the towers of churches or maybe a castle. Did ye ever see the beat of it? And the guns that are like to the grinning teeth in an ogre's head!"

Boom! The roar of an explosion behind us was as sharp as the smack of an open hand. I turned my head. So did the others. Murray was looking back, too, and the rowers rested on their oars.

A cloud of smoke jetted up from the brig's hatches. She heeled over to starboard as we watched, gave a quivering lurch and commenced to slide under by the head. We could hear the slap of the sails as they struck the waves. In two minutes she was gone.

"That was well-contrived, Silver," remarked my great-uncle. "'Sdeath, but you are a man of parts. Give way, lads!"

He nodded the length of the boat to me.

"I trust you perceive the significance of that, Nephew Robert. A certain young man, we will say, disappears from New York. A certain brig disappears simultaneously. Some might go so far as to associate the two disappearances. Frigates put to sea in search of a certain brig—but the brig is no more."

The men at the oars laughed loudly, and I made no answer. What could I say? I felt very hopeless.

The bulwarks of the *James* were lined with heads and faces as we

pulled under her counter and made fast, and even at that distance
the complexity of her crew was apparent. I saw Portuguese, Finns,
Scandinavians, French and English cheek by jowl with negroes, Moors,
Indians and slant-eyed yellow men. But what impressed me most was
the absolute silence which greeted us, a silence all the more impressive because the wind carried to our ears the bedlam of shouts,
cheers, oaths and imprecations with which the *Walrus* was receiving
Bones' boat several hundred yards away.

Murray waved me to the ladder as he set foot on the first cleat.

"Up with you, Nephew! Peter, also. The rest go to the *Walrus*."

Darby snatched at my hand as I rose.

"Whirra, whirra, but there's an ache in my heart to be from ye,
Master Bob!" he cried. "And if we was to be pirates it do seem we
might be together on the same ship!"

He made to follow me, indeed, but Silver pulled him back.

"You stays wi' us, Darby," growled the one-legged man. "Blast ye,
lad, you're our good luck. Flint'll douse the ship in rum after one look
at ye."

"We'll meet again, Darby," I said. "Never you fear."

He dashed the tears from his eyes.

"Sure, there's never a fear in me heart," he denied. "But I'm all broke
up from the parting with ye. God be good to us, and the blessed saints
spread their wings over your head! I'm thinking you're like to need
it more than me. Yes, yes, John, I'll be settin'; but—"

He was still jabbering in a mixture of grief and joy when I climbed
over the bulwarks and dropped beside my great-uncle into the midst
of another world.

Fore and aft from poop to fo'c'sle stretched the wide deck from
which the lofty spars rose like forest giants. The massive bulwarks
were shoulder-high, and inboard everything was painted red exactly
as in a King's ship. The deck was remarkably clean and in order, ropes
coiled, spare spars stowed and lashed, boats in their chocks, crates
and other gear secured. A few cannon were lashed to their ringbolts,
but the greater part of the battery was mounted on the lower deck
under cover. The hundreds of men who had watched us from the bulwarks had all sifted for'ard. We stood in the midst of an open space,
with only three others.

One of these three was a very small old man with wispy gray hair and deeply bronzed face, from which his eyes peered intensely blue and childishly simple. He had gold rings in his ears, and his dress was neat and plain.

"My sarvice, captain," he greeted Murray. "Ship's in order, I hope. —— my eyes if we've had so much as a —— o' genuine wind since the —— hussy bore away from ye off the Hook."

The effect of the unspeakable blasphemies which poured with mild intonation from his lips was ridiculous, but nobody appeared to notice it, and I learned afterward that his habit of swearing by the anatomy of the twelve apostles and various saints and sacred figures was the quaintest of several quaint characteristics of an unusual personality.

"We won't complain about that, Master Martin," replied my great-uncle. "I have brought back my grandnephew to be the mainstay of my old age. Here he is—Master Ormerod, Martin. Ah, and this is a friend of his and an old enemy of mine, Peter Corlaer," as Peter rolled over the top of the bulwarks. "He is more to be reckoned with than you might suppose, is Peter.

"Master Martin, Nephew Robert, is my mate, and as such, my right hand and arm."

Martin stepped back, and the second of the three men confronting us touched his cap. This was a square, heavy-built fellow with a dour glint to his eye, who wore a decent blue cloth coat and small clothes.

"And here is Saunders, Master Martin's second," continued my great-uncle. "A Scot like myself. My nephew should make a fine Scotsman; eh, Saunders?"

"He's a braw-lookin' laddie in seemin'," Saunders agreed cautiously.

"Your meaning is that we must prove him?" responded Murray. "Quite true. We shall. Hola, Coupeau!"

And he rattled into a string of French which I could not follow as the third man met him with a bow and a scrape of one foot. Coupeau was as brutal in looks and manner as Black Dog or Bill Bones, but without the sinister implications of speech and action that made me shudder whenever the blind man Pew approached me or spoke in my hearing. He had been branded on the cheek, and an attempt to obliterate the brand—or perhaps 'twas the superimposed scar of a wound—had made that side of his face a very nightmare. His wrists and forearms showed gouges that wound upward like snakes and suggested what other torments his clothing concealed.

"Coupeau," remarked my great-uncle, turning again to me, "is our gunner. I saved him from the French galleys, and he is not without devotion to me, that quality of devotion tinged by self-interest which is to be preferred above all.

"And now we will go aft and prepare to receive Captain Flint. Master Martin, we shall probably lie here for several hours. Have all the tops manned and a vigilant watch maintained. I have every reason to suppose we need fear no intruders, but we must be on the edge of the cruising-course of the King's ships, and I'll take no risks."

"Aye, aye, sir," assented Martin. "We ha' not sighted a sail this twenty-four hours gone."

"And before?"

"A Philadelphia packet. Captain Flint made signal to chase; but I held off as you directed, and he turned back."

"You did well, Martin. I'll not forget. Conduct Captain Flint to us when he comes aboard."

CHAPTER VII

MURRAY'S PLAN

MURRAY led us to a door in the break of the poop which was opened for us by a stalwart black in a red livery coat, who ushered us along a companionway lined with stateroom doors into a spacious state cabin stretching the width of the stern. The walls were paneled in mahogany; silver sconces were fastened at intervals, and a wondrous luster chandelier was pendant from the ceiling, itself uncommonly lofty for shipboard; several paintings in the French school hung at the sides; and there were trophies of peculiar arms and armor. Underfoot were Eastern rugs, thick-piled and soft of hue. The furniture was of mahogany, and a service of massy plate appeared upon the table that was set under the range of windows which formed the rear wall of the room.

My great-uncle surveyed this magnificence with pardonable pride. 'Twas evident it meant something to him.

"Diomede," he said to the negro, "where is Master Gunn?"

A high, piping voice answered him from the companionway.

"Coming, worshipful sir. Ben Gunn's a-coming. I jest stopped by the galley to fetch up your chocolate, a-sayin' to myself as the captain would be sharp-set account o' early business in the morning."

The man who followed the voice trotted in bearing a silver pitcher of steaming chocolate, Murray's favorite drink; aye, and food. He was a slender fellow, with a simple, open face, clad in plain black as became an upper servant. He stopped dead at sight of us.

"Set your tray on the table, Gunn," instructed my great-uncle. "This is my grandnephew, Master Ormerod, and his friend, Master Corlaer. They are to sail with us a while."

Gunn pulled his forelock and ducked.

"Sarvant, gentlemen," he acknowledged. "Allus glad to please, is Ben Gunn. Bound to oblige ye, gentlemen. You jest name your drinks, and I'll fetch 'em up from the winebins."

"Food as well, Gunn," said Murray. "And Captain Flint is coming aboard."

Ben Gunn cocked his head on one side.

"That means rum," he commented. "Plenty o' rum, says you. Jest leave it to Ben, captain."

He ducked and scraped again and skipped off into the companionway with a kind of wiggle like a self-conscious child.

"My steward," remarked my relative. "He will be at your disposal for anything you require, Robert—yours, too, friend Peter. You will find the negroes equally anxious to please."

"The man is a half-wit, is he not?" I asked.

"A natural, yes," assented Murray, tasting the chocolate.

"I should think it would be dangerous to have one so simple in such close proximity to you."

My great-uncle smiled.

"You are quite, quite wrong, my boy. It is for the very reason that the man is incapable of spying that I use him. He is more valuable for my purposes than the most intelligent member of the crew."

He broke off.

"This chocolate is by no means so well brewed as Silver's. An extraordinary fellow, that, monstrously clever—exactly the sort of man, Robert, I never permit to remain near me. Indeed, if you possess the patience and the interest to analyze the composition of my officers and crew you will observe, I believe, that there is not an independently clever man amongst them. Aye, and if you find me a clever man aboard the *Royal James*—yourself and friend Peter excepted, of course—I will thank you to point him out to me, and I will straightway make a present of him to Flint, who must have half a dozen of the *Walrus'* crew who esteem themselves equally capable with him of commanding her."

"Yet the *James* was able to get along without you for several days," I remarked.

"Ah! A shrewd thrust I am bound to admit, my dear Robert, that I regarded my recently concluded expedition as a dubious experiment. 'Twas in the light of reflections identical with those you have just detailed that I spoke of it as a problem in human equations. I was reasonably convinced that I could depend upon my men, but I should not have been greatly surprized had they abandoned me.

"I am not—by necessity I am not—regarded with affection by my followers. And on the whole, I think, I have gotten along better by means of fear than I might have by means of affection. Fear is a natural element in a pirate's career. What place has he in his life for affections?

"But we are faring far afield, Robert, into realms of philosophy in no way affiliated with our problems of the immediate moment. Hark! Do I not hear something?"

He did beyond question—an uproar of curses and shouts upon the deck outside.

"Perhaps your crew have decided to spring their revolt after your return, instead of during your absence," I suggested.

He shook his head, smiling.

"No, no. It is only that Captain Flint has come aboard. Pray take your seats. I promise you an interesting episode."

The door to the deck banged open, and a harsh, domineering voice bellowed in the companionway.

"—— me, Martin, what the —— —— —— —— d'ye think ye are? By the —— —— —— ——, ye lousy, slack-bellied swab, ye made us—"

"Stow that, ye —— —— apology for a —— —— ——," interrupted Martin mildly from the deck.

"Why, any —— —— would ha' had more sense than you!"

"Like ——! I'm my own master, I am. I—"

"Ye may be when ye stand on the *Walrus'* deck, but here you're only another —— —— —— as doesn't know better'n to veer after—"

"Belay for a —— —— lackey, ye slab-faced chunk o' rotted seahorse! I'll talk to your master!"

Slam went the door, and a mutter of curses rumbled from the companionway, preceding a tall, blue-jowled man in a flaming red coat all cobwebbed over with gold lace. He halted in the cabin entrance, hands on his hips, feet planted wide, close-set green eyes flickering balefully on either side of a long nose that seemed to poke out from a tangle of lank, black hair.

"Back, eh, Murray?" he snarled. "Two men the richer for your effort. Gut me, 'twas a fool's errand!"

"Pardon me," objected Murray, "but I am considerably more than 'two men the richer' in consequence of my run ashore—although I would not appear by these words to deprecate the importance to be attached to the acquisition of my grandnephew and Master Corlaer. Permit me, Captain Flint! Master Ormerod, my grandnephew, and Peter Corlaer."

And to me, aside:

"I fear these introductions must become boring. We shall require no more."

Flint scowled at us, flinging himself into a chair at the opposite end of the table from my great-uncle.

"A youth and a fat man!" he ejaculated. "And unwilling at that, so Bones tells me."

"Master Bones was correct in that statement," my great-uncle assented cheerfully; "but I fancy he neglected to add that the 'fat man' took his knife away from him and must have hanged him had I not intervened."

An appreciable degree of respect dawned in Flint's eyes.

"He is no butter-tub if he bested Bill," conceded the *Walrus'* captain. "Curse me, though, if I see why you should add a cub to your crew."

"Tut, tut, captain," remonstrated Murray. "'A cub!' Think again. The boy is my heir."

"All he'll fall heir to will be the rope that hung you," returned Flint. "But I'll own I did you wrong when I accused you of being but two men the better by your shore expedition. I was forgetting the red-headed mascot John Silver fetched aboard. 'Tis the first promise o' luck we ha' had! I'd never have lost that Philadelphia packet t'other day with him aboard."

"I believe I overheard something of a dispute with Martin on that point," commented my great-uncle dryly. "He obeyed my orders in calling you off, and you broke our agreement when you would have given chase."

"And why not?" roared Flint. "A ——— ——— fool agreement, if you broach it now! A ——— ——— of a ——— ——— ——— piece of idiocy! Curse me for a lubber if I see the sense in letting a fat prize slip through our fingers. And so I told Martin. Let me have him on my deck, and I'd use my hanger to him."

My uncle took snuff with much delicacy and rang a silver bell in front of him.

"Gunn is late with the liquor. I must ask your indulgence, captain, for compelling you to talk dry. But as to Martin and the prize. Indeed, you wrong the good fellow. As I have already said, he did no more than carry out my orders, and while you may experience difficulty in comprehending my reasons for stipulating that no prizes were to be taken in my absence, I am so vain as to suppose that a few moments' conversation will clear all doubts from your mind."

Ben Gunn bustled into the cabin in the course of this harangue and deposited a trayful of decanters, bottles and flasks before us. Captain Flint, without awaiting an invitation, seized upon an earthen receptacle labeled "Gedney's Jamaican Rum," pried out the cork with the point of a knife, tilted it to his mouth and drained a mighty dram.

Then he set it down beside him, wiped his mouth on his coat-cuff and cleared his throat.

"Humph," he growled. "I'm listening."

My uncle looked distressed.

"Gunn," he said, "how often have I asked you to supply Captain Flint with a goblet, beaker or some other drinking-utensil?"

The steward wiggled abjectly and pulled his forelock.

"Oft and often you has, captain, but 'taint no manner o' use—least-ways not the fust time. Captain Flint says as how he always has to take the flavor of a new flask straight from the neck."

"And so I do," agreed Flint. "Rum don't taste the same in a cup. Ye drink coffee or tea in a cup—but rum! —— my eyes if I ever see so much fuss over drink and victuals as you make. But anything to oblige, Murray. I don't ha' to eat with ye every day, thank God!"

Gunn produced a large silver goblet from a wall-cupboard, and Flint straightway filled it to the brim. I pushed a cut glass carafe of water toward him, supposing he would wish some dilution, and he laughed jarringly.

"You ha' much to learn, my lad," he jeered. "We don't spoil good rum wi' water aboard the *Walrus*. There's a cask broached this minute on the spar-deck, and all hands fillin' their pannikins as fast as they can empty 'em, wi' red-headed Darby astride the butt for luck."

"Which means you will be in no condition to make sail a few hours hence," deplored my great-uncle, wagging his head. "'Tis foolishness, Flint. This rum-swigging will yet prove the undoing of you and every man of your crew. I am no upholder of imaginary virtues, as you know, but unbridled indulgence must ultimately defeat its own ends."

"Look to your ship, and I'll look to mine," snapped Flint, quaffing a wineglassful of the goblet's contents.

My uncle stared him straight in the eye with a hard, direct thrust of power which stirred my unwilling admiration.

"To whom do you owe your present position?" he asked coldly.

Flint made a patent attempt to stare him down, but abandoned the effort and looked away.

"Some might say one thing and some another," he muttered.

"To whom do you owe your present position, Flint?" repeated Murray.

"Oh, to you, most like," admitted Flint. "Blast you!"

"Have I ever led you into difficulties?" continued my great-uncle. "Not if—"

"Have I ever led you into difficulties?"

"No."

"Have we failed in any important venture since our association began?"

"Not yet," admitted Flint sourly.

"Very well. Now I ask you: When I promise a certain accomplishment am I to be relied upon?"

"You ha' a head on your shoulders," conceded Flint.

"And you have not," amended Murray. "No, do not say any more. You are an excellent man to handle your ship, Flint, and as fearless as any of our ruffians; but you are no more capable of looking ahead a week or two than Ben Gunn."

"I take much from ye, Murray," snarled Flint, half-rising; "but think not ye can humble me before—"

"Sit down," ordered Murray. "You'll take what you deserve, which in this instance is a plain statement that you would ha' made a fool of yourself by chasing the Philadelphia packet. I doubt if you could have taken her, for your bottom is foul; but if you had, her loss must have aroused comment, and with New York already apprised that we are in these seas we should ha' had every frigate on the North American and West Indian stations a-hunting us. And what then?"

"We could lie up safe enough at the Rendeyvoo."

"Spyglass Island? I dare say—although some day 'twill be blundered upon, if not discovered. But I ask you to recall that we take no prizes when we hole up. 'Tis a losing game."

"Well, what would you?" Flint flung at him with an air of defiance, which Murray ignored.

"I would make the greatest coup we have attempted."

Flint laughed disagreeably.

"So you said when you arranged to go into New York, but you have carried back no treasure with you."

My uncle regarded him with what, under other circumstances, I should describe as honest indignation.

"You fool!" he said with a rasp in his voice—and I did not wonder that Flint pulled sidewise in his chair as if to avoid a stab. "Did you think I was to go into that huddle of a town, with its wealth in furs and groceries, and fetch out a treasure?"

"What, then?" demanded Flint, moistening his lips.

My uncle leaned forward across the table, lips drawn tight over his teeth. His eyes shot sparks.

"Knowledge, fool! Intelligence! That which wise men labor a lifetime to secure and the ignorant pass by in the gutter."

"It may be knowledge to you," protested Flint childishly; "but how'm I to know of it as never heard it?"

Murray rose from the table and commenced to stroll the length of the cabin, hands clasped under the skirts of his coat. And as he strolled he talked. Flint followed his every move uneasily, with occasional drafts of rum. Peter and I watched the two of them, fascinated by this conflict of wills, which was to exert a vital influence upon our lives—yes, and upon those of hundreds of others.

"I must speak in simple terms, I perceive, Flint," began my great-uncle.

The passion was out of his voice, and the sentences trickled from his lips slowly, with an air of detachment.

"And that I may speak simply and present adequately an important subject, I must ask you to indulge me at length."

Flint nodded sullenly, seeing that an answer was required.

"We have frequently discussed the possibility of taking one of the Spanish treasure-ships," continued Murray. "But we have never attempted the project because we could not discover the date of sailing or the port wherein the treasure was embarked. It hath been the custom of the Spaniards in recent years—in fact, since the depredations of Morgan and his brethren—to shift arbitrarily the port of embarkation from year to year, as likewise to change the date of sailing. One year the port would be Cartagena, the next Chagres, the next Porto Bello, the next even Vera Cruz. They have been known to ship the year's produce of the mines around Cape Horn. And similarly the treasure ships, which used formerly to sail invariably in the Fall of the year, now depart whenever it pleases the fancy of the Council of the Indies to fix a date."

He paused, and Flint rasped—

"So much is known to all of us."

"I conceded as much," answered Murray smoothly. "What follows you do not know. When we returned from Madagascar—"

"'Twas against my advice," growled Flint. "Ye play too much wi' politics."

"With politics! Exactly," agreed my great-uncle. "Well, perhaps I do. 'Tis true that so far I have obtained trifling advantage from the sport, excluding one substantial fortune, this vessel we are in and the information which makes it possible for me to take this year's treasure-ship."

Flint sat erect. I caught my breath. Peter, too, showed a gleam of excitement in his little eyes that twinkled from behind the ramparts of flesh that masked his solemn face.

"——— me, Murray!" swore Flint. "Do you say that in sober earnest?"

"I do. Do you remember that we cruised off the Spanish coast last Spring and Fall, and that two months since I sent a periague into the Havana? During our Spanish cruises I established connections with a group of Jacobite gentlemen who know me and placed before them the outline of a plan, the acceptance of which they communicated to me in dispatches the periague fetched to Spyglass Island. In those dispatches I was notified to meet my principal confederate in New York on a certain date. I met him. The necessary arrangements were consummated, and it simply remains for us to execute the plan."

Flint clutched at his beaker of rum and emptied it shakily into his throat.

"How—how much?" he quavered.

"One million five hundred thousand pounds."

There was a moment of silence. The clean, golden sunlight flooded through the stern windows and dappled the polished surface of the table with darting molts and beams. Flint's jaw dropped on his chest. His green eyes glared. Peter and I were as dazed as himself. Only my great-uncle remained calm, pacing quietly up and down the carpeted deck, eyes fixed upon some vision of the future.

"All—that?" stammered Flint. "'Sdeath! 'Twould be the greatest haul in our time, Murray."

"It is ours," affirmed Murray. "Upon terms."

"Terms?" echoed Flint. "What terms? Who can compel us to terms?"

My great-uncle came to a stop in front of him.

"My terms, let us say," he answered.

"Oh, aye," mumbled Flint. "But if 'tis there for the taking—"

"It will be there for the taking, as you put it, upon the terms I lay down," stated my great-uncle.

"But if ye know of yourself where it can be taken why must we bother wi' terms, Murray?" clamored Flint. "What's riches for us can be pared down to short cuts if it must be shared out right and left."

My great-uncle's laughter was wholly contemptuous.

"Observe, Robert," he appealed to me, "here was a man, who, a half-hour past, knew naught of this treasure we are discussing. It meant nothing to him. He never dreamed of obtaining it. And now that he has held out to him the possibility of looting a measure of it he waxes indignant lest that measure be too small!"

Flint refilled the beaker with rum.

The stuff seemed to heighten the uncanny blue pallor of his face, and the pupils of his eyes dwindled to pin-pricks, whether from the strong drink or excitement I can not say. But his manner was steadier than it had been.

"Why not?" he flared in reply to my relative's mockery. "If we take it, why not take all?"

"Because," retorted Murray with a burst of terrible energy, "I have passed my word as to the terms upon which the treasure is to be taken."

"What's your word?" rapped Flint.

For a moment I thought my great-uncle would strike him. He made to draw back his arm, and perspiration stood out in white beads upon his forehead. Flint feared it, too, but did not raise a hand to protect himself, charmed to immobility by the virulence of the basilisk's stare which Murray directed at him.

"It is my word," said Murray finally in a very soft voice. "No more, Flint. A poor thing, as the poet hath said, yet my own! Also—that I may chime in harmony with your mental processes—it happens that my personal interests are bound up with the observance of these terms."

"I thought so," sneered Flint.

"Ah! Did you?"

My great-uncle's tones continued dulcet.

"It is a matter we will not discuss further, since it is beyond the range of your comprehension. I shall merely say that the terms are fixed, and that you will either accept or reject them."

"What are they?"

"As to division of the spoils? One hundred thousand pounds to myself as author and architect of the plan; seven hundred thousand to our two ships; and seven hundred thousand to my friends who cooperated with me to make it possible."

Flint brought his fist crashing down upon the table.

"I'll be ——— if I accept!" he shouted. "What? Less than half to our company? And you sneaking off with a cool hundred thousand pounds in your pockets, and your friends, as like as not, splitting secretly with you!"

My great-uncle refreshed himself with snuff, contriving to invest the ceremony with an effect of distaste which I found amusing.

"Stap me, but you have a low mind!" he drawled. "Allow me to direct your attention to the fact that the plan amounts to my friends and I undertaking voluntarily to present you an opportunity to participate in the division of seven hundred thousand pounds, for which you will be called upon to do nothing except agree to follow out several stipulations I shall lay down."

"Let's hear 'em."

My great-uncle ticked off the items upon his finger-tips.

"First, 'tis highly desirable that we should lie low during the ensuing months. Activities such as we usually conduct would tend to affright the Council of the Indies and bring about a change in plan for the treasure-ship's sailing."

"What shall we do, then?"

"My counsel is to bear up for Spyglass Island and careen there. Both ships are foul, and 'twill prove an excellent opportunity to make all clean and right."

Flint nodded.

"We shall need our speed against the Spaniard," he commented.

"*I* shall," returned my great-uncle with some emphasis. "This brings me to my second point. 'Tis advisable that we do not cruise in company for the treasure. I aim to intercept the *Santissima Trinidad* before she passes from the Caribbean into the Atlantic, and to that end I shall hover on a particular meridian awaiting secret intelligence notifying me when she puts forth from her port."

The blue look became intensified in Flint's face.

"You'd leave the *Walrus* behind?" he demanded.

"I must. Figure it for yourself," argued my relative. "Two tall ships plying the narrow seas, within easy sail of Jamaica and the Havana and Martinico! We should have the frigates after us in no time. My plan is to masquerade as a King's ship, running from any ugly customers who show themselves."

"Aye," said Flint. "And after you'd taken the treasure and stowed it all below hatches what thought would you give to us aboard the *Walrus*, eh? You'd be up and off, and we might whistle for our share."

"You wrong me, Captain Flint," replied my great-uncle simply.

But Flint gave an ugly laugh. It might be the rum or the stimulus of the debate or a gradual access of self-reliance; but he was no longer to be cowed by moral suasion. If I had doubted this, the suave diplomacy with which my great-uncle proceeded to treat him must have convinced me to the contrary.

"If I wrong you, Murray, 'twould be the first time without valid cause," Flint rejoined. "Come, come! You must think of me better than that."

"I have thought of the best terms possible," answered Murray. "Mark me, 'twould be perfectly feasible for me to give you the slip any dark night, take the *Santissima Trinidad* by my lone and never account to you for a doubloon. I do not for two reasons: First, I have a feeling of common loyalty to you and your men; we have worked and fought together in the past, and I would give them their share in this haul. Second, I wish to use the Rendezvous in connection with the coup, and if you choose to look at it so, you can set down your inclusion as payment for that, as well as for your sacrificing chances at other prizes by keeping under cover."

"It won't wash," denied Flint. "What you say sounds well enough. It may be true. But I couldn't go back and report it to a fo'c'sle counsel on the *Walrus* and expect to have it believed. I have to blink myself when I think of it. ———!" He grinned evilly. "I know what I'd do in your shoes."

My great-uncle regarded him speculatively.

"What, then, is your answer?" Murray inquired.

"I don't play on those terms," returned Flint with decision. "Let me cruise with you, have a share in taking the prize, and I'll talk differently."

Murray shook his head.

"'Twould ruin the plan. I know you, Flint. 'Tis not in you to cruise for days and forego fat merchants that cross your bows, ripe to be plucked. The Philadelphia packet you were fuming over when you came in here is a case in point! Man, there'd be a dozen such chances while we awaited the Spaniard, and one of them you'd go for. No, I can't risk it. Alone, I can contrive not to attract attention. In company, we should stir up a hornet's nest."

"Curse me for a canting mugger, then, if I'll trade on it," snarled Flint. "I'll not trust you, Murray, and that's flat."

"Suppose that I gave you a hostage?" suggested my great-uncle tentatively.

"Hostage? Who could ye give me for hostage whose life would mean aught to you? No, no! Martin or any man you'd see with his throat cut, and never bat an eye."

My esteemed relative's shrug was as complete a repudiation of such a charge as might be desired. I enjoyed it with mixed feelings because I was beginning to see the writing on the wall.

"I had not Martin in mind," he replied now; "but one whose life means to me more than my own."

"The man does not live," Flint swore roundly.

"He sits across the table," returned Murray. "My grandnephew and heir. I will go so far as to assert that the only reason I concern myself with this exploit is that I may secure estate and preferment for him."

Flint eyed him shrewdly, looked from him to me and from me to him.

"Your grandnephew, you say? Humph! Long John says you're choice o' him. Still—No, I like not your terms, Murray. They offer too little."

"They are the best I can offer," answered Murray definitely. "I will add, that there may be no misunderstandings, Flint, that the odd seven hundred thousand pounds goes to promote the interest of a cause, and not to line the pockets of Spanish officials, as you may suspect; and it is highly probable that considerable of my share will follow it."

The captain of the *Walrus* wiped a rumspot from the table and tipped the earthen flask bottom up above his beaker.

"'Tis a heavy commission to pay," he said. "Eight hundred thousand pounds out of a million and a half."

"That or nothing," declared Murray.

"And I must lose how many months' cruising the while you wait for the treasure-ship?"

"Six or more."

"Gut me, but ye bargain like a Jew, Murray!"

"And like a Jew I pay well and surely, offering good security."

"I see it not," fended Flint, and drained the last of his rum.

"I pay seven hundred thousand pounds, to be divided share and share by the two ships' companies, and your company will incur no risk to win it."

Flint rose and settled his belt.

"I accept, for that I can do no better," he said. "But I must have the hostage. He's the weak point of it all; but I must take some chance, and curse me if seven hundred thousand pounds be not worth the gamble."

He snapped his finger toward me.

"Come on, my lad. We'll show you the life of real gentlemen adventurers aboard the *Walrus*."

"I'm no negro man to be bargained over and passed from owner to owner!" I exclaimed hotly. "You can make me go, but I'll not step willingly."

Flint was about to answer with a spurt of oaths when Murray interrupted.

"You anticipate matters," he rebuked his associate. "There is no occasion for a hostage yet. We shall sail at once for the Rendezvous. It will be weeks, aye, months, before I am in shape to sail west under Hispaniola. Time enough then to talk of delivering your hostage."

For an instant Flint appeared to be about to object to this view, but he evidently decided it was not worth another dispute.

"Let it go," he assented gruffly. "We'll settle the details at the island.

—— me—" this with a sudden revival of friendliness—"I knew we had not picked up that red-headed lad for nothing! 'Tis a sure sign o' luck."

And out he swaggered from the cabin, stamping and banging the door and sprinkling curses freely as he gained the deck and shouted for his boat's crew to row him back to the *Walrus*.

CHAPTER VIII

A WICKED OLD MAN'S DREAM

MY great-uncle sank into his chair with a gesture of disgust and poured three fingers of brandy into a wineglass.

"Phaugh!" he exclaimed. "At times I am nauseated by the company perforce I keep."

He rang the silver bell.

"Gunn," he said as the steward sidled in, "we are awaiting the food I ordered. But stay! Open a window before you go. This place reeks with the stench of decayed honor."

I laughed, and he put the glass from his lips, peering at me across its rim as if surprized.

"You find occasion for mirth in my remark, Robert?"

"I find myself in extraordinary agreement with you for the nonce," I returned. "You are correct. This place doth reek of 'decayed honor.'"

"Ah!"

He finished his drink, wiped his mouth carefully and set down the glass.

"You are, I suspect, attempting sarcasm," he continued. "'Tis a diversion frequently favored by the young."

"No," I said; "I am only expressing to you my feeling that you have as little claim to possession of a sense of honor as the man who was just here."

Gunn unbolted one of the stern windows, and a fine breath of salty air was blown in our faces. Murray inhaled it deeply, and Peter, whose face had become leaden in the cabin's close atmosphere, regained a touch of color and edged forward in his seat. My great-uncle turned to him courteously, ignoring me for the moment.

"I fear you have been suffering from my thoughtlessness, friend Peter. Let me recommend a draft of this *aqua vitae*. 'Tis excellent for settling the stomach."

"*Ja,*" nodded Peter.

"We shall presently have a chicken broiled over a slow fire," pursued Murray. "A few slices of the breast should be easy for your digestion and assist in the filling of the void which our rough fare on the brig was unable to satisfy.

"But Robert and I were discussing a question of honor. Pardon me if I return to it."

His large face, with its powerful, craggy features, glowed with the radiance of an intense personal conviction.

"What is honor? Or dishonor? Certes, here we have a call for close reasoning. No hasty generalities can dismiss so vexed a problem, which hath consumed the attention of gentlemen since gentility's institution."

"I should call it dishonorable to assure your grandnephew that you had kidnaped him for desire of his aid and to make his fortune, when actually you intended only to employ him as a hostage to further your personal schemes," I said deliberately.

And if I spoke restrainedly 'twas by no mean effort, for inwardly I seethed with resentment.

"The situation is susceptible to the interpretation which you place upon it," he admitted evenly. "Yet a reasonable temperament must concede 'twas necessary for me to place the consummation of my project before the claims of kinship. And though you appear not to be disposed to accept my assertions for fact, I will say once and for all that my intentions toward you are benevolent and affectionate—and this despite the contumely you have heaped upon me with no regard for the disparity of our ages."

I was nonplussed, but dissatisfied.

"If that were my only count against your honor—if, indeed, a pirate can have honor—"

"And why not?" says he sharply. "I conceive of honor as the quality of being faithful to oneself, to the ethical standard one has established for this life we pass through so precariously."

"So that if a man practices dishonesty toward all save himself he preserves his honor!" I protested.

"Now do you twist my thoughts," replied my great-uncle. "And in the same breath you raise a complementary question: What is dishonesty—or honesty? As I have told you before, I take from those who have much, those who prey upon others. I am no more dishonest than that William of Normandy, who seized upon England and farmed it out to his barons in payment for their assistance."

"You are clever with words," I sneered; "but I'll not be fooled. What have you to say of your craft in deluding O'Donnell into risking his daughter aboard this treasure-ship? Do you call it honorable to persuade a foolish unbalanced fellow to take an innocent young girl out of a convent, carry her half across the world, and then, to cloak a miserable conspiracy, plunge her into the society of such scoundrels as Flint and yourself?"

Instead of losing his temper, as I had expected, my great-uncle stared at me very earnestly throughout this tongue-lashing. A speculative look came into his eyes.

"You have seen this maid, I believe," he said.

"I met her by accident. 'Twas I saved her from walking into the Whale's Head after her father."

"You did well," he approved warmly. "And you spoke to her? Prithee, Robert, what manner of maid is she?"

"Oh, fair enough," I answered, wondering what he was driving at.

"And well-spoken?" he pressed. "I have never encountered her."

"She has the Irish way of speech."

"But is she nice in her ways? A lady?"

"Yes."

Ben Gunn fetched in the chicken upon a salver, and my great-uncle busied himself in carving. 'Twas comical to see how Peter's stolid face lighted up. As he carved Murray talked.

"She should be an exquisite chit, Robert. She has good blood in her. Her mother was a younger sister of the Duke of Leitrim, and her father's father was a younger son of Lord Donegal. She will be much to the fore when King James returns to Whitehall."

"If he does!" I jeered. "I marvel that you should use so hardly a maid of such birth."

"Hardly?" He looked up from his carving. "Why do you say that?"

"Oh, an end to your shabby deceits and subterfuge!" I shouted. "I ha' told you already I know she is to be dragged aboard your ship when you take the *Santissima Trinidad*. What good will the Duke of Leitrim and Lord Donegal and Jamey Stuart and all their string of Popish knaves be to her then? Bah! I could stomach your treatment of me, Murray. But to expose a slip of a girl, scarce more than a child, to life on this floating hell and the attentions of Flint and his lambs!"

My great-uncle pursed his lips.

"What a vehement youth! Friend Peter, I trust that chicken is done to your taste?"

"Ja," grunted Peter, plying a ready knife and fork.

"Will a thigh be satisfactory, Robert? This dish contains potatoes which were fresh when we started our voyage and should be so still. Serve Master Ormerod, Gunn. So! We will resume our debate.

"As to the maid's inclusion in our scheme, 'twas manifestly of the chiefest importance that Colonel O'Donnell's connection with me be not suspected. And the best way to cloak that was to have his daughter accompany him. Not even a Spanish official—than which there is no more suspicious breed—can carp at O'Donnell's movements whilst she is with him."

"But why?" I persisted. "Why all this devious deceit? Why mix a young maid in an unsavory intrigue? Why make her father disloyal to his master?"

Murray flushed crimson.

"He is not disloyal to his master," he replied with his first show of anger. "Colonel O'Donnell's master, my master—aye, your master—is King James! What doth O'Donnell care for the paltry Spaniard who sits in the palace at Madrid? What do any of us care for the Spaniards, who have not been men enough to live up to their declarations of support of the Stuarts? Why, this girl you mouth about would cheerfully suffer death, dishonor, any torment, to win for her king the means of power we shall afford him. And this treasure, which the Spaniards have wrung from the lands they stole from the poor Indians, we wring from them as remorselessly that we may apply it to a purpose infinitely higher than the placating of royal favorites and mistresses, which is the way 'twould go in Madrid. An unsavory business, forsooth! Boy, are you a fool?"

There was that about his rage which benumbed my own and awakened again the reluctant admiration which puzzled and embarrassed me. What was it my father had said of him?

"He is sincere in a queer, twisted way."

Past doubt, he was. I sensed a warped nobility of mind which stirred me to sympathy and pity. I felt of a sudden as if our places had been reversed, as if his white hairs were mine, and his my unlined face.

"Perhaps I am a fool," I said. "Yet if I know nothing of your plan and so am inclined to misconstrue it, whose fault is that?"

He dropped knife and fork and fixed me with his eyes, so marvelously alive and bright in their setting of crow's feet and wrinkles, so luminous with youth.

"Those are the first words you have spoken which have had any tinge of kindness to them," he answered.

"I am not kind," I denied; "but curious. You have torn me out of my natural course and thrown me into a network of intrigue of which I know nothing. You would have me think well of you and work with you, but you have not taken the ordinary pains to acquaint me with your purposes and the part you have designed for me."

Peter sat back with a sigh of content, his plate empty.

"*Ja,* Murray, you don't say much," he said in his squeaky voice. "You don't tell dot feller Flint so much as wouldt gife him der trail."

I had not observed this, and I felt secretly ashamed. My great-uncle smiled.

"Stap me, but I might ha' known you would see it, Peter!" he exclaimed. "Now, tell me: Why did not Flint ask me the treasure-ship's course and port o' sailing? Did he not think to in his fuddlement with the rum? Or did he know I would not tell him and reckon to save his tongue?"

"He knows you, *ja,*" answered Peter.

Murray nodded.

"Yes, that would be it, and it took you to see it. You have not lived with the red Indians for naught, Peter. But this doth not answer Nephew Robert's question. 'Tis my fault you are so far ignorant,

Robert, and I will endeavor to repair the error. I did not seek to delude you when I told you I carried you from New York because I needed your assistance, and that is so far true that I admit without hesitation I must have your help before I can achieve aught of my future plans for bettering your station in life. In fine, Robert, I need you at this time being more than you can need me; and your hostage-ship with Flint is but the least of the services I hope from you."

"That is frank," I replied. "And I will match it. I have told you I'll not help in piracy; nor will I. The taking of this treasure-ship is—"

"Bide, bide," he interrupted. "Before you commit yourself further let me tell my story. I ask only your promise to hold it secret from all men on these two ships."

"I'll promise that," I said.

"*Ja,*" assented Peter.

"So be it."

He left the table and took from a cupboard in the wall a rolled map which he spread upon the table between us, shoving aside the plates and glasses to make room for it. I saw at a glance 'twas a chart of the Carribbean Sea and the Spanish Main and the islands which stretched from the tip of the Floridas to the Brazils.

"This is for reference," he remarked. "My story begins in Europe, and we require no map for that. Your father, Robert, was a stout Jacobite at your age. He has since changed his convictions; but we say nothing on that score. I, on the contrary, was born a Jacobite and am one still, heart and soul. I shall never rest until the Hanoverian usurper has been displaced.

"I was on the other side of Africa when I first had word Prince Charles had raised the White Cockade in Scotland in the '45. I sailed for home, as you have heard, and was many months too late to be of service. But I established touch with friends in France who work for the cause, and so learned that the good work was going merrily on. We all know now that Prince Charles might have remedied his plight after Culloden had he been more fortunate in his advisers. I will tell you beyond that that the disarming measures in the Highlands have been a failure and the clans have only turned sullen from the oppression they have received. All that is wanted for another rising is money—gold!"

His luminous, dark eyes looked from one to the other of us, and I
thought the tawny flecks in the pupils increased in brilliancy as he
cried out that last word on a rising note that thrilled and disturbed
me.

"Gold!" he said over again. "Why, there is one little hoard of treasure Prince Charles had to leave behind him—the Loch Arkaig treasure they call it. Cluny MacPherson and Locheil's brother have had
the keeping of it, and you'd scarce believe the source of trouble it
has been to the English! And it not more than forty thousand louis
at the beginning, and dribbling fast before it was turned to account.
It has set all the Highlands by the ears—forty thousand louis, spent
by fives and tens, a good bit of it going to feed gillies in the heather
or gambled away in some *clachan* of the Cameron country, if what
I hear be right.

"Think what a real treasure would accomplish! Think what—But I
am going too fast."

He paused, and a slow, strange smile shadowed his face as he drew
a finger across the map upon the table.

"I said I would tell you a story," he went on. "But after all 'tis only
a dream—a wicked old man's dream, Robert. 'Tis so you think of me,
I know—and your father—and Peter there—and—I wonder what the
little maid you spoke with would think! Or the poor, throneless old
king who huddles over his brazier for warmth in the dreary palace
in Rome that is all he has left of his majesty! Or Prince Charlie, who
flits back and forth from France to the Low Countries, scheming and
plotting and always curbed for lack of—gold!

"Gold! We stumble for lack of it in every enterprise. With sufficient
of it you may upset kingdoms, buy pardons, obtain patents and hon-
ors and place. 'Tis a definite substance, mark you, hard and shining
and heavy in the hand—not such thistle-down as dreams are made
o'.

"But the virtue of dreams, Robert—" he addressed himself direct
to me, seeming to forget that Peter was present—"is that they can be
transmuted into that which is palpable and finite, aye, even into gold.
And the dreams of a wicked old man may become as efficacious to
right wrong or to throw down the mighty or to redeem the weak
and the persecuted as the gold which Indian slaves mine under the

whip of Spanish masters. For the dream may lead to the gold. What is the ancient saw? 'First the thought, then the deed.'

"When was the thought born? I can not say. Flint and I had often sought the yearly treasure-ship, but never had sight of her. Then one day the idea came to me to utilize my Jacobite friends in France and Spain. They leaped at the suggestion, for to say truth, Robert, both Spaniards and Frenchmen have treated our party shabbily. An intrigue was set afoot through the medium of a cardinal who is partial to King James, and so we gained access to the Council of the Indies. A bribe, which I supplied, procured for O'Donnell, already an officer on the regular establishment of the Spanish forces, appointment as an Inspector of Fortifications of the ports on the Main. And with the prestige of this post and the assistance of our friend the cardinal 'twas easy for O'Donnell to secure complete information as to the Council's plans for the dispatch of this year's treasure-ship."

His forefinger explored the chart before us and came to rest upon a dot on the flank of the narrow neck of land which joins the two Americas.

"There is Porto Bello, which was the port of the old treasure galleons and discarded as such by the Spaniards after Morgan sacked it. But later they restored and strengthened the fortifications, although in the late war our Admiral Vernon carried it by surprize. At that time Cartagena was the treasure center, and when Vernon attempted it he was repulsed with loss. Two years since the Council of the Indies decided to resume sailings from Porto Bello, which is the most advantageously situated of all ports on the Main for the collection of the treasure.

"See! 'Tis about midway betwixt Mexico and Peru, and the mines of Veragua are at its back door. The treasures of the South Sea islands can be fetched by sea to Panama and thence carried overland by the *recoes,* the royal mule-trains which are the link betwixt Panama and the West Coast and the cities of the Main. The Peruvian treasures come by the same route. Those from Mexico are fetched south from La Vera Cruz by a ship under escort of the Garda Costas and transferred at Porto Bello to the ship for Spain, which puts forth about the beginning or middle of September.

"This is a strong ship and well manned, but the Spaniards have been taught by centuries of experience to accept no risk for her. Her identity is never known in advance, even to her captain. He sails from Cadiz for the Main under sealed orders which he doth not open until mid-Atlantic is passed, and these orders do but carry him to Porto Bello. There a strict embargo is laid upon him and his crew, and the port is rigidly closed the while the assembling of the treasure is under way. So soon as that is accomplished 'tis laded aboard him, and he sails in the night, the hour known to no more than the Governor and higher officers; and to make assurance surer the port is kept closed for two weeks additional."

"Then how shall you have word of her sailing?" I broke in, swept off my feet by the rush of this amazing narrative.

"That is O'Donnell's task. He will reach Porto Bello during the Summer and be so concerned for the state of the fortifications that he'll refuse to leave until he has put them in defensible condition."

My great-uncle gave me a chiding smile.

"You ha' been vastly concerned for the well-being of the maid his daughter, Robert—and I am bound to say your feeling is highly becoming—but you might better fret for her health in that —— hole at the most pestilent time o' year. I hope, for her sake, she will be sent away with the officers' ladies into one of the mountain retreats the Spaniards have erected for their refreshment."

"Better Porto Bello and pestilence than a pirate ship," I muttered angrily.

"You will harp upon that word," he answered sorrowfully. "I am yet far from converting you, I perceive. Well, well! To my story again.

"Whilst he is there he will receive dispatches from Spain summoning him home on urgent affairs. He will elect to embark upon the treasure-ship because she is large and commodious and likewise safe. And thanks to his position, he will have accurate knowledge some days in advance of her sailing-date. When he has obtained this fact he will convey it secretly to one Diego Salvez, an agent I maintain in that port, as I maintain others in almost every place of importance along the coast of the Main and in the islands. Diego, by O'Donnell's help, will get out of the town and put to sea in a fast sloop be hath in a little river near where was the ancient town of

Nombre de Dios, so that we shall have sure tidings of the *Santissima Trinidad*'s coming and be prepared for her."

"But what of her course?" I scrutinized the map. "There are three several exits from the Caribbean into the Atlantic."

And I pointed them out in order: The Straits of Florida to the north of Cuba; the Windward Passage between Cuba and Hispaniola, with the great island of Jamaica lying to the westward of it; and last, the Mona Passage between Hispaniola and Porto Rico.

"She would never point up for the gaps between the lesser islands in the south," I added.

My great-uncle chuckled with a keenness of relish that was new to him.

"You read the chart well for a landsman, boy," he said. "What say you, Peter? Here is a stout sailor in the making."

"*Neen*," answered Peter earnestly. "You stick to der landt, Bob."

And for the first time my great-uncle and I laughed together, so comical was the Dutchman's repudiation of the sea and its folk.

"You have clapped on to the nub of our problem," said Murray. "'Twas the piece of information I was at most pains to obtain. The *Santissima Trinidad* will head for the Mona Passage. I will show you why. The first aim of the Spaniards is to conceal her voyage; she sails a course which keeps her as much as possible in open seas. And the best exit for that purpose is the opening between Hispaniola and Porto Rico. There are no islands in the Caribbean on that course, and once through the passage she fetches south and east of the Bahamas and so beats up for the Cape Verdes.

"My intent is that the *Royal James* shall ply off the westerly mouth of the passage from about the end of August, avoiding all intercourse with shipping and keeping as far out to sea as is practicable. When Diego appears we will restrict the space of our beat, and 'twill be impossible for the treasure-ship to escape us. If she runs we can catch her, and at fighting I can take any don under a ship-o'-the-line."

"So much I heard you declare to Colonel O'Donnell aboard the brig," I said. "But what comes next? You take the *Santissima Trinidad*— and then?"

He moved his forefinger over the surface of the map and brought it to rest in front of a tiny outline sketched in ink on the expanse of sea east of Cuba and somewhat to the north of Hispaniola. Northward of this spot stretched the far-flung myriads of the Bahamas.

"That is what you have heard Flint and me refer to as the Rendezvous and Spyglass Island," he answered. "It has other names, I believe. Some have called it Treasure Island, although I know of no treasure upon it. In truth, its one value is that it doth not appear upon any map, and its comfortable isolation and sheltered havens supply an excellent resort for such outlaws as ourselves. 'Tis said that Kidd discovered it, and certes, others of the old-time buccaneers were wont to maintain themselves there. Flint had the secret of it from a tarry-breeks who claimed to have sailed on the *Adventure* galley. We are bound thither now to refit and careen, and when we have the treasure safe under hatches we will return to the island to divide it and concert arrangements for delivering their share to Colonel O'Donnell's friends."

"What will Flint say to your fetching in strangers to your hiding-place?" I asked.

A furrow deepened betwixt my great-uncle's lambent eyes.

"He'll not like it, Robert," he admitted. "I have O'Donnell's word to betray none of our secrets, and indeed 'tis to his own interest to keep hidden his part in this affair; but Flint may well make trouble. 'Tis a determined dog, and a greedy. Look you, boy, will you stand by me in the affair? For the girl's sake, if for no other reason?"

"Why not leave her aboard the treasure-ship?"

He regarded me askance.

"It may be we must sink—"

I started up.

"Now, that I'll ha' naught to do with! I ha' told you I'd fight if you butchered the defenseless."

He waved me back.

"Peace, peace! We can not carry off all the Spaniards in any case, and—"

He hesitated.

"—O'Donnell must be protected," he concluded.

"Against what?"

"Wagging tongues. I tell you his part must never be known. The

Santissima Trinidad disappears, and with her the treasure and all her company. There's no other way."

"But if O'Donnell and his daughter survive to reach Europe there must be talk," I pointed out.

"True," he agreed; "but they will have their story ready. A shipwreck, perhaps, and they alone contriving to reach shore."

"Who beliefes dot?" Peter interjected contemptuously.

"What else can we do?" countered Murray.

"Take the treasure, if you must," I retorted; "but do not stain your hands with the blood of men who have not harmed you."

"I must slay some of them in all probability," returned my great-uncle. "What difference between that and slaying all?"

I remembered the thrill of reprobation with which even the most devoted adherents of King George had heard of the butchery of the Scots wounded after Culloden.

"'Tis not yourself alone must bear the disgrace of such a deed," I tried again. "'Twill attach an irremovable stigma to your cause. No honest Jacobite can ever afterward call Cumberland butcher. Aye, and if I know aught of Misstress O'Donnell she will refuse to have anything to do with so horrible a crime. Be sure 'twill bring a trail of ill-luck will swamp the Pretender and all his train."

He took snuff with his accustomed fastidiousness.

"Your arguments carry weight, I am bound to admit," he said, returning the box to his pocket. "What alternative have you to suggest?"

"Cripple the ship to give you time to escape."

"That's well enough," he argued; "but you take no thought to Colonel O'Donnell's plight. What will be said of him after he is brought aboard the *James?*"

The idea which came to me then I put away as distasteful, but rack my brain as I would I could produce no substitute for it.

"There's but one thing to do," I said. "You must make pretense of bearing off the daughter, and you can imprison the father, too, in order to silence his objections."

"A fit rôle for a pirate captain," mused my great-uncle. "*El capitán* Rrrip-Rrrap and how he devoured the virgin! I can hear the stories that will be told in the Havana wine-shops. But I must have my price,

Robert. If I spare such Spaniards as escape our great guns and the boarding-cutlasses, will you agree to stand back of me in the division of the spoils with Flint?"

"I'll not become lieutenant in your piracies, if that be your meaning," I returned.

"No; my meaning is plain, boy. I wish you and Peter to help me to get clear of Flint with the O'Donnells and their portion of the treasure."

"But why return to the Rendezvous at all? Bear off with the O'Donnells, and land them and their treasure before you deliver Flint his share."

My great-uncle shook his head.

"'Tis not so simple as all that. The action with the *Santissima Trinidad* will require cannonading, and that will be heard. Probably we shall be seen sailing away. We may be pursued. The surviving Spaniards, whom you will have me spare, will speedily have out their frigates after us. We must remain under cover for a period. And finally, for various reasons too complex for discussion, I can not make delivery of the treasure to my friends in France before the Spring. Seven hundred thousand pounds in gold and silver bullion is no easy mass to handle. Preparations must be made for its landing and transportation.

"No, Robert, the Rendezvous is necessary to my plans. Furthermore, I am surprised that you, who prate so much of honor, should seek to encourage me to act dishonorably toward my associates by withholding from them, for however short a time, their just share of our spoils. You will grant me, I hope, the credit of being at least an honorable pirate."

He spoke at the last with a kind of mincing solemnity which was vastly funny, and both Peter and I fell a-laughing for it. Read me for a fool or a knave if you will, but I protest I was conscious of a growing inclination for my relative. So whimsical a scoundrel could not be altogether without redeeming qualities; and sure, his courage and resource by themselves were sufficient to set him apart from ordinary men.

"Very well," I said. "I will do what you ask for the maid's sake—if Peter is willing."

"*Ja,*" assented Peter.

Murray caught my hand in a quick, firm clasp.

"Good!" he cried. "'Twill be the first o' many times we stand shoulder to shoulder. Ah, Robert, I ha' dreamed a splendid dream, and any man who helps in its achievement will not have lived in vain. We'll take this gold and build an avenue of victories for the king's ride to Whitehall. What will we not do? We'll rouse the claymores from the hills! We'll carry the Irish Brigade to London town! We'll fetch home the Wild Geese from their haunts of exile! We'll ha' the beacon fires ablaze from end to end of the Three Kingdoms! And the White Cockade over all!

"There'll be no talk of pirates then! 'Twill be my Lord Duke of Jedburgh, Marquis of Cobbielaw and Earl and Baron Broomfield; aye, and an English peerage to boot. We'll ride high, Robert—aye, with the highest!"

He broke off short, and the glow in his eyes charred out.

"'Tis not a bad vision for a wicked old man to dream; eh, boy? Remember it when you hear the crowds a-cheering us in the Strand."

Almost he made me believe him, this outlaw of the sea. But Peter broke the spell.

"Me, I don't beliefe in dreams," yawned the Dutchman. "*Neen.*"

Murray glared at him.

"What you believe is of little account, Corlaer," he said curtly, and strode from the cabin.

Peter took a sip of *aqua vitae.*

"He is a great dreamer, Murray," he squeaked. "*Ja,* all der time he dreams. He dreamed when we fight wit' him before, me andt your father, Bob. It is not goodt to dream too much, *neen.*"

He sighed.

"My stomach is better. We finish der chicken, *ja?*"

CHAPTER IX

THE ISLAND

ONE DAY was like another aboard the *Royal James,* although to a landsman the routine of duties, work and varying weather was charged with unending interest. My great-uncle held his pack of wolves on a short leash and exacted from them all the efficiency of a man-o'-war's company. Indeed, he rather fancied himself in the status of admiral upon a private establishment, and occasionally indulged in visions of the *James* gazetted to the roster of the royal fleet and himself flying a broad pennant in a line-ship at the head of a squadron.

"His Majesty could scarce make me Lord Admiral, Robert," he would say, pacing the poop with hands clasped behind him and spyglass tucked beneath his left arm. "I am one for maintaining the rights of tradition, and the Howards have an inalienable claim to the place. But a regular commission—that would be vastly different. Admiral of the White, let us say—or if that grade be filled, perhaps of the Red. I understand there to be considerable jealousy amongst the sea-dogs of the Navy over the rankings on the White, and I am a reasonable man. Military or naval fitness must never be sacrificed to political ends. 'Tis a canker will wreck the most powerful State in time."

Each morning he inspected the ship from stem to stern, accompanied by his officers, and he was not slow to administer rebukes for shortcomings or oversights. Later in the forenoon the men were exercised at the great guns, and in the afternoon there was pike and cutlass drill. The watch was rigorously maintained. We carried lookouts day and night at all three mast-heads and on poop and fo'c'sle, and every one of them was equipped with an observation glass. The handling of the sails was astonishingly smart to me, who, of course, had had no previous experience to go by.

The cleanliness of the decks and living-quarters was beyond any peradventure of criticism. Even the men of the crew—as choice a collection of hangman's favorites, jailbreakers, road-wanderers, hedge-thieves, pickpockets, murderers and mutineers as could have been mustered upon one deck—were kept personally tidy and clothed with a rough similarity in wide trousers of tough canvas, gaudy shirts of calico and round-jackets of Irish frieze.

There was plenty of food, and of far better quality than is served on King's ships, as I have since learned, and enough rum to keep all hands in good humor without being drunk. None of this broaching a cask on the spar-deck according to Flint's habit, but a full pannikin three times a day. And in tropical waters, so Master Martin told me, Murray was at great pains to keep the ship stocked with fresh fruit to prevent the scurvy and the wasting fevers of the hot latitudes.

The officers lodged for'ard of the cabin in what answered, I suppose, for a gun-room. Murray had the poop quarters to himself, with only Peter and me for company, aside from Ben Gunn and the two negro lackeys, who were more for show than aught else, seeing that the steward did practically all the work.

With our accommodations I could find no cause for quarrel. My great-uncle had promised me I should fare like an admiral, and certes, like an admiral or a princeling did I fare. There was a stateroom each for Peter and me, and whilst constricted in space by shore standards, they were spacious beside the cubby-hole we had shared aboard the brig.

The main cabin I have already described, but I may add that in addition to its artistic decorations it possessed a well-chosen library of Latin, French, Italian, Spanish and British authors, including such recent works as our own Cadwallader Colden's "History of the Iroquois Nations," which my father esteemed a masterpiece of historical authority; Smollet's novels, several pamphlets and slim volumes dealing with the experiences of spirited gentlemen who had participated in the struggles of the '45; and a variety of philosophical studies and disquisitions upon political economy. Perceiving that I displayed some interest in it, my great-uncle commended to my attention Monsieur de Montesquieu's "Spirit of Laws," Cervantes' "Don Quixote," the "Satyricon" of Petronius, Carte's monumental "Life of the Duke Ormond" and Clarendon's "History of the Rebellion."

"There, Robert," he remarked of the last, "is an object-lesson in the success to which a man may attain by application, diplomacy and native genius. My Lord Clarendon began life as a commoner; yet he lived to see his daughter married to the brother of the King of England, and only by the obscure bafflements of fate was he prevented from beholding the offspring of her body occupying the holy eminence of the throne. I have derived much satisfaction from the contemplation of his success in moments when I might have despaired of the future's reward of my own efforts."

He was particular that I should be well garbed, and forced upon me several suits out of his abundant wardrobe which were given the necessary alterations by a former journeyman tailor who had escaped from Newgate on the eve of execution for the murder of a scolding wife. He would have done as much for Peter also; but the Dutchman refused to be parted from his salt-stained buckskin shirt and leggings; and an odd figure Corlaer made, in all conscience, striding the decks of the *Royal James* in the costume of a forest-runner, even to the knife and hatchet hung on either thigh.

We were fortunate in our weather until we had gained the latitude of Florida, when a northwesterly storm drove us some hundreds of miles out of our course and separated us for several weeks from our consort. By reason of this misadventure we were obliged to beat back to the north in order to take advantage of the trades to run down upon the island from the nor'east, which was highly essential, so my great-uncle said, else we must be compelled to thread the dangerous mazes of the Bahama group or sail uncomfortably close to the eastern coast of Cuba.

To the west of the Bermoothes—within sight of which we never came—we encountered the *Walrus* again, Flint having had substantially the same experience as ourselves, and thenceforward we continued in company. Other ships we occasionally sighted from the mast-head; but as Murray was particularly anxious to avoid calling attention to his presence the cry, "Sail ho!" was the signal for our bearing off upon any course which would fetch a compass around the strangers. This fact, together with the time lost through the storm, protracted the voyage near a month beyond what might have been expected, and we were eleven weeks out of New York when a cluster of rocky peaks soared above the heat-haze dead ahead.

My great-uncle, after a single squint through his object-glass, handed the instrument to me.

"'Tis the island," he said. "I'd know those peaks anywhere."

The double lens etched distinctly a rugged spread of land, shelving up out of the sea from a succession of yellow beaches on the east to a series of small hills which culminated in a range of considerable height along the westward side, running almost due north and south. The interior seemed to be heavily forested; the trees climbed the mountains to within the last few hundred feet of their summits, which were bare rock, precipitous in the case of the midmost and highest, a cloud-hung giant which dominated the island.

"That is Spyglass Hill," said my great-uncle, noting the intentness of my survey of it. "'Tis there we maintain our lookouts whilst we are in harbor, and some men give the name of the hill to the island. But in truth the place hath no set name, and is dubbed by each to suit his fancy. You may judge this to be all the more so when I add that Spyglass Hill is known likewise as Mainmast Hill. Do you see the two other high peaks in line with it, north and south? That to the nor'ard is called Foremast Hill, and its twin in the south is Mizzenmast Hill."

We were on the la'b'd tack, clawing off to work eastward of the island's mass, and as he spoke we opened up a sizable bight. Rocky headlands fell away to tree-clad shores, and I caught the gleam of a little river which flowed into the upper end of the basin.

"Is that our haven?" I asked.

"No, 'tis in no sense as secure as that which we customarily use," replied Murray, "although safe enough in storm. It is called the North Inlet. The principal harbor is known as Captain Kidd's Anchorage, and is bitten into the so'east corner of the island. We shall not open it for another two glasses."

The breeze was dwindling, which was fortunate for us as we required plenty of sea-room to weather the island; and the east coast, though flat and sandy, offered no feasible harbor or roadstead. The surf boomed up on the beaches with a steady roar which we could hear above the creaking of our vessel's cordage and the shrieking of the sea-birds whose countless flocks wheeled overhead as we approached. A half-mile astern of us the *Walrus* was bouncing in our wake. Seaward in every quarter the horizon-line melted into the infinite expanse of the ocean.

To me, used to the busy life of a bustling little town or the tossing treetops of the forests of the wilderness, cloaking beneath their restless boughs all manner of wild and savage life, there was something appalling in the isolation of the blotch of land ahead of us.

A continent in miniature, complete with capes, bays, inlets, rivers, mountains, woods and fields, it was yet so utterly desolate in its setting of blue-green water. Actually, I believe, 'twas as much as three leagues in length from north to south, and perhaps better than a league across at its widest. But as I stared at it from the poop of the *Royal James* it seemed less than the green dot of Nutting Island,[1] which lies in the mouth of the East River over against New York. And what scenes of heart-rending cruelty it had witnessed! What acts of ruthless perfidy!

Nearing its shores, I descried the tangled masses of trees which clothed most of its surface. A few conifers shot up to goodly stature, but the greater part of the forest growth was gnarled, wind-tortured dwarfs, misshapen abortions of trees. The whole effect of the place seen from offshore was sinister and forbidding, repulsive as the silent ferocity which emanated from the blind man Pew.

The crew of the *Royal James* eyed the unfolding shoreline with a slackness of interest which surprized me. Men did not talk together. There was no jesting. The bracing of the sheets and trimming of the yards brought forth no more than the customary amount of shouting and yo-ho-hoing without which the sailorman is powerless for good or ill.

I commented upon this; and my great-uncle, silently contemplative beside me, smiled.

"If the ensuing weeks meant leisure and carousing it might be we should be put to it to maintain our standard of discipline," he said. "But as it chances, our crew find confronting them a task of difficulty and duration, the which they know and realize. And therefore, Robert, are they silent, and not because of the spell of evil deeds which you think to decipher from our surroundings. Evil enough the island hath

---

1 .*Governors Island.*

known, I doubt not. What place could not as much be said of? But men, and especially seamen, reck little of an evil past if land be usefully available for their needs. No, no, my boy; you shall sleep securely tonight in Captain Kidd's Anchorage, for all the ghostly memories it contains. And Peter shall eat without a qualm, for the *James* will lie as still as the dry land in the haven's shelter."

"We get some fenison, *ja*," spoke up Peter, with marked enthusiasm for him.

He pointed toward the slopes of a hill this side of the Spyglass, and I had a brief glimpse of a string of white dots which leaped from crag to crag.

Murray laughed.

"You have keen eyes, friend Peter," he observed. "But if you will accept the aid of my glass you will perceive that what you saw were goats—the descendants, we are told, of a flock left here by the old buccaneers, to whom we owe an appreciable debt therefor. Goatflesh is not venison by long odds, but it hath much to commend it over salt beef and pork, and the tender bits of a young kid seethed in the milk of its dam—we are not obligated to obey the Mosaic code— might appeal even to an epicure of as unquestioned taste as yourself. There are, too, certain wildfowl and a breed of duck not to be despised; and we shall have much store of fish and shellfish. Yes, I can assure you additions to our diet which should go far to reconcile you with your lot."

Peter's face shone.

"Dot's goodt," he said. "*Ja*, now I fill oop my stomach wit'out it yumps from der wafes."

Several miles south of this mountain we sighted a white rock on a point of land and beyond it an islet and beyond that a much larger island. Murray ordered the helmsman to edge away to the east, and presently we bore off on a long tack to the so'east to fetch us around a patch of shoals. A man was ordered into the forechains with a leadline, and several others relayed his soundings aft along the deck to the poop. The water shoaled rapidly from ten fathoms to five and a trifle less; but Murray conned his way coolly, the *Walrus* scrupulously exact in our wake, and of a sudden we went about on the starboard tack and opened a wider, deeper harbor even than the North Inlet, on the right hand the shores of the smaller island, on the left the main itself.

My great-uncle turned over the conduct of the ship to Martin and crossed to where Peter and I stood, staring about us. Already we were under the lee of the smaller island, and the ship was making less way as the force of the wind was decreased. The water seemed strangely quiet—instead of bouncing us up and down, it did no more than purr and ripple as the bow cleaved through it. And the heat of the sun, unrelieved by the free sweep of the wind, became intense. In a few moments the decks were hot to the touch, and we might not lay our hands with comfort upon the bulwarks.

Here were no beaches; only mud-banks covered to the waterline with twisting, many-rooted trees, their foliage of an ardently soft green presenting impenetrable, whispering barriers to the eye. The channel curved, following the contour of the smaller island, and we sighted the mouth of a little river similar to that which had flowed into the head of the North Inlet.

"Starboard, Master Martin!" called my great-uncle as he joined Peter and me. "Starboard your helm, if you please. Aye, on to this shoal here. We shall have three fathoms and less to careen in. Bid them drop the anchor."

Martin bawled an order. A whistle piped, and there was a great clatter and rustling of rope running loose, a mighty splash that drove the birds in tumult into the air; and the *Royal James* swung to her cable close under the lesser island's shore. My great-uncle waved one hand over the bulwark.

"Skeleton Island this is called, Robert," he said. "I tell you because you demonstrate so gruesome an interest in the more horrifying episodes of our past. But I regret I must confess that I know of no authentic detail to account for the nomenclature. Pirates have a way of naming a spot to suit themselves, without rime or reason, if the fancy once moves them."

"May we land?" I answered, ignoring his gibe.

"Suit yourselves," he returned with a shrug. "I must have all my men busy aboard here, however, and can spare none to guide you."

"*Ja, ja,*" urged Peter. "We shoodt some goats, eh?"

"If you please," agreed Murray. "Ben Gunn will find you a brace of light muskets preferable to our rack-blunderbusses. I'll have the gig put overside, and you may row yourselves, if you will."

"Are you not afraid we may plan to escape?" I asked curiously.

"How?" he countered. "Look about you."

"We might fashion ourselves a vessel," I declared. "A raft, at the least."

"And whither would you go?" he pressed me. "These seas are unfrequented and tempestuous. Also, I do not think that you would be able to construct a vessel in the amount of uninterrupted time I should allow you. And finally, my dear nephew, I must remind you that you have promised your aid to me in a certain matter."

"I need not consider that binding in event of an opportunity to escape," I retorted.

"You need not perhaps," said he. "Yet you would."

And with that he walked off and bade Saunders order the gig lowered overside. Nor did he say another word until we had secured our weapons and a packet of food from Ben Gunn and returned to the deck. Then he gave over supervising the cock-billing of the mainyard and joined us at the gangway.

"I desire above all things, Robert," he said, "to deal gently with you. Therefore I ask you to believe I am considering your own safety when I require your promise to be aboard again not later than an hour after sundown."

"Why, what harm——"

The *Walrus* slatted past us, her canvas in a slovenly mess alow and aloft, a dozen men howling orders and counter-orders from poop, waist and fo'c'sle, Flint in his red coat strutting the poop and adding his own bellow to the din whenever the confusion showed signs of dissolving. Pew was huddled over the wheel, the green eyeshade masking his powder-burned eyes, John Silver tall beside him, a-leaning on the carven mahogany crutch, his cool, pleasant voice the one sensible sound in the tumult on those disordered decks.

My great-uncle's eyes strayed across the narrow gap of water betwixt the two vessels.

"Well, damme, it's been a —— of a voyage, Murray!" shouted Flint.

"We are here," returned my great-uncle urbanely.

"Aye, and what to do wi' ourselves?" Flint called back. "Blast me for

a —— —— —— if I can see what five hundred —— ——
—— are to do wi' months on their hands, and naught but rum-
drinkin' xand quarrellin' for diversion."

"There's your ship to clean, man," replied Murray. "She needs it."

Flint answered with a curse. The *Walrus* had slid on too far for all
his words to be distinct, but I heard a fragment of the beginning.

"—use o' cleaning' ship? Only a —— —— swab o' a ——
—— Navy officer 'ud think to —— —— his—"

My great-uncle indulged in one of his essentially Gallic shrugs and
dusted a pinch of snuff into his nostrils.

"Captain Flint doth not agree with me, it seems. A strange character, and eke a forceful one, Robert, for all his inherent stupidity and
blindness of view. But to return to your question. You were about to
ask me what harm could befall you ashore. I answer you that I do not
know, but that in all candid truth we are here, to quote my associate,
some 'five hundred —— —— ——,' and accidents may happen.
Therefore, I suggest that you be aboard not later than an hour after
sunset. On second thoughts, Robert, I regret that I shall be unable to
permit you to leave the ship save upon your parole on those terms."

"You have it," I answered shortly, and followed Peter down the side-
cleats into the gig.

We rowed up the estuary for the mouth of the little river which
we had seen from the *James*' deck, and our course took us under the
yellow hull of the *Walrus*. A shrill voice hailed from a gunport, and
Darby McGraw's red head was thrust out beside the frowning black
muzzle.

"Glory be, Master Bob, and do they let ye go free wherever ye will?
Sure, it's yourself must be one o' the grand favorites over yon. Are ye
an officer yet?"

I was about to answer him when Flint gloomed down at us from
the towering poop.

"Gut me!" he sneered. "'Tis Murray's by-blow, no less! What d'ye
make o' this, Billy?"

The brutal face of Bones showed above the bulwarks.

"He's a pris'ner," jeered Bones. "Only he ain't; d'ye see, Flint? Into
New York Murray went to crimp him, and now, by —— ——
—— he gives him shore-leave!"

"Come aboard here, my hearty," Flint hailed me.

"We are going ashore," I answered; "and I have reason to hasten."

Flint scowled.

"Well, ye'll come soon enough. And when I get ye I'll learn ye a thing or two! There's too much politics and favoritism aboard the *James* to suit me, and ye can tell your great-uncle or granddaddy or whatever he may be, blast him for a —— —— —— —— ——, that John Flint says so!"

Darby bobbed up on the poop beside him very much out of breath.

"Och, will ye let me go along o' Master Bob, captain?" he cried. "Do now, avick! Sure, I hain't seen him this long three-month gone."

"That I'll not," snarled Flint, turning his back to us. "Isn't this ship good enough for ye, Darby? Ain't you our luck? Will I let you go and ruin it by rounding up wi' Murray's by-blow?"

"Troth, he's no more'n the old master's son that I worked for in New York, captain darlin', and him that good to me always I had a main likin' for him, indeed and indeed I did! And I'm fair crazy to be ashore after the weeks and months we'll ha'—"

Flint clapped him on the shoulder, abruptly jovial.

"Ah, if it's ashore you'd be that's a different matter," says he. "I'm for goin' ashore myself. Bill, call all hands away for the boats, and we'll have a grand goat-hunt up Spyglass. John Silver shall barbecue 'em for us. And break out a couple o' casks o' rum. Lively now, my lads! We'll enjoy ourselves like the honest pirates we are!"

A frenzy of cheering answered him, and I backed water with my oars.

"You heard, Peter?" I said over my shoulder.

"*Ja;* dot's badt."

"We can't go where they do."

"*Neen.*"

I reflected and examined the surface of the main island, rearing itself before us on the opposite side of the estuary. A half-mile, perhaps, eastward of the river we had been heading for a second and less inviting stream oozed its way into the haven through a succession of swamps. Beyond it toward the island's eastern shore the country was sandy and open. The Spyglass and the intervening hills were miles to the west, clear across the island and the two streams.

"There we'll be safe, Peter," I said. "They're not going in that direction, and if they do by chance come after us we'll be able to see them."

"Maybe we better go back to der ship," he answered doubtfully.

"Not I," I returned grimly. "We won't look for trouble; but if it comes our way we'll meet it."

"*Ja*," he said, and bent to his oars.

We did not enter the second stream, because the swamps along its course presented no landing-place, but ran our boat aground on a sandy bank on the far side of a point which concealed us from the *Walrus.* Then we took our guns and walked inland through the trees up a graduated sandy slope to the top of a little hillock whence we could look off through the aisles of pines and see the *Walrus,* with boats putting off from her sides and pulling into the mouth of the first of the two streams, and over a spur of Skeleton Island the topmasts of the *Royal James.*

"This would be a good place for a fort," I mused.

"*Ja*," said Peter. "You got water, too."

He pointed to a streak of green vegetation along the sandy slope of the knoll which we traced to a spring issuing from the summit.

"Now we got water, we better eat," he added.

"But what about the goats?" I cried. "We were to—"

"No," he insisted subbornly; "we don't shoodt. If we shoodt, der pirates hear us andt come. We waidt until they are all ashore. Then we go back to Murray."

"I'll not be driven from the first pleasure we have had in months," I protested childishly.

"We do it again," replied Peter placidly. "Next time Murray he come wit' us himself, *ja.*"

"Yes, but—"

"Now you be sensible, Bob. Der Injuns is goodt friendts beside them fellers, *ja.* We go back to der *James.* Soon all o' them be ashore andt drunk. Drunk, they like to kill us, but they can't row—*neen.*"

And we rowed back to the *James* ingloriously in the dusk, the shouts of the *Walrus'* carousers echoing to us from the shore.

CHAPTER X

HOSTAGES

THE WATCH aboard the *Royal James* challenged us as we made fast by the larboard side-ladder, and when we climbed over the bulwarks to the deck Master Martin flashed a lanthorn in our faces with a gust of oaths in his absurdly gentle tones.

"By the —— —— —— ——, but I hoped 'twas that —— —— Flint come a-seekin' mischief," he complained.

"Where is Captain Murray?" I answered.

"In his cabin."

And in the same mild manner he continued to his men:

"To your stations. Remember cap'n's orders. Now these two are aboard, ye'll fire at any boat that approaches and challenge afterward."

The negro lackeys stood aside as we came to the cabin entrance under the poop; the door was open. Down the dark tunnel of the companionway with its stateroom doors on either hand Peter and I could see my great-uncle sitting at the table in the main cabin, a glass of wine at his elbow, a chart spread out before him. He raised his head as we entered.

"You were cheated of your sport, I conclude," he greeted us. "The watch informed me a half-hour since they had heard no shots ashore."

I recounted briefly our conversation with Flint and the determination Peter and I had reached in consequence. He nodded agreement with it.

"You did quite right, Robert. Peter did not exaggerate the dangers inherent in the situation."

"You appear not to feel any too safe yourself," I answered sarcastically, "with sentinels posted on your decks ordered to shoot into any approaching boat."

"I do not," he assented with perfect equanimity. "'Tis true I should be surprised did our confrères of the *Walrus* undertake to assault us, but I have had too much experience with desperate men, especially when they are under the influence of liquor, to discount the possibility of their adopting any atrocious idea which might enter their heads."

"Do you mean that you live in perpetual fear of treachery from Flint's crew?"

He considered the question, sipping at his wine.

"Perpetual is too strong a word for the occasion," he decided at length. "Let us say rather that the experience to which I have previously referred has taught me that under certain circumstances—such as the license practised after the tedium of a long voyage—a band of men who recognize no authority save the strong arm may be induced to excesses they would not otherwise attempt."

"Then we don't shoodt no goats?" asked Peter sorrowfully.

"On the contrary, friend Peter. We most certainly shall. 'Tis not only a question of securing you the opportunity of sport which I promised you, but of varying the diet of my crew, with an eye to maintaining all hands in good health at a time when we can not afford incapacity. Tomorrow morning I shall be occupied in organizing the work of careening the ship, so that her bottom may be cleaned; but in the afternoon we will take a party of beaters to aid us and arrange a battue in the Continental fashion. By that time, I anticipate, Captain Flint will have returned to his senses—recovered from his debauch, in other words. If he has not—"

He shrugged, and I gathered that the contingency would not be a happy one for Flint.

"You will excuse me," he went on, "if I return to my studies. I have much upon my mind."

We bade him good night and went to our staterooms, weary enough from the unwonted exercise of rowing. As I shut my door I noted that he was measuring distances in the Caribbean with calipers and jotting figures upon the margin of the chart.

In the morning, as he had said, all hands were occupied with the task of careening the ship. In the first place she was to be hauled over to starboard to expose her larboard bottom, and all her guns and movable stores and heavy equipment were shifted to starboard to give her a list on that side. Then her yards were cockbilled to keep them clear of the water, and heavy cables were run from her masts to the shore, looped around trees and carried back aboard, and the crew by main force, a few inches or a foot at a time, canted her over. The tide, as it dropped, aided them by bedding the keel in the estuary's soft mud floor, and gradually the *James* came to assume a most lopsided appearance.

'Twas when the work had gone so far and was proceeding satisfactorily that my great-uncle bade Martin tell off a dozen hands who were good shots and call away the longboat.

"I marvel that you dare to leave the *James* in this defenseless condition," I said to him as the longboat pulled off up the anchorage past the silent bulk of the *Walrus*. "If there was danger last night—"

"—there need not necessarily be danger this afternoon," he interrupted. "'Tis all quiet ashore, and I doubt if there is a man sufficiently sober aboard the *Walrus* to carry a carton of powder from the magazine."

"But by evening they'll ha' slept it off," I insisted.

"True, and with it their lust for bloodshed—for the time being, at any rate. Our problem then will be to turn Flint's mind to some undertaking which will divert his attention and occupy him until we need no longer be concerned for his whimsies."

We landed south of the first river, below where Flint's party had held their carouse, and proceeded inland through a wooded valley, with hills rising to right and left of us and the Spyglass towering in the distance. The day was very clear, and the mountain's summit was a gray cone against the blue of the sky. A soft wind whispered in the trees; the beat of the surf came to us faintly; the severity of the sun was tempered by the shade; and the pine-mast was springy to our feet. Even our sullen, hangdog escort of seamen became almost cheery under the influence of their changed surroundings, and with the sight of their first goat they began to whoop and shout like schoolboys. Murray, despite his age, was as spry as the youngest of us, and he never wasted a shot.

At his suggestion we turned north along the lower flanks of the Spyglass, circled the intervening hills—foot-hills they might be called—crossed the headwaters of the first river, traversed another patch of forest and forded the second river at a point where it ran shallow and clear between two of the marshy stretches which were its distinguishing characteristic. This route brought us over to the eastern side of the island some distance north of the hillock Peter and I had visited the preceding evening, and when I remarked this fact my great-uncle expressed interest and requested that we should visit the place. We had by now shot sufficient goats to load down all our bearers, whilst Peter carried half a dozen brace of various birds, to the eatable qualities of which Murray bore testimony.

We had maintained a brisk pace on our wanderings, and we reached the site of the spring well before sunset. My great-uncle surveyed the situation with a calculating eye, estimated the stand of timber on the hill's sides, and exclaimed that there was no neighboring eminence whence an enemy could command it.

"'Tis all you have asserted it to be," he said. "Moreover, it gives me an idea of a way in which we may occupy the energies of Captain Flint and his lambs for the ensuing weeks of our stay."

I asked him what he intended, but he would not answer me, striding off with his head sunk on his chest after his manner when plunged in thought. The seamen, who had awaited us at the foot of the hill, fell in behind us, and we retraced our steps across the swampy river and the intervening belt of forest to the first and larger stream. This, too, we recrossed, but instead of continuing on as we had come Murray turned down the course of the stream in a southeasterly direction. A thread of smoke trickled up beside the mouth of the rivulet in the woods along the estuary, and I indicated it to him.

"There is Flint," I said.

"Yes," he replied absently, and kept on.

The shadows were lengthening as we stepped out of the forest into a glade on the river's bank. Several additional fires had been kindled, and around each were huddled groups of pirates much the worse for the last night's drinking-bout. John Silver was the only man who appeared to have any animation left in him; he hopped on his crutch from one fire to another, supervising the roasting of the haunches of goat, which were spitted in front of the flames with pieces of hardtack placed beneath to catch the dripping juices. 'Twas he first saw us, and evidently spoke to Flint, who sat with Bones and several other cronies at the smallest of the fires. He swung toward us as Flint rose unsteadily and tacked in his wake.

"Come a-visitin', captain?" Silver inquired cheerfully. "Mighty kind o' ye, sir, seein' as how most o' our lads is a bit the worse for liquor and blood-lettin'. My duty to ye, Master Ormerod. I hopes I sees you and your friend well?"

"Blood-letting?" repeated Murray, ignoring the balance of his remarks. "The old story, eh? Well, well! You'll never learn. How many for the sailmaker's palm and needle?"

"Three, captain. And main lucky we are as—"

Flint lurched up beside him.

"Stow that, John," growled his captain. "I'll do the talkin'. What's your trouble, Murray?"

My great-uncle took a pinch of snuff with his inimitable knack of expressing acute disgust without moving a muscle of his face.

"I have been a-hunting," he replied. "Shooting for the pot. We stopped on the way to our boat to pass the time o' day with you, Flint."

Flint snorted.

"Time o' day! ——! 'Tain't like you to take the trouble."

"I am a person of most uncertain proclivities," replied my great-uncle. "I hear from Silver that last night's episode was accompanied by the usual fatalities."

"Three," assented Flint. "Two o' 'em could be spared—lousy dogs. The other was Toby Welsh, as stout a fellow as we had."

"Not bad for one night's work," commented Murray.

Flint was obviously in no very belligerent mood; he could scarce stand. But he flamed up at this.

"Aye, and what d'ye expect? How many months did ye tell me I must bide here wi' a crew that knows naught but how to brew the Devil's broth? And how many men d'ye think will be alive by the end of the time? Gut me, but 'twill be like the song we sing o' the Dead Man's Chest!"

"I fear it will," agreed my great-uncle. "Unless you take measures to prevent it."

"Measures?"

Flint cursed with the fluency of the man who enjoys his work.

"There's a deal to be done in keeping twelvescore men from fighting on this chunk o' earth and rock!"

"There's your ship to be cleaned," said my great-uncle tentatively.

"I'd ha' mutiny on my hands did I call for it! They're all for a run ashore, and there'll be no working them aboardship until they ha' had their fill o' woods and mountains."

"Ah!" said my great-uncle. "Doubtless that is so. Well, if they must remain ashore a time, is it not in their own interest to erect themselves some shelter from the elements?"

Flint stared at him curiously.

"Ye've an idea in the back o' your head, Murray. Out with it!"

"We have often said that some day we should build ourselves a fort on the island," answered my great-uncle.

"We ha'."

"I came upon the ideal spot this afternoon—a sand hillock overgrown with fine pines and oaks eastward of the swamps. It hath the airs from the ocean, a good prospect of the anchorage and the nearer waters, and there is a spring at the very top."

"And I'm to do the work!" snarled Flint.

"Your men are to do the work," corrected Murray. "I should gladly assist them in it but for the fact that my own crew will be occupied aboardship during the duration of our stay. We of the *Royal James,* I may point out, are laboring in the common interest no less than your people will be if they undertake the construction of the fort."

"Blast me for a —— —— fool if I care two —— —— —— for the common interest!" cried Flint. "But 'tis true there is need of the fort, and if the men will bide ashore they should ha' a roof to their heads and a better place to camp than down here in the river vapors. I'll see what's to be done, Murray. Not tonight—there's no man of us, except Long John, curse him! can put two thoughts together. But in the morning 'twill be different. We'll fetch off a boatload o' axes and shovels, and I'll turn 'em to. I think it can be done. —— me, it must be done! I can't lose three men a day for the next six months!"

"You'll not regret it," replied my great-uncle. "I shall be glad to lend you aught I possess in the way of tools or advice."

"—— your advice!" snapped Flint. "The tools I'll take. Is that my hostage wi' you?"

"'Tis my grandnephew, yes."

"Ye may as well leave him then. We can use him on the fort. He's not too proud to hand and haul, is he?"

Murray stepped so close to him that notwithstanding the dimness of the twilight their faces were clearly discernible to each other.

"When the time comes for it my grandnephew will be placed in your hands, Flint," he said quietly. "And I shall hold you strictly accountable for his treatment."

His manner chilled.

"D'ye hear, man? Strictly accountable, I said. The feckless knave that lays a finger to him, who has my own blood in his veins, shall be flayed alive and bound to the bowsprit of the *James.*"

"Oh, aye," mumbled Flint, and faded into the shadows.

Long John Silver, who had tarried within earshot throughout their dialogue, stumped forward again.

"It grows sudden dark in these 'ere latitoods, captain!" he said. "Will ye ha' one o' our boats to take ye off?"

"I thank you," replied my great-uncle. "We shall have no difficulty in finding our boat."

He did not speak again until we were pulling across the star-flecked waters of the anchorage.

"I think," he announced casually, "we need have no cause to worry over the defenseless condition of the *James.*"

"A dozen shot under water—" I started to say, when Peter spoke up.

"He gets them all ashore, Bob. *Ja,* dot's it! All der time they work, andt so they don't think about der *James.*"

"A singularly acute mind our Peter has," commented my great-uncle.

His strategy was completely successful. The building of the hilltop fort appealed to some boyish strain submerged beneath the surface villainy of Flint's scoundrels. They went to their task with positive enthusiasm, clearing the hillock of timber, sawing and squaring the logs and erecting a substantial house of the more massive logs and after that an open stockade or paling of sapling stakes six feet high. The house-walls were loop-holed for musketry, and Flint commenced to talk of a pair of bastions to hold six-pounders; but this was after the work had gone forward two months and his men were becoming weary of ax and saw.

Toward the end of our sojourn the *Walrus'* crew were committed
to a serious effort to exterminate the goats of the island, and since
this occupation was to be preferred to the extermination of one
another, which was their favorite sport when their energies were not
otherwise diverted, nobody was inclined to stop them, my great-uncle
least of all.

His personal object was already accomplished. The *Royal James*
was back upon an even keel, her bottom scraped clean, her hull fresh-
painted inside and out, her rigging overhauled and canvas in order,
spars tested and a weak topmast replaced, guns varnished, stores
checked and stowed, sufficient great-cartridge for three actions prepared by the gunner, ballast aboard and distributed with a careful eye
for sailing trim.

"As sweet and proper as though she was just from the hands of
the dockyard fitters at Portsmouth," was Murray's comment on an
evening about the beginning of August.

The three of us sat at table in the main cabin, Peter still occupied
with the fragments of a wild pigeon. Through the open stern windows drifted a tag-end of song from the *Walrus,* lying a cable's length
higher up the anchorage:

> "The Frenchman took Moon's knife in the throat—
>   Yo-ho-ho, and a bottle o' rum!
>   But all they found was a rusty groat—
>   Yo-ho-ho, and a bottle o' rum!"

"That is Flint's voice," continued my great-uncle. "I am glad he is
aboardship. 'Twill save us the inconvenience of a journey ashore."

And to the query of my raised eyebrows he replied:

"The tide ebbs on the break of dawn. I purpose sailing then."

"And you must deliver the body of your hostage beforehand," I
answered as disagreeably as I could.

"Even so," he acknowledged. "'Tis regrettable, Robert, yet the time
will come, I venture to predict, when you will look back with pride
upon the inconvenience you suffered."

"I'll accept the inconvenience if I may escape the rascals alive," I
retorted.

"Of that you need have no doubts," he said earnestly. "I shall accompany you, and you may hear my parting instructions to Flint. Friend Peter, will you indulge me for the space of half an hour whilst I visit the *Walrus* with my nephew?"

"*Neen*," answered Peter, and pushed away from the table. "I go too."

"No, no—"

"I go too."

"But naught was said of two hostages—"

"If Bob goes, I go," insisted the Dutchman. "*Ja.*"

Murray shook his head.

"For you I might not be responsible, Peter."

"I be responsible for myself," said Peter. "I go to der *Walrus* or you go oudt der window."

My great-uncle stared at him for a moment, then burst into laughter.

"By gad, you would! And after become captain in my place, no doubt. You are unmatchable, Peter. What do you say, nephew?"

"I'd not have Peter risk his throat with mine," I answered uncomfortably, the words of Flint's song still ringing in my memory.

"I go wit' you, Bob," repeated the Dutchman.

"You see!" cried Murray. "'Tis useless to object. Go with you he will. Well, you'll have company at least—and I shall lack a companion whose presence is not the less valuable for his silence. A good friend is Peter, Robert. I would he were mine!"

Peter rose.

"We go," he said. "*Ja.*"

On deck Murray had the longboat called away, and we embarked in silence. 'Twas a hot night, with very little air stirring, and the ribald uproar on the *Walrus* was amazingly distinct. The *James* was like a tomb by contrast. Not a sound came from her, and the only lights she showed were in the waist and the main cabin. The *Walrus* was a blaze of lanthorns from poop to fo'c'sle, but Murray hailed the deck twice before he had an answer.

"Boat ahoy!" responded a husky voice then. "Why'n —— don't ye come aboard?"

"'Tis Captain Murray to see Captain Flint," replied my great-uncle calmly.

"Aye, aye, sir," answered the husky voice on a quaver of fear. "We'll call him directly. Will ye come aboard, sir?"

My great-uncle turned to Peter with one foot on the side ladder.
"Are you certain you must go with Robert?" he asked. "I can assure
you no harm will come to him."

"*Ja,* I go."

My great-uncle's reply was a shrug of indifference, and Peter and
I climbed after him to the deck. The noise of revelry stopped dead
as he appeared, but the visible evidence of it was plain to see on
every hand. A cask of rum with the head knocked out stood by the
foot of the mainmast. There was a pool of blood on the deck-plank-
ing by the fo'c'sle companionway, and a pallid-cheeked fellow was
binding up his arm in a dirty headcloth and spitting oaths at another
man who composedly wiped his knife clean on a frowsy coil of rope.
Fore and aft men had been gaming, drinking, quarreling and singing—
and all abruptly halted whatever they were doing to stare at us.

Murray returned their stares with an undisguised repugnance which
I discovered myself to share. The *Walrus* was a revelation after the
ordered discipline of the *Royal James.* In a word, she was pig-dirty.
Her deck was littered with all kinds of rubbish; her rigging was slack
and spliced in a fashion which seemed lubberly to me, who was a
lubber; her canvas was torn, poorly patched and wretchedly furled;
boats, barrels, lumber, spare spars and cables lay about in entire confusion. The planks we trod on were slippery with grease. The paint
was peeling from the bulwarks. There were spots of rust on the muzzle of a chase gun, which itself was hauled out of its proper position.

Flint came swaggering down to us from the poop in a condition
which was in harmony with his surroundings. Like most of his men,
he had discarded coat, shirt, stockings and shoes to accommodate
himself to the heat of a tropical Summer. His loose canvas trousers,
identical with those the seamen wore, were streaked with dirt and
tar. His bare calves and forearms were covered with dried blood
where they had been scratched by brambles in his shore expeditions;
out of the matted hair on his chest was thrust the head of a tiger,
most marvelously tattooed in black and yellow. His hair was a lank
frame for his saturnine face, stubbly with a week's growth of beard.

Sure, the contrast was as sharp betwixt him and my great-uncle,
immaculate in figured black satin, hair sprucely dressed, as betwixt
the two ships. He sensed it himself.

"What d'ye seek, Murray?" he growled. "Come to look us over?"

"I am come to fulfil my contract with you," replied my great-uncle. "I am sailing with the morning ebb, and I bring you, not one hostage, but two."

Flint stepped closer and scrutinized Peter and me.

"Two, eh? What do I want wi' two? What good's this fat man to me? He means nothing to you."

"On the contrary," denied my relative. "Master Corlaer is an old and valued enemy of mine, of whom I have hopes of making in time a friend."

"Well, he's no good to me; gut me if he is!"

"You will take both or none," said my great-uncle in the voice like a dripping icicle which he knew so well how to assume.

"Nasty, are ye?" rasped Flint. "Blast ye for a ———"

A light in Murray's tawny eyes kindled like a flame under the reflection of the battle-lanthorns which were hung from the lower spars.

"Two it is," Flint ended hastily. "But ye'll never see either one o' 'em if ye don't make good on your bargain. I ha' supported much from ye, Murray, but—"

"You'll support more for sufficient gold," rebuked my great-uncle. "Tut, man, I read you like a book. When we first encountered you were proud to be mate of a trading-brig. I have put you in the way to rank and fortune, if you know how to exploit your opportunities."

"Rank and opportunities!" jeered Flint with an ugly laugh. "Aye, ye took me when I was an honest young man and made a pirate o' me. And the only opportunity I'll win through you will be to kick the air in Execution Dock."

My great-uncle helped himself to snuff, tapping his box as Flint talked.

"Hark ye," he broke in when the *Walrus'* captain had got so far, "I am pressed for time. I have but two things to say to you. Guard well and cherish carefully these two persons I commit to you, and in two months I'll hand over to you three hundred and fifty thousand pounds."

"You said seven hundred thousand," snapped Flint.

"I said seven hundred thousand to be divided betwixt the two ships."

"Oh-ho! And ye'll take captain's share o' the *James'* half, eh? As well as your hundred thousand slice?"

"My terms are perfectly clear," returned Murray. "Now for my second point. When I return it may be we shall have need of swift keels. I recommend you to get your ship in decent condition. As she stands, you could be carried by a Portuguese slaver."

A shrewd look dawned in Flint's face.

"And where are ye a-goin' to pluck this million and a half o' treasure from?" he demanded. "You ha' said much of it, but you told me little. What course doth the treasure-ship sail? Where do you lurk for her? There's wide seas betwixt the Main and the Atlantic, and ye can't stop every hole, Murray."

"You may safely entrust that portion of the task to me," replied my great-uncle dryly.

He offered me his hand, and somewhat to my own surprize I found myself inclined to accept it.

"Robert," he said, "I regret exceedingly the necessity I am under of inflicting this unpleasantness upon you. I shall endeavor to provide you adequate reparation. You also, friend Peter. Remember, we are working for a greater cause than our personal enrichment."

He vaulted lightly to the top of the bulwarks and dropped out of sight on the farther side. His shoes clicked on the ladder-cleats, and we heard the rattle of oars as his boat put off.

"Gut me, but there's times I think he believes all he says," swore Flint.

CHAPTER XI

PETER PLAYS AT BOWLS WITH DESTINY

DARBY McGRAW'S red head shone in the lanthorn-light.

"Whisht, but it's Master Bob again! Now ain't this the mighty forchune to have ye with us! Ha' ye left the old devil yon for good?"

He nodded his torch of hair at the vague hull of the *James*. Flint exploded with raucous laughter.

"'The old devil yon,'" he repeated. "——— me, but it takes Darby to

put the right word to a man. 'Tis what he is, blast him for the ——
—— —— he sets himself up to be!"

Darby proffered him a huge silver beaker of rum.

"I fetched this from the cabin after ye, captain," said the Irish boy
in his wheedling brogue. "Troth, say I to meself, if the captain must
talk with Murray he'll ha' a bad taste in the mouth o' him to be
washed out, and I'd best ha' a sup o' sugar-juice handy for his needin's."

Flint seized the rum, threw back his head and drained the fiery
stuff as if it had been wine.

"You said right, my lad," he answered sourly. "And I'm thinking I'll
maybe need all the luck that red head o' yours can bring me. Where's
Billy Bones?"

"Dhrunk under the cabin table," returned Darby promptly.

"Gut him for the souse he is! And Long John?"

"Sure, captain dear, 'twas yourself sent him ashore to keep the lads
up to the fort from carvin' theirselves."

"So I did. Well, I'll see to the prisoners myself then."

"Pris'ners!" protested Darby, wide-eyed. "Troth, himself is the nevvy
or what-not o' the old devil. For why'll be makin' him a pris'ner? More
by token, he was me friend in New York, and Peter too. Grand pirates
they'll be, if ye do but give 'em time."

"Prisoners I said, and prisoners they are!" glowered Flint. "D'ye
know what a hostage is, Darby?"

"One that'll be by-ordinary wicked?" answered Darby.

"More'n likely," assented Flint with a pardonable chuckle. "Well,
these is hostages, Darby. Likewise prisoners."

"Och, captain, ye won't be hard on Master Bob! He's as kindly a
young gentleman as ever I see—and Peter there is a grand fightin'
feller. Ye should hear to tales they tell o' his murtherin' and slayin'
with the red Injuns."

"I'll be as hard as they make me be," returned Flint. "But for tonight
I must have them safe."

Darby plucked at his sleeve.

"I'll say naught if ye must put Peter away—though a good friend
I ha' called him. But be aisy wi' Master Bob and let me take him below
for a sup for old times' sake. Troth, there's no harm in nature in him.
And if he has a chance at education in the right way 'tis a fine, brave

pirate we'll make o' him that can fight two men at once wi' knife and
tomahawk."

Flint's eyes narrowed.

"Ho-ho!" he exclaimed. "Is that the kind of cockerel ye are, Master
Ormerod or whatever ye may be called? I'm main thankful for the
tip-off, Darby. I knew Buckskin was dangerous, but I'd never ha' been
on my guard for the young 'un, except for you. Gut me, if I take
chances wi' two such champions!"

I saw that Darby was doing more harm than good by his spon-
soring of me, so I spoke up for myself.

"You need not take what the boy says for truth," I said. "He means
well, but—"

"And if I didn't see ye knock the hatchet from Tom Trumbull's hand
the while ye were fending Dick Varje's knife—and could easily ha'
stabbed him, fightin' earnest, as Peter said—may I be hornswoggled
for a lubber!" proclaimed Darby indignantly.

"That's enough for me," snarled Flint. "No lies, if it please you, my
fine gentleman! The time may come we'll boasts to—"

"I have not boasted."

"Keep your tongue behind your teeth! Hold still, the two o' ye, or
I'll give ye a bellyful o' pickling-brine."

He signaled up a dozen or so of the nearest of his men, all of whom
had been observing us with a mingling of interest and hostility.

"We'll put these knife-fighters in the lazaret for the night," he
announced. "They're a desperate pair, and we'll watch 'em close until
they are under hatches."

"Oh, whirra, whirra!" sobbed Darby. "Do but see what I did to ye
with my tongue that wags from the middle both ways! Sure, captain
darlin', ye don't need to hold against Master Bob what I said. All he
seeks is to be a grand, murtherin' pirate. Troth, we talked o' nothin'
else in the old days."

"Don't be foolish, Darby," I said.

And to Flint, as the group closed around us—

"Captain Murray bade you—"

"I know, I know!" he interrupted impatiently. "The treatment you
receive will be whatever you earn for yourselves. I'm an easy skipper, as any man aboard the *Walrus* will tell ye, my lad. But you are

my stakes in a rich venture, and I'll be ——— ——— if I take any
chance on losing ye or your fat friend as goes with you. So stow your
gab, and come wi' me willingly, and no blows struck or feelings
injured. Tomorrow the *James* will ha' sailed, and then we'll deal a new
hand all around."

His narrow green eyes, squinting out on either side of his thin
nose, surveyed me with a kind of appraisal.

"I have an idea we may yet find interests in common," he concluded. "But that's to be seen."

Peter, at my elbow, spoke for the first time.

"*Ja, ja.* We go. I hafe a wish to sleep."

"Sleep, is it?" jeered Flint. "That ye shall, my hearty! Come along o' me."

He led us aft, the others following, Darby in the rear almost in
tears. We entered the poop quarters, stumbling over empty bottles,
broken platters, discarded garments, boots, articles of equipment and
weapons. At the end of a dark passage Flint unhooked a lanthorn from
a wall and one of his men heaved up a trapdoor. Below was a pool
of shadows that scuttled and swayed as if to escape the feeble light.
There was an odor, also, none too pleasant.

I drew back.

"Certes, you could lodge us securely otherwhere than this," I
protested.

"No, no," answered Flint. "There's not a door aboard hath a lock
would hold Darby, let alone you two. I'm sorry for ye, lad, if it's no
fault o' yours that you're here; but for tonight at least you must lie in
the lazaret. Come, come; don't make me use force. Here, ye shall ha'
the lanthorn to keep the rats off, and in the morning we'll manage
different."

Peter pushed past me, and took the lanthorn from his hand.

"We go, *ja,*" he squeaked. "Come, Bob."

I followed him without another word, already wondering at his
extraordinary docility.

"Do ye see your way, my masters?" Flint called after us, mimicking
the servile tones of a tavernkeeper to the considerable amusement
of his body-guard. "Mind the low roof, an' it please ye, sirs. The beds
ha' not been aired, but then we had no expectation o' your company."

A guffaw of rough merriment, pierced by Darby's Irish wail, and the trapdoor crashed down. A hasp clacked home in a bolt, and foot-steps thudded away. I sat on the bottommost step of the ladder and peered hopelessly around me as Peter, swinging the lanthorn as high as the low deckroom allowed, prowled around the limited area of our prison.

A black rat as large as a cat rushed across my feet. Squeaks and rustlings sounded in the corners. There was the *lap-lap-lap* of water against the vessel's hull, the creak of the rudder and the strange moan-ing noises which any ship emits, whether at anchor or under way.

Peter returned to the ladder-foot, deposited the lanthorn on the floor and plumped himself beside it.

"What you t'ink, Bob?" he said blandly. "Do we stay or get oudt?"

I frowned at him.

"'Tis no joke," I snapped. "I had reasons for—"

"*Ja,*" he agreed. "Der little gal."

The Dutchman said so little and revealed such scant interest in what went on about him that he frequently surprised even those who knew him best, as my father never tired of maintaining. He had not spoken, up to this evening, of Murray's plan to employ me as a hostage to conciliate Flint. He had never suggested that he would accompany me. He had never betrayed by any hint a supposition that I might pre-fer to remain aboard the *Royal James* during the cruise after the trea-sure-ship. But on all these points he had done considerable thinking as he now proceeded to demonstrate.

"How did you know!" I exclaimed.

"I know," he replied with his simpering imitation of a laugh. "You t'ink der little gal is a goodt gal. You t'ink it is not goodt dot she be taken aboard der *James.* You want to be there andt be sure dot she is safe."

"'Tis true as gospel, Peter," I groaned. "I hoped to the last this ridicu-lous plan of Murray's would fall through in some manner, but the man has a damnable determination."

"*Ja,*" agreed Peter. "I t'ink he takes der treasure-ship, Bob. Dot's easy."

"Easy? I see not how!"

"*Ja,* it is easy to take her. But after comes his troubles. Much trea-sure is bad for pirates. We hafe troubles after."

"'We!' We won't be there. Very likely we'll be dead, Peter, slain in one of the *Walrus'* knife frays."

"Suppose we get oudt tonight," answered Peter persuasively. "Suppose we get oudt and back to der *James. Ja?*"

I looked around me skeptically at the heavy planking and stout timbers of the sides and for'ard bulkhead.

"It can't be done. 'Twould take a week to break out of this—and the *James* will be sailing in five or six hours."

"*Neen,*" said Peter. "We get oudt—any time we get oudt."

"How?" I demanded.

He picked up the lanthorn and led me for'ard to the bulkhead. The light showed that one of the oaken planks was slightly sprung, leaving an infinitesimal crack between its edge and the uppermost of its fellows.

"Are you planning to pry that off with your fingernails?" I taunted him.

"*Neen,*" he answered, and conducted me to a corner whence the rats scudded as we approached.

He stirred his foot amongst some rubbish and turned up several long, wrought-iron spikes, such as are used to bolt together the heavier ship-timbers.

"Dot's plenty," he said.

I could hardly control the gush of relief that welled up in me.

"I believe it is," I whispered. "But, oh, Peter, there is such little time!"

"Enough," he grunted. "Come! We begin."

We listened at the bulkhead for signs of life on the opposite side, but not a sound came through to us, although the clamor on the upper deck and in the poop cabin seeped into our dungeon from overhead. 'Twas stiflingly hot, and Peter's first care was to strip off his buckskin shirt and leggings.

"We got to swim," he said, eying them regretfully. "You don't need clothes tonight, Bob."

So I followed his example, and we fell to work with our spikes upon the sprung plank, the sweat pouring in rills of moisture from our half-naked bodies, our crude tools slipping in our greasy fingers as we pried and pushed and fought for every inch of space betwixt the plank and the upright it was nailed to. Peter did all the work. It was his tremendous muscles that fretted and teased the point of his spike into the tiny gap that awaited us, that gradually enlarged the advantage. All I could do was to hold whatever space he won, giving him opportunity to improve upon it until a smashing drive of his great shoulder tore the plank loose at one end.

We waited, then, gasping for breath, wiping the sweat from our eyes, fearful lest the wrench of the wood as it was ripped free should have attracted the attention of some member of the crew. But nobody appeared, and the uproar on deck was audibly decreased. Even the crew of the *Walrus* found occasion for sleep.

The most difficult portion of our task was immediately ahead. We had to pry loose now a plank which was nailed fast to the uprights, and we dared not resort to the use of any substitute for a hammer because of the noise. 'Twas necessary for Peter's fingers to force the point of a spike between plank and upright and slowly wedge the two apart. He did it, with the palm of his bare hand for a mallet, his muffled grunts the only indication of the energy he expended.

But this was a matter of several hours, for I was less able to assist than I had been before. My puny strength was wholly inadequate to the wrestle with seasoned wood and tempered iron which he must carry on in cramped quarters and semidarkness.

As the last nail yielded to Peter's shoulder the thin clangor of the bell of the *Royal James* stole down to us out of the night. Four times it rang—two o'clock! No answering strokes sounded on the deck above us. Ship routine was a thing of caprice aboard the *Walrus.*

"Get oudt, Bob," whispered Peter.

I wriggled through the gap in the bulkhead, and he passed the lanthorn after me. Its flame was burning low, but I had sufficient light to determine that I stood in a stores-hold crammed with casks of rum, salt meat and ship's biscuit. A door in its for'ard bulkhead led to another hold of the orlop deck, where were a hatch and ladder leading up to the gundeck. I crept as far as the foot of the ladder and listened to the snores of the scores of men who slept in hammocks slung between the great guns of the battery. That way lay our only path of escape.

I returned to Peter in a mood that was none too cheerful; but he was already at work with his spike, hissing like a kettle on the boil as he prodded away with its blunted point. I was able to be of more assistance to him this time, since from the farther side 'twas possible to exert a greater leverage, once the plank was sprung loose. Yet the *James* sounded seven bells before we were successful. Peter grunted his satisfaction.

"We got time," he said. "Whoof! So much I sweat I slide me t'rough dot hole."

The lanthorn's flicker was little more than a pin-prick of flame in the darkness of the ship's bowels, but I lighted my shirt from it and held this aloft to help him see his way. He was stripped to the buff, and his pink, hairless body was all a-glisten as he rolled into the opening. His head and shoulders made it easily, but I saw with dismay that his immense paunch was an insurmountable obstacle. He heaved and shoved and twisted. 'Twas no manner of use. He could not pass that gap without the removal of another plank, and there was not time for that. At any moment the *James* would ring eight bells. And at any moment then she would be under way.

Peter backed out of his predicament to an accompaniment of squeaking grunts, and I followed him, too bitterly disappointed for words. Escape had seemed so easy—and now we were condemned to two months aboard the *Walrus,* very likely to exceedingly uncomfortable deaths, for I fancied that Flint was the sort of man to lose his queer mixture of fear and respect for my great-uncle as soon as they were out of touch.

"Hold der light here, Bob," said Peter, squatting on the litter of the deck, and he proceeded to extract a splinter from his foot.

"*Ja,* dot's goodt," he went on, standing up. "Well, we don't get oudt dot way."

"Are you sure we could not tear off another plank?" I answered. "I might find a hammer—or a chisel—"

"Andt der noise brings der watch! *Neen,* we got a better chance."

"What, Peter?"

"You see!"

He felt his way toward the ladder to the cabin-hatch.

"Always there is another way, Bob. If one way is not goodt, der other maybe is better. *Ja!* You see."

He climbed the ladder silently in his bare feet until his great shoulders were directly beneath the square of the hatch, and I heard a faint grinding of straining metal, the crackling of tortured wood.

"*Ja,*" he panted, desisting. "We do dot. Now you be ready, Bob. Jump oop, quick. Maybe we got to kill some fellers, andt if we do we don't let them holler."

I could feel his legs quivering above me; the ladder itself vibrated under us. There was a whine, a sudden pop—and the hatch flew up in the air. Peter caught it on the flats of his hands before it could settle again and lifted it back. He was out in a flash, and I was hard on his heels.

We crouched on the main-cabin floor, staring about us for a sign of the pirates. The lights had all burned out, and it was several minutes before our eyes became adjusted to the star-shine that sifted through the stern window.

A snore from the settee which ran along beneath the windows brought both of us to our feet, and I bent over the table, fingers crooked, to clutch the throat of whoever it might be. But I was put to it not to laugh aloud as I looked into the flushed face and open mouth of Darby McGraw. Poor Darby! A little rum went a long way with him, and he loved to ape his elders.

"'Drink an' the devil—done for th' rest,'" he hiccoughed in his sleep.

"He's safe," I murmured.

"*Ja,*" whispered Peter, and busied himself reshutting the trap-door and arranging the bolt and hinges so as to conceal the fact of its having been forced.

We tiptoed into the companionway, and a very cannonade of snores assailed us from the staterooms on either hand. The doors stood open, and we looked in upon the prickly of Flint, Bones' mottled cheeks and two other drunken underlings. Flint held a cocked pistol in his right hand, which was flung across his chest. Why he did not shoot himself only an obscure Providence can explain.

At the exit to the deck we tarried to reconnoiter our situation, and 'twas lucky we did so. Eight bells rang out from the *Royal James,* and a voice most astonishingly close muttered a curse.

"Ye might think they 'ad a blarsted admiral aboard," answered a second voice.

"I'll lay ye a castellano there was a whole watch awake on her the night long," said the first speaker.

A whistle shrilled, and the gruff voice of Saunders reached us quite distinctly ordering the topmen aloft.

"There they go, Jemmy," returned the second man. "We'll be free o' the swabs in another glass."

"And good riddance, says I," declared Jemmy, spitting into the scuppers.

I saw where they were then, leaning against the starboard poop-ladder and peering overside at the vague hull of the *James*. Peter's little eyes had identified them, too, and his fingers sank into the flesh of my arm, signaling me to stay where I was. He glided past me on to the deck, his body ghostly in the gloom.

"I'm —— if I can see as why we has to keep our peepers open," growled the second man.

"'Tain't long now till morning," replied Jemmy. "What d'ye s'y to a dash o' rum, matey?"

He half-turned, and saw Peter's enormous white bulk hovering over him, and his teeth gleamed as he opened his mouth involuntarily to scream.

"I don't care if—" the second man said.

The Dutchman leaped, and his two arms whipped out. Jemmy's scream died in a guttural cough. Peter grappled the throat of each. He held them poised for a moment, then brought their heads together with an odd hollow smack like the cracking of egg-shells. They collapsed inert on the deck.

I darted for the rail, but Peter stayed me.

"*Neen, neen,*" he objected. "First I get me some pants, Bob. Andt we drop these fellers overboardt."

He was divesting the larger of the two of the single garment each one wore the while he talked, and, conquering an instinctive sensation of repugnance, I did likewise.

"Dot's better, *ja,*" remarked Peter complacently. "A little tight; but I don't like it to be naked, Bob. *Neen!*" He rose to his feet, buckling the dead man's belt around him.

"They'll splash!" I warned him as he picked up the big one.

"Nobody hears," he answered.

He lowered the body over the rail feet first, and the splash was less than I had expected. The second body followed with equal expedition, and Peter laid hold of one of several ropes that trailed untidily over the *Walrus'* side.

"Now we go, Bob," he said.

We entered the water almost together, and swam side by side down the anchorage toward the *James*. I realized at once that the tide had turned, for the ebb sucked us along at a rate vastly swifter than we could have achieved by our own unaided efforts, although Peter, despite his discomfort at sea, was a remarkably powerful swimmer, thanks to his lifetime in the wilderness country of the frontier.

"The tide will take care of the dead men," I panted, stroking for all I was worth to keep pace with the Dutchman.

A whistle shrilled again aboard the *James*.

"*Ja,*" said Peter. "Der anchor goes oop, Bob. We hurry!"

He was a dozen strokes ahead of me at the end. I found him hanging on to the heel of the rudder and calmly treading water. For'ard the capstan was clanking to a steady yo-ho-hoing and trampling of feet. Yards were banging, sails were slatting, men were shouting and calling.

"Anchor up-and-down, sir!" called Saunders.

My great-uncle's voice answered him.

"Very good! We will weigh. Oh, Master Martin, are you sure there is no boat from the *Walrus?* I could have sworn I heard the splash of the falls."

"Aye, aye, sir," replied Martin. "I'll be ——— ——— ——— ——— for a ——— ——— ——— if there is so much as a man awake aboard the ——— ——— craft."

I looked up at the stern windows, so high above us. From our precarious perch on the rudder the *James* towered like Spyglass Mountain, touchable but unattainable.

Almost I could have cried out to my great-uncle and hailed him to have us hauled aboard. But common sense warned me he would certainly seize upon the opportunity to send us back to the *Walrus* as clinching evidence of his good faith. And I had no desire to face Flint with those two dead men to account for.

"What's to do?" I whispered to Peter, whose eyes were roving over the lofty stern. "We can not bide here. Once she has way on her, we'll be tossed off."

"*Ja,*" agreed Peter. "You see dot shiny picture oop there?"

He indicated a golden sunburst, carved across the stern beneath the cabin windows. 'Twas a minor tragedy in my great-uncle's life that he was without the gold-leaf to make this part of his ship as immaculate as the rest. The constant battering of following seas had cracked and diminished the gilding, but the ridges and niches of the carving were still visible.

"Yes," I answered, puzzled.

"I climb oop on der rudder, andt I holdt me on to der roundness in der middle. Andt you climb oop on my shoulders andt into der cabin windows, *ja.*"

"You can't hold me up in that position, Peter!" I exclaimed. "'Twould be all you could do to maintain yourself."

"I do it, *ja,*" insisted Peter.

"But you? How will you—"

"You t'row me a rope."

He scrambled on to the rudder and slowly spread-eagled himself upward against the scrollwork which covered the stern. His hands, feeling blindly above his head, sought for and found a deep indentation in the rays below the center of the sunburst, and with this to cling to, he climbed a foot or two higher on to a shallow ridge which ran across the stern, a shelf scarce wide enough to give him toehold. His grip shifted with lightning precision, his fingers clamping themselves about the embossed figure of the sun, deeply carven for relief.

"Now you climb, Bob," he grunted.

I obeyed him without objection, for every breath was precious and the *James* was already adrift, her anchor merely pendulous weight for'ard.

The rudder I surmounted with ease, standing erect with a hand on one of Peter's legs to steady me. I stepped up to the ridge upon which the Dutchman stood with no more difficulty, holding to his leather belt. Then I changed my hand-hold to a ridge in the carving, and by his direction braced the toes of one foot in the slack of his belt as I heaved myself upward. Peter grunted. That was all.

I found a new hand-hold and brought my other foot up on to

Peter's shoulder and stood erect there. Reaching upward now, better than two tall men's height above the waterline, my groping finger-tips were still below the level of the stern windows. Peter sensed my difficulty.

"On my headt," he grunted.

I carefully lifted one foot, selected another band-grip and mounted Peter's tow locks. Again I explored upward with one arm stretched to the limit of safety, but I failed by inches to clutch the sill of the stern windows.

"Jump," sobbed Peter.

"But you!"

"Jump!"

The rudder clacked as it was put over, and the *James* heeled slightly to the breeze. The water commenced to purr as she gathered way.

I jumped. Peter sagged beneath me, but the fingers of my right band fastened upon the ledge of the window. I heard a splash, and caught hold with my left hand.

"Ooop!" spluttered Peter from the water.

The rest was child's play compared to what had preceded it. The carving afforded toe-holds in plenty, and soon I had a leg over the windowsill and looked down at Peter trailing in the *James'* wake as he clung to the shelf which crossed the stern perhaps a foot above the water. He dared no longer hold to the rudder.

His big face was so white that it frightened me, and I tumbled inboard without stopping to make sure the cabin was empty. But my luck was with me, and I scurried around to find a rope. This was a hopeless quest in that luxurious apartment, so I ran up the compan-ionway and just inside the door to the deck came upon a lead line, coiled and hung to a hook, which I appropriated.

Altogether these movements consumed less time than is required to describe them; but when I returned to the stern windows Peter was gone. I leaned out and stared back at the *James'* creaming wake— and a white arm flashed in a gesture of appeal twenty feet astern. I cast the lead behind him, and he caught the line as it settled into the water, cut the lead free with the dead man's knife at his belt, looped the slack under his shoulders, and with my feverish help hauled him-self back to the shelf above the water line.

I lacked the strength to draw him up; but I fastened my end of the line to the cabin table, which was bolted to the floor, and then, foot by foot, Peter toiled upward. He was so weary at the last that I must pull him through the window, and he fell in a heap across the table, puddling the polished surface with the sea-water that streamed off him and the blood from his scarred hands.

A bottle of the *aqua vitae* my great-uncle favored stood by his place, and I took this and poured a liberal tot between Peter's lips. He staggered to his feet, blinking his eyes and red as a school miss.

"All right, Bob," he squeaked. "I be all right, *ja.*"

His eyes chanced upon the lead-line, still fast to the table's leg, and be stooped and unknotted it and dropped it out of the window.

"We better not stay here," he muttered. "*Neen!* If Murray sees us—"

"Oh, my Gawd!"

Ben Gunn goggled at us from the companionway.

"Drowned, they be!" he gasped to himself. "He done for 'em, Flint did!"

I was afraid he would run out on deck and cry an alarm, and I started for him to prevent this. But the poor creature was fettered by superstitious fear.

"Dear Christ!" he mumbled. "It's a-comin' for me. Oh, sweet Lord, don't 'ee let the ghostie take Ben Gunn. Don't 'ee, now! A good, pious lad I was, as went to church reg'lar and said my catechism, and if my old mother could—"

"Be still, Ben," I said. "We don't mean to hurt you."

He plucked up a little courage when I spoke.

"'Tain't right for ye to talk," he objected. "I never heard tell as how sperets—"

"We're not spirits," I answered. "We are as alive as you are. Here, feel this."

He shrank back as I placed my clammy, wet hand upon his neck, but the touch reassured him.

"Ye ain't sperets, says you," he repeated amazedly. "Nor ye ain't ghosts. And consekently ye ain't dead. And seein' as you're here, why, it do stand to reason as how ye ain't aboard the *Walrus,* which is where ye was and where ye oughter be."

He shook his head.

"'Tain't right, Master Ormerod, and don't follow in nature nohow."

"'Tis perfectly natural," I retorted. "Master Corlaer and I have escaped from the *Walrus.*"

Ben came a step or two into the cabin and stared hard at Peter. Then he turned a disapproving eye upon the pools of water we had sprinkled on the table and the rich carpet.

"Well, it do look to be 'ee two," he conceded grudgingly. "But ye ha' mucked up the cabin awful, and the captain will be like to ha' me triced to the main for a round dozen wi' the cat."

"Not if you work quickly with a bucket and mop, Ben," I said, for I was as anxious as himself to conceal the traces of our entrance from Murray.

"Maybe so," he agreed. "But he won't like it that ye come aboard this way."

I seized upon his opening without scruple.

"Yes, he'll hold it against you, Ben. 'Tis a shame."

He shivered, and I appreciated what my great-uncle's wrath must be.

"Ye wouldn't let him now! Master Ormerod! Oh, say ye wouldn't! Ye don't want poor Ben Gunn to be screamin' on the triangle."

"That I don't," I assented warmly. "You must hide us, Ben. Hide us and clean up the cabin, and he'll never know we are aboard."

"Aye, but then?" he asked shrewdly.

"Oh, then 'twill not matter. Nobody will know that you had aught to do with our coming aboard; and indeed Captain Murray will not care, I think. 'Twas not of his own will he gave us to Flint."

"If 'tis so, why don't 'ee go up on the poop and tell the captain now?"

"He'd have to send us back to Captain Flint. You wouldn't like to be sent aboard the *Walrus* to stay, Ben."

Ben Gunn cocked his head on one side.

"I ain't so sure," he answered. "Maybe Flint would let me wear seaman's gear and tar my hair."

Despite the urgency of our plight I was interested in the humor of the steward's ambition.

"Aren't you satisfied with your lot?" I inquired.

"Not I!" he replied with unexpected determination. "Look 'ee,

Master Ormerod, I went to sea for to be a swearin', cutlass-lashin' pirate, and they put me in a livery-shuit! All my life I been wearin' livery o' one kind or another. Now if you, or Cap'n Flint, we'll say, was to hail Ben Gunn and argyfy as how ye'd take him out o' livery—never a livery-shuit again—and make him a reg'lar sailorman as pulls on ropes and climbs masts and holds a wheel and swabs decks—if you was to do all this, why, maybe Ben Gunn, he'd do 'most anything for you—or Cap'n Flint, if so be as Flint spoke fust."

"'Tis I speak first," I replied. "If I ever command a ship you shall be a tarry sailorman aboard her, Ben. Or if I don't have a ship of my own I'll help you to a berth on another such as you desire."

He came close to me, and his eyes bored into mine with an earnestness that was pathetic.

"That's a solemn-honest promise, ain't it, Master Ormerod? Ye wouldn't go for to fool Ben Gunn, would 'ee, now?"

"No, no," I promised. "But if you don't hide us quickly, Ben, I'll never be able to make good on it."

He caught my hand in his.

"You jes come along o' me. Ben Gunn knows a thing or two, he does. I'll show 'ee, my master. You jest come along o' me."

Peter and I sopped after him up the companionway to a door for'ard of the staterooms we occupied, which led by way of a steep flight of ladder-stairs to the galley and service quarters, a space partitioned off from the vast sweep of the gundeck. Ben unhooked a lanthorn from the wall, opened a trap in the deck and signed us to follow him. At the bottom of a second ladder we found ourselves in a lazaret such as had been our prison aboard the *Walrus*. But there was this difference in our surroundings: That they were clean. The walls were whitewashed, and around them were ranged kegs and pipes of wines, ale and rum, and racks laden with bottles of various liquors.

"'Tis Murray's wine-cellar," I commented aloud.

Ben Gunn deposited the lanthorn in the middle of the floor and approached his mouth to my ear.

"Aye, and he keeps his treasure 'ere—when so be he has any," he whispered throatily.

"Doth he never come here?"

"Not he. Nor the naygurs, neither. Only Ben Gunn."

"What shall we do for food?"

Ben wiggled with embarrassment.

"Jest you leave that to Ben Gunn. He'll feed ye well, my master, as spoke kind to him and promises to take him out o' livery-shuits. Aye, that he will. And fetch ye clothes from the cabin. But don't 'ee forget the promise, sir. Oh, say ye won't!"

"I won't," I assured him. "But you must get back to the cabin and tidy up the mess we made. Haste, man!"

He scampered up the ladder as if the devil were after him—or Paradise within view.

And during the two days of our stay in the wine-cellar of the *Royal James* he was as good as his word. He fed us well. He brought me a sufficiency of clothing. And he procured for Peter a quantity of linen and cotton cloth, with thread and needles, with which the Dutchman fashioned himself garments to cover his inconveniently large body.

On the evening of the second day, having learned from Ben that the *James* had logged several hundred knots since leaving the Rendezvous, we decided 'twould be safe to appear before Murray, and we took an opportunity whilst Ben was serving his dinner to ascend through the galley and present ourselves in the main cabin.

My great-uncle was poring over the chart of the Caribbean which so frequently engaged his attention, but he glanced up as he heard the shuffling of our feet on the carpet. A furrow of perplexity was dug betwixt his eyes. Otherwise he revealed no astonishment.

"So! You two have taken matters into your own hands! Did you by any chance slay Flint?"

"We might have," I answered. "But we did not."

"A pity in the circumstances," be ruminated. "'Odsblood! Here is a pretty coil! Peter, I'll wager I have you to thank for it."

"*Ja,*" said Peter, and sat himself in his accustomed place at the table.

"'Tis true," I agreed, "that without Peter we might not have escaped, but the responsibility is equally mine."

"How did you compass it?"

I told him, and he stared curiously at Peter, placidly eating across the table from him.

"I might have known it, Peter. No man ever held you in constraint against your will. I might have known it. What a mess! My plans and combinations all askew! Peter, y' have played at bowls with destiny! A half-hour since I saw my way clear. Now I must plot it fresh. Stap me, what a coil!"

He rose and started to walk the cabin, hands clasped behind him, head on his chest. Suddenly he paused in front of me.

"What moved you to such a desperate course, Robert?"

His tawny eyes glowed with the light of inner speculation.

"Was it to be with me? Or was it O'Donnell's lass?"

I hesitated, frankly loath to hurt him.

"I was concerned for her," I admitted finally. "This ship is no fit place for a maid, as I have said before."

"'Tis better than some," he answered.

But my reply did not seem to annoy him. His gaze dwelt upon my face for several moments longer.

"Well, well," he said as he began to pace the carpet again. "We must make the best of it, lad."

CHAPTER XII

THE TREASURE-SHIP

THERE WAS no hint of triumph in my great-uncle's manner as the sloop came about and lay to under our lee quarter; nor did he exhibit excitement when she unloosed the small boat she towed astern and a half-dozen swarthy fellows commenced to pull it toward us. He indulged in a pinch of snuff and took his station by the starboard rail at the break of the poop. Peter and I followed him. Besides us there was only Martin, who stood aft by the man at the wheel. For'ard on the spar-deck men slouched away from the starboard bulwarks as Murray appeared. The gunports were all closed because of the swell which rolled the *Royal James* until it seemed she must dip her yard-arms under. So I think—aside from the lookouts lashed in the crosstrees of all three masts—we on the poop were the only ones who watched the little boat come sliding across the great, heaving mountains of water that surged out of the misty reaches of the Caribbean as if they would overflow the shores of Hispaniola, which loomed purple in the north beyond leagues of indigo sea.

The rowboat was as infinitesimal as an insect in those tossing wastes; but the man at the steering-oar guided it with uncanny skill, up the toppling crests that threatened to crush it, down the dizzy steeps that bade fair to hurl it to the ocean's oozy bottom, and brought it to rest a scant fifty feet from the *James'* hull, his long sweep fending and twisting to maintain the position. He was very dark and lean, with bare, corded limbs and a sinewy trunk covered by the remnants of a cotton shirt and trousers. His hair was a stringy black. His voice, when he spoke in answer to a sign from my great-uncle, was harshly rhythmical, but what he said I could not understand, for both he and Murray used Spanish.

My great-uncle asked two questions, both brief, and he answered as briefly. My great-uncle waved his hand again; he dug his steering-oar into the crest of one of the monstrous surges, and the little boat shot away like a roundshot from a gun. A few moments later we saw them make fast to the sloop and leap aboard, one by one. The sloop hauled her wind and beat off to westward in long, slanting tacks, and the *James* was once more alone in the western mouth of the Mona Passage, Hispaniola a blur in the north and Porto Rico somewhere out of sight southeast of us.

Murray dusted a second pinch of snuff into his nostrils as he turned from the rail.

"Our three weeks' waiting hath not been in vain," he said. "The *Santissima Trinidad* was to sail from Porto Bello within the forty-eight hours after Diego put forth. She will be up with us in another five days—before the week is over at the latest."

I was conscious of a conflict of emotions.

"She may slip by you. 'Tis a wide gut—and what's to do if she comes in the night?"

"She can not slip by," returned my great-uncle. "For all the leagues of channel and the darkness of the nights, she can not slip by, Robert. The fools have delivered her into our hands. By her sailing-orders, so Diego told me, she must hug the south shore of Hispaniola, that she may be within easy run of Santo Domingo in case of accident. As for the nights, she'll be lighted up like Bartholomew's Fair."

"*Ja*, it's all right if dot Englishman we sighted last week don't find a frigate," said Peter.

Murray's face fell a trifle.

"Yes, we have always that to reckon with," he acknowledged. "Stap me, I see not what the fellow could have suspected to send him kiting from us. But with any luck he'll not flush a frigate this side of Jamaica, and that should give us time."

"If he suspected us, why not some of the other craft that have passed us on our beat?" I interjected. "There ha' been plenty."

My great-uncle pointed to the white ensign floating from the mizzen-truck.

"They were all Spaniards or Frenchmen," he answered. "They took us for a King's ship. No, there's little chance of interference. If there is—" his jaw squared—"I'll hunt the *Santissima Trinidad* into Cadiz port."

He broke off abruptly.

"Master Martin!"

"Aye, aye, sir," responded the mate, stepping for'ard from the wheel.

"I would have all lookouts notified that I shall give ten onzas to him who first hails the deck for a large Spaniard of forty-four guns coming from the west. She'll show a red-and-yellow light o' nights at her fore-peak. You will also see that all men sent aloft carry night-glasses."

Martin touched his forelock.

"Aye, aye, sir! I'll pipeclay the —— —— —— who misses the —— —— dago. Curse me for a lubber, but I knew there must be fat game a-comin' after such a spell o' idleness."

"She'll be the fattest prize we have ever boarded," rejoined Murray. "You may tell all hands as much."

There was no formal mustering of the *James*' crew; but Martin evidently had his own means of circulating information, for the polyglot seamen had shaken off their lethargy and sullen quiet within a glass of the sloop's departure. All around the decks men were oiling pistols, sharpening cutlasses and whispering in secret. Coupeau was busier than ever about the battery, testing breech-ropes, pinning tighter carriage-wheels, filing glassy-smooth a pile of shot for the chase-guns that might be called upon to lop a vital spar at extreme range.

But nothing happened that day or the next. And so three more days passed with increasing tension. The lookouts in the crosstrees were relieved every two hours, that the men's vision might be fresh and unstrained. The sight of a sail anywhere on the horizon sent the crew scampering to the guns and swung the ship's bows in that quarter; and four times in those five days the *James* boomed down upon Spanish fishermen, a Martinico brig, a Yankee schooner and a Plymouth snow, tacking away again the moment she identified each one as impossible to be her prey.

The sixth day was like its predecessors, blazing hot, bubbling the pitch out of the deck-seams, a gentle sou'east breeze barely sufficient to keep the sails drawing. The swell, which had bothered us for several weeks, had almost disappeared, and the Caribbean might have been a landlocked lake. Daylight found us farther to the south than we usually plied, since Murray feared the Spaniard might have missed his reckoning and shifted the designed course he was to follow.

For the first time in days we could descry the shadowy hills of Porto Rico as we wore around and beat north again. As the sun rose higher a haze danced along the horizon's rim. Porto Rico was swallowed up; Hispaniola's soaring peaks were buried before we had come within normal view of them.

Noon observation saw us returned to our customary station, and to guard against the possibility that the *Santissima Trinidad* had passed us in the heat-haze whilst we were beating up from the south my great-uncle ran down the wind into the mouth of the passage for several glasses. We encountered a fishing-periagua then, and the Indians of its crew shouted back to Murray's question that no great ship had entered the passage that day. So back again we beat to windward the whole weary afternoon.

Night brought rest to nobody. Even my great-uncle paced the poop by the hour, snatching an occasional nap upon a pallet which Ben Gunn laid for him where it would catch the breeze. Peter and I dozed on the deck-planks with the crew.

In the shadowy hour that precedes the dawn the hail came from the mast-head—

"Lights ho!"

Murray was on his feet as quickly as any of us.

"How do you make them?" he trumpeted.

"Red and yellow, over and under," answered the main crosstrees.

"Very good," replied my great-uncle. "Master Martin, you will single out that man and present him this purse."

He handed it over.

"Pipe all hands to breakfast, and serve an extra ration of rum."

"Aye, aye, sir," sighed Martin. "And here's to luck, ——— ——— my eyes!"

The dawn came all at once, as if a magician had waved his wand. A crimson glow in the east, soft at first, then spreading and deepening, and the light expanded almost like an explosion in the night. The red disk of the sun lifted over the horizon. And it was day. Westward, perhaps half a league, a great ship was wallowing toward us before the freshening wind. The coloring of her figurehead sparkled in the level rays which touched her dingy canvas and turned the sails to cloth-of-gold. The gaudy banner of Spain flapped with a splendid insolence in the pure light. The spray which was tossed over her bowsprit as she buried her stem in the easy swell was transformed into threaded amethysts, turquoises, emeralds!

"She is heavy-laden!" exclaimed my great-uncle, staring at her through his prospect-glass.

"Heavy-armed too," I added, pointing at the band of cannon along her sides.

"We'll make light of that," he answered. "But I shall have to pay somewhat for my Quixotic promise to you, Robert, to spare her crew. Ho, Coupeau!" he hailed the gunner who was passing on the spardeck.

The former galley-slave turned his terrible face to the poop and saluted.

"Pass the word, Coupeau, that the prize must not be pierced betwixt wind and water. I would bring down a spar or two at the beginning of the action, but concentrate your fire upon her decks."

"Oui, m'sieu'."

"But what of O'Donnell and his daughter!" I exclaimed. "On a shot-swept deck!"

My great-uncle regarded me curiously.

"'Tis not a game of lawn bowls we are about to play, Robert," he replied. "I ask you to remember that the Spaniard carries forty-four cannon which he will discharge against us, with some probability of slaying certain of our people, including perhaps ourselves."

"But the girl!"

He took snuff.

"Tut, tut, my boy! You concern yourself needlessly. 'Tis a risky business and can not be otherwise. Yet she'll probably come safe through it. What part do you and Peter purpose to play in the action?"

I was about to answer hotly that we would have naught to do with piracy when Peter said—

"Maybe we better go aboardt der Spaniard and catch der little gal, *ja.*"

"An excellent idea," returned my great-uncle, looking expectantly at me. "I shall lead the boarders myself, and in the confusion I may be hard put to it, single-handed, to direct the fighting and save the O'Donnells from injury. If you two—"

"We'll do it," I said ungraciously. "'Tis of a parcel with your crazy notions that you can not even safeguard your accomplice without aid."

"That is quite true," he agreed mildly. "I am free to admit, Robert, your presence takes a load off my mind, notwithstanding your escape from Flint hath created other difficulties for me to contend with. However, I shall be sufficiently grateful to you if you will assist me. My notions, whether 'crazy' or not, are not easily carried into execution."

I nodded to the white ensign at the main peak.

"Will you fight under false colors?"

"They are not false," he retorted with tightened lips. "We fight for England today."

"England and Flint and Long John Silver and Bill Bones and Martin and Coupeau and—"

"Myself? Perhaps. But if those you have named share in the rewards of victory 'tis that England may profit thereby and the Good Cause triumph. What doth it matter if King James return to London?"

"What indeed?" I echoed sarcastically, yet impressed against my will by his deadly earnestness.

"'Tis not my way, Robert, to fight under false colors," he proceeded, as if determined to argue me over to his viewpoint. "Any sailorman will tell you that, whatever other slander he may relate of Captain Rip-Rap. As for the Jolly Roger—pho! 'Tis a tradition required by any pirate crew. I look upon it as a somewhat humorous attempt to terrify the timid; but I ha' fought under it without shame, since 'tis the only emblem of the sea outlaw. But today 'tis different. We fight, not as pirates, but as servants of King James."

A white puff of smoke jetted from our fo'c'sle, and a crackling explosion smote our ears. Coupeau had fired the first shot from one of the chase guns, long eighteens, beautiful bronze pieces of prodigious range. Involuntarily we all focused our eyes upon the treasure-ship, and a cheer from the gun-crews applauded the flapping rent that showed in the bulge of the Spaniard's foretops'l.

"Excellent!" murmured my great-uncle.

The *Santissima Trinidad* staggered for an instant like a man who has been struck unexpectedly by one he supposed to be a friend. Then she yawed to give us a full view of her colors; and as she yawed, broadening the target, Coupeau fired again. 'Twas a low shot, fired as the *James* dropped into the trough betwixt two waves, and all we could see of it was that apparently it plowed into the waist.

The Spaniard fired a gun to leeward and put over his helm, aiming to cross our bows and head up for Santo Domingo. Plainly he did not know what to make of the incident. To all appearances the *Royal James* was a King's ship. She showed the English naval ensign. To a Spanish eye, at any rate, she might well seem to possess the solidly rakish aspect which was the usual keynote of an English frigate. So he evidently decided that hostilities must have broken out between the two countries, and in obedience to his sailing-orders endeavored to avoid a fight and make for the nearest fortified Spanish port.

But the *James* sailed two feet to the treasure-ship's one; and, splendidly handled, we overhauled her within a glass of first shot. In the meantime Coupeau kept pecking away at her, and as we came within range of our main battery her foretopmast crashed, covering her fo'c'sle with a tangle of top-hamper.

This was too much for her people, and she put up her helm, brought her entire battery to bear and let fly at us with all her starboard metal. 'Twas a poorly managed salvo, yet three or four round-shot swished across our decks, and an eighteen-pounder smashed a couple of men to jelly just for'ard of the poop.

Murray stepped to the poop-rail to examine the damage and shouted to Coupeau:

"Hold your broadside, Master Gunner! He must come to to clear his decks."

And to Martin, who was conning the ship:

"Bear up! Bear up! He still hath the weather gage of us."

Coupeau, working like a madman with his chase guns, was firing both together, laid on the same target, and now he succeeded in cutting down the foremast about twenty feet from the deck, sending the heavy spar and billowing canvas a-tumbling after the fallen topmast. The bulk of the wreckage fell overside, dragging the *Santissima Trinidad* down by the head and forming a sea-anchor to hold her stationary.

My great-uncle smiled with grim satisfaction.

"Ho, Saunders!" he hailed the second mate, who was stationed amidships. "Rig grappling-irons on the larboard bulwarks. We'll round the Spaniard as he lies."

The *Royal James* forged abeam of the treasure-ship, approaching at an angle which diminished the effectiveness of her second broadside, and as we entered the filmy cloudbank of smoke from her guns Murray gave the order to fire.

"Let go your broadside, Coupeau!" he called.

The gunner ran to the open main-hatch and bellowed the order down to the gun-deck. The planks seemed to spring under our feet. A thunderous series of detonations shook the *James'* whole fabric. The smoke-clouds were first driven away, then thickened to an impalpable mist, and the acrid stench of saltpeter and brimstone was choking in the nostrils. I had a wavery glimpse of a vast gilded figurehead, a heap of torn canvas and rigging.

"Sta'b'd your helm, Master Martin!" shouted Murray.

We headed up into the wind with much creaking of yards and slatting of sails, and I heard faintly a clamor of wailing outcries from the smoke-bank that masked the *Santissima Trinidad.* Almost at once our broadside roared again, the red flames from the gun-muzzles licking out like hungry tongues. Another dim vision of shot-rent bulwarks and towering sails, and the gray gloom became denser than ever. Figures on our own deck were indistinct in it.

The Spaniard blindly returned our fire as the *James* felt her way toward him, the thunder of the two broadsides overpowering, numbing, like the roaring of two beasts fighting in the night. I felt my great-uncle's hand on my arm; his voice was low, but distinct.

"We shall soon be broadside on with her," he said. "The O'Donnells will be on the poop. You had best get for'ard, Robert. If we board from abaft the foremast 'twill place you strategically to seize upon them. Where is Peter?"

The Dutchman leaned through the smoke-whorls.

"We better go aboardt der Spaniard, *ja,* Murray?" he answered calmly.

My great-uncle chuckled as he dusted snuff into his nostrils.

"We had, friend Peter. And you and Robert had best carry arms. I fear the Spaniards will not seek to differentiate betwixt you and my wicked self."

"*Ja,*" assented Peter. "We go."

Amidships we encountered Saunders and a horde of men pouring up from the gun-deck to augment the boarding-parties. Peter and I tarried to select weapons from a rack by the main mast. He took a boarding-pike, and I contented myself with a cutlass.

Murray, having inspected the grapplings and ascertained that hooks had been rigged from our yard-arms to clutch the Spaniard's rigging, rejoined us. He was dressed with usual exquisite taste in watered gray silk, with white stockings and gray shoes with jeweled buckles. He wore no hat, and his white hair was clubbed and cued. The only weapon he carried was a dress-sword, which he held unsheathed.

"An end to our immediate worries soon, Robert," he announced cheerfully. "The action has gone perfectly. I would not have varied a move so far. We have not lost a dozen men."

A final blast from our guns tore the smoke-clouds to shreds, and a vagrant wind-puff snatched them aside. 'Twas like the drawing of the curtain at a play. The treasure-ship lurched helplessly not twenty fathoms distant, her rigging in tatters, her spars split and wounded, her fo'c'sle and foredeck one red litter, her bulwarks splintered, gunports blown in, guns dismounted. A handful of men were laboring to cut loose the wreck of the foremast, and a few other brave fellows were still fighting a couple of guns which raked us as the bowsprit of the *James* nudged over her rail.

The two ships jolted together, and in response to wind and helm the *Royal James* swung broadside on against the Spaniard, our bowsprit becoming entangled in her mizzen rigging. A dozen grappling-irons clattered in air and ground their hooks into her bulwarks. There was a brisk popping of small-arms, an exchange of threats and shouts of defiance.

My great-uncle, regardless of the firing, mounted the breach of a cannon which elevated him above the bulwarks, and Peter and I climbed into the forerigging, whence we had a fair view of both decks. The larboard bulwarks of the *Royal James* were crowded with men. Stripped to the waist, their lowering faces smutted with powder-stains, their hairy chests barred with tattooing, their backs more often than not scarred by the cruel welts of the lash, they tussled for first place and clung with their bare toes wherever there was a bit of running gear or an inch of space, gripping cutlasses in their teeth to leave hands free for pistol work or to steady themselves as they waited an opportunity to leap the narrowing gap between the vessels.

My eyes strayed to the Spaniard's decks. Little knots of men ran about confusedly. A stolid-looking fellow aimed a pistol at me, and a ratline over my head fell apart. Officers were driving the sailors forward to meet us. A man in a laced coat and periwig was shouting orders from the poop, and my pulse quickened, for at his shoulder was the lanthorn-jawed face of Colonel O'Donnell—aye, and in rear of both a skirt fluttered in the midst of a huddle of raven-black figures, priests and nuns.

"Jump!" squeaked Peter in my ear.

We jumped together, but my great-uncle was ahead of us. He leaped all of ten feet, sword in hand, alighted on the Spaniard's bulwarks, poised himself a moment and dropped into the center of a ring of foes. Before he had recovered his balance he parried the slash of a

cutlass and pinked an antagonist in the throat. And he beat down a
leveled pistol as I gained the treasure-ship's deck, inclined his head
to avoid a murderous blow, ran the man through and almost in the
same breath stepped a pace to the right to engage a fourth opponent—and all this with the cool precision of a fencing-master, unhur-
ried, a flush of obvious enjoyment on his pallid cheeks.

But I saw no more. My task was to fight my way aft and protect
the O'Donnells, and Peter and I turned our backs upon the struggle
amidships. One wave of the pirates stormed in Murray's wake; the
rest followed Peter and me. They were as brave as they were vicious,
and we made rapid progress and were nearly at the foot of the poop-
ladder when Murray's whistle shrilled behind us. I realized too that
both O'Donnell and the officer in the laced coat were shouting vol-
ubly, the one in English and the other in Spanish, trying to make themselves heard above the din.

"—asks parley," came in broken phrases from O'Donnell. "—can
not understand—regrettable mistake—"

"Der Spaniard wants quarter," grunted Peter.

Indeed, those of the *Santissima Trinidad's* men who had been
resisting us promptly flung down their arms, glad of the excuse to
quit the fight; but the wolves of the *James'* crew were not schooled
to show mercy, and they killed three poor fellows before Peter and I
could knock up their cutlasses.

Murray's whistle blew a second time. There was a sudden hush,
punctuated by the grinding of the two vessels, the thudding of unshod
feet as more of the *James'* pirates dropped aboard the treasure-ship,
the gagging cries of the wounded, the nasal singsong of a priest pat-
tering Latin prayers.

I seized the opportunity to look around. We were too close under
the poop to see what went on beyond the rail directly overhead; but
the maindeck, fore and aft, was a pitiful spectacle—cluttered with
wreckage and dead men and bits of men and men wounded in every
conceivable fashion, its yellow-sand carpet gemmed with carmine
pools and rivulets.

My great-uncle, as immaculate as when he had ascended the *James'*
bulwarks, stood a little ahead of the mass of his followers, his serene
face and rich clothing in startling contrast with their nakedness and

frank brutality. A trickle of blood dripped from the point of his slender sword. His attitude was that of an honorable man who wishes to be reasonable in a difficult situation.

"I believe I heard an appeal for quarter," he said quietly.

"Sir, you did," replied O'Donnell. "I have spoken for the gentleman beside me, Señor Don Ascanio de Hurtado y Custa, who is captain of this vessel."

"I am honored, sir," returned my great-uncle. "And yourself?"

O'Donnell did not altogether relish the playing of his part. He bit his lip and hesitated an instant before he answered.

"I am Colonel O'Donnell, an officer in the service of his Most Catholic Majesty."

"Ah; and what can I do for you, gentlemen?" inquired my great-uncle.

O'Donnell hesitated again and conferred with the Spanish officer.

"Sir," he said then, "Don Ascanio asks you by me: Since when have your country and Spain been at war?"

"To the best of my knowledge, they are not at this present," my great-uncle answered blandly.

"Then to what cause must we attribute this—this—ah—unwarrantable attack?" demanded O'Donnell.

"I am afraid," replied my great-uncle almost with sorrow, "that I am unable to satisfy your curiosity upon that point."

The Spaniard burst into a declaration of passionate intensity, which Murray interrupted.

"I am so fortunate as to comprehend the noble Spanish tongue," he said. "Would you be so kind, Colonel O' Donnell, as to acquaint your friend with the fact, and to assure him that I regret he must accept the situation as it stands? I am desirous of sparing the lives of those of his people who survive, but at a pinch I will slay them all to compass my intention."

"And what is that?" asked O'Donnell.

"To relieve Don Ascanio of the consignment of treasure he carries," answered my great-uncle. "When it is aboard my ship he shall be at liberty to continue his voyage."

O'Donnell proceeded haltingly to translate this statement. He never finished it. The Spaniard launched a fresh torrent of curses, broke his sword across his knee and tossed the pieces overside. My great-uncle nodded sympathetically.

"'Tis an unpleasant plight, I know," be said. "Had Don Ascanio not discarded his sword I should have been delighted to yield him an opportunity for such satisfaction as one gentleman may give another.

"However—I must stipulate further, Colonel O'Donnell, that the crew of the *Santissima Trinidad* shall be placed in confinement for so long as suits my purpose. Any resistance must cause additional bloodshed, which, I am sure, you will agree is unnecessary."

"Don Ascanio will say no more," returned O'Donnell. "He washes his hands of the whole proceeding. Abandoned by his crew—"

"Enough," interrupted my great-uncle.

He rattled off a sentence in Spanish, and there was an answering rattle of arms thrown on the deck. He spoke again, and the *Santissima Trinidad*'s men all shifted to starboard and marched into the fo'c'sle, herded by a bristle of pirate cutlasses.

Murray walked aft to where Peter and I still stood, uncertain what to do next.

"Have you seen her?" he asked.

"I think she is in that group of priests and nuns under the stern lanthorn," I said.

He compressed his lips, a habit he had whenever he must turn to some task he did not overly care for.

"'Tis a trick I shall find as distasteful as O'Donnell did our collo-quy just now," he said shortly. "But we must be about it without delay. Our cannonade will have been heard ashore in Hispaniola with this wind. We must gather our loot and away."

CHAPTER XIII

TROUBLE BOARDS THE Royal James

THE SILENCE was oppressive as we ascended the poop ladder. A last babble of Latin ended on an hysterical note. The Spanish captain glared his hatred, gnawing at his hands as he leaned against the rail, and when my great-uncle drew a laced handkerchief from his coat pocket and began to wipe clean his red blade 'twas more than Don Ascanio could stand. He stalked to the far side of the deck, rumbling curses, and fixed his gaze upon the purple hills of Hispaniola. Behind the steering-wheel the black flock of religious gathered closer under the great, gilded lanthorn which crowned the high, pulpit-like recess intended to protect the helmsman; and amongst those cowled shaven-heads and shapeless swathed forms the slim grace and sunny, blue eyes of Moira O'Donnell were as patent as the growing fear with which her father met us.

My great-uncle nodded a satisfaction I was unable to comprehend.

"A fair maid, Robert!" he exclaimed. "Well, well! This is fine. I might ask no better. I congratulate you, *chevalier*," he added to O'Donnell. "Your daughter is as dainty a little lady as I have seen in a long life."

O'Donnell understood his mood no better than I.

"I wish she was out of this," he growled resentfully. "Don Ascanio has placed the conduct of matters in my hands. What is next? Must you—"

He gestured expressively toward the vessel beneath us.

"It seems—I—I find myself—'Tis a nauseating prospect—Several hundred men—and priests and nuns, Murray—Aye, a cardinal sin, one I'll never have absolution for, whatever betide—"

"You concern yourself without cause," said Murray soothingly. "We have arranged it differently, and to that end I shall act a part with your daughter which you must support; aye, to the offering of violence. And now, tell me, where is the treasure?"

"In the lazaret."

"Master Saunders!" called my great-uncle.

The second mate thrust his way to the front of the mob of pirates on the main deck.

"Take fifty men and break out a quantity of treasure from the lazaret of the prize."

"Aye, aye, sir," returned Saunders, and the pirates fell over themselves in their alacrity to have a hand in his business.

My great-uncle concluded the cleaning of his sword, crossed to the larboard railing and tossed the bloodied handkerchief overboard.

"Oh, Master Martin," he hailed the mate on the poop of the *Royal James.*

"Aye, aye, sir," answered Martin. "—— —— —— —— my gizzards for a —— ——, but we ha' done a clean job this morning."

"I find myself in agreement with your sentiments, Martin," replied my great-uncle. "Be so good as to have a whip rigged from the fore-yard-arm to sling aboard the treasure which Saunders is breaking out. You will also tell off a score or two of men to make any essential repairs at once. I would have the ship ready to sail as soon as we cast off, which will be the moment the prize's cargo is transshipped."

"Aye, aye, sir, I'll attend to it all myself," Martin assured him. "—— my eyes for a —— —— —— and all the Twelve Apostles, blast 'em for a —— —— lot of —— —— ——."

"A pungent fellow, Martin!" commented my great-uncle, recrossing the deck. "But we must play our little comedy here. You, *chevalier,* are cast for the *Anguished Parent.* I am the *Aged Libertine.* Peter is the *Mute* with the bowstring—be gentle, Peter. Robert—humph! I scarce know how to describe your rôle, Robert. You, shall we say, are to be *Youth?* Ah, yes! *Youth,* immortal, selfish, impulsive, acquisitive, mendacious—"

Colonel O'Donnell regarded him as if he had lost his sanity.

"What folderol is this?" he broke in.

"You shall see," answered Murray. "'Tis our way of carrying you off without focusing the suspicion of Don Ascanio and his people upon your personal participation in this interesting episode. But to continue the enumeration of our cast. Your daughter, of course, is the *Innocent Victim.*

"And this, Robert, leads me to recast you. I shall deny you the satisfaction of virtue—which after all, the clergy tells us, is its own reward. You shall be *Youthful Wantonness,* and did we adopt all the exigencies of the plot 'twould be necessary for you finally to strive with me for the possession of the maid. But we will wave that anon. Play up to me, nephew! You, too, Peter!"

He left us and walked with a mincing gait, entirely different from his real catlike prowl, up to the black-garbed cluster surrounding Mistress O'Donnell.

"Stap me, a fair piece, this!" he drawled. "Too fair to bloom unseen. Come hither, mistress!"

A fat monk spat an ejaculation at him in Spanish, and two of the nuns threw their arms around the Irish girl. Murray replied to the monk in his own tongue, and with a virulent fluency which inspired the whole group with pitiful terror. But the maid answered him so dauntlessly that it made the blood prickle in my neck.

"A black shame on you, old enough to be the father of me and these others here! I know you for what you are, Captain Rip-Rap, and if you will be thinking I am one to fear you it is a sorry wakening you will have. Oh, you might better be down on your knees, asking pardon for the wickedness you have wrought, than plotting fresh evil, and threatening holy folk with your dreadful torments!"

The fat monk lifted a crucifix like a weapon and shook it in his face, and Mistress O'Donnell put the two nuns aside and stood forth in front of the group, with her arms spread wide to shelter them.

"So you recognize me?" said my great-uncle. "'Tis an honor, mistress. But I fear you have heard much to my prejudice, and I must press you to visit my ship and learn the contrary. Certes, you should be the first to rejoice to disprove such foul allegations against an aged man."

"Step forward, colonel, and defend her," I muttered under my breath to her father.

He had the grace to blush, but he acted upon my suggestion with a semblance of sincerity.

"Sir, sir, what is this you do?" he cried. "Certes, there is some limit to your law-breaking! The maid is my daughter."

My great-uncle went through his snuff ritual with an artful exaggeration which was comical to one who knew him.

"Unfortunate!" he drawled. "I could sympathize with you, sir."

And to me—

"Robert, you will conduct the lady to the *James*."

For the first time Mistress O'Donnell's glance lighted fair upon my face.

"Master Ormerod!" she gasped.

I jumped toward her with as roughly peremptory a manner as I could assume.

"You'd best come quietly, mistress," I snapped.

She flung out her hands to fend me off, and the fat monk and the two nuns cast themselves upon us, the monk striking at my head with his heavy crucifix and the nuns scratching and clawing so that I was put to it to protect my eyes. They were surely three of the bravest people who ever lived, and but for Peter they would have worsted me.

The big Dutchman waded stolidly into the confusion, shoved O'Donnell from his path, upset the monk and pushed the two nuns out of the way.

"You take der little gal, Bob," he squeaked.

She struggled with all the strength in her lissome body, but I pinned her hands and tossed her over my shoulder—and then her father attacked me with the Spanish captain, whose patience had been exhausted by this last outrage.

Murray drew his sword and forced the Spaniard back, and Peter slung O'Donnell over his shoulder as easily as I had the maid.

"I got him, *ja*," he announced to Murray.

My great-uncle sheathed his sword.

"Carry him along," he said. "Since he is so much concerned as to his daughter's fate, we will permit him to watch it. Afterward, it may be, he can afford us some additional amusement. Stap me, a most persistent fellow!"

The fat monk picked himself up from the deck, waving his crucifix, and launched a tumult of invective which my great-uncle received with raised eyebrows and an occasional humorous interjection. But I had my hands full controlling my prisoner, and paid no more attention to what happened on the poop after I reached the main-deck ladder.

A line of pirates staggered across the deck, backs stooped beneath burdens of portly casks and iron-bound chests, wirewrapped and pad-locked, each a-dangle with leaden seals impressed with the arms of the Spanish king. They leered at my writhing captive and grinned openly at the ridiculous spectacle presented by Colonel O'Donnell's lank form draped over Peter's shoulder. But they all looked quickly away as my great-uncle descended to us.

"Can you manage her alone?" he asked me curtly.

My temper was thoroughly aroused by the false position in which I had been placed, and I vented it upon him.

"I'll manage her or go overboard with her," I barked.

He smiled.

"The right spirit, lad! Tut, tut, mistress," as she wrenched a hand free and dug at my eyes. "You concern yourself for nothing. We have but played at a game. Observe your father's attitude."

"The greater his shame!" she hissed. "That he should have suffered you to take me alive!"

"We are friends," urged my relative, lowering his voice. "'Tis but a pretense we make—"

"Friends!"

Her white teeth clicked in an effort to bite my ear.

"Ah, you are friends to the Powers of Evil."

"Be patient a little longer, Moira," pleaded her father from his perch on Peter's shoulder. "I'll explain—"

She went of a sudden entirely limp and burst into a passion of weeping.

"Oh, *padre, padre,* to think of you a coward! 'Tis worst of all!"

O'Donnell swore helplessly.

"Let me down till I settle her mind," he begged.

But Murray rebuked him.

"They are watching you from the poop, *chevalier.* Struggle as much as you please—'tis all one to Peter—but if you value your future secu-rity in Spain do not seem to give in to us."

I climbed by way of a carronade on to the larboard bulwarks, hold-ing Mistress O'Donnell with one arm the while I hooked a strand of rigging with the other; and even as I collected myself to jump the gap that separated the two vessels she twisted free of me and would have slid overside—to be crushed to death, most likely, for the two hulls were continually grinding together. I caught her in the nick of time, letting go my clutch upon the rigging, and was near to being dragged down with her, teetering back and forth as aimless as a feather blown by the wind. So that, what with her struggles and my own loss of balance, I gritted my teeth and jumped most precariously, hit or miss, and, I am bound to admit, landed upon the *James'* bulwarks rather by good fortune than skill.

I dropped to the deck in no very pleasant mood. Faith. I could have slapped the tear-stained face that was pressed against my shoulder; and in the excess of my disgust I thrust her from me.

"An ill recompense for one that hath been at pains to spare your father's reputation, mistress," I growled, as surly as any pirate of the crew. "You might ha' been my death."

She looked at me, too surprized to answer at once, and before she had recovered herself my great-uncle and Peter joined us, Peter still placidly carrying Colonel O'Donnell like a flour-sack.

Murray cast a swift glance of appraisal around his ship.

"We have come through very creditably," he remarked. Martin hailed him from the poop.

"By your leave, sir, we're whole aloft, 'ceptin' a few ropes as the topmen are splicin' and a rent in the mizzen royal."

"That's well," replied my great-uncle. "How many casualties?"

"We ha' put twelve overside, and there's two as'll follow, and twenty —— —— —— lubbers as must nurse their carkisses."

"Very good, Martin. I shall be in the cabin. Let me know so soon as the prize's treasure is all aboard."

He turned to us.

"The curtain is ready to fall upon our comedy. Will you accept my arm, Mistress O'Donnell? A glass of wine and a bite of sailor's fare will taste better than Robert's ear, which your hunger prompted you to nibble. Fie, fie, my lass!"

She stared at him with utter horror, yet suffered him to place her hand upon his arm. The spirit was gone out of her, exhausted by the strain she had been subjected to. And I forgot my anger at sight of the agony of dumb fear mirrored in her lovely eyes. She was like a butterfly spiked on a thorn.

Something of the same sensation must have affected my relative, for he patted the limp hand on his arm with a truly paternal kindness.

"Come, come, did I not say the comedy was ended?" he chided her. "I have played the *Aged Libertine,* 'tis true, but the role is now abandoned. You are as safe here as in your Spanish convent. But the deck is too public for our revelations. We will seek the seclusion of the cabin, and there the complete tale shall be unfolded for your reassurance, with your father a witness to support it."

She shook her head.

"I—I—know not what you mean."

"To be sure," he agreed. "But you soon shall."

Peter, behind us, grunted to command Murray's attention.

"Does der colonel walk or ride?"

"Stap me!" exclaimed my great-uncle, "I was forgetting your father's present plight, mistress."

"I feel like a fool!" snarled the Irishman.

"How unreasonable!" deplored Murray. "Have you not been acting the part of an *Outraged Parent* who sacrificed all in defense of his daughter? My dear *chevalier,* what role could you select more heroical?"

"Give over your mummery," protested O'Donnell. "I'll not be made a mock of, sir!"

"Rightly spoken!" cried my great-uncle. "You shall not be, *chevalier.* Peter, good friend, prithee take three steps within the companionway and there deposit Colonel O'Donnel with decent propriety upon the two limbs Nature intended for his locomotion. Ah! Excellent! Allow me, mistress!"

Peter and I followed the three of them up the dark tunnel of the companionway.

"We are past one danger-mark, Peter," I whispered. "What's to come?"

"Trouble," mumbled Peter.

"Trouble?"

"*Ja.* To get der treasure, I saidt dot was easy, Bob. But to divide der treasure—dot's trouble. Andt now we got a woman on der ship—andt dot's more trouble."

Ben Gunn and the two negro lackeys ushered the party to their seats. Mistress O'Donnell sank into hers with a weariness that was pathetic. She was quite regardless of her surroundings. 'Twas as if she was become reconciled to whatever misfortune was in store for her. And she did not so much as glance at her father, who sat morosely upon Murray's left hand across the table from her. Peter took his accustomed place at the opposite end, and I sat beside her.

"Let me give you a glass of this *aqua vitae*, my lass," said my great-uncle. "'Tis efficacious for fatigue and the migraine. See, I taste it myself. 'Tis quite all right. You, too, *chevalier?* Excellent! Perhaps you will pass the flask to Master Corlaer yonder. You gentlemen should know each other after your recent intimate contact. And Master Ormerod yonder—my nephew. But I believe you and your daughter have had previous acquaintance with him."

O'Donnell muttered something none too civil, but the maid bestirred herself, and her eyes examined me again with the mingling of horror and stupefaction which governed her mood.

"How come you here?" she asked. "You—you—are you also a pirate?"

"I am a captive as surely as yourself," I returned. "Aye, more so."

"A captive!" she exclaimed, her interest fanned alight. "But surely you—"

My great-uncle interrupted her.

"Please, Mistress O'Donnell! Our tale is sufficiently complicated. Let us not make it more difficult to comprehend by confusing it at the beginning with side-issues."

"Gunn!"

"Yessir!"

The steward ducked and scraped.

"Give us whatever food you have prepared, swiftly. And fetch up some wines—port, burgundy, claret, madeira."

"Yessir."

Ben Gunn writhed himself into the companionway. Murray resumed his discourse to the Irish girl.

"First, that there may be no misunderstanding, mistress, 'tis true that I am he who is known as Captain Rip-Rap."

She shrank away from him in a renewed access of terror.

"I have already told you that you have no cause to fear me," he

went on gently, "and to prove that to you I will add that I am an outlaw—what is called a pirate, although I detest the word myself—
because I am a Jacobite. I believe, too, I may claim your father as my
friend."

He looked inquiringly at O'Donnell. The Irishman drained his glass.

"'Tis true," he assented. "This gentleman is one Andrew Murray, who
was out in the '15 and was afterward in trouble in New York Province
on the score of intrigues with our friends and the French, Moira. He
hath been a good servant to King James."

"But for why will you have been the death of all the poor folk on
the *Santissima Trinidad?*" she cried. "And your men will be lifting the
treasure that is Spain's, and Spain a safe haven for the exiles the
Hanoverian will not suffer to serve their rightful king and dwell in
Britain!"

"'Tis regrettable that Spaniards had to die, lass," answered my great-
uncle, lowering his voice to a proper depth of emotion. "But I call to
your mind that Spain has not helped the Good Cause as she might
when there was a bonny chance of fetching the Stuarts home."

"That is God's truth," she admitted with quick passion.

"Therefore," pursued my great-uncle, "some of us have concerted
it to seize a portion of Spain's treasure and turn it to the purpose of
winning back for King James his crown."

"I am thinking 'tis not overhonest," she said doubtfully.

"You are no more than a lass," rebuked her father, emptying his
second glass. "'Tis not for you to be saying what is honest and what
is not honest in politics, of which you have no knowledge."

"Indeed," interposed my great-uncle, "the question as to what is
honest and what is dishonest in politics is one upon which men have
been unable to agree since the times of Aristotle."

"Yet even politicians can not honestly confuse the dishonesty of
taking one man's gold for another man's profit," I put in.

Mistress O'Donnell gave me a sidewise look.

"We are speaking of kings, not of men," my great-uncle pointed out.

"I am afraid I will be of Master Ormerod's way of thinking," said
the Irish maid.

"You talk nonsense, Moira," blustered her father. "Is it not better that this treasure should be employed to recover England and all the lands pertaining to the English crown for their rightful rulers—who will assist in the restoration of the True Faith—than that it should be poured into the pockets of the king's favorites at Madrid? You are only a child, and 'tis not fitting for you to know all that goes on in world; yet common sense, ordinary religious devotion and affection for your king might tell you so much. Why, lass, there are great lords, aye, a prince of the Church, no less, that set the seal of their approval to what we do."

Moira O'Donnell hung her head.

"Sure, I am only an ignorant lass as you say, *padre,* one that knows no more than the sisters taught her in the convent; but there's that in me cries out stronger than learning or creed or loyalty."

Colonel O'Donnell hammered his fist upon the table-top—he had just drained a third glass.

"And this is the child of a race that have been pulled down from the high places of the land by the tyrant, and their heads and limbs strewn God knows where, and those who escaped death driven to poverty and exile! Girl, you know not what you say. The people of Spain will be thanking us for the use to which we turned their trea-sure—and then we'll pay it back," he added with a happy inspiration.

"Odds, that we will!" endorsed my great-uncle. "What's a million and a half pounds to royal Spain? Aye, or to an England that waxes grandly prosperous under wise Stuart rule?"

"'Twill be the difference betwixt honor and dishonor," I cried hotly. "As for prosperity, England was never richer, as any man who earns his living honestly would tell you. King George may be a Dutch-man and talk with an accent and spend more time in Hanover than London; but he keeps his hands off trade, and that means wealth for all who'll labor."

Colonel O'Donnell favored me with a fishy glance.

"It seems we must both reckon with disloyalty in our families, Murray," he remarked dryly.

"Never give it a thought, sir," replied my great-uncle. "Tut, tut, *cheva-lier,* they are young and shall learn by experience. Let them argue it between themselves, eh? That should fetch them around."

"I'll not suffer any to call me disloyal!" exclaimed Moira. "I am all for the Stuarts; but I'd not have them resort to dishonest means to win what is their own."

"Humph," said my great-uncle. "To win their own, my lass, they must have money. If you will tell us where else in the wide world they are to obtain it, I'll transship this treasure back aboard the *Santissima Trinidad*."

She was silent.

His suave manner conveyed subtly an implication of the importance he attached to her approval.

"I would not inflict a dose of the material philosophy of age upon one so young and charming, my dear," he went on; "but possibly you will forgive me if I indicate to you the regrettable circumstance that the ideal is seldom attainable? In other words, mistress, to obtain the greatest good for the greatest number of people it is occasionally necessary to inflict misery, suffering, even death, upon a lesser number. As in the present case, in order to secure the means for reëstablishing King James and what your father so quaintly terms the True Faith in the British Isles, it hath been necessary for a gentleman of questionable legal status—myself—associated with others of yet more dubious antecedents and repute, to procure the death of divers Spanish persons, who, of themselves, had never wrought any harm against us or the cause we served.

"Paradoxical, I must admit, involving an apparent denial of the essential elements of divine justice, and in an ordinary light a gross breach of the world's laws and conventions. But 'tis by precisely such contraventions of precedent and lettered laws that epochal events are brought about. I trust my reasoning is clear?"

"Faith, sir," she answered simply, "I think you will be poking fun at me."

My great-uncle took snuff.

"I was never more serious," he asserted.

O'Donnell emptied a fourth glass with an impatient growl that masked an oath.

"You are wasting time, Murray. Moira is a good lass, and my daughter; but what she thinks of this venture—"

"—is of considerable importance to me," my great-uncle protested.

"I was compelled in the beginning of our acquaintance to give her a wrong impression of my character, and I am extremely desirous to have her good opinion."

"You'd better work on your nephew first," the Irishman snapped.

"'Tis to earn his good opinion that I am so solicitous of her's," my extraordinary relative admitted serenely, and the shadow of a smile brightened her face.

"Troth, sir," she retorted, "I am thinking that is the wisest thing you have said, for the young man appears to be the one of you that has a prejudice for the plain truth—I can say nothing for the large gentleman, since he has not opened his mouth."

Murray laughed.

"I will take to myself some of the credit you heap upon my nephew," he said. "As to the 'large gentleman,' 'tis his custom to be silent; eh, Peter?"

"*Ja,*" said Peter.

"But why is he—" she blushed a trifle—"why is Master Ormerod a captive? Why does he say I am a captive, if—"

"You are not a captive," returned my great-uncle. "At least, I say that under the impression that, as your father's daughter and a devout Jacobite, you would not, whatever your personal feelings might be, undertake to interfere with our plans."

He waited, and after a pause she nodded her head.

"My grandnephew on the other hand," he continued, "as well as the 'large gentleman' yonder, are not political sympathizers with us—not yet."

"Nor will they ever be," I corrected him.

"I shall beg leave to differ with you, Robert," he replied. "Nevertheless, in justice to you, I will go on and acquaint Mistress O'Donnell that I carried you by force aboard my ship, Peter accompanying you of his own free will, for reasons which sufficiently commended themselves to me."

"I am wondering are you all mad," she said blankly.

"You may well say so!" I exclaimed. "The truth is this, mistress: Master Murray hath besides his own ship's company a second band of pirates the which are restless beneath his thumb. He desired me to be his lieutenant to help him hold them in restraint, and—"

"You restrained them bravely aboard the *Santissima Trinidad!*" she said. "My faith, but I am caught in a network of lies!"

"Moira!" gurgled her father, sopping his cuff as he finished his fifth glass. "Ye talk like a—like a—" his brogue thickened—"a besom or what not at all. I'll not have it! I'll not have it, I say!"

"That was to save you!" I declared.

"Troth, and I'm saved," she echoed sarcastically.

"Yes, you and your father," said Murray gravely. "Colonel O'Donnell risked everything on this coup of ours. To protect him 'twas essential it should never be known he was privy to it. We had the choice of two means to that end. One was to sink the *Santissima Trinidad* with all hands except yourselves—"

She cried out in expostulation and clapped her hands to her eyes as if to shut out the vision the words evoked.

"The other," he continued, "was to arrange to remove the two of you in such fashion as to establish your innocence. I am free to say the first was the easiest course. The dictates of humanity, however, prevailed."

How he rolled that last sentence!

"And what do you know of humanity that soaked the decks of the *Santissima Trinidad* with blood?" she answered. "You that the Spaniards cite as a byword for cruelty and wickedness! I will not believe a word that you say. I will not believe any man here. You are all smirched with the same badness."

"Blessed Virgin guard me!" whimpered O'Donnell. "And did any ever hear a daughter tell off her father the like of that? Glad I am the mother that bore ye—"

Peter leaned his great bulk forward upon the table.

"Don't talk no more, you," he commanded the Irishman. "*Neen,* I talk! Little gal, Bob andt I we don't come wit' Murray because we like to. He makes us. *Ja!* He uses us. He uses your fat'er. He uses you. But when we are wit' him we do what we can to take care of you. It is not goodt for little gals to be on pirate ships. *Neen!*"

He leaned back.

"Dot's all."

Her blue eyes dwelt seriously upon his vast, flat face, with its insignificant features blobbed here and there.

"I believe *you*," she said.

"Stap me," jeered Murray. "Our Peter is discovered a squire o' dames—a *preux chevalier.* Peter, you ha' disguised your talents. We must know more of them."

"*Ja*," said Peter vacantly.

Mistress O'Donnell rose from her chair.

"Sir—" she addressed my great-uncle—"you will be excusing me if I do not linger for more conversation. What you do hath no concern with me. I am very distraught, and my heart is sick with the black sorrow, and I—I—" she swayed a little—"I would lie me down and—and—weep."

I slipped from my seat and steadied her. Her father, opposite, blinked at us through maudlin tears.

"A sweet maid!" he hiccuped. "She's all I ha' left from following the Lost Cause. Curse the Hanoverian—"

"Take her to your stateroom, Robert," said my great-uncle. "You must lodge with Peter."

He rose, himself, bowing with the fine courtesy which became him nobly.

"What we can do to serve you, dear lass, that will we right gladly. In the mean time, do you rest and forget the nightmare scenes I would have spared you had I known how."

I guided her as far as the stateroom door. She thanked me faintly as I opened it for her, and I was abruptly impelled to recover her friendship.

"What I tried to tell you was the truth," I murmured, the words spilling fast from my tongue. "Indeed it was so! Peter Corlaer had the right of it. We two are no pirates, and all that we ha' done has been intended to make smooth your way."

There was a wistful light in her eyes as she lifted them under long, black lashes.

"God send you be honest, sir," she said. "I—I must wait to judge. The world is gone all twirly-round. Even the *padre*—"

She choked back a sob.

"You will not misunderstand," she ended with quiet dignity, "if I say no more that maybe already ha' said too much."

CHAPTER XIV

THE DEAD MAN'S CHEST

WHEN I returned to the main cabin Ben Gunn was placing the food on the table, and my great-uncle was removing the liquor from Colonel O'Donnell's reach.

"We have had sufficient to drink, Ben," he said and, heedless of the Irishman's disappointed face, waved away that which had been before them as well as the new array of bottles one of the lackeys bore upon a silver tray.

Nothing more was said until the steward and the negroes had retired. Then Murray sat forward in his chair.

"There is a certain matter of importance to be discussed, colonel," he announced. "I must have your attention."

O'Donnell nodded sulkily.

"As you know, the crew of my associate, Captain Flint, some of whom you saw in New York, are not under the same discipline as my own men. Captain Flint saw fit to express jealousy of the terms I arranged with your principals for the division of the treasure, and in order to conciliate him and assure him of my good faith I gave him my grandnephew and Master Corlaer as hostages. They went unwillingly and succeeded in escaping before we sailed, returned aboard the *James* and secreted themselves for several days. I dared not risk the time to return them to Flint, and I anticipate that he will receive me now with augmented suspicion."

"I said all along ye were crazy to let a low fellow like him have any hand in the affair," fumed O'Donnell.

"We need not go over that again," rejoined my great-uncle. "I must have the security of the Rendezvous, and for that I must needs pay Flint. Also, I may have need of him in other ways. This venture is not yet consummated. There is likewise the consideration that we have worked together in the past, and I owe him a modicum of loyalty."

"Loyalty to the Cause should come first," declared O'Donnell.

"True, sir, and I yield it. But I must look to the future. 'Tis contrary to my policy to break with Flint if it can be avoided. 'Tis similarly contrary to my instinct to trust him farther than I must, and in this immediate case I am loath to trust him."

"What's to do?" rasped O'Donnell. "Raise his price?"

"No, no. My suggestion is that we should stow away our friends' portion of the treasure before we return to the Rendezvous."

"Where?"

"I have been turning that in my mind for several weeks. There is an island south of Porto Rico in the Virgin Group, a barren dot, hated by all seamen for sorry memories of shipwreck and suffering. They call it the Dead Man's Chest."

I remembered the deep, swinging chorus I had first heard in the Whale's Head tavern the night I sought O'Donnell for his daughter. It sounded like a fit place for pirate treasure.

The Irishman frowned.

"What? Dump this gold we have risked so much to win on a sandbar for the first passing fellow to—"

"I have said no man will go there if he can help it."

"I like it not!" scowled O'Donnell. "My friends would have ugly things to say did the stuff slip from our hands in that way."

"'Tis less likely to slip from our hands on the Dead Man's Chest than aboard the *Royal James*," answered Murray. "Bethink you, *chevalier!* To begin with, there is Flint to reckon with. He will be nasty, as nasty as he dares, depending upon the temper of his crew and the quantity of rum he has consumed. Second, there is always the chance that we might fall in with a frigate too swift for us. On all scores 'tis preferable to get the treasure off the *Royal James*. 'Twill give us time to let the hue and cry of the Spaniards die down and to arrange with your friends for its reception."

"Whatever you say, 'tis a miserable alternative," protested O'Donnell. "Let us rather hold north and set the treasure ashore in France."

"To run the gauntlet of French and English cruisers?" my great-uncle demanded scornfully. "'Odsblood, man, you are out of your mind! And when you had landed it, what would you do? How much of it would go to your friends and how much to grease the pockets of French officials? A great treasure is not so easily disposed of."

"Ja," spoke up Peter, "dot's right, Murray. But what goodt is it to go back to Flint? He makes trouble, always he makes trouble—andt if he don't, his men does. It's better you go anodder place."

My great-uncle took snuff, tapping the box thoughtfully after he had dusted the powder in his nostrils.

"To be strictly honest with you, gentlemen," he remarked at last, "I am disposed to return to Flint because I foresee a possibility of my desiring to sacrifice him to cover our tracks. I have no definite plan in mind, but a situation might shape itself in which it would be desirable to supply a fugitive for Spaniard, Frenchman and Englishman to chase. I should vastly prefer—as I am sure you would, too—that the fugitive be the *Walrus* and not the *James.* Also, until that situation arises, the Rendezvous is the safest hiding-place I know this side of Africa."

O'Donnell eyed him with involuntary respect.

"I should hate to have ye set on my track, Murray!" he exclaimed. "Is not Flint your friend?"

My great-uncle considered this question.

"Scarcely my friend," he decided. "Say, rather, associate. And the fellow is troublesome occasionally. I should have no hesitation in sacrificing him to secure the stake we play for."

"And there is no real feeling of loyalty in your heart!" I gibed. "'Tis simply a question of using him to your best advantage."

"Yes and no, Robert," he retorted coolly. "As you grow older you will learn that as naught is wholly bad neither is it wholly good."

A step clumped in the companionway, and Martin stuck his grizzled head in the cabin.

"Last o' the —— —— ruddy-boys is comin' aboard, sir," he said. "What course will ye set?"

Murray looked at the Irishman.

"Here's the moment for decision, sir," he said. "'Tis for you to say what shall be done."

O'Donnell's long face seemed to grow longer.

"Sure, and how will I know what to say that never gave thought to the matter before?" he parried dubiously. "Do I understand you to suggest Captain Flint might attempt to possess the entire treasure?"

"I should consider it likely," assented my great-uncle.

"He is more likely to make trouble if you come to the Anchorage after disposing of half the gold," I thrust in. "'Twill only serve to stimulate his suspicions."

"There is reason in what you say," agreed my great-uncle. "Nevertheless, permit me to indicate that if we have not the half of the treasure 'twill be impossible for him to secure it by any means."

O'Donnell smacked his open hand upon the table top.

"A truce to arguing!" he exclaimed. "I am in your hands, Murray, whether it pleases me or not. Do whichever you think best."

My great-uncle turned to the mate.

"Cast loose from the prize, Master Martin, and make all sail. The course is so'east by south. I would have you stand off out of sight of the Porto Rican shore."

"Aye, aye, sir."

Martin hesitated.

"And the treasure, cap'n?" he added.

"Ben Gunn will give you the keys of the lazaret. 'Twill go there as usual."

"Aye, aye, sir."

There was an interval of silence after he had gone. The shouts of the pirates echoed from the deck, with the creaking of halyards and flapping of sails. The *Royal James* seemed to shake herself as she sidled free of the battered hull of the *Santissima Trinidad,* and through the stern windows showed the bowsprit and fo'c'sle of the Spaniard, still smothered beneath a mess of canvas and broken spars and rigging. Slowly we drew past her, and I was amused to see that men leaned from her ports and on her bulwarks, watching us with the idle curiosity to be expected in any friendly meeting at sea.

The Spanish flag still flaunted at her main where it had stayed throughout the action. Don Ascanio, her captain, still stood with folded arms and furious mien on the poop. The group of religious were all on their knees in prayer. The fat monk raised his crucifix with a threatening gesture as we glided under her stern.

"Observe the fallacy of religious conviction," commented Murray. "The monk curses us for a crime we have not committed."

"There is enough evil to your credit to warrant him, even so," I answered.

O'Donnell crossed himself.

"Leave religion alone, Murray," he said sourly. "'Tis a bid for ill-fortune to mock the Church and holy men and women."

"Prejudice, my dear *chevalier!*" protested my great-uncle. "Yet any sane view of mundane affairs must recognize religion hath its uses to mankind."

He rose.

"If you will pardon me, I have much to see to on deck. Should you desire any refreshment do but ring that bell and state your wants to the steward. Robert, if you and Peter can so far submerge your Hanoverian sympathies I should appreciate such aid as you might render in the accounting of the treasure."

Peter and I went with him, as much to escape the company of the Irishman as to satisfy our curiosity regarding the chests and boxes we had glimpsed in transit across the *Santissima Trinidad*'s deck. And certes, the scene that awaited us was worth going far to see. The maindeck, immediately for'ard of the poop, was jammed with the tents of the Spaniard's lazaret, piled helterskelter as working-parties had hastily shifted it from one ship to the other.

Murray produced tablet and ink-horn; a desk was arranged for me atop of a water-butt, and one by one a procession of pirates filed past, each with his load of gold or silver, minted and in bullion.

'Twas a marvelous concentration of wealth. The columns of figures I set down upon the tablet never condescended to detail—5,000 pieces of eight, they would run, or 10,000 doubloons, 12,000 onzas, 20,000 castellanos, 25,000 eights, and so on. One cask we opened was filled with quaint Eastern coins, some square, some oblong, some cubical, some round, inscribed with spidery characters, a consignment from the Spanish possessions in the South Seas. There was upward of two hundred thousand pounds in bar silver, fifty-pound ingots sheathed by threes in thick canvas jackets to facilitate their transport by mule-trains—each mule carrying a load of three hundred pounds. There was a quantity, too, of gold bullion, each ingot of eighty pounds in its own canvas jacket. There were a chest of precious stones, the value of which we could only guess at, and three chests of plate.

The total value, by the Government estimates upon each package, chest or keg, was £1,563,995 in English money, exclusive of the jewels and the plate; and we did not conclude the accounting and bestowal of the treasure in Ben Gunn's wine-cellar until an hour past dusk, when Murray dismissed all hands with an extra ration of rum and instructed Saunders, who had the watch, to allow his men to sleep on deck, except those actually needed for lookouts and the wheel.

In the cabin we found Colonel O'Donnell asleep, sprawled on the table with his head rested on his folded arms, a puddle of wine by his elbow. My great-uncle's eyebrows twitched upward.

"This gentleman is a chamberlain to King James, Robert," he remarked, "a Knight of Malta and of Santiago in Spain, a colonel of Spanish engineers and lord of I know not how many bog-manors in Ireland if he had his rights. And look at him!"

He was not a pleasant sight, I'll own; but my redoubtable relative's perpetual air of omniscience grated upon me.

"Who brought him to this?" I retorted.

"Not I, my boy! To intrigue is not necessarily to license appetite. Well, well, 'tis doubtly fortunate I induced him to fetch along the little maid."

"'Twas well nigh your most dastardly act!"

He took snuff, deliberately pondering the charge, and despite the toil of the day his face preserved its uncanny fulness of outline.

"The appearances are against me," he answered. "Yet I am inclined to believe that in the long run you will concede I acted for the best. Consider her plight in a Spanish convent, if anything happened to her father."

"Consider her plight in a pirate ship, if anything happened to him!" I jeered.

He appealed to Peter, whimsically humorous.

"Stap me, the boy wears upon my nerves! Was ever a youth so callow in his assurance of righteousness?"

Peter's little eyes twinkled.

"He is right, andt you are right. But we better put der colonel in his bed, *ja.*"

"'A Daniel come to judgment!'" cried Murray. "Now what might you mean by that, friend Peter?"

"You know what I mean—andt I know what you mean," returned the Dutchman solemnly. "You are a big rascal, but dot time maybe you was right."

"Don't be an idiot, Peter," I rasped.

"'Tis you are the idiot," affirmed my great-uncle. "Here are you and Peter—two honest men if any ever were—and myself, with less claim to virtue perhaps, but as acute an interest, if the truth be known. And all three of us a-hungering to safeguard the lass. What mother might ask more?"

"And Flint," I amended. "He'd protect her, I suppose."

"He'll never have the chance, Robert," he answered gravely. "You and Peter have played ducks and drakes, between you, with my plans; but John Flint is not the man to overreach me. Give him rope, lad— and we'll present him his chance to hang."

"*Ja,*" said Peter. "We take care of der little gal—andt so we put der colonel in his bed."

And so we did, to an accompaniment of stammered oaths and tags of Jacobite ditties.

Afterward, in Peter's stateroom, I asked him what he had been hinting at in his exchange with Murray.

"Oh, we just talk," he replied, rolling into his berth with a ponderous sigh of satisfaction.

"I heard you," I snapped. "But of what?"

There was a dim light in his eyes, buried behind rolling flaps of blubber.

"We just talk," he murmured. "Murray talks, andt I talk. Murray, he likes to talk, *ja.*"

I was up early in the morning, but Mistress O'Donnell and my great-uncle were before me. As I climbed to the poop I saw them standing by the weather rail, Murray expressing deference in every line of his straight figure and handsome, old-young face, the little maid eying him with a comical mixture of antipathy and respect.

The wind had veered in the night, providentially for us, and we were running free, the *James* riding the easy swell with the dash of a race-horse. We were out of sight of land.

My great-uncle clapped his hand on my shoulder in his best paternal manner, and Mistress O'Donnell gave me a shy look that I read to reflect a double attitude of mind similar to that she evidenced for him.

"Here is my nephew, who will settle all your remaining doubts, Mistress Moira," proclaimed Murray; "and with your leave I'll be about my morning inspection—for we must maintain a high level of discipline, since we sail on the king's errand and are therefore the king's ship."

She watched his retreating back with a kind of fascination.

"Sure, I never met the like of him," she said at last. "He puts me in mind of the grand gentry the *padre* brings to see me in Madrid—and him a pirate! Glory, what a tale I could be telling the girls if I ever see the four walls of St. Bridget's again! Whiles I talk with him he makes me feel there's none other so grand and fine in the broad world. And again I'll remember the screaming on the *Santissima Trinidad* and what Frey Sebastian said of him—and then the shivers turn me winter-cold. But I'm thinking yourself will be the same queer sort, Master Ormerod, you that can be generous and gallant to a foolish maid and as cruel as the wildcat the Indians showed us in the hills up behind Porto Bello."

"It must seem so to you," I answered. "But the truth is that I am as much the sport of Fate as yourself."

"Do you tell me so?" she replied politely.

"I do," I said with energy. "Let me tell you the whole story—it begins on the night I accompanied you to the Whale's Head—"

"Ah, that was a night of nights!" she exclaimed. "The first breath of adventure ever I drew, and I was thinking to myself as I hugged the memory afterwards I could never get enough of that same savor. But yesterday was the curing of my hunger."

And her blue eyes clouded with tears and the corners of her mouth quirked downward most dolefully.

"Do but let me tell you my story," I pleaded, "and you will think better of that night and maybe of some things that happened afterward."

"Why, sir," she said, "here are you with a ready tongue, and me with two ears wide open. There's naught to stop you. But as to believing—that will be a story for me to tell and you to hear."

So I began at the beginning and told her all from the moment

Darby McGraw had run into the counting-room in Pearl Street—and how remote in time and place that seemed as we stared out upon the blue-green rollers of the Caribbean and the tropic sun warmed toward its noon intensity! She listened with mounting interest, never interrupting save for an occasional "Glory!" "Oh, blessed saints!" "Holy Virgin, can such things be!" But when I came to the escape from the *Walrus* she broke in upon me.

"And you did that to be handy by if I had need of you! Oh, sir, forget the wicked suspicions I owned! 'Tis a true friend you will be—and the large gentleman, too. What is he called? Master Corlaer? Alas, I am heavy in your debt, and always shall be. But the only payment I ever can make will be just my bare thanks and the prayers I'll say on my bended knees my life long."

She was wholly trustful with Peter and me from then on and spent most of her time with us. Her father, when he was not drinking, was engaged in conferences with Murray. They worked for hours at a time with quill and paper, figuring the strength of clans, costs of muskets and powder and lead and the number of field-cannon to be stowed in a ship's hold, as also the individual requirements of chiefs and nobles and the amounts for which several persons would "sell out." And as they worked my great-uncle's confidence increased, and Colonel O'Donnell's long, horsey face took on a flush over the cheek-bones that was not alone the result of four bottles of madeira at a sitting.

On the seventh morning after the action with the *Santissima Trinidad* we raised a low, sandy islet, densely choked with low trees and bush growth, bare of any characteristic that invited human habitation. Its only distinguishing feature was its roughly oblong shape, which might, by a stretch of imagination, enable it to be likened to a sailor's chest. Murray approached it with caution, a man in the chains dipping the lead continually, and we came to anchor under its lee and a mile or more offshore.

In the mean time Martin and a party of some fifty men had been passing up treasure from the wine-cellar or lazaret, the mate checking the amounts withdrawn upon the list I had prepared, the pirates muttering amongst themselves in a way not at all to my fancy as they gaged anew the size of the fortune they had won, without, so far, any benefit or reward. Martin was a competent officer, and he kept them at work, for all their grumbling and discontent, until the anchor cable ran out and Murray issued an order to lower all the small boats. The next thing we knew the fifty had hurled the mate into the scuppers and were swarming up the starboard poop ladder, a giant Northcountryman at their head.

Murray, who had been talking with O'Donnell, leaped to meet them, as unperturbed as if the incident were a part of the ship's routine.

"Get back there, men," he ordered quietly.

The leaders halted, sullenly irresolute, cowed at once by the red glare in his tawny eyes, the cold power that radiated from his white face.

"We'm on'y seekin' a bit goold," said the first man hoarsely.

My great-uncle calmly produced a small, double-barreled French pistolet from an inner pocket, shot the fellow in the head, leaned forward and pushed his body off the ladder.

"Master Martin," he called, "be so good as to have that carrion cast overboard. Go about your work, men, or I'll flog the lot of you at the triangles."

They tumbled down the ladder and disintegrated like a pack of sheep, and not one raised a hand when Martin came at them, cursing grotesquely in his gentle voice and striking right and left with knotted fists. Two of them obeyed his order to throw the dead man's body over the rail, and they went straight to the boat-falls without another mutinous word or act.

Yet when Murray turned to face us I noted the tiny wrinkle betwixt his eyebrows which was a sure indication that he was worried.

Moira O'Donnell, who had been standing with Peter and me, listening to my recital of the song about the island, was the first to speak.

"Will you have had to shoot that man?" she challenged

"'Twas that or maybe the deaths of all of us, my lass," he replied, unwontedly grim. "A shipload of men like my crew are a volcano of lawlessness held in restraint by fear. Let them once break the spell of discipline—which is maintained by fear—and they in their numbers would soon overpower us. This incident is relatively unimportant, but it points a lesson I should be reckless not to heed.

"To be brief, my friends," my great-uncle summed up, "I dare not leave the *Royal James* whilst any of the treasure is aboard; nor would it be safe for me to entrust any of my crew with the location of the hiding-place."

He took snuff, staring contemplatively at the sand-hillocks of the Dead Man's Chest.

"Here, then, is my plan," he pursued. "I will have eight hundred thousand pounds set ashore in the boats—my own share of one hundred thousand, *chevalier,* as well as the seven hundred thousand pounds guaranteed to your friends. I will then land you four, with sufficient provisions, and bear away in the *James* to the so'th'ard, returning in five days to pick you up. In the intervening period you should be able to transport the treasure to a safe spot and bury it. In that way, *chevalier,* its safety can be assured until we are able to return for it with the *James* or some other craft dispatched by your friends."

"Your plan is maybe the best in the circumstances," answered O'Donnell, "but I'd have ye remember, Murray, that of the four people who will know of the gold's location two are Hanoverians and the third is my daughter, who is a weak maid."

My great-uncle laughed.

"You need have no fear on the score of those three. You little know Mistress Moira if you call her a weak maid; and as for Robert and Peter, they are men of honor—and best of all, are not likely to be submitted to the temptation to reveal the treasure to their political friends. No, no, colonel; by my plan the treasure will be safer than in a bank."

There was more talk back and forth, but the end of it all was that O'Donnell accepted my great-uncle's plan, and Moira was won over likewise by the argument that so long as the treasure was stolen it had best be assured to a worthy purpose. Peter and I agreed for a complex of reasons—because of the little maid for one thing, and for another, because there was an excitement in the burial of treasure which neither of us had tasted before, and also, of course, because, when all was said and done, we were prisoners and we must. But I'd never seek to deny that we had pleasure from the thrill that came to us late in the afternoon of that day as we stood on the narrow beach of the islet beside a great stack of kegs and chests, axes, pickaxes and shovels, barrel of water and boxes of food from Ben Gunn's larder, watching the boat that had landed us pull back to the *James*.

The ensuing five days demanded an amount of manual labor which extracted wails of indignation from Colonel O'Donnell, much uncomplaining effort from Moira and all the strength Peter and I possessed. Indeed, without the big Dutchman we might never transported that amount of treasure, dug a hole for it and concealed the location, all within the time-limit Murray had allowed us.

The first afternoon and evening we spent in selecting a hiding-place in a shallow valley protected from the terrible storms which sweep those seas. Colonel O'Donnell and Moira were detailed to do the digging, as neither was as capable as Peter and I of managing the weighty bulk of the casks and chests. And after that we worked unremittingly, except for a couple of hours at midday and a short snatch of sleep about dawn; for the starlit nights, with their bracing sea-winds, were the most comfortable times we had. Yet the tops'ls of the *James* were within sight before we had disposed of the last spadeful of sand from the hiding-place and replanted its area with the trees and bushes we had removed with every care to preserve their roots.

O'Donnell had an unconquerable aversion to laboring with his hands, but his engineering knowledge enabled him to survey crudely the site we used and plot certain angles which fixed it in our memories—a precaution highly necessary, as when we had finished there was no more evidence of what we had done than a slight instability about several trees. We had even gone so far as to transplant an enterprising colony of land-crabs to scuttle back and forth over the fresh-turned sand. And in a month, we knew, the luxuriant growth would have obliterated the narrow slash of the path that zigzagged across the sand hillocks to the valley's lip.

CHAPTER XV

SUSPICIONS

FROM THE Dead Man's Chest the *Royal James* headed northwest into the Atlantic. Murray knew that the *Santissima Trinidad* must have sent the tidings of his feat the length and breadth of the Antilles. By now the Spanish squadrons would have put to sea from San Juan de Porto Rico, Santo Domingo and the Havana, and the Caribbean would be aswarm with *garda costas;* but more to be feared than all the Spaniards' efforts would be the consequence of the complaint sure to be dispatched to the port admiral at Kingston. The Jamaica frigates would carry a hunting-call to every English cruiser on the West Indian station.

As it was, we were chased by a strange sail in the latitude of southern Hispaniola, whose heaping canvas and lumbering gait bespoke the ship-o'-the-line; and off Cuba we sighted three sail—a frigate and two sloops—who chased us two days and a night to the eastward. And the day after that we encountered the Brazils fleet, under convoy of two sail of the line and half a dozen small fry, but my great-uncle, nothing daunted, displayed his white ensign, fired a salute to the Portuguese admiral and sailed through them.

Then we picked up a smart so'easter and ran our westing down packet-fashion, with never a sail in sight for a week, until a morning when the sun came up at our backs like a burnished copper plaque and we saw the cone of the Spyglass lifting out of the haze ahead. A league or two farther on the whole island shaped itself beneath its spine of hills, and a column of smoke from the Spyglass told us that Flint's lookout had detected us.

The wind had continued strong through the night, but after dawn it turned puffy and 'twas nearly noon when we passed into Captain Kidd's Anchorage on the last of the flood. There was a great bustle aboard the *Walrus,* with boats plying to and from the shore, and as our anchor splashed, the longboat put off from her side, Flint's red coat like a flame in the stern sheets.

"Glory!" exclaimed Moira O'Donnell, her blue eyes wide with delighted horror. "There's one I'd not need to have pointed out to me to know him a pirate—or the dreadful knaves that do be rowing the oars. My faith, look to the color of them, as red as Indians with the sun, and they without the clothes any heathen would be by way of wearing."

She clapped her hands.

"But I like the kerchiefs on their heads. See! All red and green and yellow and blue. And the marks they have done in their skins."

Her father was otherwise impressed. He glowered down at the heap of treasure kcgs, chests and packages which Murray had ordered fetched on deck that morning, and then stared off at Flint's gaudy figure.

"And 'tis to scoundrels like yon ye'll be trusting the lives of all of us, Andrew Murray!" he snarled. "By times, man, I think there's a green madness in your brain. Why, the view of that gold and silver below would be sufficient to tempt better men than they to commit murder."

My great-uncle took snuff.

"Your diagnosis is correct, *chevalier*," he retorted. "They would cheerfully commit murder for a coveted knife or a sixpence with a hole in it. My design in revealing to them the entire extent of the treasure we carry is to impress them at once with my good faith and benumb their acquisitive faculties by the sight of greater wealth than they ever dreamed of obtaining at one time."

A snort from Peter diverted attention to the Dutchman.

"You do not agree with me?" inquired Murray mildly.

"*Neen!* A t'ief is a t'ief. He steals to steal."

"Plausible," assented my great-uncle. "Your idea is?"

"If Flint has der feel for it it don't matter what you show him. He wants all."

"Ah!"

Murray regarded more attentively the boatload of pirates just rounding up to our port quarter.

"I see that Captain Flint has with him John Silver and the red-haired Irish boy he calls his luck. Humph! You may be right, friend Peter. But I should not be greatly concerned over that. In many ways—"

He broke off, considering. Colonel O'Donnell caught him up.

"Yes? Yes? What new deviltry are you planning?"

My great-uncle smiled.

"Certes, 'tis no deviltry to plan in a good cause—in the Good Cause. Eh, Mistress Moira?"

She shook her head.

"You will be too quick with your wits for me to fathom them, Master Murray," says she. "I am but a young maid that knows no more than that right is right."

"I protest you underrate yourself," he answered.

"What Moira thinks is of no consequence," interrupted O'Donnell. "You have not answered me."

"True, *chevalier.* I was thinking. My thoughts are not completely shapen, but 'twill do no harm if I reveal that it occurred to me that in many ways it might simplify our problem did Captain Flint resort to force."

The Irishman counted the gunports in the *Walrus'* side.

"He seems to carry as heavy metal—"

"But on the sea, as on the land, 'tis the brain which overmatches brute force, *chevalier.* You, who are an engineer, do not need to be reminded of this axiom. However, we are not yet come to the issue, and I am never one for engaging in a search for trouble. All I know clearly at this moment is that we can not afford to wander far afield from the island, with the cruisers of three nations quartering the seas for us."

"We are in an *impasse,*" reflected O'Donnell gloomily.

"Not at all," rejoined my great-uncle. "We have played our hand with entire success so far in the game. 'Tis now for us to sit back and await the plays of other participants. What they do must determine our next—But Captain Flint is come aboard. This conversation is without purpose, since fact must now displace conjecture."

He eyed us all somewhat gravely.

"I have but one word more to say," he added. "Whatever happens, leave me to do the talking."

"Ye'd do it whether we would or no," growled O'Donnell.

Flint climbed over the bulwarks with a racket of oaths and swaggered up to the poop. Martin dropped a whip from a block on the mainyard, and John Silver was hauled up in its bight, his crutch hanging from his neck. Darby and the rest scaled the side ladder and mingled with the *James'* crew. Their eyes popped from their heads as they circled the heap of treasure, Long John stumping with them, listening avidly to the accounts of the *James'* men, hefting the weight of the packages of bullion and painfully deciphering the inscriptions on the kegs and chests of coin.

Their chief was equally frank in revealing the lust of greed the picture wakened in him. His green eyes flickered hotly on either side of his thin, beaked nose, and his blue jowl was bluer than ever, the weather-worn skin over his cheekbones laced with a network of crimson veins that brightened as his excitement increased.

Yet he forgot the treasure the instant his gaze fell upon Peter and me.

"So your hostages returned to ye, Murray? Gut me, 'twas a pretty trick ye played us! Ye'd keep faith wi' me, ye would! Oh, yes! Ye'd give me two hostages, instead o' one. You'll fulfill your contract, you will. There's no need for it, to be sure, but ye'll do anything to prove good faith to me! And take both or none, says you. Both or none! Well, ye fooled me that time, Murray, but ye never will again, by thunder—not if my name's John Flint!"

My great-uncle heard him out in silence, waiting until he had stepped off the poop-ladder and stood facing us.

"I am not responsible for your losing the hostages," he replied then in his iciest tones. "Stap me, Flint, I warned you your ship was in a disgraceful condition. With all hands drunk, did you think to keep fast two men of strength and intelligence?"

"Drunk or sober, we were promised them," asserted Flint, a trifle less belligerently. "And sure, ye could ha' turned 'em back to us—not that that will do me any good for the two men they killed, they or whoever helped 'em to break from the *Walrus.*"

"Nobody from the *Royal James* assisted them," said Murray. "You have my word for that. I can not say as much for your own ship, although they told me when they discovered themselves to me, several days after our sailing, that they had acted alone."

"Alone or not, where's my two men?" blustered Flint. "Good hands don't grow on trees."

"No; aboard the *Walrus* they stab one another to death," agreed my great-uncle. "Come, come, you have no proof in support of your charge."

"No proof?" howled Flint. "These two broke out of my lazaret, and the same night the two men on watch—"

My great-uncle raised his eyebrows.

"Tut, tut! Really, now! 'Two men on watch!' What would you have? Silver and Blind Pew could have escaped from such slender guards, let alone two whole men, one of them the strongest ever I knew."

"Well, two broke free and two died," insisted Flint. "And if the two who broke free were not the means—"

"What proof have you of it?"

"Proof?"

"Aye, proof, I said. Their bodies, what of them?"

"Why, we never—"

My great-uncle shrugged his shoulders.

"You see? You have been talking loosely, I fear, my friend. But you must suffer me to repeat that if you left your ship all night with a watch of two men on deck you deserved to lose your hostages and the lives of the watch. At any rate, you'll not have my sympathy."

Flint's fingers twitched on his hanger-hilt.

"I tell ye, Murray, there's a foul smell about this whole business. You were all for giving me hostages—'twas no idea of mine. And then they no sooner come aboard my ship than they're away again. I like it not. Here's trickery or ye may gut me for a preacher."

"Had I found your hostages on the *James* before sailing or within a day after, you should have had them back again," said Murray firmly. "But there is no point to this argument; for hostages or no hostages, you see me returned with the treasure, as I promised."

"——— me, ye've been long enough gone," complained Flint. "It hath been a month more than ye promised."

"For that I had excellent reasons," answered my great-uncle. "I was chased twice on my way hither."

Flint was impressed by this—also, his eyes strayed, as if lured by a magnet of irresistible power, back to the heap of treasure on the deck below.

"Ye must ha' had rare success," he admitted unwillingly. "We ha' the gold o' the Indies here!"

He looked up and happened to meet the awe-struck gaze of Moira O'Donnell. A sneer curled his lips.

"But ye carry passengers, I see," he insinuated. "Gold and women! 'Tis a fine combination, Murray, but there's a rule in our Articles you were all for establishing. Number Four, eh? It sticks in my crop, for ye called it once on me.

"'And that there may be less occasion for broils amongst our company, we do further decree that gaming may be prohibited at any time when in the captain's judgment it becomes dangerous to our harmony, as likewise, that at no time and under no circumstances may women be taken and kept as spoil aboard our vessels or any vessel upon which our company may chance to fare.'

"What d'ye say to that? What of Rule Four now?"

"I wish it was observed as strictly aboard the *Walrus* as on the *Royal James*," returned Murray. "As to gaming, it seems that you allow your crew full license."

"I'll govern my own ship," responded Flint sourly. "Ye ha' yet to answer my questions."

My great-uncle took snuff.

"This lady," he said, with the slightest emphasis, "is the daughter of my friend here, Colonel O'Donnell, a gentleman who represents in our venture the group of my friends who made it possible for me to intercept the treasure-ship."

O'Donnell, whose face had been growing redder and redder throughout this conversation, plucked his daughter by the elbow and led her away.

"I'll be thanking ye to let me know when the time comes there's an end o' mangy curs in these parts," he remarked over his shoulder. "'Tis not to be hearing my daughter insulted and my own self explained to the scum of the sea that I'll be standing quiet and idle in front of as—"

"Peace, *chevalier!*" interrupted Murray, and there was a ring in his voice that compelled obedience.

Flint's blue jowl took on a sickly greenish pallor and the tiny veins over his cheekbones commenced to beat.

"—— me for a —— —— —— if I'll stand for such from any sneaking, longjawed, Irish Papist ——"

"That will do," said my great-uncle without raising his voice.

Flint subsided.

"Colonel O'Donnell and his daughter are my guests," my great-uncle continued. "They have played essential parts in our capture of the treasure. I must insist, Flint, that you accord them a courtesy similar to that which I should extend to friends of yours in a like situation."

"They're no friends o' mine," growled Flint. "This is more o' your cursed political blethering. Well, I'm sick o' it, Murray, and I care not who knows it. First, ye carry us north to America, just to crimp two men, with not two hundred pounds in booty to show for the voyage. Next, ye shut me up here for the better part of six months for my men to rot with fever and drink and my ship to foul her bottom—"

"On both these counts you have your own negligence to blame," put in my great-uncle.

"—and last," Flint fumed on without heeding him, "ye bring to the Rendeyvoo a man and a woman who are not of our company, and who, for all ye know, may go hence, and loose a King's ship on us some day when we are careened and helpless."

"Not you," returned Murray sarcastically. "You'll not careen, Flint. That would mean work for your crew. But you concern yourself needlessly. Colonel O'Donnell has reasons for keeping his share in our enterprise under cover. He is more safely to be trusted in the circumstances than many another."

"I care not who he is or what you may have on him," cried Flint, working himself into a fury. "Ye ha' introduced four strangers into our midst without the let or permission of others of our company."

"I do not recognize the right of any other to tell me what I shall or shall not do," replied my great-uncle haughtily. "Such as it is, this company is the creation of my efforts, and I venture the assertion, Captain Flint, that it will not long survive my leadership. The four strangers of whom you complain have been essential factors in enabling me to win the treasure before you—which now awaits your convenience for division, according to the terms I originally stipulated."

If Murray's last words were intended to stimulate Flint's cupidity anew they succeeded. The captain of the *Walrus* opened his mouth to shout defiance, then let his eyes wander again to the pile under the break of the poop.

"How—how much?" he asked, almost fearfully.

"Seven hundred and sixty-three thousand, nine hundred and ninety-five pounds in coin and bullion, without counting a chest of jewels and three chests of plate," replied my great-uncle promptly. "You will note that I have favored our people in the division, allotting to them all in excess of the million and a half pounds the *Santissima Trinidad* was expected to carry."

A cunning look crept into Flint's face.

"Where's the rest?" he croaked.

My great-uncle took snuff.

"Quite safely disposed of, I assure you," he answered.

"Down below?"

"No, 'tis no longer aboard."

Flint swallowed hard.

"Ye mean it ain't here? It ain't aboard the *James?*"

"Precisely, captain."

"Gut me!" roared Flint. "Ye divided it by your lone? Wi'out a man from the *Walrus* to stand by and see fair play? I'll not support it, Murray. Curse me if I will!"

My great-uncle tapped his snuff-box.

"Your suspicions are quite unnecessary," he said. "Had I intended to defraud you, be sure I would not have enlarged the sum intended for division betwixt the two ships by sixty-three thousand pounds and more. Indeed, figuring in the jewels and plate, there must be an excess of better than one hundred thousand pounds."

"I know your tricks!" yelled Flint. "May I be —— —— for a —— —— —— if any lousy swab of a sea-lawyer politician is a-goin' to cast dust in my eyes. 'Twould be the very thing you'd do, Murray, to attempt to cozen me into believing seven hundred thousand pounds had been set aside for your 'friends' by throwing in an extra hundred thousand pounds for our division. 'Friends!' By thunder, the only friend ye know is yourself, ye dried up wisp of a—"

"That will do," said my great-uncle in his still, level voice.

Flint opened and shut his mouth rapidly without a sound issuing forth.

"I bar personalities, captain," warned my redoubtable relative.

One hand barely touched his sword-hilt.

"I trust there will be no occasion for me to repeat the warning," he remarked.

Flint's baffled rage was comic to behold.

"Aye, you and your fine gentleman ways!" he choked. "I know ye! Gut me if I'll support it to be swindled thus. A woman and strangers aboard! And eight hundred thousand pounds missing! 'Safely disposed of,' says you! I'll warrant. Safe where you can collar it any time you please. I knowed it as soon as I marked the flutter of a petticoat. A woman and gold—"

Long John Silver swung himself up on to the poop from the head of the port ladder and stamped toward us.

"Beggin' your pardon, Cap'n Murray, sir!" His pleasant voice broke through Flint's diatribe.

"My duty, Master Ormerod. And Master Corlaer, too. Like old times, ain't it, gentlemen, all of us together? I hopes as how ye'll overlook my boldness, Cap'n Murray, but I ha' a word to speak to Cap'n Flint— fo'c'sle council, sir."

My great-uncle took another pinch of snuff.

"Ah, yes," he observed dryly. "I recall that aboard the *Walrus* the fo'c'sle council must be heard. I trust that you can instil some common sense into your captain's head. He hath need of it, Silver."

Flint glared, but Silver snatched whatever reply he intended out of his mouth.

"Thank 'ee, sir. You just let me an' Cap'n Flint ha' a word in private, and maybe we'll see a way out o' this tangle."

"Suit yourself," said my great-uncle with a shrug.

Silver pulled his forelock, and his large face lighted up as if a considerable favor had been conferred.

"We won't be no time at all, sir. Thank 'ee kindly."

He put his free hand under Flint's elbow, and I marveled to see

the ease with which he was able to bend his captain to his will.
Accustomed as I was to Murray's autocratic discipline, it was a revelation to establish contact again with the free-and-easy spirit of the
Walrus, where any man might become commander if he was able to
muster a majority of the fo'c'sle to raise cutlasses in his behalf. Flint
obediently followed his quartermaster to the sta'b'd side of the poop,
and there they laid their heads close and collogued for a quarter-glass,
Silver at first arguing and Flint resisting him.

"Silver is no man to let hard on four hundred thousand pounds
slip through his hands," I said.

"Andt maybe he says not to let eight hundred thousand pounds
get away, needer," commented Peter. "*Ja,* I t'ink so."

Murray nodded slowly.

"You are more like to be right than wrong, friend Peter. Of all the
Walrus' people he hath the most acute intelligence. A choice knave!"

Colonel O'Donnell stalked back to us from the extremity of the
stern with Moira on his arm.

"Did ye put a flea in the rascal's ear, Murray?" he demanded. "By
the Mass, I never thought to hear ye tolerate such impudence on your
own deck."

"I am no man for quarreling without an adequate end in sight,"
returned my great-uncle. "Never threaten unless you must, *chevalier,*
and then smite with a sure aim."

"Words!" grumbled the Irishman. "'Tis time we had a little action."

Moira disengaged herself from her father and came to stand betwixt
Peter and me.

"If there's to be more fighting," says she, "I will have a pistol and
cutlass and do my share. I'll not stand idly by to be shot at the way
I was on the *Santissima Trinidad*—more by reason that if I must sail
with pirates I'll be preferring Captain Murray to the fellow yonder in
the red coat."

There was a high gallantry about her that drew a chuckle even
from Peter.

"Some time I take you to der wilderness country, andt we shoot
us bears andt scalp Injuns," he promised.

She clasped her hands.

"I am all for that, Peter," she cried. "Sure, I'd sooner fight Indians than pirates. But see, Bob! There's the red-headed boy will be making signals to you from the larboard ladder."

Darby McGraw's flaming top-knot projected just far enough above the level of the deck to show his eyes and a hand that jerked mysteriously at me.

"Come up, Darby," I invited him.

But he shook his head vigorously, so I crossed to his side.

"What is ailing you?" I asked.

"Sorra a trouble in the whole of creation," he returned in his rich brogue. "But I'd walk my two feet over the galley-stove as soon as stand so near the old devil as yourself, Master Bob. My troth, he's the terrible cruel feller, and him that ancient old he'd oughter been waked these many years past."

"He's no more to be feared than Flint," I answered, laughing.

"Ah, there's little ye know to be saying the like of that!" exclaimed Darby. "With Flint 'tis a blow and a curse and 'take it or leave it!' But him! He'd put the evil eye on the lot of us if the notion but came into the head of him."

"I rather be his friend than his enemy," I admitted. "Do they fear him so aboard the *Walrus?*"

Darby squinted sideways at me.

"Whiles they fear him. And then again when the rum is flowing— But I'll be saying what maybe I'll be sorry for later. I see ye found the elegant young maid that went to the Whale's Head with ye. My faith, ain't she the pretty creature! Will she be a pirate, too?"

"No more than Peter and me."

"Do ye tell me that same! And ye took her along with the treasure, the lads do be saying below. That was the grand haul! But they say, too, a good half of it ye buried on that island Long John do be always singing about."

"So you have heard that!" I cried.

"Troth, yes. They was telling Long John and me before he come up to speak with Cap'n Flint. God save us, who'd think there was so much money in the world? But here comes John and the cap'n now. I'd better be skippin'."

He slid down the ladder as he spoke, and I rejoined the group about my great-uncle. Flint strode across the deck, his face like a thunder-cloud. Silver, at his elbow, exhibited a countenance wreathed in smiles.

"We'll divide what's below," said Flint abruptly.

"I rejoice that you have come to your senses," replied Murray.

Silver spoke up.

"He's a main jealous cap'n, Cap'n Flint is, sir. Allus has a lookout for the interests o' his crew. A kind o' gardeen for us, ye might say. But we're all mighty beholden to yourself for counting in the *Walrus* same as the *James*; and speakin' on behalf o' the *Walrus,* I make bold to say as we won't forget it, Cap'n Murray, sir."

My great-uncle listened to this with the shadow of a smile on his face.

"I thank you, Silver," he acknowledged blandly. "I was confident you would appreciate the situation. Will you divide at once, Flint?"

Flint growled in his throat, then mastered his temper by a substantial effort.

"We'll appoint the usual committee o' six to check over with your men, Murray," he rasped. "I'll send my boats to shift our portion."

And he turned on his heel. John Silver pulled his forelock and nodded to all of us.

"Thank 'ee kindly, Cap'n Murray. My duty, sirs. And the young lady. Mighty nice to ha' a sweet, pretty face in the cabin, ain't it? Well, gentlemen, there's no excuse now for any o' us if we don't go home and make them happy as we left for the sea."

"Not the slightest," agreed my great-uncle. "I take it you are returning to your dear old mother, Silver—or is it your fondly waiting wife?"

Silver grinned.

"'Tain't neither, sir. But there's a sightly gal in St. Pierre in Martinico as I could set up shop with. A bit o' color in her, but then—"

He swept his arm in a liberal gesture as he stumped off to the ladder and hopped lightly down to the maindeck after his commander.

CHAPTER XVI

TREACHERY

THE CANDLES burned with a steady, spear-shaped flame, undeviating, motionless, so that the shadows were cast upon the paneling of the cabin walls in solid blocks like streaks of a darker coloring in the polished woodwork. The air was so still that we could hear the sea-birds calling down the inlet, the seethe and suck of water about the rudder, the splash of a fish, the patter of the feet of the watch.

Mistress O'Donnell had retired to her stateroom with the appearance of the wine, for both her father and Murray held punctiliously to the polite usage of society in this respect, Colonel O'Donnell, I think, because he dreaded lest she should witness one of his periodical bouts when he would saturate himself to a state of insensibility, and Peter and I must carry him to his berth, as we had done the first night he came aboard the *Royal James.*

My great-uncle, for want of other diversion, had undertaken to teach Peter to play chess, with some saturnine advice and comment from the Irishman; and to my amusement—as likewise to Murray's, I must admit—Peter proved himself a most redoubtable tyro, and once he had been coached in the rudiments presented a shrewd defensive gambit.

"Check at last!" exclaimed my relative, sinking back in his chair—of the four of us, he alone wore coat and stock and still contrived to maintain an air of cool well-being in that humid atmosphere. "You pushed me, Peter. Stap me, but you did! I'd not like to match my game with yours six months from now. Had you developed your queen's knight eight moves back—But 'tis futile to argue concerning what might have been. As well seek to prognosticate the future of our own lives."

Peter giggled and muttered that he was "no goodt, *neen.*"

"I would we might say, 'Check!' in this weary coil we are caught in," grumbled O'Donnell. "I see not that we are any farther forward with your confederates yonder."

He waved his hand out of the stern-window.

"They carried away their four hundred thousand pounds, but every man of them was as glum in the face as though 'twas so many bodeens instead of a prince's ransom. St. Patrick! When I think of what four hundred thousand pounds would do with the English Parliamentmen that will be selling their souls to whoever bids them the highest!"

"We have paid a price, *chevalier*," returned my great-uncle. "If we receive what we purchased, well and good. If not—"

He spread out his hands in deprecation.

"I am bound to concede, however, that I do not augur the best from what little information we have to go upon. Have you noted, gentlemen, that still as is the night, we hear no sounds of carousing aboard the *Walrus?*"

'Twas true, and had been true since the last boatload of treasure was transferred to Flint's ship shortly after dusk.

"You think he will fight then?" I asked from my seat under the stern windows, whence I could see the lights of the *Walrus*, dimly yellow in the thick, velvety, tropic darkness.

"I *hope* he will fight, my dear nephew," my great-uncle corrected me. "I fear Captain Flint has outlived his usefulness to me, and if my fears are well founded, the sooner we can smash him the better I shall be pleased. But I make it a rule never to think on the possibilities of the future. Rather I prepare for whatever eventualities may arise and let it go at that."

"And are ye prepared tonight for treachery, if this fellow Flint will be turning upon ye?" demanded O'Donnell.

Murray indulged himself with a pinch of snuff.

"Within reason, *chevalier*, yes. We have a strict watch, and the battery hath been cast loose and provided. More I can not do. The one advantage which Flint possesses is that I must wait upon whatever line of conduct he devises or his crew dictate to him."

The Irishman downed a goblet of brandy in a single gulp.

"Bah!" he cried. "'Tis easy enough for you to be talking the like of that. But I tell ye I am thinking we'd maybe better choose the now whether we'll push the fighting to Flint or pass out to sea."

My great-uncle shook his head.

"That would be poor tactics, either way. A fight means loss of life and ship damage, and if it can be avoided without loss we are by so much the gainer. Also, the seas are dangerous for us, as you should know, *chevalier*—and for another reason, Martin agrees with me the weather is working up for a violent storm."

"St. Patrick aid us!" protested O'Donnell. "I'm not able at all to make out how ye stand, Murray, and that's the naked truth. One moment you're crying for a fight with Flint, and the next you say to avoid it, if that can be managed."

"Quite true, *chevalier*," assented my great-uncle calmly. "And I fail to see that my position is a false one. I prefer not to force the issue. My policy is summed up in that."

"But you don't know what der *Walrus* will do, dat's der trouble," said Peter, looking up from the chessmen with which he had been toying on the table-top.

"And that, too, I have admitted, friend Peter," answered Murray.

"One night Bob andt me swam in der water from der *Walrus* to der *James*," pursued Peter as if my great-uncle had not spoken. "Maybe we could do dot again, *ja.*"

"Ha!" cried O'Donnell, smiting the table with his fist. "The very thing."

But my great-uncle sat unmoved.

"It could be done!" I exclaimed. "And none besides ourselves have knowledge of it."

Murray's wonderful, tawny eyes settled upon my face.

"Aye, it could be done," he agreed. "But there is danger, lad. 'Tis a still night. You can hear the fish leap."

"And Flint's people keep a slovenly watch," I replied. "But Peter and I are good swimmers. We'll not make a sound."

Peter commenced to blow out the candles.

"*Ja,*" he said. "Me, I don't like der water when it makes waves, but quiet it is nice."

My great-uncle smiled in the dwindling light.

"I should be a hypocrite as well as a fool, did I refuse your offer, gentlemen," he said. "'Tis not only our own lives are at stake, but Mistress Moira's too."

A groan came from Colonel O'Donnell.

"Ah, didn't I tell ye the way we would be left to the mercy of your cutthroats and latch-drawers, Murray? And now 'tis yourself must admit it! A sorry business it is, and I wish to God I'd never heard your name or gone forth of Spain."

Murray himself blew out the last candle.

"Well, well, *chevalier*," he answered a little tartly, "forth of Spain you went, and aboard the *Royal James* you are, and the one hope of life you have is that you stay aboard the *Royal James*—and this is saying naught of the obligations we owe to your friends on the other side."

Peter's great bulk glided by us.

"I go get a rope," he squeaked.

"A rope!" hiccuped O'Donnell. "And if we don't end in the noose of a rope, we'll likely be walking the plank. I care little for myself. I'll have seen my life and had my fling. But it was an ill day, Murray, you prevailed on me to fetch Moira along. I can't think what was in your mind—a young maid in a pirate hold! 'Tis wicked past belief."

"Tut, tut," remonstrated my great-uncle. "My reasons were of the best, and have been vindicated by events. But here is Peter. You found the rope?"

"*Ja*," answered Peter, and knotted an end around a leg of the table as I had done the night of our surreptitious entry.

O'Donnell sought solace in another glass of brandy. Murray assisted Peter and me to undress, and accompanied us to the stern windows.

"No needless risks, remember," he whispered as I crawled over the sill. "And above all, avoid discovery. Better learn nothing than be found out."

I had wrapped my ankles around the pendent rope and was prepared for a cautious slide into the water when a faint chuckle escaped him.

"What is it?" I asked.

"I was but thinking what a sturdy pirate you are become."

He withdrew his head before I could answer, and I dropped into the tepid water, with care that there should be no splash. An instant later Peter was beside me, and we began to swim with long, slow strokes in the direction of the blobs of light which were the only indication of the *Walrus,* so impalpable was the texture of that breathless night. There was not even a star in the sky—and the sky itself was invisible.

The hull of the pirate ship did not take shape until we were under the sheer of the stern. A single, guttering lanthorn seemed to burn in the main cabin, which was tenantless. And we paralleled the sta'b'd side, attracted by a hum of voices for'ard.

Peter's hand on my shoulder detained me as we swam beneath the heel of the bowsprit.

"Here you climb oop," he breathed in my ear. "They are all on her deck. I t'ink dey smoke der pipe in council, *ja!*"

I trod water, and explored with both arms above my head.

"There's no rope within reach," I told him.

"Dot's all right. I lift you."

He was clutching the cutwater with both hands and bracing his feet against the swell of the bow.

"Come on," he urged. "Oop on to my shoulders. I hold you, *ja.*"

"But if we splash?"

"No splash. You go oop; I go down under der water. Dot's all."

I forged alongside of him and gingerly climbed his immense shoulders, using a grip on his hair for haulage. Then I reached overhead again, and this time got my hands upon a stay of the bowsprit which ran from midway of the spar to a turnbuckle on the bow.

"Steady," I whispered. "I'm going to jump."

"*Ja!*"

I threw my legs upward and twined them around the stay, hanging like a monkey from it, and Peter went under with a gurgling ripple which might have been made by a fish. Presently he came to the surface and swam beneath me.

"Can you climb, Bob?"

"I think so."

"Goodt! I waidt."

The stay was fortunately dry—had it been slippery-wet I could never have swarmed it—and I was able, after much effort, to secure a grip on the bowsprit and lift myself astraddle of it. From here ordinarily the deck should have been visible, but in that intense darkness I could see no more than a vague loom of spars and a blur of light in the waist. The hum of voices was more audible, but still indistinct.

I worked down the bowsprit to the lift of the bows; but still I could see nothing, even on the fo'c'sle. 'Twas plain, however, that here was no watch to fear, and I dropped to the deck and crawled aft on my hands and knees toward the hum of talk, which I made certain now came from the waist.

The fo'c'sle was littered with spare cables, water-casks and other sailor's truck, which I had to avoid displacing; but I had my reward, for as I advanced the hum of voices dissolved into words and phrases.

"—a foxy 'un, Murray is," said a seaman's voice.

"And they *James* fellers'll fight us, whatever 'ee say," added a second.

"O' course they will!"

This was Silver's unmistakable oily speech.

"Who wouldn't fight for the grandest fortune as any gentlemen adventurers ever had a chance at?"

I wriggled behind a chase-gun, and peered over its breech into the waist. Two battle-lanthorns were suspended from the mainyard, and their yellow glare revealed the *Walrus'* crew squatted in serried ranks around the butt of the mainmast, where Flint, Bones, Silver and several others sat on upturned rum-barrels.

Flint leaned forward, wrathfully insistent, as I propped myself against a trunnion.

"Gut me if I thought to find such skulkers in my crew!" he snarled. "D'ye think to take any prize wi'out loss?"

"Aye," said a third seaman doggedly, "but we ha' never yet fought wi' Murray. Them as does don't ha' luck."

A murmur of assent answered him.

"Ah," struck in Silver, "but there's a first time always, mates. Murray's like the rest o' us. A ball or a cutlass-edge will finish him. And I say again, who wouldn't risk death for more'n a million and a half o' pounds in good gold and hard silver as'll buy every man jack o' us such pleasures as few men ever comes by, mates?"

"But there's only as much aboard the *James* as we ha' here," objected one of the first speakers.

"True for you Tom Allardyce," said Flint. "But the rest's safe enough, ain't it?"

"There's only them few knows o' it," returned the man. "They said on the *James* there was but the three men and the girl was landed to bury it."

Flint's answering laugh was horrible.

"And d'ye think that out o' four people, not countin' Murray—and one o' the four a girl—we can't make one talk? I tell ye, Tom, the stuff is as good as divided."

"Ye ha' first to catch Murray," retorted Allardyce.

"And why won't we?" demanded Silver. "Didn't we take what he was ready to give us and thank him for it like blessed lambs? And if he does suspect, what good'll it do him? On a night like this he'll never know where we are until we're on him. Two good broadsides, and then we'll sweep his decks."

Nobody spoke for a time.

"When does the ebb make?" asked Flint with a stretch and a yawn.

"Another two glasses yet," said Bones.

"——, I must ha' a bit of sleep," growled the pirates' captain. "Come to a vote, lads, and be done wi' it. Will ye go or won't ye? Ye all know what mercy Murray'll give ye, if he ever hears o' this council—and there's them as would like to blab, be sure o' that."

Silver pulled himself erect, cuddling his crutch under his arm.

"Quartermaster speaks for the crew," he said. "And my view is as how the crew is for fightin' for their just rights. The *Walrus* has played second fiddle long enough, and here's a chance as isn't likely to come again."

There was a second brief interval of silence.

"Nobody contrary," announced the one-legged man cheerfully. "Council's over! Keep quiet, mates. No drinkin', no fightin'. There'll be plenty o' both later."

The squatting ranks broke up into groups, and a number of men strolled for'ard toward my hiding-place. But I did not await them. From the shelter of the chase-gun I hunched myself back behind a water-cask, and so regained the bows, slipped overside and slid down the anchor-cable to the water.

A huge white shape floated up to me.

"Is dot you, Bob?"

"Yes. They're for attacking the *James* when the tide turns."

He headed down-stream without a word. We were halfway to the *James* before he spoke.

"Dot Murray, he is a lucky feller. Always he gets what he wants."

"What does he want?" I panted.

"Now he gets rid of Flint andt der *Walrus* crew, *ja.*"

"But he'll lose their half of the treasure if—"

"Maybe; maybe he don't. Andt after dot he gets rid of der *James.*"

"You're crazy, Peter," I said indignantly, trying my best to keep pace with him. "He'd be stranded here."

"Oh, he don't do dot here—maybe he don't do dot at all; maybe der tdefil stops helping him, *ja.* But if he gets der chance, you watch him, Bob. He gets rid of der *James,* and maybe he gets rid of us, *ja.*"

"Well, why do we help him, then?" I snapped, recalling my great-uncle's parting gibe.

"Dot's where he is smart, Bob. He makes it so we got to help him to safe our own skins, *ja.* Andt der little gal, too. For him and der Irisher dot drinks like a Lenape squaw I ain't got no use. But you andt der little gal—dot's different."

"Do you mean he intends to sacrifice all of us? And carry away the whole treasure for himself?"

"I don't know, Bob. Murray, he is a funny feller. Very funny! He likes you. He likes der little gal. Maybe he likes me—I don't know. Andt he is honest about dot oldt king dot lifs in Rome. But if any of us come in his way, he would push us aside. Dot's him now!"

The stern of the *Royal James* rose before us, and in one of the open windows my great-uncle's fine white head showed like a faded picture in a frame seen across a darkened room.

"Once before he planned too big," Peter whispered on. "Maybe this time *Gott* speaks loud to der tdefil andt stops him."

My great-uncle's voice floated down, quietly distinct.

"They are gone overlong. Gadzooks, *chevalier,* if they do not shortly return I'll slip my cable and take advantage of what remains of the flood to come at the *Walrus* and finish matters off-hand."

O'Donnell's reply was simply a querulous echo from the interior of the cabin.

"That sounds as though he had some use for us," I murmured to Peter, noiselessly treading water beside me.

"*Ja.* Use he has for us. Maybe he needs us when he gets rid of der *James,* eh? If der tdefil fails him, he can have use for honest men, Bob."

"We'll soon know," I retorted, and twitched the rope which dangled by the rudder-post.

"Who is there?" challenged my great-uncle, instantly alert.

"Robert," I whispered back, and commenced to climb.

Both Murray and O'Donnell—the latter for the time being stirred out of his habitual gloom—assisted me over the window-sill, and it affected me oddly to note my great-uncle's unconcern for the water I dripped on his silken coat.

"You ha' suffered no hurt?" he asked eagerly.

"No, no," I answered. "Make haste to help Peter up. They are coming against us with the making of the ebb."

He was betwixt me and the window, and I could see the faint smile of satisfaction on his face.

"'Tis what was to be expected of them," he remarked. "We must improve our watch. 'Tis no compliment to our people that they failed to suspect aught of your going and coming."

Peter squattered into the cabin like an enormous toad.

"Oof!" he squeaked. "I haf bubbles under my skin. We haf a fight tonight, Murray, *ja?*"

"Thanks to you and Robert, friend Peter, 'twill be rather in the nature of a chastisement than a fight," he answered urbanely. "If you will pardon me, gentlemen, I will go and complete the necessary arrangements."

A tinkle of glass told me that O'Donnell was refilling his goblet.

"What's a fight to the likes of him?" muttered the Irishman dolefully. "Treachery and scheming and murdering, aye, it's a fine night for such! Oh, blessed saints, where'll we be this time the morrow?"

"Safe, beyond question," I sought to encourage him as I drew on my breeches. "'Tis never the *Walrus'* scaly crew will overcome us."

"Be not too sure, Master Ormerod," he retorted with unusual vehemence. "I am thinking there is the curse of high Heaven on this venture and all connected with it."

Nevertheless he buckled on his sword and accompanied us to the deck when we were dressed. Men were scurrying silently to and fro, and from an open hatch came the whine of tackle as a piece was shifted on the gundeck. Aloft, squads of topmen were unfurling shreds of canvas to give the *James* steerage way at need. On the poop my great-uncle was issuing his final orders to Martin, Saunders and Coupeau.

"You, Saunders," he said, "will stand by the anchor cable with a broad-ax and upon my giving the word hew it asunder. Your position, Martin, will be in the waist. Keep men on the fore and main yards, ready to make sail when the cable is cut. Coupeau, of you I expect an initial broadside of crushing effect and a second fire if circumstances permit. Now to your stations, and above all things instruct your men to preserve silence. The man who makes a noise I will blow from a gun forthwith, and let that be my declaration to Flint!"

The officers gave their acknowledgments and flitted away. Simultaneously Peter pointed up the inlet.

"See!" he exclaimed.

The *Walrus'* riding-light winked out. An interval of minutes, and one of the waist-lights followed it. Another interval, and she disappeared completely in the black maw of the night.

My great-uncle sneezed delicately.

"In the dark one is clumsy," he observed. "I fear I have abused my nose with an over heavy dose of Rip-Rap. Well, well! Perhaps there is a parable in the incident for such clever fellows as Captain Flint.

"I must ask you not to move about, gentlemen. We have the better part of a glass to wait for the ebb, but caution is our watchword!"

CHAPTER XVII

THE STORM

WE HEARD the *Walrus* before we had sight of her—the slatting of a head-sail, a rattling block, a vague creak of cordage. Then an impression of a mighty shadow, a towering spiderweb of spars and lacy rigging, stealing ghostlike from the enshrouding dark.

She floated nearer. Nearer still. And nearer. It seemed that the two vessels must collide, and the suspense became unbearable. I wondered at my great-uncle's restraint. Would he never—I gasped with relief as his cool, even tones clove the silence.

"Touch off, Coupeau."

Crash! The deck leaped underfoot; the anchored hull surged forward. A red sheet of flame girdled the *James*' side, and in the instant's glare the *Walrus* was revealed in stark detail against a setting of glittering, black water and low, forested shores. I saw a man in her foretop, aimlessly balancing a grenade. I saw men staring curiously from the gunports as our broadside smashed into them. I had a glimpse of the brutal face of Bones, peering over the bulwarks, a cutlass in his teeth.

The darkness returned, and a multitude of echoes dinned back and forth across the inlet. There was a rending and cracking of timbers, with such screams as I never hope to hear again, the screams of wicked men who face an unexpected death, oaths and blasphemy and piteous appeals, all blended into one terrible, heart-searching whole.

My great-uncle's level voice dominated the confusion as easily as it had the silence.

"Cut your cable, Saunders!"

Flint's bellow answered from the *Walrus*.

"Give it to 'em, ye cowardly swabs! Stand to your guns!"

The red tongues of the *Walrus*' guns licked out at us; the staggering roar of their discharging smote the night. The fabric of the *Royal James* quivered and shook as the iron hail lashed into her. A moaning and screeching rose from waist, fo'c'sle and gundeck:

"Oh, God!"

"My leg! My leg!"

"It hurts! Sweet Christ, how it—"

"They're out! My guts are a-runnin' out!"

"Where's my arm? Oh, God, where's my arm?"

But a third time my great-uncle mastered the uproar.

"Make sail, Martin!"

Coupeau had reloaded his guns, and the *James* fired a second broadside with the same crushing unanimity as before. The *Walrus* receded as if our fire had had the effect of physically repelling her from us. Clouds of smoke came between the ships, and I perceived that we were benefiting from the severing of the anchor-cable. The ebb tide was already sweeping us down the Anchorage toward the open sea.

The *Walrus* shot off another ragged broadside, which for the most part splashed water or scattered mud, and then settled to a pegging chase, the Long Toms on her fo'c'sle barking fitfully as they tossed the twelve-pound shot athwart our decks. Our guns were silent. Our gundeck spewed forth men, whom Martin hustled to the yards to shake out every sail to catch the errant wind that veered gustily from southeast to southwest.

Colonel O'Donnell waved his fist at my great-uncle.

"What madness will have taken ye now, Murray?" he cried. "There was the grand chance ye had to finish the rascals once and for all. Are ye feared of them that ye turn tail—you that ha' struck first blow; aye, and second, too?"

"Not at all, sir," rejoined my great-uncle. "Having struck first blow and second blow, as you so aptly phrase it, I am of a mind to strike also the *coup de grace*. And this with as trifling damage to my own vessel as is possible."

"Man, you'll never have another such chance as that ye cast away," mourned the Irishman.

"For a soldier, *chevalier*, you reveal astonishing lack of judgment," returned my great-uncle. "Had I remained to finish conclusions with Captain Flint in the narrow space of the Anchorage I might conceivably have gained the victory, but it must have been by means of subordinating brains to brawn, and with loss in proportion thereto. I prefer to force him to sea, where, by maneuvering and proper strategy, I can secure the same object at a half or a third of the cost."

"'Tis all the same," retorted O'Donnell. "If ye sink him, ye lose his treasure."

"Quite true," assented Murray. "But what would you say to driving him ashore, eh?"

What O'Donnell would have answered to this I know not; for there was a sudden drumming of feet on the deck, and Moira cast herself into his arms.

"Oh, *padre*," she cried tearfully, "and are ye safe from the cannon? I waked in my bed with their roaring, and it came over me we were on the *Santissima Trinidad* once more, and poor Señor Nunez, the apothecary, groaning from his death-wound—and him that was looking forward to the quiet end of his days in the little house by Alcantara!

"And then I was thinking 'twas all a horrid dream. But the cannon blatted again, and the ship trembled, and there was a shriek at my very door. So out I ran in my shift, and Diomede the blackamoor was lying in his blood on the cabin floor, and Ben Gunn beside him a-praying. And with that I put on me enough clothing for decency's sake, and came to find ye, for my four bones are clattering with fear, and that's Heaven's truth!"

O'Donnell drew her close.

"There, there, *acushla*," he said with a tenderness he had only for her. "The worst will be over. There's naught for ye to fear."

She reached up and stroked his face.

"Troth, and I was thinking that same if I could but come at you, *padre*," says she. "But 'tis terrible fearsome to be sleeping by your lone self, and awake in the midst of a sea-fight."

Her father swore under his breath.

"Ah, 'tis I was the weak, foolish fellow to drag you into such a venture! There'll come a day I must answer—"

She stopped his mouth with her hand.

"As if I'd be anywhere else than just here!"

I turned my head, not wishing to be prying into their affairs, and a quarter-mile astern I saw a jet of flame and heard the smacking report of one of the *Walrus*' chase-guns.

Moira said something more that I did not hear, and he interrupted her.

"Get ye below, my maid until we—"

There was a harsh, whistling sound in the air, and the hairs on one side of my head rose up, and on the heels of this came the thud of a shot as it struck timber.

"Close, egad!" commented my great-uncle.

O'Donnell swayed strangely and drooped over his daughter's shoulder.

"Padre!" The dazed grief in her voice was tragical. "Why won't ye

stand? Are ye hit? Oh, blessed Virgin, there's no sense left in him! Bob, Master Peter, help me! He's so—so—heavy."

Peter and I jumped to aid her, and Murray was not far behind us. We lowered O'Donnell's tall body to the deck, and I ran for a lanthorn. When I returned with it my great-uncle had assumed command of the situation.

"We can feel no blood or broken bones," he said. "Hold your light here by his head, if you please, Robert."

The yellow glow played over the Irishman's long face. His lips were drawn back in what had been a smile; his eyes were fixed and glassy; no pulse beat in his corded throat. Moira crouched beside him, chafing his limp hands and crooning a medley of endearments in English, Irish and Spanish. Murray, opposite her, thrust exploring fingers into the bosom of her father's shirt. A startled look appeared in my great-uncle's lambent eyes, but his features preserved their immobility.

"'Tis useless to cry to him, lass," he said gently. "He doth not answer, you see."

"But he will!" she protested. "Sure, ye must soon be finding what is wrong with him, sir. It may be a sup of brandy would bring him round."

My great-uncle reached across and plucked from her grasp the hand she had been rubbing.

"Come," he said, rising, "we will ask Peter to carry him to his berth, shall we?"

"But—but—we must bring him to!"

"We can not bring him to," he answered kindly.

She stood up, bewildered.

"Not—bring—him—to? But why?"

"Because his heart no longer beats," said my great-uncle. "Quick! Catch her, Robert."

She lay like a tired child in my arms.

"Dead!" she murmured faintly.

"He can not be dead!" I exclaimed. "There's not a wound on him."

"*Neen,*" said Peter.

He picked up the lanthorn from where I had dropped it on the deck and directed the light upon the upper part of Colonel O'Donnell's head. A blue bruise like a scar was spread across the Irishman's left temple.

"A graze-shot," pronounced Peter. "Der cannonball came dot close. *Ja!*"

"But the skin is not even broken," I objected.

"*Ja,* but dot don't matter."

Murray bent over and fingered the bruise.

"Peter is right," he said. "'Twas the concussion affected the brain. I have heard of such a freak shot, but never seen it happen before."

Moira clung to my arms.

"And he is really dead? The *padre* is really dead? And he unshriven, without a comfort of the Church! Oh, holy saints, be his advocates! Sure, was there ever a crueler end?"

She collapsed in a passion of weeping.

"Conduct her below, Robert," said my great-uncle. "We will follow you."

She suffered me to lead her from the poop without objection, more like a child than ever, sobbing and protesting and repeating the same things over and over again, in an abandonment of grief which only the Irish can attain.

"'Tis you are the kind friend," she stammered when we had reached her stateroom. "And oh, Bob, I have the sore need of you, I that am an orphan in a pirate ship. Troth, I haven't a friend in the wide world unless it be you and Master Corlaer. But I am the bad, selfish girl to be thinking of my own plight, and the father that loved me this moment gone up to Peter's Gate, and him without the holy wafer to his lips or so much as a prayer said over him. Ah, what ill deed did we do, either one of us, that he should be taken from me so, without a word of parting? The sisters were always after saying we must reconcile ourselves to God's mercy, but 'tis little mercy has been shown to me."

I quieted her at last, brought her a swallow of brandy and induced her to lie down.

"I mustn't be crying the way I will have done," she apologized, gulping her sobs. "Himself will be needing all the prayers I can say, and a boiling of candles, too. Do you go on, Bob—only promise you'll not leave me by my lone if there's more fighting. I could never stand to hear the thundering of the cannon after—after—*that*—and no one by to bid me take heart o' grace."

The gray dawnlight was seeping through the stern windows when I rejoined my great-uncle and Peter in the main cabin. Peter was as placid as ever, puffing industriously at a long clay pipe; but my relative displayed more concern than I remembered to have observed in him at any time in the past.

"I trust you were able to calm the poor lass?" he greeted me. "Stap me, what a sorry business! I'd never have chosen O'Donnell for a traveling companion, but without him I know not what to do. The whole venture—"

He shook his head and stared out the window beside him, clicking the lid of his snuffbox open and shut.

"But we have first to attend to the *Walrus,*" he added presently. "I shall do so with the less reluctance after that last shot. The cursed luck of it! A beaten enemy's blow in the dark, blindfolded, by gad! And to think it must strike down of all men the one most essential to my schemes. I could—Well, well, no matter! We must triumph over the unexpected. 'Tis the chasm all great leaders must cross to win the final victory."

I found myself somehow instinctively hostile to his attitude.

"What have you done with Colonel O'Donnell?" I asked coldly.

"Peter carried him to his stateroom. We will give him decent burial when we return to the island. And perhaps some day we can come for him in state with a squadron of King's ships and bear him home to a grave in the land he was exiled from."

My great-uncle's spirits brightened noticeably as he contemplated the picture his words presented.

"Yes, yes," he murmured half to himself. "What O'Donnell could have done surely I can do. Our friends in Avignon will help. And Robert!"

He turned to me.

"Ah, my boy, this unfortunate incident is my best justification for pressing you in my cause. What should I do without you and Peter? 'Twill be for you two, with Mistress Moira, to establish our connections with the king's agents in France."

"You seem to forget I am no Jacobite," I answered unpleasantly.

"Tut, tut, you shall be as stout a Jacobite as Prince Charles himself."

"Not I!"

He smiled.

"We'll leave that to Mistress Moira."

"Maybe you forget der *Walrus,*" interposed Peter.

"Not so, Peter. I shall dispose of the *Walrus* within the next few hours."

"Andt *Gott,*" added Peter as if Murray had not spoken.

My great-uncle laughed merrily.

"My dear Peter, men of judgment will inform you that there is no God—or, if we concede a God, there is every reason to assign a superior degree of power to the inevitable Devil representing the opposing virtue of godliness. Indeed, did I incline to bow down before any superhuman authority I should elect Satan by preference. But a ripe experience has inclined me to the view that the Devil is as much a figment of men's imaginations as God. Since the beginning of recorded time a priestly caste— But here we are drifting into a philosophical discussion; and as you very properly reminded me, the *Walrus* awaits our attention. Let us go on deck."

"Der wise man don't know eferyt'ing," answered Peter. *"Neen!"*

"Essentially true," agreed my great-uncle. "I must confess myself ignorant of such staple points as why we are here, the excuse for human existence, the relative significance of this world of ours, the utility of the differing qualities of goodness and evil. But any serious consideration, friend Peter, must convince as profound a thinker as yourself that the very existence of men and women is of itself *prima-facie* evidence that there can be no Divine Author of omnipotent or sentient powers."

"We better go on deck," said Peter.

"After you," protested my relative as we rose. "'Tis a pleasure to debate with you, Peter. Take care, pray! Gunn has not removed all of the evidence of Diomede's passing. Strange, is it not, how a black fellow like Diomede and a man who hath been the confidant of princes like O'Donnell should both be abolished by a simple organic disruption? That alone, Peter, should suffice to disprove the humbug of an all-wise Providence. An all-wise Providence, forsooth! Here am I, arranging to reconstruct for the better a most unhappy trio of kingdoms, with consequences bound to improve the well-being of the entire world, and my plan is suffered to be placed in jeopardy by an ignorant sailor's blind shot in the dark! What could be more absurd?"

Peter did not answer him, and we passed out upon the maindeck, where sailors were busy removing the traces of the *Walrus'* first broadside which had wrought a certain amount of minor damage and caused the deaths of several men. 'Twas now light enough to see about us, but the light was of a quality I had never known before— hard, coppery glare, with the sun obscured from view. The sea was quite flat, and the wind continued intermittent, veering from one quarter of the south to the other. Spyglass Island lay to larboard, its contour amazingly distinct—as if it were bitten into the frame of steel-blue sea and dully shimmering sky that encompassed it. The *Walrus,* like the *James,* had cleared Captain Kidd's Anchorage, and was running due north before the wind betwixt us and the islet called Skeleton Island.

Murray bent a shrewd eye aloft and hailed Martin.

"How is it you carry no sail on the mizzen?" he demanded.

"Account o' that there ———— ———— ————shot, cap'n, answered the mate, tugging his forelock. "If ye look to it ye'll see as how a ———— ———— twelve-pounder bored into her."

We all followed his pointing finger to a gouge beneath the mizzen yard. The shot that had grazed Colonel O'Donnell's head had done more than graze the mizzen. The mast was whittled away to a depth of several inches as cleanly as if a giant's ax had chopped into it.

My great-uncle took snuff very slowly.

"What luck! What luck!" he muttered.

And then louder:

"'Twas an expensive shot for us, gadzooks! Well, Martin, we must fish the mast at our earliest opportunity, but we can make shift to corner Flint without it. The *Walrus* is foul and heavy in the water. The *James* can sail circles round her in this wind."

There was a worried look in Martin's weather-beaten face.

"Askin' your pardon, sir, I don't like this ———— ———— wind. We're in for a ———— of a storm or I'm a ———— ———— ———— lubber."

My great-uncle shrugged his shoulders.

"Storm or no storm, Martin, the *Walrus* carries nigh four hundred thousand pounds."

"Aye, sir; and by your favor, best sink her and be done wi' it and run for shelter."

"Sink her! Man, we'd lose the treasure."

"Better lose the *Walrus*' treasure than go down ourselves," insisted Martin doggedly. "Have it your own way, sir, but I'm a —— —— ——if it ain't fixin' to blow up one o' these here tarrible Caribbee storms as pluck the hairs outn your head."

Murray regarded the four quarters of the sky for several moments.

"With your prognostications I find no quarrel, Martin," he said finally; "but I believe we have ample time to head the *Walrus*. Flint dares not run south because he knows the hornet's nest we have stirred up in those seas. My purpose is to box him in and force him to beach. If this wind continues we should bring him to book on the north coast of the island, and so soon as the *Walrus* has taken ground we will wear and beat in for the North Inlet. Doth that satisfy you?"

The mate hesitated.

"You be cap'n, sir. But if 'twas my say we'd head back in to the Anchorage, *Walrus* or no *Walrus*."

My great-uncle stiffened.

"'Tis impossible," he replied haughtily. "However, we will bear up for the *Walrus*, and you may bid Coupeau to see what harm he can contrive against her with his chase-guns."

Martin saluted and went for'ard. My great-uncle led us to the poop.

"Your old sailor is eke much of an old woman into the bargain," he remarked perfunctorily, climbing the sta'b'd ladder ahead of me. "Let him but sniff the approach of a tempest, and he is all for the nearest haven—aye, the hardiest buccaneer no less than the law-abiding merchantman."

"O'Donnell was right, it seems, when he advised you to finish the task you had begun in the inlet," I snapped, none too pleased, myself, with the outlook.

"In that case, my dear nephew, a half of us must have perished," retorted my relative. "You have had some experience of these wolves of ours when their lusts are roused. No, no; I am no milk-and-water fighter, but I prefer to batter my enemy safely at long range rather than give him an equal opportunity to tear my throat."

Peter grunted.

"You said?" Murray inquired courteously.

"*Neen,* I saidt not'ings. But I t'ink—I t'ink it is all right if you get der *Walrus* and yourself come safe. If you don't do bot' it don't matter if you do der odder; *neen.*"

My great-uncle raised his prospectglass.

"You have ably stated one of the primary rules of success in any branch of warfare, friend Peter," he said. "Captain Flint is making better going of it than I had expected. Apparently by some perversity of our continuing ill-luck he hath a more constant wind close under the island than we out here. Ah! I hear Coupeau's bark."

A cloud of smoke rolled aft as the long eighteen on the la'b'd side of the *James'* fo'c'sle boomed. The shot dashed up a fountain of water a few feet ahead of the *Walrus,* which was now running neck and neck with us. Flint replied with one of his long twelves, but the shot fell short, and he edged away as much as he dared, which was very little, for Murray had seen to it that he had bare sailing-room. Our chase-gun barked again, and this time the round shot ricocheted from the water's surface and slapped into the *Walrus'* hull.

"Neat," commented my great-uncle; "but what we require is a fair hit on a spar."

Coupeau realized as much, as was evidenced by his next two shots going high and striking the water beyond the target. But I was distracted from watching his efforts, for at the fifth discharge Moira O'Donnell crept up the poop ladder, her eyes wide with misgiving. "Troth, yourself promised only a few minutes since you'd not leave me by my lone was there more fighting, Bob," she reproached me.

"'Tis no fight," I answered.

"Aye, we do but seek to drive yonder knaves ashore," Murray assured her. "They can not reach us at this distance."

She surveyed the scene with a doubting eye and was constrained to credit us.

"But why is the light so strange?" she demanded. "'Tis as if the door of a cookstove was ajar."

"We are in for bad weather, sweet," replied my great-uncle. "You must go below."

But she shrank away from him and clutched firmly an arm of Peter and me, each.

"No, no, I'll not be going down there again," she cried. "On the inside of a door I can think of naught but the sorrow that is come upon me. I'll stay up here in the open."

"Certes, this will be no safe place in a storm," I urged.

But she clung the tighter to us.

"I'll not go down. I'd sooner be taken by the pirates than go down. Down there the noises of the water and the ship will be like the cry-ing of the banshee in the Green Room where grandfather died. No, no! In the cabin there is only death, and the light is dim, and the noises will be whispering at my elbow the livelong time. I'll have none of it! Sure, I care not what danger there is, if I can stay up here and meet it in the open."

"We let you stay," said Peter soothingly. "*Ja,* we better let der little gal stay, Murray. Bob andt I, we take care of her."

"That will we," I endorsed him.

My great-uncle eyed me a thought quizzically.

"You are, it seems, subject to change of opinion, Robert," he remarked. "By all means let Moira remain with us. I daresay she'll be none the worse for a wetting."

But the storm held off throughout our morning-long chase down the east coast of the island and then out to sea to herd the *Walrus* in from the north. Coupeau hulled the miserable craft again and again, and shot away her foretopmast; but she steadily clawed offshore and made desperate attempts to steal ahead of us and win a clear path before the wind, and when, toward noon, the breeze died completely the positions of the two vessels were practically the same as they had been from the beginning of the cat-and-mouse game that Murray played.

The *Royal James,* by nimbler handling, had gained in the last hour, and was more than a cannon-shot to the northwest of the *Walrus,* with the northernmost of the island's chain of hills—the one the pirates called the Foremast Hill—almost due southeast of us. If the wind sprang up again in anything like the same quarter the *Walrus* was fast in Murray's trap. She would have the choice of two alterna-tives: She could stand on and fight, with the practical certainty of destruction for all hands, or she could drive ashore, in which case the crew might take to the woods, with every prospect of eluding pursuit, unless Murray made a determined effort to comb the island's craggy recesses. After the long-range battering they had received all morning, on top of the hammering in the action in the dark, there was not much doubt that the *Walrus'* disorderly crew would take the decision into their own hands and choose the latter as offering a fair chance of life, no matter how circumscribed.

The helmsman had just turned the hour-glass, which lay beside the compass in the hooded box in front of the steering-wheel, when a shout came from Martin, who was half-way up the main-rigging, sweeping the horizon with a glass. My great-uncle had been pondering the desirability of getting out the boats and undertaking to tow the *James* within range of the long eighteens, and he called back—

"Is it wind?"

"Aye, aye, sir," roared Martin—and there was no mildness now in the old fellow's tones. "There's the —— ——est blow o' wind as ever came out o' the —— —— bowels o' the sky or I'm a —— —— swab as ever was."

He tumbled from the ratlines and ran aft to the break of the poop, his face lifted earnestly in appeal.

"Best let me lay an ax to the mizzen, sir," he called.

My great-uncle took snuff, calmly deliberate.

"Curb your fears, Martin," he answered. "I have weathered a lifetime of gales in the *Royal James*. Take in sail, of course; but if we sacrificed a mast needlessly 'twould cripple us for weeks. Where away is this wind?"

Martin waved an arm across the northwestern arc of the horizon.

"Look for yourself, cap'n. I be an old man, and I never seed the like."

Murray's reply was to swarm up the mizzen rigging with the uncanny agility of which he was capable, and I climbed after him. We were some fifty feet above the deck when we saw clearly with the naked eye a vast purple canopy arching forward across the northern sky, a thing of splendidly colorful intensity, savagely beautiful. Jagged streaks of lightning flashed forth from its mirky depths. A tattered fringe of storm-clouds whipped out ahead of it like the tentacles of some monstrous sea-creature. And it advanced at an incredible speed, covering miles of sea and sky in the few moments that we watched it.

My great-uncle's jaw squared grimly.

"'Tis too late to sacrifice the mizzen," he said. "We'd not have time to clear the wreckage."

His commands rang through the ship.

"Aloft, topmen! Strip her to a storm-jib! Hola, Coupeau! Double-lash your chase-guns and be certain the broadside batteries are secured and the ports closed. Batten all hatches, Saunders!"

'Twas as much as I could do to keep pace with him as he descended to the poop.

"Fetch a coil of light rope, Robert," he ordered briefly. "We shall all require to be lashed fast."

"Shall I carry Moira below?" I asked.

He hesitated.

"No, she will have a better chance—"

He checked himself.

"Let her bide on deck. Here we can aid her at need. Haste, boy! We must have the rope before the wind strikes us."

I slid down a stay to the maindeck and dug the rope out of a chest of spare gear which was bolted to the cabin bulkhead. My great-uncle's last words had impressed me even more than the spectacle of that baleful curtain across the northern sky; and I was thrilled, too, by the tense celerity with which the entire crew leaped to the task of preparing the ship to meet the tempest. There was almost no noise—a few shouts of command and hails of acknowledgment; but every man worked as if his life depended upon it. When the jib-sheet fouled Martin slashed it free with his knife, and the sail came down with a run. By the time I had regained the poop the upper spars already were bare.

Murray was standing with Moira and Peter beside the helmsman, and while they stared, fascinated, at the oncoming storm, his eyes were upon the *Walrus.*

"Flint must be sober," he said bitterly. "He is taking in sail. Stap me, what a fit end to a luckless day! In the hollow of my hand, and now— Aye, 'twould be all ways fitting did he escape, whilst we—"

A snarling moan, as of great winds tortured and confused, came to us from the belly of the storm. The sky darkened. A gust of air, sulfurous and warm, ruffled my hair. The moan became a howl, a clamor.

My great-uncle snatched the clasp-knife from the belt of the helmsman, a splay-footed Easterling, whose flat, gap-toothed face had remained impassive during all the excitement since Martin's warning shout had announced the storm's approach.

"Give me that rope, Robert," he exclaimed. "I am a fool to stand talking. Here, Peter!"

He flung the Dutchman a length of it.

"Bind Mistress Moira to those ringbolts—and best knot her to yourself as well. She'll not be able to stand alone. Aid me with this fellow here, Robert. We must tie him to the wheel."

One of the clouds in advance of the storm curtain reached out over us with a crackle of lightning-bolts and spatter of rain, and our fingers flew as we secured first the helmsman and then ourselves. The voice of the tempest was become a sullen, animal roar, riven at intervals by the crash of the thunder. And the immense curtain of its front overhung the *James,* impenetrably sooty at the base, opaquely purple as it toppled forward. The *Walrus* was a specter ship to leeward, and disappeared in the gloom as I watched.

"Oh, holy Mother!" gasped Moira. "'Twill be the end of all things."

And so it seemed. The *Walrus* was gone. The northern coast of the island dimmed and vanished. For an instant the peak of Foremast Hill hung in the upper air. Then that, too, was blotted out. The purple twilight deepened. Rain sheeted down from clouds scarce higher than our mast-heads. A lurid glare of lightning flickered and was quenched in the sea. And the wind smote us with a mad howl of exultation, sucking up into its embrace everything that was not fastened to the deck.

The *James* shuddered under the blow, bearing down by the head and heeling to starboard. My great-uncle and I were pushed forward on our faces. The helmsman was doubled over the wheel. Peter bent to cover Moira, crouching above her on hands and knees.

Presently the ship righted herself; but as she neared an even keel there was a prolonged *craa-aa-ack!* of breaking wood, and the wounded mizzenmast went by the board, crushing a score of men in its fall and brushing as many more through the hole it stove in the starboard bulwarks.

A wail of agony pierced thinly the tumult of the storm, and the

James was jarred from end to end as the big spar, with all its litter of yards and top-hamper, lunged at the hull like a trip-hammer, its dead weight dragging us broadside on into the path of the waves which followed the wind's first irresistible rush. Steep walls of water dropped on us from as high as the mainyard, thudding hollow on poop and fo'c'sle. Giant combers crowded so fast that we choked beneath their deluge. The waist was a lather of creamy seas that wrenched and battered at hatchcoamings and bulwarks.

Murray staggered to his feet and set his lips to my ear.

"Must—cut—free—mizzen—breach—hull—"

So much I understood, and assisted him to slash the rope, which bound us to the deck. Peter saw what we were up to and loosed himself, taking care in his deliberate fashion to strengthen Moira's lashings. Then the three of us fought our way down into the hell-reek of the waist, where small boats and water-butts and dead men swirled fore and aft in a torrent of pounding seas.

There were axes in the box from which I had procured the rope, and we equipped ourselves with them, waded thigh deep through the tangle of water and wreckage and attacked the maze of stays and rigging that united the dangling mizzenmast to the ship. Not a man helped us. There was not a living man in sight aft of the mainmast, and it was as much as a man's life was worth to try to work aft of that point, for on the one side there was a wide breach in the bulwarks through which the waves poured, and opposite was the gap the mizzenmast had crushed. Whoever crossed the deck there must have been carried overboard, one way or the other.

Where we were we had some slight shelter from the poop, but 'twas sufficiently hazardous in all conscience. I can see my great-uncle still, in his black silk coat and breeches, all adrip with the salt water as he labored with the energy of a man of half his age, always swift to perceive the strategic center of the tangle, always first to wade into the tricky web of cordage where a misstep meant a plunge overside.

Twice Peter rescued him from certain death, and once the Dutchman saved me when a mountainous sea curled down upon us over the *James'* bulwarks and was like to have carried me off in its passing. And it was Peter whose brute strength and cool-headedness made the most of my great-uncle's agility of wit, and hewed and hacked the mizzenmast from its moorings. Aye, and none too soon; for when we clambered back on the poop Moira met us with hands clasped in terror and pointed to leeward where a rocky headland loomed through the gray rain.

Murray gave it one look and leaped for the wheel. The Easterling was bent over in the odd, huddled posture he had assumed from the moment the storm hit us, and he lolled sidewise as my great-uncle grasped his shoulder, his body all askew from the small of his back upward. He made no response, and slipped lower in the coils of rope that bound him to his post; his gnarled fingers slid off the spokes; his feet went out from under him.

"His back is broken," shouted my great-uncle.

The *James* had begun to gather headway; but as the wheel was released from the dead helmsman's grip her head fell off, and she dropped sluggishly into the trough of the seas which surged over the shattered waist, and one green hill of water burst squarely on the poop, hurling us to the deck. Peter recovered his footing before either Murray or I, shoved the Easterling's body aside and gripped the wheel in his own hands. Slowly, the buoyancy all out of her, the *Royal James* swung around in response to the rudder's thrust and lumbered off before the wind.

The headland Moira had sighted faded into the mist; but my great-uncle shook his head sadly.

"We are making water," he shouted to me; "and the island is to leeward. We scarce can weather it, and if we do—"

A faint hail reached us from the fo'c'sle.

"Land—"

And a rent in the storm-clouds showed a second and lower headland fair over our larboard bow.

Peter started to put the helm down to enable us to bear off as much as possible and have whatever chance there was of clearing it; but Murray caught his arm.

"No, no, Peter!" cried my great-uncle. "Head up! Head up! 'Tis the North Inlet! If we can pass in to sta'b'd of that spit we are safe."

"*Ja,*" squeaked Peter, and his iron muscles forced the rudder over until it neutralized the drive of the wind and sea; and foot by foot the

Royal James made her southing, passed the east spit with half a cable's length to spare and opened a narrow, bottle-shaped roadstead, with tree-clad shores that offered protection from any storm that blew.

The rain was still pelting down. The surf was foaming on the outer beaches; the wind whistled shrilly in the rigging. But to us that prospect was the fairest ever seen. Moira sank to her knees in prayer beside the dead pirate. My great-uncle stepped to the rail and bade the survivors of the crew get sufficient sail on the ship to give us steerage way. And I—I tried to shake Peter. He blinked at me solemnly.

"I t'ink *Gott* spoke out loudt to der tdefil today, Bob," he said. *"Ja!"*

CHAPTER XVIII

DISASTER

ANOTHER less self-assured than Andrew Murray must have been dismayed by the series of misfortunes which had beset him. We were safe, but no more. The *Royal James* was taking in water so rapidly 'twas necessary to beach her on the mud-flats at the south end of the inlet. She leaked like a sieve where the mizzenmast had thumped her side, and her upper works were in splinters. In the fight with the *Walrus* and the storm we had lost eighty-odd men, but more serious than this were the deaths of the two mates. Martin's body was found near the stump of the mizzen; he had been struck down by the mast he so distrusted. Nothing was ever seen of Saunders, and we could only suppose that he had been swept overboard.

The crew were apathetic and sullen, inclined to be mutinous and resentful of my great-uncle's authority. For the first time they had reason to question his omnipotence, and it required a full display of his ruthless temper to reduce them to subjection—an accomplishment to which he was aided considerably by Coupeau, and I am free to admit, by Peter and me, who could not afford to risk the brutal license which would certainly follow a successful revolt of the gundeck's polyglot horde. The former galley slave was a redoubtable ally with the nine-tailed cat, and a bruiser whose fists were as deadly sure as the long eighteens he handled so deftly.

The rain and wind ceased with the approach of darkness, and my great-uncle had the men mustered under the poop, many of them still bleeding from the punishment they had received. And of all his feats I deem that the most remarkable: To face, practically unaided, upward of a hundred and fifty men, who had just been curbed in the act of mutiny, without even sufficient light to enable him to exploit the compelling gleam of his tawny eyes. He beat them down—held them down—by sheer power of will and fearlessness.

"You stand upon the deck of a wrecked ship," he said bleakly. "Under hatches lies sufficient treasure to make every one of you comfortable for life, to buy you dissipation or place or fortune, whichever you prefer. One man can lead you to repair the ship and conduct you where the treasure will be of use to you.

"I am that man. Without me you are doomed to spend your days chasing the goats on those hills; and if there is any repetition of the disorder exhibited today I shall maroon all of you save a number required to handle the ship.

"Get to work. Before you rest I expect the maindeck to be cleared and stagings rigged overside for resheathing and calking."

He drove them until midnight, then sent them reeling to their hammocks.

In the morning a systematic plan of occupation was arranged. By Coupeau's advice a handful of the more amenable of the crew— mostly negroes, Portuguese, Italians and Frenchmen of the south— were organized as an after-guard, and the remainder were divided into squads headed by men selected for skill at some special trade. One squad were to overhaul the sails and cut and sew from spare canvas a suit for the new mizzen, which a second squad were to hew on the slopes of Spyglass Mountain and transport to the ship. A third squad were to repair all exterior damage to the hull; a fourth were to recalk the started seams; a fifth were to attend to whatever internal repairs were necessary.

Coupeau was placed in charge of the work aboardship, and the rest of us carried Colonel O'Donnell's body to the top of a small hill east of the head of the inlet. There, in the midst of a grove of pines, we laid him to rest. 'Twas a noble situation for a wanderer who had never reached his goal, with the clashing boughs and the distant thunder of the surf to sound a requiem until the end of time and a view over green meadows and dwarf woodlands to the white rim of the beach and the blue sea, shining in the sun.

Yesterday seemed years past. I blinked my eyes, looking from the peaceful garb of nature to Moira's slim body huddled in prayer beside the mound of raw earth amongst the pine needles. On the edge of the grove the men who had dug the grave were playing a gambling game with the pine-cones. Peter leaned on a musket, gravely compassionate. My great-uncle, his eyes puckered in thought, was staring out to sea. As I watched, he twitched my coat sleeve and drew me to one side.

"I shall leave you to amuse yourself as you choose for the remainder of the day," he said. "'Tis for you and Peter to safeguard the maid. I must ascertain, if possible, what hath become of Flint."

"And then?" I asked.

"Then?" His eyebrows arched in surprise. "Why, then, Robert, we shall continue as we have done hitherto."

"You must pursue this insane scheme?"

He was as patient with me as if I were a fractious child.

"'Tis no 'insane scheme,' but a coup of high politics of fascinating import, my boy. I own to disappointment it doth not appeal to you more readily. What? Shall we cry quits, simply because of shipwreck? And after every move hath turned as we plotted it should!"

I shook my head hopelessly, but decided to try again.

"Bethink you," I argued, "the longboat can speedily be made weather tight. In her we might reach—"

"Put it from your mind," he interrupted with a hint of iron in his voice. "You little know me, Robert, if you reckon me one to turn back from what I have begun—in especial, this matter which consummates the ambition of my life."

"But we—"

This time the iron was uppermost.

"Boy, you are essential to my plans. Much as I love you, I—But we'll not talk on that plane. I am none for threats. Let it suffice that you are not to mention the subject again."

He wheeled around and left me, and with his escort of tarry-breeks strung out behind him was soon buried in the undergrowth on the lower flanks of the hill.

The sun was past meridian when Peter and I induced Moira to abandon the unmarked mound, and to divert her mind we led her on a tramp to the shoulders of the Spyglass, where a score of the *James'* men already had felled a giant fir and were lopping the branches from the trunk preparatory to removing the bark. In the forest near by we killed a mess of birds, and Peter skilfully broiled them over an open fire, and after that, since she professed to enjoy the silence of the mountainside, we pressed on, beyond hearing of the ringing ax-blades, and finally came to the foot of the steep pinnacle of rock which was the lens of the Spyglass.

Here we would have halted, but Moira had heard the story of the watch the pirates maintained from the summit, and she insisted on completing the ascent, despite the lateness of the hour. And we, because we were for doing anything that would please her that day and relieve her grief, consented.

It was more difficult than it looked, and the sun was low in the west when we reached the platform at the top, stained and blackened by the beacon fires that had burned there. But the view was glorious. The island was spread out beneath us like a map on a table, from the Foremast Hill on our left all the way southward along the rocky spine of the west coast to Mizzenmast Hill and a cape to the west of that which old Martin had called Haulbowline Head. Eastward the irregular shore ran north and south to the indentation of Captain Kidd's Anchorage, the tree growth matted and thick except for several savannas midway of the island and the silvery loops of two or three small rivers.

We identified the masts of the *James,* rising above the headwaters of the North Inlet, and the opening in the trees north and east of Captain Kidd's Anchorage that was the site of the fort Flint had built. And then Moira cried out:

"Oh, blessed saints, will that be a ship? Do but see, Bob! Peter!"

She pointed eastward; and there, sure enough, was a ship, or rather, the tops'ls of a ship barely lifting over the horizon's rim. If it had not been for the fact that the sun's rays were striking level across the ocean floor, and so were reflected from the sheen of the canvas, we should never have seen it, not even with a glass.

"Aye, 'tis a ship," I said.

"*Ja*," nodded Peter. "It is Flint."

Moira shivered.

"Troth, and who would it be else?" she demanded. "There'll be no friends of us come a-calling, I'm thinking."

"It might be a King's ship—" I began.

"No, then," she denied, "if this island is gone all these years without the King's ships finding track of it, 'tis not like they will come upon it sudden in this moment."

"'Tis a ship indeed," I agreed unwillingly. "Aye, a full-rigged ship."

"*Ja,* a ship like Flint's," said Peter.

We were silent for an instant, the three of us, dazed by the suddenness with which our whole outlook on the future had been changed by this unexpected loom of tops'ls leagues away.

"He must have weathered the storm," I said foolishly.

"And now the red fighting will begin all over again," cried Moira. "My soul, will there not have been deaths enough for this treasure? Every piece of it must be specked with men's blood."

"We better tell Murray," said Peter, moving toward the lip of the rock platform.

"But how could Flint be back so soon?" I protested. "'Tis impossible, Peter. He could not—"

"He could, *ja,*" returned the Dutchman imperturbably. "Der storm was by in two glasses—andt der ship is yet maybe ten leagues off, *neen?*"

We descended the Spyglass in silence. Twilight overtook us in the forest at its base, and we were obliged to retrace our course with extreme caution, so that eight bells rang from the *Royal James*—so exact was the restored discipline on that stranded hulk—as we stepped from the trees on to the shore of the North Inlet and hailed for a boat.

My great-uncle met us at the gangway, immaculate in plum satin coat and blue plush breeches, white silk stockings and black pumps, silver-buckled, his hair neatly tied with a black silk ribbon.

"Well, well," he greeted us, "you have made a long day of it. I trust you are not overtired, sweet?"

This to Moira.

"I have delayed sitting to dinner in hopes that you would be here. You can see—" he waved an all-inclusive hand—"that we have not been idle aboard the *James*. We begin to look like a ship again, eh? Did you by chance see the new mizzen?"

"You better come to der cabin," said Peter abruptly.

"I beg your pardon?" answered Murray.

"We have something to tell you," I said. "It can not wait."

His eyes plumbed mine, and I think he knew in that instant what our news was. He clicked open his snuff-box and dusted a pinch delicately into his nostrils.

"So?" he murmured. "Sets the wind in that quarter!"

And he offered Moira his arm with the fine, stately dignity he achieved to perfection, and led the way aft to the main cabin.

"You may place the viands upon the table, Gunn," he said to the steward when we were seated. "We will serve ourselves."

He turned to Moira.

"I recommend this fish. 'Tis fresh-caught, and Scipio—" the remaining blackamoor—"is a master at such dishes; he hath stuffed it, you see, with greens he procured from the woods."

"We have scant time to eat, let alone to admire our food," I interposed roughly. "From the peak of the Spyglass at sunset we sighted the tops'ls of a ship in the east."

"I presume that you believe her to be the *Walrus?*" he returned.

"*Ja*," said Peter. "It is Flint."

"My faith, and who else would it?" asked Moira.

"Doubtless you are right," he assented. "Indeed, I do not question it. Our examination of the northern and eastern beaches today failed to disclose a trace of evidence to indicate what had become of the *Walrus*, and had she sunk some wreckage must have washed ashore. Yes, yes, my friends, our ill-luck is still with us. Flint rode out the storm. But that, Robert, is no reason why we should not secure the maximum of satisfaction from this tasty meal—all the more particularly so when we consider 'tis like to be the last for some days we shall eat in such comfortable surroundings."

"You take it coolly!" I exclaimed.

"And why not? 'Tis a disaster, I grant you, yet irritation will not aid me to redress it."

"You don't stay here, *neen?*" said Peter.

"Quite right, friend Peter. The *Royal James* in her present plight would be a death-trap. I shall abandon her tonight and shift to the fort Flint was so obliging as to construct for us by the anchorage."

"And the treasure?" I asked.

He held up his wineglass to the light and studied it reflectively.

"Obviously, we must be where the treasure is," he returned at length. "Or, if you please, put it the other way round: The treasure must be where we are. I foresee a busy night for our people."

Moira thrust out appealing hands toward him.

"Oh, sir, why won't ye just be after calling out to this ship when she comes and bid them take what they will and go? Sure, that would be better than—"

"Tut, tut," he rebuked her. "A part of this treasure is to supplement the eight hundred thousand pounds intended for your father's friends —and they, my lass, are King James' friends. You are a good Jacobite, I trust, and would not see our Cause deprived of a single doubloon that might buy muskets in Lyons or swordblades in Breda?"

"Ah, 'tis little enough I feel for King James or any of them that will have sent the *padre* to his doom!" she cried. "And what is a Jacobite or a Hanoverian, or what worth King George or King James, that you must be murdering and slaying and he that was a good man and kind—when he wasn't in liquor—should lie in heathen ground?"

She leaped up, quivering with passion lashed aflame.

"Jacobite! The toe of my boot to the word and them that use it! Little enough hath it meant to me but poverty and exile and the death of her that bore me and now—and now—the *padre*—and now—"

She fled from the cabin in tears, and her stateroom door slammed after her.

"Poor lass! Poor lass!" sighed my great-uncle. "It hath been a trying day for her. We must be lenient."

"You should be down on your knees, beseeching her forgiveness, you who wantonly dragged her into this danger!" I snarled at him.

"'Wantonly,' Robert?" he objected mildly. "Certes, you should know better by now. My reasons were of the best, my motives of the highest."

He rang the silver bell in front of him, and when Gunn appeared said—

"Send Coupeau to me."

Then he turned to me again—

"You, of all persons, Robert, have least cause to censure me for Mistress O'Donnell's presence."

"I have most!" I retorted hotly. "I am so unfortunate as to be related to you, and therefor must be in some measure a sharer of the obloquy attached to your deeds."

He wagged his head sadly.

"Words! What rash, unreasoning words will not youth sponsor in its blind prejudices! Peter, I appeal to you: Doth not my grandnephew lie in my debt for my conduct in arranging for him the opportunity to squire our little Irish maid?"

Peter drained a glass of brandy.

"You better not say any more, Murray," he grunted. "*Neen!* Maybe you say too much."

"I had supposed myself the model of diplomacy," protested my great-uncle.

Peter's little eyes twinkled behind their protective rolls of fat.

"*Ja*, you been pretty smart, Murray. But der smart feller, he has to look oudt or he gets too smart. *Ja!* Andt when he gets too smart he is in trouble."

Coupeau's hideous mask of a face showed in the companionway entrance.

"*Oui, m'sieu?*" he growled.

"Ah, Coupeau," answered Murray. "A strange sail approaches the island, perhaps Flint, perhaps another. To us it matters not. We must entrench ourselves ashore. The treasure and sufficient stores for two weeks' sojourn will be shifted to the stockaded fort on the hill north of Captain Kidd's Anchorage. The men must work all night again if necessary. Do you understand?"

"*Oui, m'sieu*," replied the gunner.

"That is well. You will rout them out at once."

"*Oui, m'sieu.*"

And Coupeau clumped off down the companionway. A moment later his hoarse voice split the quiet of the ship as he commenced to bark his orders.

"A stout fellow, Coupeau," commented my great-uncle. "I have never regretted the salvaging of him. But perhaps it would be as well if we went on deck and lent him moral support."

As a matter of fact, there was less disposition than we anticipated on the part of the crew to object to this new labor. And the reason was not far to seek. The transfer of the treasure to the fort by the Anchorage furnished them an opportunity to establish an intimacy of contact with it they had not known previously, an intimacy alluring, stimulating, discomposing. True, they already had transferred the entire cargo of the *Santissima Trinidad* once, had removed the half of it from the *Royal James* to the Dead Man's Chest, and only two days since had broken out the remainder for division with the *Walrus.*

But that was very different from shifting the squat, weighty, little chests and kegs and the canvas-jacketed bars overland in the darkness, along brush-paths dimly illuminated by occasional lanthorns and torches, into a corner of the log block-house which was the citadel of Flint's ramshackle fort—very different, too, from the realization that the treasure's well-nigh fabulous wealth was outside the charmed hull of the *Royal James,* where Murray's personality and the arbitrary divisions of rank and intellect had reared an insuperable barrier betwixt it and themselves, lying instead in a promiscuous heap without a door to guard it, where any one of them could gloat over its bright mysteries.

Peter and I, with Moira and Ben Gunn and Scipio, followed the main column of the evacuation about midnight. Coupeau had led the first contingent, some of whom we met returning to the ship, to fetch a second load of stores. My great-uncle was to come after us with these and the remainder of the crew, leaving behind on the *Royal James* only some twenty-odd men who had not yet recovered sufficiently from wounds received in the two actions with the *Santissima Trinidad* and the *Walrus* to permit of their removal, and who were made as comfortable as possible on the gundeck.

I noted uneasily that the groups who passed us were talking eagerly amongst themselves, with no appearance of the surliness to be expected normally from any sailors put to extra work, although they fell silent as soon as they saw who we were.

"They have never been drinking," I muttered to Peter.

"*Neen,*" he answered. "But they get drunk on der treasure."

"Do but see how it is a fell curse upon all who touch it," said Moira.
"Ah, blessed Virgin, that it were all in the depths of the ground where
God first planted it!"

Our misgivings were justified when we toiled up the sandy slopes
of the hill upon which the stockade was built. The glare of an immense
bonfire showed through the trees, and rude voices were chanting that
sinister sea-song which had been my introduction to the pirate broth-
erhood:

> "Fifteen men on the Dead Man's Chest—
> Yo-ho-ho, and a bottle of rum!
> Drink and the devil had done for the rest—
> Yo-ho-ho, and a bottle of rum!"

I had never heard it sung by the *James'* crew before.

As we approached the palisades we descried through the open-
ings a score or two of them, comical in their broad pantaloons, their
belts bristling with cutlasses and pistols, prancing around the fire like
Mohicans dancing a scalp.

They paid no attention to us, and we crossed the cleared area
inside to the door of the blockhouse, where Coupeau lounged against
the log wall.

"*M'sieu le capitaine* ees com'?" he inquired.

I told him yes.

"Ees com' queeck?" he insisted.

I shrugged my shoulders to this, and he grunted.

"Maybe so we mak' —— com' at those rrrascal," he suggested.

"Have they had any rum?" I asked suspiciously.

"*Non.* They have zee fire—and they see much trrreasure."

He paused.

"Maybe so you com'," he said, and without waiting for us to answer,
strode alone toward the fire.

I shoved Moira inside the blockhouse, and Peter and I started after
him. I made to draw a pistol, but Peter caught my arm.

"*Neen,*" he said. "We do this wit' our fists andt our voice, Bob—or
we don't do it at all."

Such were Coupeau's tactics—but he relied mostly upon his fists.
He waded into the dancers, smiting right and left, and Peter and I

came behind him. Several men reached for their cutlasses, but these we got to before they had time to draw steel. In the middle of the row Murray's voice flashed out from the shadows like a sword, and our opponents cowered away.

"'Sdeath," he drawled. "Will you fellows think to take advantage of me because I turn my back upon you for an hour or two?"

He came forward into the circle of light.

"I warned you no longer ago than last night," he went on icily. "It should have been sufficient. Coupeau!"

"Oui, m'sieu."

"Who began the trouble this time?"

The gunner fastened his awful visage upon the whitening faces of the group of trouble-makers.

"That man."

He pointed.

"Heem. Heem. Heem. Heem."

"Very good," said my great-uncle. "Most of us prefer to sleep, seeing that we confront the certainty of a busy morrow; but I have no wish to disappoint those who would amuse themselves tonight. Nay, I will provide entertainment for them. Take those five, Coupeau, and the fellows who broiled with them, and stand by whilst their followers lay on a hundred and fifty lashes with the cat for each."

There was an instant's silence, then a gasp of terror, and one man commenced to sob.

"Oh, Gawd, cap'n, sir, we'm can't stand no hun'erd'n' fufty lashes! No mortal man could. Doan't 'ee say it, sir! We'm'll crawl to 'ee, cap'n, sir, 'deed we will."

"You should have thought of that beforehand," replied Murray, unmoved.

"Not a hun'erd an' fifty, cap'n," pleaded a second man. "'Twill kill us, sure."

"I should not be surprised if it would," agreed my great-uncle, taking snuff. "In fact, were I in your shoes I should hope that it would. Take them away, Coupeau—out of earshot, if you please."

CHAPTER XIX

THE ATTACK ON THE STOCKADE

DAYLIGHT revealed the *Walrus* heading in toward the mouth of the Anchorage; but the smoke from our cooking-fires obviously puzzled her, and she heaved to and lowered a boat which pulled up the channel to investigate. 'Twas impossible from our hill-top to see what the boat's crew did; apparently they turned back so soon as they had convinced themselves the *James* was not lurking in ambush. And the *Walrus* took the boat in tow and bore off to the northward under full sail.

"She is bound for the North Inlet," commented Murray, pocketing his glass. "Flint will find the *James* and be with us again by mid-afternoon."

"When his battery will make short work of this gimcrack fortress," I said disagreeably.

"You are unduly pessimistic, Robert," he reproved me. "'Tis impossible for a vessel of the *Walrus'* draft to lie so that she can bring a full broadside to bear."

"Why not make terms with them?" I argued. "You have the eight hundred thousand pounds safe."

"I stated my opposing reasons last night to Mistress O'Donnell."

"But you had not then been compelled to flog five knaves to death," I objected. "This is no crew to fight a forlorn hope."

"They and their like have fought for me these thirty years," he replied placidly. "Nor do I consider the approaching struggle a forlorn hope. Let me involve Flint in an attack upon us here, and I promise you he'll not bring off enough men to work his ship. Also, you err in your first assertion, Robert. Only three of last night's mutineers have died. The other two are yet alive—albeit uncomfortable, I fancy; exceeding uncomfortable."

"And how they must love you!" I sneered.

"Fear me, you should say," he corrected. "As I have told you, I have developed my opportunities in life rather by stimulating men's fears than by angling for their affections. Affection, Robert—and the argument is applicable alike to that tender sentiment which arises periodically betwixt the sexes—is a most unchancy emotion. Fear, on the contrary, once aroused, is never forgotten."

"*Ja,*" said Peter, "andt from fear grows hate."

My great-uncle smiled.

"I find myself, as always, moved to admiration of the philosophy you have distilled from your wide range of experience, friend Peter," he answered. "But suffer me to remind you that, in the language of the alchemists, fear and hate are mutually reactive principles, the one consuming and neutralizing the other."

Peter chewed a grass-stem without replying, and after a courteous pause to allow him ample opportunity, Murray inquired:

"Shall we ascertain if Mistress O'Donnell hath completed her toilet? I own to a normal morning hunger."

"Your mention of her is the mightiest argument for a settlement with Flint," I protested. "What hope is there for her, if you—"

"Robert," he interrupted gently, "you speak to no purpose. The maid's entire future is entangled with my success—and of my success there can be no reasonable doubt. What? Shall I bow the knee to that misbegotten crew of gallowscheats aboard the *Walrus?* You have seen them!"

His voice rose.

"You know how much of discipline there is amongst them. Do you think that men of their stamp can overcome me? 'Tis incredible, I say! I can not fail."

"*Ja,*" said Peter, spitting out his grass-stem. "Once you failed."

"Failure is a word of relative significance," retorted my great-uncle. "By that which you term failure, Peter, I was impelled to adopt the career which hath nourished me to this pitch, that I am the center of a conspiracy which shall overturn kingdoms. Failure! You will be telling me next that I am lacking in godliness!"

"*Ja,*" said Peter, unperturbed.

"I concede the point!" exclaimed my great-uncle, chuckling. "And seeing that we are at last in agreement upon one point, let us sink our other differences in a pot of chocolate."

There was no more to be said, and however unwillingly, Peter and I were constrained to do all that we could to aid in strengthening the position. 'Twas Peter's idea that the men be set to digging shallow pits behind the stockade to provide additional shelter against musketry fire from the border of woods and undergrowth at the base of the hill. 'Twas likewise Peter who suggested, vastly to her indignation, that we construct for Moira a shot-proof cubby-hole of treasure chests and kegs in one corner of the blockhouse.

We had scarce finished these preparations when the *Walrus* reappeared and tacked up the Anchorage to the elbow where it bends sharply around the larger island which covers the entrance. Farther she was unable to go because of shoal water, and for the same reason she was obliged to anchor practically bow on to us, which meant that, as Murray had predicted, she could train on the hilltop only her chase-guns and two or three of the carronades mounted for'ard on her gundeck. But she showed no immediate disposition to use her battery. Her people seemed to be concerned entirely with the task of disembarkation, and in the space of a glass we reckoned that all of a hundred and fifty men were landed and straggled irregularly into the forest.

Then there was a lull in Flint's activities, and we made our final dispositions for the anticipated attack. Murray stationed his men all around the circuit of the stockade, except for those included in what I have termed the after-guard. These fellows, about twenty in number, were held in the blockhouse as a reserve to be thrown to the support of any part of our line which might require assistance. Murray himself with Coupeau, Peter and I stood in the center of the enclosure where he could keep watch upon all that went on.

The afternoon was warm and drowsy. The *Walrus* looked like a toy ship on the oily-smooth surface of the inlet. There was not a sign of life aboard her, and the forest that spread betwixt us and the shore hugged silently whatever secrets it covered.

My great-uncle frowned thoughtfully.

"This is not like Flint," he remarked. "He must always fly bull-headed to the attack."

The words were hardly out of his mouth when a shout came from the side of the stockade fronting the inlet.

"Here be Flint's Redhead!"

And conflicting cries:

"Shoot mun!"

"'Tis flag o' truce!"

"Ta lucky lad!"

We ran forward to the stockade, bidding the men withhold their fire, and Peter boosted me up on the cross-bar that bound the logs together. From this height I could survey the denuded slopes of the hill and the jungle growth of scrub trees and bush that cinctured it. And forth from the forest wall projected the unmistakable flaming locks of Darby McGraw, with one arm which flourished diligently what once had been a white shirt. At the first glimpse of me he scrambled into the open.

"Will ye be letting me come in, Master Bob?" he called.

"Why, that depends," I answered him. "Are you for spying upon us?"

"Sure, the thought was never in me mind. I ha' a message for himself."

"Who?"

"Himself—him that's uncle to ye."

"Well, seeing that we hear each other excellently as we are, suppose you speak your message from the spot you stand on," I said.

"Troth, that will suit me fine," he replied with alacrity. "And 'tis easy said. Flint will ha' Cap'n Murray shift the treasure to the foot of the hill, and that done, the *Walrus* will take it and go. If he won't, we'll be takin' it anyways—or if by chance we don't, we'll blow the *James* out o' the water and leave ye all marooned."

He waxed confidential.

"Aye, and he means that same, Master Bob. Ye may take me word for it. We're a wild, angry crew for the surprize ye give us in the dark."

"'Twas a fit reward for your treachery, Darby," I said with some heat.

He hung his head, digging with his toe in the sand.

"Ah, but that's what pirates will be doing," he said. "And what way will there be kindness betwixt men if they do be fighting? Or wanting, the one, what the other has?"

"Maybe we haven't the treasure here at all," I suggested.

"We know dif'rent. The wounded men in the *James* were afther tellin' us."

I looked down inquiringly at my great-uncle.

"If they seek terms, they are uncertain of success," he said. "Send the boy away."

"But if they destroy the *James?*"

"First they will attack—and after that we will deal with the problem of protecting the ship."

And as I hesitated—

"Be so good as to answer him at once, Robert, or I shall have him shot as he stands."

"Go back, Darby," I called. "Captain Murray will have none of your offer."

"God save us!" he exclaimed involuntarily. "I'm thinkin' that will be the death of many a tall feller, Master Bob. Well, good luck to ye and to Master Peter and the elegant young maid. If we all come out safe—"

My great-uncle leaped upon a tree-stump and fired a pistol over Darby's head. The boy stood motionless a moment, mouth agape.

"The old devil!" he howled then, and fled down the hillside for all he was worth.

Flint did not wait to receive Murray's verbal answer; that pistol-shot was sufficiently explicit. Three musket-shots echoed it from the foot of the hill, and at once there was a renewed bustle of men on the fo'c'sle of the *Walrus*. A puff of white smoke blew up from the deck, and the crack of a long twelve started myriads of seabirds from the seaward marshes. The shot sang over us and crashed into the forest beyond. The other chase-gun bowled a shot into the enclosure, where it simply buried itself in the soft sand. Two carronades, with lower mounts and shorter range, discharged missiles that fell short of the stockade. And that first salvo might pass for a chronology of the bombardment to which we were subjected until sunset.

One man was killed, and no material damage was done. The carronades were unable to reach the blockhouse with their heavier shot, and the Long Toms lacked the power to penetrate the green wood of the walls. Most of the round-shot plumped into the sand. Three posts of the stockade were knocked over and promptly set up again. That was all. The noise was most impressive, with the echoes reverberating across the island from the sounding-board of the Spyglass, but the net result was to imbue me with a confidence I had not previously entertained. When darkness intervened and the firing ceased we felt that we had been the winners of the first bout of the struggle.

In the mean time we had not seen a trace of the landing-party from the *Walrus,* and as the night shut down we all peered curiously through the posts of the stockade, expecting momentarily to discover a rush of crouching figures. But hour after hour passed without a sound to disturb the silence, and even Murray, whose nerves were of forged steel, became uneasy as he up-ended the hour-glass for the third time since sunset and decided to inspect the circuit of the defenses.

"There is another hand than Flint's behind these Fabian tactics," he observed. "Perhaps John Silver's. 'Tis a clever rogue, and a cunning. We can not be too vigilant."

Moira, poor lass, was asleep beneath the stack of gold and silver inside the blockhouse. Ben Gunn and black Scipio, equally frightened, were huddled on the doorstep; and the men of the after-guard were sprawled in the sand, some of them asleep, some of them gambling— the pirates of both crews were inveterate gamblers—at pitch-penny or with pebbles and shells or at a kind of mumbletypeg with their clasp-knives.

Coupeau joined us on the southern arc of the stockade. He reported dim flittings and shadowy movements on the lower hillside, but naught in the nature of an advance or a threat of one. Elsewhere the men rose from their burrows and sullenly or stupidly, according to their dispositions, affirmed they had seen no enemies. On the north side we came to a pit which was empty, and in the one next to it a man lay on his stomach as if asleep.

Murray prodded him with his sword, and the fellow groaned, but did not stir.

"What is the matter with this man?" demanded my great-uncle.

"Please, zur, 'tis Job Pytchens," answered the man next beyond.

"I asked what was the matter with him," said my great-uncle coldly.

"He'm wur one o' they as had a hun'erd 'n' fufty lashes, cap'n, zur."

I shuddered. My great-uncle took snuff.

"And who is gone from this vacant place?" he pressed.

"Tom Morphew, zur. He'm dead, zur."

"Was he shot?"

"No, zur, cap'n. He'm had a hun'erd 'n' fufty lashes, too."

"Where is he?"

There was a barely appreciable pause.

"Please, zur, us buried him," the man answered.

"Where?"

The man waved an arm vaguely over the sandy top of the hill.

"Ah! Well, you will leave unburied the next man who dies, be he Job or another—else I shall have the cat administered to all of you who have abandoned your posts without permission."

"'Iss, zur. Thank 'ee, zur," replied the man—but there was no thanks in his snarling voice; his face was masked by the darkness.

"Stap me," said Murray, turning away, "but these rascals are becoming as slack as Flint's tattertails!"

Across the clearing a musket exploded. Then another and another. A volley crackled from the lower slopes, and our men replied. A hoarse yelling underscored the firing.

"At last!"

Murray's voice vibrated with exultation.

"Now we shall scoop the rogues like so many grains of sand. The fools! A night attack is fatal with undisciplined men."

We ran past the blockhouse, where the after-guard were scrambling to their feet and Moira was wringing her hands in the doorway.

"Ye won't be leaving me!" she cried to us.

"You must remain under cover, my dear," said my uncle kindly. "'Twould distress all of us had we to be concerned for your safety."

"'Tis not lead or steel I will be fearful of," says she, "but the cruel memories that do be creeping from the treasure boxes. My troth, I'd liefer be here in the open than within."

My great-uncle hesitated, plainly exasperated by her persistence in remaining outside.

"Where is Gunn?" he asked.

"Oh, him!"

Moira's laughter trilled as lightly as if there were no messengers of death in the air.

"He's where ye would have put me first—under the treasure. And he's welcome to it."

"Be that as it may," he snapped, giving rein to his exasperation, "here you shall not stay, my lass, and we are pressed—"

A great roar of firing burst out upon the northern front of the stockade, and mingled with the reports of the muskets were shouts of:

"Down arms, *Jameses!*"

"Step aside, *James* lads!"

"All we want is old Murray!"

And a wailing voice cried over and over again—

"Here be Tom Morphew 'n' his bloody back, mates!"

The firing sputtered and dwindled and was succeeded by a prodigious scuffling and clatter of cutlasses.

"We'll do 'ee no harm, *Jameses!*"

And now I recognized Silver's voice.

"Strike arms, *Jameses!*"

Three men, one of them with a broken arm, raced up to us.

"Long John's in," sobbed one.

"Tom Morphew let 'em in," panted a second.

"Excellently planned," drawled Murray.

I heard the click of his snuffbox.

"Yet observe how fate hath tricked our opponents," he went on. "They timed their second attack to catch me on the southern side of the stockade, whereas, thanks to the perversity of womankind, I am strategically disposed to exploit the disorder which attends their success. I think we shall teach the clever Master Silver a lesson."

"Yes, if your men are loyal," I said angrily.

"Any crew are loyal in victory, Robert," he answered.

"*Ja*," spoke Peter, "but you better not let dot feller talk about his bloody back."

"You are squeamish, it seems, Peter," murmured my great-uncle. "Well, I shall even seek to humor you. Coupeau!"

His voice hardened.

"*Oui, m'sieu.*"

The gunner stepped from the huddled ranks of the after-guard.

"We attack."

But indeed the attack was made upon us. We had not advanced four paces from the shelter of the blockhouse when fifty or sixty of the invaders stormed out of the night, howling and waving their cutlasses. We fired one smashing volley that dropped a fourth of them, and charged. A few pistol-shots met us, but most of the *Walrus'* men had discarded their muskets, preferring to fight sailor-fashion with the cutlass, and they were utterly disheartened by the unexpectedness of the reception we gave them.

Murray's slender dress-sword was a bodkin of death which pricked a path through the densest ranks. On one side of him Peter swung a clubbed musket which shattered heads and limbs at every step. On his other side Coupeau wielded a cutlass with equal effect.

A yellow crescent moon was riding over the treetops, and we halted in the gap the attackers had torn in the stockade to survey our situation by its light. Half-way down the hill a group of the *Walrus'* men rallied and commenced to fire up at us; and Coupeau was for pushing after them, but my great-uncle checked him.

"No, no, Coupeau! Yonder is John Silver, astraddle of the stockade. See, he is helping up another fellow. They have been cut off by our charge, and if you please, we'll deal with them first."

I will admit a pang of sympathy for Silver. He was not more than twenty yards from us, and by dint of well-nigh incredible efforts, with the other man to boost him, he had succeeded in scaling the stockade and was sitting there, with his one leg dangling inside. When we discovered him he started to swing his leg over the top, evidently intending to abandon his companion. But whether because of something the other man said or because he feared he must injure himself in dropping the eight feet to the ground without any one to check his fall, he abruptly changed his mind and faced about toward us very resolutely, seizing hold of the crutch which hung from his neck by its thong.

The man at the foot of the stockade gathered himself together like a coiling serpent and plucked a long knife from his belt. He had been in the shadow until then, but now the moonlight shone over his torso and we recognized him for the blind man, Pew. He had lost his green eyeshade, and his pockmarked face was cadaverous in the yellow glow. His eyes were open, and they seemed to smolder dully as they strained at us. His knife glinted in his hand.

"Will you be assisted down and be hanged whole, or must we cut you down, Silver?" hailed Murray.

He, like the rest of us, ignored the blind man. Our attention was fixed upon Silver, his broad face very calm in the moonlight.

"Them there ain't exackly tempting terms, Cap'n Murray, sir," Silver answered temperately. "Couldn't ye be a mite more generous?"

"I am serving you a dish no more highly sauced than that you intended for me," returned my great-uncle dryly.

"Now, sir; now, sir," remonstrated Silver. "How can ye say that? All we done was to try and persuade ye to give us our share o' the treasure—you havin' eight hundred thousand pound stowed away special, accordin' to your own story. And if we come in by the back door a'ter it, why that was so's we'd hurt ye least."

"You'd argue yourself to a block of ice in Hell, Silver," rejoined my great-uncle amusedly. "Throw down that crutch! Drop that knife, you, sirrah, Pew—or whatever your name is!"

Sword in hand, he advanced ahead of the rest of us, who were strung out all the way from the gap in the stockade. Coupeau was at his elbow, and Peter and I close behind.

"Come," he adjured them a second time. "I'm in no mood to talk terms, and if you delay 'twill make your end the more painful."

Silver's face went livid in the moonlight.

"Aye," rasped the one-legged man, "ye'll lash us bloody-raw like the lads as let us in tonight."

And as Murray continued to advance, he struck out with his crutch.

"Keep off," he shrieked. "Keep off!" And then: "I can't reach him, Ezra. Let him have it!"

Pew crouched with his knife-hand drawn back.

"Aye, it takes blind Pew to let him have it," he croaked in his hateful voice.

His hand jerked forward. There was a flash in the moonlight, and my great-uncle staggered, the flung knife buried to the hilt in his side.

"I am stabbed," he gasped.

Silver brandished his crutch over his head.

"Pew's stabbed Murray!" he shouted. "Come on, *Walruses!* Lay off, ye *James* lads—we'll not harm ye, mates. Treasure for all, and no more tyranny!"

Peter and I caught my great-uncle as he fell. Coupeau jumped at the blind man with a bellow of rage, cutlass raised to strike; but as he came within reach Silver poised his crutch like a spear, leaned over and drove the sharp spike of the ferrule through the gunner's eye into the brain. Coupeau dropped in his tracks.

"I ha' done for Coupeau," Silver shouted again. "Don't make Long John do it all, lads!"

There was such a rush of enemies, such a howl of exultation, as took my breath away.

"Do you hold Murray, Peter," I said. "I'll finish that precious pair."

And I ran in at Pew, albeit more warily than Coupeau; but the blind man—and certes, if he was blind his hearing was so marvelous as to make up for it—retained a clubbed pistol, which was a serviceable weapon at close quarters, and Silver covered him overhead with that deadly crutch. I shouted to the after-guard to shoot them, but our people had not reloaded their pieces, and many were already engaged with the party we had just driven out, who swarmed in again through the same gap. Those of the *James'* men who were nearest were palpably lukewarm, and Silver, atop of the stockade, perceiving his advantage, thrust his crutch at me and continued trumpeting his rallying-cries.

"Murray's a goner, mates! Coupeau's shark-bait! There's only the two Buckskins left. Go easy wi' they *Jameses.* Naught for ye to fight about, *James* lads! We'll divide square with ye."

Men swirled toward us from all sides of the stockade, the *James'* crew mingled with the *Walrus'* and where our people fought at all 'twas faint-heartedly and to no purpose. We were pressed back, and presently were put to it to avoid being surrounded.

"We go to der house, Bob," squeaked Peter. "Der *James* men don't fight for us no more."

He had Murray's limp body slung over one shoulder and still retained the iron barrel of his musket—the stock had been demolished; but he ran easily beside me through the sand.

There was tremendous confusion within the stockade enclosure, and but for this and a considerate cloud which draped the new-risen moon we should never have gained the blockhouse. Our men disappeared at every yard. Two were slain in the beginning of the retreat, and the continuous cries of "stand off, *Jameses*—us won't hurt 'ee," sapped the remainder of such loyalty as had survived the vicissitudes of the last few days.

We reached the blockhouse alone on the side opposite the door, and circled it cautiously, no little concerned for Moira's safety, for pistols were popping and cutlasses clashing in several directions close at hand. With the moon obscured we could not see a musket's length ahead, and as I turned in toward the black oblong of the doorway I tripped over a corpse.

"'Tis on your own head your death will be, my man," said a cool voice. "I can hear you fine, and if you're not after—"

"Moira!" I exclaimed.

"And is it you, Bob? Oh, blessed saints, but I'm that glad. I thought you were—Is that Peter?"

"*Ja*," said Peter.

"And what will ye have on your shoulder? A dead man? Is it him I shot a few minutes back?"

"'Tis Captain Murray," I answered, making way for Peter.

"Oh, Queen of Heaven! Sure, we're in bad case."

"We are," I assented grimly as I followed Peter inside. "Have you a light?"

She took a lanthorn from under a cloth, and its scanty rays played hide-and-seek with the shadows over the rude log walls and the piles of rum barrels and kegs of hard-tack and the clumsy stack of treasure.

"Where are Ben Gunn and Scipio?" I asked.

"They made off after I shot him that lies outside. They were mightily feared of what Captain Flint would be doing to them did he find them here, and one of his men dead at the door."

Peter laid my great-uncle gently upon the earthen floor—there was no softer bed—and began cutting away the garments from around the hilt of the knife, which was still fixed in his right side.

"And why didn't you go with them?" I asked. She gave me an indignant look.

"And be leaving the two of ye! I am not that kind of friend, Bob."

Peter looked up from his task.

"You got to watch dot door, Bob. Andt, Moira, you bring me some rum. Maybe Murray gets back his sense before—"

I suddenly found myself unwilling to believe it could be so.

"He can't, Peter!"

"*Ja*," replied the Dutchman patiently. "Pretty soon he goes. He bleeds inside."

I stumbled to the doorway with my head in a whirl. Murray dying? 'Twas incredible! That tremendous personality, so masterful, so aloof, dominating all with whom he came in contact, saltily compounded of wickedness, greatness, wisdom and naive vanity! And explain it how you will, I suddenly discovered an admiration for him which had been growing for months beneath my surface resentment. Up to this moment I had detested him. But I choked now at the thought of his death. Whatever he was, he was no coward. And there was about his end in this sordid, haphazard fashion, stabbed by a blind man in the dark, a redeeming touch of high tragedy. He, whose ambitions had vaulted the stars, to perish by the hand of Pew! And in a moment when apparently he had snatched victory from defeat!

Mechanically I carried chests of gold and silver ingots from the heap of treasure and built a barricade across the doorway. There were several spare muskets and pistols, and I loaded these and placed them handy, then knelt behind the barricade and waited for what was to come. But nothing came. Feet shush-shushed in the sand all around the blockhouse; voices called, questioned and argued; an occasional shot was fired—no more. Flint's triumph had been too amazingly complete for him to grasp, and evidently there were dissensions in the pirates' ranks as to what the next step should be.

The hour-glass we had fetched from the *Royal James* stood by the door, and I remember that I turned it twice before Peter tapped my shoulder.

"He wants you," he said.

Murray lay with his head in Moira's lap. On his face was stamped a waxy pallor. His nostrils were sunken and pinched in. A crimson froth showed at the corner of his mouth. But his tawny eyes blazed with the unconquerable fire of his spirit. As I stooped over him a mocking gleam radiated from their black depths, and his lips moved in almost voiceless speech.

"Sorry, eh?"

I nodded, and the mockery became more pronounced.

"Would have—won you—boy—in—time."

Moira wiped the dreadful bubbles from his lips.

"You—won't—carry—out—plot?" he asked.

"'Twould be dishonest to promise," I answered. "And I doubt if we are like to live much longer than you." The fingers of one hand fluttered strangely.

"Tut, boy—never—lose hope. Win—yet—myself."

His colorless lips parted in a ghastly smile at the shocked disbelief in my face.

"This—will be—end—of Flint. Kill me—kill himself."

His fingers fluttered again, and Moira whispered—

"'Twill be his snuffbox he's after wanting, Bob."

And as I fumbled for it in the wreck of his coat she added—

"But 'twill be his death does he use it the once."

I hesitated, but the look in his eyes impelled me to give it to him. "Good lad!"

And his fingers closed lovingly on the jeweled trinket, picking at the lid he was wont to click open and shut in moments of perplexity. The tawny eyes flirted toward Moira.

"Take care—maid—good blood—in—her. Family, Robert—breeding—landmarks in—mad world."

"I'll do what I can," I promised, seeing he expected an answer.

"Might do—worse—or more," he replied with the shadow of a smile. "Pew's knife—kept you—being—duke—Moira—"

A pause whilst Moira wiped his mouth.

"A mad world," he repeated. "What will—Prince Charles—say?"

His eyes clouded, and he murmured a snatch of song, one of those ranting Jacobite ballads that spread like wildfire after the '45—

> "Cope sent a challenge frae Dunbar,
> 'Charlie, meet me an ye daur'—"

A coughing fit interrupted him, weakened him so I thought he was sped; but the ghostly voice went on with a hint of the gay, reckless tune:

> "Hey, Johnnie Cope, are ye waukin' yet?
> Or are your drums a-beatin' yet?
> If ye waur waukin' I wad—"

His voice strengthened.

"Ah, your Royal Highness! The procession is ordered—the heralds —waiting—my Lords—Commons—"

He struggled so to rise that to save him I propped him against my shoulder.

"A glad day—this—and long coming. Do you use snuff—sir? 'Tis Rip-Rap—a sound brand."

He opened the box and raised a pinch to his nostrils.

"A glad day—sir—but a mad world."

And so he died.

CHAPTER XX

PRISONERS

"AHOY, the blockhouse!"

Moira stayed her weeping, and I rose from my knees as the hail thundered from the night.

"Dot's Flint," whispered Peter. "You talk to him, Bob, *ja.*"

"What is it?" I shouted back.

"Is Murray with ye?"

"He's dead," I answered after a moment of reflection.

"And that's ———— —— lucky for him! Here's Tom Morphew ready to give him a taste of the cat."

A shrill howl echoed the words.

"Don't 'ee believe mun, Cap'n Flint! 'Tis all a lie! And 'ee promised I should ha' t' beatin' o' mun."

"'Tis true," I said wearily. "After sunrise you can send in a man to see for himself."

"Ah!" jeered Flint. "But ye see I'm not waiting for sunup or moon-set or aught else, my Buckskin. We know how many o' ye there are; and if ye don't surrender, why, we'll put a torch to the blockhouse and roast ye out. Fire won't hurt gold and silver, but 'tain't friendly to live meat."

"'Twill cost you something first," I retorted.

"Not so much as ye might think."

"Dot's right," squeaked Peter beside me. "*Ja*, you better make a bargain wit' him, Bob."

"A bargain," I repeated. "What on earth can we bargain with?"

"Der treasure on der Dead Man's Chest."

"But that is—"

I turned to Moira.

"In a manner of speaking, that treasure is yours. 'Twas in your father's name, to be held in trust for others. Are you willing—"

"My faith, any cause will be the better without it," she interrupted. "What has it done but bring bloodshed and suffering upon all who trafficked in it? If it will just win us our lives, Bob, 'twill be the one good deed to its credit."

"Time's runnin' short," shouted Flint. "If ye won't surrender we'll start the fagots."

"Suit yourself," I replied with as much confidence as I could muster. "There are three of us here, and 'tis we know where the treasure lies on the Dead Man's Chest. If you won't even promise our lives we'll make the bitterest fight we can and carry the secret with us."

There was a gabble of protest at this, several others joining their voices to Flint's, among them Silver.

"Naught's been said o' slayin' ye," declared Flint. "Give up the treasure, and we'll part friends."

"Aye, aye, Master Ormerod," called Silver. "Cap'n Flint puts it straight. There ain't a man of us would wish to be your enemy."

I looked hopelessly at Peter.

"What more can we win?" I asked. "'Tis a mockery to place credence in their promises."

"*Ja*," nodded Peter. "We don't trust 'em. But we know dot, Bob. We don't be fooled. Andt now anyway we get off alive. Afterwards—"

He shrugged his mountainous shoulders.

"If we do but get off this terrible island we are that much improved in our circumstances!" exclaimed Moira. "Glory, but I'll wear the skin from me knees when I see another woman's face—not that I'm ungrateful to the two of ye here, that are as brave cavaliers as any maid ever owed her all to."

What she said set me to pondering again, and I called to Flint—

"Mistress O'Donnell must have every consideration she is accustomed to, with decent lodging in the cabin and we two to attend her."

"Gut me!" roared Flint. "D'ye think we conduct a nunnery aboard the *Walrus?*"

"I am thinking she is a young maid by her lone, which is hard enough, let be she must dwell with pirates," I answered.

"There's Rule Four of our Articles," he sneered. "Ye will ha' heard it before. It should be assurance for any maid."

"You have heard my terms," I said. "Take them or leave them. There's eight hundred thousand pounds to be gained from treating us kindly. If you do not so, as sure as I am here we will die, the three of us, before we yield you the secret—and you should know the years 'twill require to dig over the Dead Man's Chest."

"We'll take you," he replied ill-naturedly. "And such a argufying swab I never listened to or will again, —— my eyes. Are ye fixed in your mind, Buckskin?"

"Yes."

"Drop your arms and bide where ye are, then. We're comin' in to look ye over."

Torches flickered around the circuit of the stockade, and as they drew nearer Peter and I tore down the barricade of treasure I had built across the doorway. Figures appeared in the wavy light, naked to the waist, scratched by the jungle growth; uncouth, grizzled faces lowered at us.

"Keep back," I warned them. "We'll let no man in until Captain Flint is here."

"Careful, ain't ye, Buckskin?" he mocked me from behind a clump of pirates. "Make way, shipmates. Ye'll all ha' a chance to see the treasure, soon or late, and we'll share in it equal and regular, accordin' to the Articles."

The group split to make way for him, and he strode up to the door. Bones was with him, and Silver, and the man they called Black Dog, who carried a torch, as did Bones. And behind them all limped an awful creature, whose grimy face was a mask of pain, whose bare back and flanks were crisscrossed with festering welts. In one hand he held a cat-o'-nine-tails, the pendent rope lashes with their jagged knots stained a dark claret hue.

Bones flourished his torch as they entered the low door, and the light shone into every corner of the big hut.

"Is that Murray?"

He pointed to the body that lay beneath the hacked remnants of the plum satin coat which served as shroud.

"Yes," I said, and Moira shrank betwixt Peter and me as they crowded forward, staring open-mouthed at the cold clay that represented the man they had so feared and hated.

"Gut me," swore Flint. "I never thought to see Murray lyin' stark."

Silver's eyes glinted from his slab of a face.

"He don't figure much now, do he, mates?" he said.

"Let's have a look at him," spoke up Bones abruptly. "Here, Black Dog, bring up your light, too."

The man with the sore back limped after them, drawing the tails of his cat through the fingers of one hand with a kind of lingering caress.

"Let me at mun," he muttered. "I'll flay mun, I will! I'll learn mun t' murder sailormen. Five o' us, and—"

Bones brushed off the plum satin coat with one toe, and Murray's gaunt white face smiled up at them, faintly satirical, the snuff-box still clutched in one hand.

"—— me, 'tis so he looked ever!" gasped Flint.

"'Tain't right nor natural," said Bones. "He looks like he knowed we was here—and couldn't harm him none."

Silver said nothing, peering down at the dead man with a puzzled frown as if he were trying to read something that was hidden behind the impassive features.

"He'll look dif'rent when I lash mun," whined the man with the cat, pushing past Black Dog. "Wait till t' cat slices into t' back o' mum, cap'n. I'll cut t' grin off'n t' devil's face o' mun."

'Twas Silver caught the poor fellow's arm as it was raised to strike.

"No, no, Tom!" he cried. "Murray's dead."

"Dead?" answered the man dazedly. "But 'ee promised I should ha' t' beatin' o' mun!"

"Aye, Tom; but ye can't beat a dead man."

"Why? He beat me till I was like t' die. He beat three o' my mates till they died, an' Job Pytchens is a-dyin' out the sand right now."

But Flint himself snatched the cat from the man's grasp with unaffected horror.

"Ye can't beat a dead man, Tom," insisted the *Walrus'* captain. "'Tis bad luck. And look at the good luck we ha' had since we found Darby McGraw! I can tell ye, mates, I'm a-going to hang on to my luck."

Bones growled assent, and Silver added—

"Aye, aye, cap'n; and if ye'll be guided by me ye'll lose no time in puttin' Murray underground."

They all exchanged superstitious glances, and Bones said hoarsely—

"He *were* close to bein' more'n human, weren't he?"

"They do say as how ye can chain down a ha'nt by drivin' a stake through the body," suggested Black Dog—and he shook so that his torch scattered sparks.

"Ye couldn't pin Murray down that way if he was of a mind to ha'nt ye," answered Silver. "Not that I believe in ha'nts myself."

"It's bad luck to mutilate the dead," objected Flint. "No, no, we'll bury him quick and be done with it."

"But 'ee promised I was t' beat mun," sobbed Tom Morphew. "I let 'ee in, Long John, and 'ee promised!"

"How was I to know he'd be dead?" returned Silver. "Don't ye take on so, Tom. We'll give ye a double handful o' onzas for what ye done, and when your back's well ye'll ha' a rare spree wi' the yellow boys, eh?"

But Morphew refused to be comforted. He limped from the hut, trailing his whip behind him.

"'Tisn't goold I want," he wept. "'Tis to lay my lash to t' back o' mun. Aye! Till he do be bloody raw, same as Job Pytchens and they other lads as is under sod. Oh, my pore back!"

There was an interval of silence after he was gone.

"It's bad luck to touch the dead," reaffirmed Flint. "No, no, the thing to do is to bury him quick. You take half a dozen men, Bill, and plant him anywhere—so's he's deep enough."

"And what about the treasure?" called one of the men by the door.

"Aye, aye," chimed in a second. "When do we shift it aboard and divvy up?"

Flint stroked his chin, considering.

"Why, there's no hurry about the treasure, mates," he answered finally. "'Tis safe here. What we all need now is a dram o' rum and two watches below."

There was a general murmur of assent with this sentiment, and he crooked his finger at me.

"Come along, Buckskin. We'll put the three o' ye aboardship, out o' harm's way, seein' as ye're so precious o' your skins. Long John, I'll leave it to ye to guard the prisoners. Give the girl a stateroom for herself—less'n ye might wish to share it, Buckskin?" he added with a leer that fetched a ruddy tide to Moira's cheeks.

He guffawed.

"Dainty, ain't ye, my lass? Well, the *Walrus* is a pirate, not a private man-o-war, and maybe ye'll learn a thing or two."

Silver motioned us to precede him into the night, and as we passed out he gathered together a party of men who formed loosely around us.

"If so be as ye'll give me your word to come peaceable, Master Ormerod, I can make things easier for ye," he offered when we were clear of the hut.

"What do you say, Peter?" I asked the Dutchman.

"*Ja.*"

"That's enough for me," announced Silver cheerfully. "And very sensible of ye, too, gentlemen. Not quite so fast. I'm only a crippled sailorman, and I ha' labored hard this night. Aye, it were such a seesaw o' fortune as kep' my heart a-poppin' in my throat. I thought ye had me on the stockade; but there's none like Pew wi' the knife, and he can smell his man when he can't see him. Well, well, who'd ha' s'posed when we met in New York we'd come to aught like this, Master Ormerod?"

I lacked the heart to answer him, and we stumbled through the woods in silence to the shore of the Anchorage. Here one of the *Walrus*' boats was launched, and we were rowed out to where she lay, her hull squatting like a rock in the quiet water. Men hailed us from her deck, a whip was sent down for Silver's convenience, and the rest of us climbed the side ladder, Moira as agile as any after her months at sea.

"Here we are, safe and snug on the old *Walrus*," remarked Silver, still aggressively cheery; "and them as is here can call theirselves fortunate, 'cause there's a plenty as ha' kept Murray company. Aye, blast me for a swab, but it ha' been a bloody night. Get for'ard, mates."

This to the men who had come off with us.

"I'll see to the pris'ners. Now then, gentlemen—*and* mistress—you come along wi' me, and I'll make ye all as comf'table as if ye was in a Bristol packet."

He prodded a muscular forefinger into my chest.

"You mind that, Master Ormerod. You mind that Long John was your friend. 'Cause why, says you? 'Cause there's never a man could see through the sand in the hourglass, could he now? And we'll ha' queer times ahead o' us—aye, queer times. How queer, says you? Ah, how'm I to know? All I says, and I stands on my words, is there'll be queer times—and you mind Long John was kindly and stood your friend, hearty and free. D'ye see?"

He plainly desired an answer, although I was not very certain of what he was driving at with this rigmarole.

"I'm afraid I don't," I said shortly.

He cocked his head on one side.

"Ye don't? Humph, there's things best left unsaid, but I'll put this to ye. Here's the *Walrus,* and here's a treasure, and here's Flint, and here's maybe twelvescore lads as don't all think alike, and here's Bill Bones—and here's me. A goodish bit might happen, my master. And who's to say what will start it a-happenin'? Not me! Nor who might come out on top a'terwards."

And with a parting wink he stumped aft, crooking his finger in sign that we should follow him across the untidy deck.

"Glory!" sniffed Moira, her nose in air. "This will be more the like of a stable than a ship."

She did not exaggerate. The *Walrus* was dirtier than she had been the night Peter and I were committed to her as hostages. Her decks were foul with grease and all manner of filth; her paint was cracked and peeling; a cloud of flies buzzed around a tub of fish-guts which nobody would take the trouble to cast overside; from an open hatch poured a sour, acrid stench. A strange contrast with the *Royal James!*

Inside the companionway under the poop we tripped over the

usual litter of broken bottles, pistol-flints and odds and ends of cast-off clothing. Silver balanced himself on his crutch against the wall, struck flint and steel to a slowmatch and ignited the wick of a whale-oil lanthorn which depended from a hook. Holding this above his head, he surveyed the double line of stateroom doors, very similar to the plan of the cabin quarters of the *James*.

"Room for all," he pronounced. "This here to larboard is Flint's, and Bones' berth's opposite. T'others are full o' junk, but ye can soon clear 'em out."

Inspection revealed that the junk was mostly Jamaica rum and other strong liquors, which we removed to the main cabin. But the crusted dirt of years was not so easily dispossessed. Silver, to do him justice, was tolerant of our initial efforts, and went so far as to procure us a bucket on a rope which we could lower over the side for water; but he wearied of such fruitless work after a time and hopped away to his hammock with admonitions to us to be satisfied "there ain't no nipper-bugs in them bunks."

We did the best we could, which was very little, and then persuaded Moira to risk lying in the cleaner of the two rooms—we had chosen it for her because it had a bolt on the inside of the door and offered her a degree of privacy—while Peter and I berthed across the companionway, Peter on the floor by reason of his bulk, and I in the one cramped bunk. And I marvel to say that we went promptly asleep and did not waken until the noon sun was flooding through the grimy panes of the cabin windows.

A rumble of snores assured us that Flint and Bones were in their berths, but the sound of a familiar brogue drew us aft to the main cabin.

"And what way will ye ha' cause for complaint that ha' seen men walk the plank and been to Madygascar and the East Indies and Afriky where the naygurs come from? On me soul, ye sicken me with your whining! Holy ——, man, do but look to me that am a pirate these many months, and all the fighting they will ha' throwed in me way was with other pirates—and them great, powerful rogues that give as good as we sent. Sure, I haven't been at the scuttling of any wan—"

"But ye had a cutlass to your hand and a musket on your shoulder," protested another familiar voice. "And ye walk the deck wi'out shoes to your feet, and ye ha' a fine bright kerchief to the head o' ye, and if ye seek to haul on a rope or hold to the wheel there's no man will say ye nay, Darby. But wi' me it's been lackey's work an' livery-shuits since the first day I went to sea. It's 'Ben, clear the table!' or 'Fill up the glasses, Ben Gunn!' or 'Fetch me the 'backy, Gunn!' I'm no more a pirate than the Irish maid—"

"Don't ye be naming her, or I'll lay the end o' a rope to ye! I won't ha' ye talkin' the way ye were betther nor ye are. Didn't the cap'n give ye to me for me sarvant? Sure, he did! '———— me,' says he when we took ye, 'Darby, you're a good cabin boy and main lucky. I'll give ye the feller to be doin' your work for ye.'"

"Well, there was one promised to take me out o' livery-shuits," answered Gunn doggedly, "and if he—"

He broke off as we entered from the companionway, writhing with the excess of embarrassment which visited him when in the presence of several persons. Darby McGraw was no less surprized and leaped up from the chair in which he had been lounging, bobbing his head to Moira with the vigor of a heathen kowtowing to an idol. All the boy wore was a pair of canvas trousers belted about his waist and a kerchief from which straggled his carroty locks. A cutlass slapped his thighs, and three pistols were stuck through his belt.

"Master Bob!" he exclaimed. "And Master Peter, too! And—and— Misthress O'Donnell—sure, there's a harp within me does be strummin' pretty music this instant!"

He grinned; and for all his months aboard the *Walrus,* his grin was as sunny as in the counting-room in Pearl Street.

"Ye'll be forgivin' me, ma'am, that am Irish meself, and must think o' the lakes o' Wicklow when I look to your eyes."

Moira clasped her hands.

"Wicklow!" she cried. "'Twas in Wicklow I was born, and my mother before me."

"Ah, then, 'tis glad I will be I met ye this side o' the world," he answered, clapping his hand to his cutlass-hilt very hardily. "For if we'd come on each other in Wicklow I'd be no more nor a gossoon of a bog-trotter and ye one o' the grand gentry-folk."

Moira's laugh had the note of fairy chimes I had not heard since her father fell on the *James'* deck.

"'Tis you are the lad with the silver tongue," she said. "But if ye come from Wicklow, Darby, it will be almost as if we were of the same family."

She suddenly sobered.

"And I, that might be elder cousin or maybe sister to you, must be asking why ye are a pirate? Were ye not honest-born?"

Darby's embarrassment was almost as painful as Ben Gunn's.

"Why, ye see—There was in me always the wish for the sea—I was no more nor a bound-boy—And Long John, he says—"

"Darby," she interrupted sternly, "how long will it be since ye confessed?"

He poked at his bare toes with the tip of his cutlass-sheath.

"Why, maybe—oh, a month this way or maybe that, I'd say—well, troth, if ye put it to me—"

"A many months," she asserted.

"I'll not deny it," he admitted, shamefaced.

"And you from Wicklow, Darby!"

"'Tis no fault o' mine when I couldn't come at the priest."

"Maybe no, if you held your ways in places a priest would frequent; but who would be expecting a priest in a pirateship? And what would the priest say did ye go to him and confess what ye ha' done? Oh, Darby, ye will be a monstrous wicked boy!"

Darby was overwhelmed.

"On me soul, I never meant to be! Troth, there's none will ever be repenting better nor me—if I do but get the chance. But do ye see, misthress, it will be the like o' this: Whiles ye lives wi' pirates ye must be main wicked, and aftherwards, when ye break free o' them, there'll be lashin's o' time to make up for it."

He sought to cover his confusion by rounding upon Ben Gunn, who had stood trembling to one side throughout this dialogue.

"What way will this be that ye act, ye lackey?" he demanded with an excellent imitation of Flint's manner. "Will ye be too stupid or feared to see we are waitin' our bite and sup?"

"Stop! Stop!" I intervened as poor Gunn started to scramble from the cabin. "How comes it you are here? Do I understand you have been relegated to your former duties by Captain Flint?"

"I don't know what relegated means, Master Ormerod," replied Gunn forlornly; "but I'm doin' my former dooties, yessir. I figgered last night 'twas all up wi' Cap'n Murray, which same I hears is true, and so I says to myself, I says, 'Ben, you go and tell Cap'n Flint here's a man as is glad and willin' to j'in up and serve him handsome, a man as is as good a sailor, give him a chance, as any afloat.'"

He shuffled his feet a moment, regarding me sidewise.

"Ye see," he amended, "I figgered as how with Cap'n Murray gone 'twouldn't hardly be possible for you to give me the new ratin' we talked about once. And then bein' the circumstances it seemed all ways fair as I should make the best deal—"

"Yes, yes," I said; "but what did Cap'n Flint say?"

Ben Gunn scratched his head in some perplexity.

"He said summat as how I was too good a lackey to spoil. And then he called to Darby and told him a good cabin boy desarved his own sarvant and here I was. And here I be, sir! Unlucky I were born, steppin' into a livery-shuit as page-boy, and unlucky I ha' lived. And unlucky I'll die, I reckon, sir. But I won't die in no livery-shuit, no, sir!"

With which he shuffled off.

"The ignorant natural!" snorted Darby disgustedly. "Him to be a pirate!"

CHAPTER XXI

FLINT'S WAY

BONES swaggered into the cabin whilst we were still eating, and his leathery face crinkled in what he intended for an amorous grimace as his eyes fell upon Moira.

"This is what I calls proper homelike," he declared. "You come and sit on Billy's knee, my pretty, and cut up this here goat for me."

I started to rise, but Darby was ahead of me.

"Do ye so much as put a finger on her, and I'll send a bullet into the black heart o' ye," he challenged in his shrill boy's voice.

"Oh, ye will? Ye red-headed ———"

"Me head's the ship's luck," boasted Darby. "The less ye say on that score, the betther for ye."

"We'll see to that!" snarled Bones. "You're the cabin boy, my lad, and no more; and I ———"

He tugged at his cutlass-hilt, and Darby, in no wise daunted, hauled forth a pistol as long as his arm. But before one could assail the other Flint shoved in from the companionway and caught Bones by the shoulder.

"What now, Bill?" he demanded. "Ain't we got enough to face wi'out you fightin' in the cabin?"

"And would ye ha' me take impidence and worse from this red-headed land-rat as Long John picked up in New York?" shouted Bones.

"I'd not," returned Flint. "Darby, you may be my good luck and a lad o' promise, but I'll lay the cat to your shoulders if you go for to make trouble."

"'Twas him was after makin' the throuble," answered Darby sturdily. "Wasn't he botherin' Misthress O'Donnell? Sure, I'm Irish, the same as her, and I'll kill the rogue that does be givin' her cause for to weep a tear—that I will. And I care not who he may be!"

"Easy, all," admonished Flint. "What's this, Bill?"

"Blow me for a dock-swab if I can see as how she'd oughter be set apart," blustered Bones. "I'm mate, I am, and if I—"

Flint's bloodshot eyes focused upon him with something of the silent force that I had seen Murray employ against his wild crew.

"You know better nor that, Bill," he said quietly. "Here Long John's just been to tell me the crew ha' demanded a fo'c'sle council, and God knows what Allardyce and his gang will be up to. And you want to bust into the middle of Rule Four. Gut me! There's many things I held against Andrew Murray, but one thing he did as was the wisest any gentleman adventurer ever done—and it's to his credit no less because Bart Roberts done it before him—and that was Rule Four."

"A woman's a prize, same as treasure," grumbled Bones.

"Oh, no, she ain't! A woman's trouble—she's no prize. You know what happens when there's women aboard a buccaneer. Jealousy, fightin', and as much blood spilled as in an action. We can't afford to lose no more men, Bill. Here we are wi' a bare ship's company left out o' five hundred men! I tell ye I'm for sendin' down the plank any man as draws a knife from this day."

"Much good it'll do ye," said Bones.

"We'll see to that. Anyhow, I'll ha' no fightin' over women."

He scowled himself.

"I'd throw the wench overboard if it weren't that she's my best chance to find the stuff Murray hid."

"If harm comes to her you'll get no such knowledge from any of us," I interposed.

"Oh, belay that!" he rasped. "You're lucky to be alive, and the one reason for it is that ye know what ye know."

He turned to Bones again.

"Now, mark me, Bill, lay off her. When we get this treasure cleaned up ye can take all the time ye fancy for wenches or aught else."

"Aye, when we do!"

"And that'll be sooner than ye think," retorted Flint.

"Wi' the crew all shoutin' for disbandment? Allardyce talkin' of goin' home tomorrow? I ha' seen ye handle some bad times, John Flint, but you're no Andrew Murray!"

The gibe annoyed Flint. His face turned blue, as it did when his temper was fanned or he was in liquor.

"Watch me," he snapped. "I'll learn 'em a few things yet. No Andrew Murray! Maybe not. But I ha' my own way, Bill. Aye, Flint's way! And it ain't so bad."

He suddenly remembered us.

"Keep your mouths shut, d'ye hear? No sneakin' up to John Silver or any one else. And as for you, my wench—" he frowned at Moira— "keep under cover, for your own sake as well as mine. This is a rough ship, a pirate ship, and—"

"Don't ye worry about Misthress O'Donnell," said Darby loyally. "I'll see to her."

"Oh, ye will!"

Flint laughed.

"You're beginning young, Darby. Gut me, what a lad! Well, you keep her out o' harm's way, and when we divide the treasure maybe there'll be an extry allowance for ye. How'd ye like to have her, eh?"

"She'll be better worth the havin' than all the treasure there is," flashed Darby. "And do ye be mindin' what I'm afther tellin' ye, Cap'n Flint. If harm comes to her, or sorrow into the heart of her, 'twill be the end o' your luck—aye, lucky ye'll be do ye come off wi' a neck ye can breathe through."

Flint went pale.

"Now, now, Darby," he wheedled. "Don't ye talk that reckless way. 'Tain't good for our luck. And I ha' been main kind to ye, and—"

"'Tis you would be the ruin of our luck," said Darby. "All I'm for tellin' ye is to be gentle in' handlin' an eligant young maid as ye ought to be on your two knees before this moment for the throuble and sore dismay ye ha' wrought wi' her."

"She's safe enough, Darby," Flint answered. "I'd never harm her. We'll keep her until we ha' lifted what's buried on the Dead Man's Chest, and then she and her two buckos can take a small boat and fare how they please, and—"

"And I'll be with 'em," added Darby.

"Oh, no, not you, Darby! Think o' all the red gold ye'll have aboard the *Walrus*. And there's your luck we'll still need."

"Me luck!" fumed Darby. "May the ——— curse me luck! 'Tis more of a nuisance than a help."

"Ah, that's no way to talk."

Flint was nigh frantic.

"Lad, would ye lose all your red head has brought us? And look ye, too, if the maid's to be safe, 'tis I alone can keep her so, for wi'out me there'll be ——— to pay, and none to stall the reckoning."

"And that before this glass is out," affirmed Bones with saturnine emphasis.

The mate knocked the neck off a flask of rum with his cutlass-hilt and poured the equivalent of a water-glass down his throat, gurgling it lustily that he might secure the full savor of the fiery liquor.

"I'll take the rest o' that!" exclaimed Flint eagerly. "Aaa-aah! There's naught like good rum to put heart in a man, Bill. Here, Darby, you finish it. That's the lad! And don't talk no more about losin' your luck. We're goin' to need that luck mighty bad these next few days. Aye, this very day, as Bill says. For here's Tom Allardyce and a batch o' chicken-hearted ——— ——— a-cryin' we should be satisfied wi' what we got, disband and save our necks. And I don't know what more bilge-slush."

"'Tain't Allardyce I'm 'feared of," said Bones wisely, "but Silver. He's got a head on his shoulders, Long John has, and all the men'll listen to him after the way he carried the stockade."

Flint nodded.

"True for you; but what you're amiss on is that John feels same as I do about disbandin'. After the treasure's all lifted, look out for squalls. But right now, Bill, Silver's as strong for pullin' together as you and me."

"Maybe," said Bones with more of doubt than conviction.

"Maybe? Gut me for a lubber if I'm not right."

Flint rose from the seat he had assumed.

"You come along on deck, and I'll show ye. You, too, Darby. No, no, lad—" when Darby would have hung back—"I want ye by me. I tell ye that red head o' yours is the best beacon I ever steered by."

At the exit to the companionway he halted and spoke to us over his shoulder:

"You mind what I said about the girl. Keep her under cover."

"Must we all remain below decks?" I demanded with some heat.

"That's as ye may happen to feel," he replied carelessly. "So long as ye don't try to suck up to any o' my men and make trouble you can go and come around the ship; but let me find ye up to mischief, and treasure or no treasure, I'll keelhaul ye."

His green eyes twinkled evilly.

"Maybe Murray told ye what that might mean."

He gave Darby a push before him.

"Run out and call the men aft," he commanded. "That's the boy! Bill, ——— ye for a low-hearted ——— ———, plaster a grin on that mug o' yours and pipe up a song. We mustn't let them swabs for'ard figure us to be worried none, eh?"

And his voice boomed hollow betwixt the confined walls of the companionway:

"Oh, a fine, tall ship was the *Elephant*
  As ever sailed the seas;
She came down-Channel apast Ushant
  Bound for the East Indies.

"And Dicky Lamb, he says to the crew—
  He was the bosun's mate—
'Pickle my guts! Will ye do what I do?
  Be game, says I; tempt fate!'"

Bones joined valiantly in the sweep of the tune:

"We are forty-five before the mast,
  And ten green clerks berthed aft,
With the cap'n, the cook, the mates and last,
  Simmy, the boy, who's daft.

"That's fifteen hands against forty-five.
  Christ! What an easy lay!
We'll take 'em at night, and dead or alive,
  Pitch 'em in Biscay Bay.

"Oh, that was a night the wind howled free,
  The sails froze to the mast,
And Dicky Lamb and the Portugee,
  They bound the cap'n fast."

They were out on deck now, and Flint stayed the song long enough to roar:

"Lay aft, ye swabs! Ye asked for a fo'c'sle council, and ye shall have it. ——— me, Bill, can't ye sing louder?"

"Louder!" I muttered to Moira and Peter. "Certes, ye might hear them on the Spyglass."

"Ssh!" reproved Moira. "I will be wanting to hear the rest of it. There, Darby is singing now—and others."

A score of voices took up the savage lilt:

"Sandy Grant bashed the mate in the head
  And dropped him overside.

The second mate they stabbed abed,
And so the ten clerks died.

"The cook they choked on his own salt pork;
But Simmy they couldn't find,
For Simmy was daft, and their evil talk
Had addled his feeble mind.

"He groped his way to the darkest hold,
With ax and bit and saw,
And laughed with glee as the waters rolled
In through the hole he tore.

"Oh, that was the end of the *Elephant*—
She's under the Biscay seas,
And she'll never more slant past Ushant,
Bound for the East Indies."

By the time they came to the last verse the whole crew must have
been singing. The roar of voices made the dishes quiver on the table
before us.

"A proper song, *The Elephant*," commented Flint's voice. "Barrin'
'Fifteen Men' 'tis the best I know. I ain't no preacher, but I can't help
bearin' in mind that every crew has some feller like Simmy, some
feller as always wants to scuttle the prize for his own satisfaction,
and never mind what his mates thinks."

There was no answer to this, only the slapping of bare feet on the
deck and the rustle of men crowded close together.

"Well, speak up, fo'c'sle," he went on with a note of satire. "What
d'ye seek? I've heard tell as how there was talk of givin' me the Black
Spot—whatever that may be—and sailin' home by your lones and
dead reckonin'. What's the argyment, I say?"

The companionway acted like a voice-tube to carry the deck-noises
to our ears; but hearing was not the same as seeing, so Peter and I
persuaded Moira to slip into her stateroom and ourselves advanced
to a position immediately inside the doorway issuing upon the main
deck, where the council was being held.

The scene was almost identical with that which I had witnessed a few nights previously when I spied upon Flints preparations to surprize Murray. Flint sat, as he had then, upon an upturned barrel, with Bones, Silver, Pew and two or three more. The remainder of the crew were squatted on the deck, a semicircular pattern of coppery faces and tattooed chests. The weather had turned warm after the storm, and practically all of them wore Darby's costume, a pair of trousers or breeches, usually slashed off above the knees.

Foremost in the ring of seamen was a tall, lanky fellow with rather long, yellow hair and a belligerent expression. 'Twas he who sustained the burden of the debate with Flint, supported to some extent by a group of a score or so, who sat behind him.

"Aye, aye, Tom Allardyce," Flint was saying as we reached our aerie. "You was the man all against attackin' Murray."

"Wasn't I right?" retorted Allardyce. "Didn't all happen as I said it would? Butchered, we was."

"Everything don't go right from the beginnin'," answered Flint. "But just look where we be now, mates."

"It ain't your doin'," asserted Allardyce. "'Twas only blind luck as the storm wrecked Murray and we rode it out."

"Ah!" said Flint agreeably. "Luck is right. The very words I'd use myself, Allardyce. For see ye, 'tis luck counts for the most, and I ha' been main lucky o' late. No man can deny that. Whatever I put my hand to turns out well."

This received a murmur of endorsement, and the yellow-haired man cried out—

"Luck is well enough, but all luck comes to an end, and I am saying that ye ha' stretched yours overthin, cap'n."

"That's moderate," admitted Flint. "I'd say myself as I'm for doublin' my luck. Ye see, mates—" he appealed to the several hundred men who thronged the deck—"my luck has won us eight hundred thousand pounds, and I'm for using it to win eight hundred thousand pounds more. And that's askin' less o' luck than ye might think, seein' the heaviest part is accomplished. We ha' three prisoners as know the secret o' Murray's cache, and all we need do is sail to the Dead Man's Chest, land a party and ferry the stuff aboard."

"Aye, and s'pose a frigate jumps us?" called one of the men sitting with Allardyce.

"Depends on the frigate, man," answered Flint equably. "A Spanisher I'd fight. A King's ship I'd run from. A Frenchy—I don't know."

"The ship's foul. We couldn't run," said Allardyce. "No, mates, I say we ha' eight hundred thousand pounds, and we'd better be satisfied wi' that. 'Tis a couple o' thousand pounds apiece."

"Aye, aye," came from a number of men. "Disband while the luck's wi' us."

"Disband wi' eight hundred thousand pounds more as good as in our pockets!" exclaimed Flint. "I never heard crazier talk."

"Better live wi' eight hundred thousand pounds than lose a third o' us to win twice that," insisted Allardyce doggedly.

"Not while I ha' aught to say about it!" roared Flint. "Gut me if I'll lose riches we all ha' worked and fought for just to please a handful o' swabs as haven't got the courage to risk a bit more."

There were expressions of opinion both ways upon this; the company was fairly well divided. And Allardyce proceeded to press his advantage.

"If ye talk about losin' riches, cap'n, 'tis you are willing to risk losing the eight hundred thousand pounds we have in hand. Ye'd go for the other treasure and most likely lose what we already have."

Flint squinted reflectively at the yellow-haired man.

"Now that might be a good argyment, Allardyce, if 'twas true," he remarked. "But it ain't. The truth is, I am all for makin' the treasure we have safe before we go cruisin' to the Dead Man's Chest. Treasure is a poison on shipboard if ye ain't got a sure use for it. That's why I had ye leave ashore the lot Murray moved to the blockhouse. It's out o' the ship."

Allardyce lost his temper.

"Aye, ye want it where ye can get your hand on it, and give us the slip!"

"How'd I do that, Allardyce?" inquired Flint softly.

"If I knowed how you were plannin' to do it I'd stop ye."

"Ah, stop me, would ye?"

"I would! There's other men ha' marooned or murdered the half o' a ship's company that there might be fewer to share in the prize."

"That's kindly of ye," said Flint. "I take that real kindly! There's some, Allardyce, as might draw pistol for that. No, no, put up your weapon! I'm a-goin' to prove to ye, whether ye like it or not, that I mean well by ye. I'll tell ye what I'll do.

"First off, mates—" he addressed the whole crew—"do ye or don't ye want to win eight hundred thousand pounds more wi'out havin' to fight for it?"

A fair majority were in favor of this.

"Second, mates, are ye willin' as the treasure we have shall be buried here on the Rendezvous until we ha' fetched back the part that's on the Dead Man's Chest?"

"Who's to bury it?" put in Allardyce sullenly. "'Tis easy for a few men to bury treasure so's none save theirselves can find it—and if they disappear suddenlike, what'll their shipmates do?"

"There's sense in that," agreed Flint. "Let's say as you and me bury it, Allardyce."

The yellow-haired man shook his head.

"There'd be one o' us come back—and 'twouldn't be me."

"Got a great idea o' me, ain't ye?" mocked Flint. "But s'posin' ye took along some friends? Would ye feel safe then?"

"How many?"

Flint turned to Silver, whose hard eyes had been studying the faces of both parties to the debate.

"How many would ye say, Long John?"

Silver's big face split in a smile of derisive quality.

"Seein' as you're one o' the party, cap'n, maybe we might say five—six includin' himself."

"Ye think he'd be safe from me wi' five friends along?" asked Flint earnestly.

"Six is a good number for buryin' treasure," replied Silver, grinning broader than ever. "And with you 'twould be seven—and seven's lucky."

Flint regarded him admiringly.

"Wouldn't ye know 'twould take Long John to think o' that? Seven is lucky, says he! Ah, yes, and who for? Well, Allardyce, what d'ye say? Will ye feel safe wi' six friends?"

Several men laughed.

"Yes," answered the yellow-haired man.

"Then that's settled," said Flint. "Pick 'em now. We'll start settin' the treasure ashore at once. You and your friends and me, we'll go off soon as that's finished. Bill Bones will take command o' the *Walrus.* Bill, ye'd better take her out east o' the island and stand off and on, weather permitting. If ye lie up here wi' naught to do, there'll be trouble, and men will be comin' ashore, and so we'll get no work done."

"How long will ye be?" asked Bones, smiling in a knowing way.

Flint hailed Allardyce, who was already deep in conversation with his group of supporters.

"How long d'ye figure it should take to stow away the two lots of treasure, Allardyce? We'll put the gold and coined silver in one cache and the bar silver in another."

"How do I know?" snarled Allardyce.

"'How does he know?' says he," Flint echoed gravely. "Tell ye what, Bill, you just stand off and on like I said, and when we're ready to come aboard we'll row out o' the Anchorage. That's simple enough, ain't it? No chance for misunderstandin' or aught goin' wrong."

Peter and I ducked into our stateroom as the two came aft. They went into Bones' room, which was next to Moira's, and for some time we could hear them talking in low tones. When they came out Flint was saying:

"Mind, Bill, an easy rein, but give 'em no slack. And leave the wench alone. 'Twould only make endless trouble wi' the crew."

Bones replied with a blistering string of curses.

"And ye were a fool," he wound up, "to let Long John make odds o' six to one. Why, even Murray—"

"Stow that!"

I could feel an edge of temper to Flint's voice.

"I'm sick o' hearing you prate Murray this and Murray that. I'll show this crew that Flint's way is as sure as Murray's."

"It's plum duff to Silver if aught happens to ye," remonstrated the mate.

"Don't ye worry, Bill. There'll be no man in this crew willing to lift a finger after I come aboard again. Where's my Flemish pistolets?"

When they were finally gone I looked an unspoken question at Peter.

"*Ja,*" he said.

"But six to one! Why?"

"He wants der treasure where only he can reach it. *Ja,* dot's it."

The morning of the sixth day I was awakened by a considerable clamor on the deck, and Darby McGraw danced into my stateroom, so excited that his brogue was nigh incomprehensible.

"Haste ye! Haste ye, Master Bob!" he cried. "'Tis Flint comin' off, and him by his lone."

I roused Peter, and we threw on our clothes and ran out upon the maindeck, which was crammed with pirates, staring in rapt suspense across the sta'b'd bulwarks. The sun was just rising, and the island shelved upward, darkly portentous, from the creamy lather of the surf. The *Walrus* was standing south, with the White Rock on her sta'b'd quarter and the entrance to Captain Kidd's Anchorage ahead. Outside the entrance, and pulling to meet us, was the gig we had left behind for the convenience of Flint and his companions. A single figure with a light-blue scarf wrapped around his head, rowed at the oars.

"But how be certain 'tis Flint!" I exclaimed. "His back is toward us, and at this distance—"

"Beggin' your pardon, Master Ormerod," said Silver at my elbow, "we ha' made him out wi' glasses. Bill—" he waved his free hand toward the poop, where Bones strode up and down by the helmsman—"is sure o' him."

The one-legged man sniggered and lowered his voice.

"Ye ain't surprized, are ye?" he asked.

"Six to one!" was all I could think to say.

"*Ja,*" agreed Peter, chuckling.

Silver sniggered again.

"Aye, six to one. A strong, desperate feller is Flint. Now what d'ye reckon he'll do wi' the map?"

"What map?"

"When ye bury treasure ye draws a map," Silver explained oracularly. "If so be as one man knows where 'twas buried and he has the map that treasure is safe till doomsday—'nless some one else gets the map."

"Well, he won't give me the map," I returned shortly.

"No-oo-o, it ain't likely. But if he ever stows it where ye can lay your hands on it or ye see him give it to anybody else you just remember as Long John stands your friend, gentlemen. Friend is the word, remember. And the old saw says as a friend in need is a friend indeed."

His black eyes glinted icily as they rested in turn upon Peter's face and mine. Then he stumped aft, shouting:

"Rig them boatfalls, mates. Stand by to hoist the cap'n's gig aboard."

Presently we rounded into the wind and came to, and Flint pulled under our lee, rowing slowly, with long, leisurely strokes like a man who is very weary but intent upon finishing a difficult undertaking. Now that he was so close we could see that the scarf around his head was crusted with blood. His coat and shirt were torn to shreds, and his shoes and stockings gummed with mud.

A man heaved him a couple of lines, and he knotted them carefully to bow and stern before he began to climb the cleats of the side ladder, moving stiffly but with unerring precision. As his face lifted above the bulwarks the men nearest to him gasped and trod back upon the toes of those behind them. Such a face I have never seen. 'Twas not alone the terrible blue color and the congested veins that bulged redly under the skin, but a suggestion of experiences beyond the pale of ordinary human understanding. His eyes glared savagely. His mouth was fixed in a grimace of hatred. In his tanned cheeks were riven lines of fear, of anger, of revenge, of cupidity, of insensate ambition—aye, and of remorse.

He dropped to the deck and peered watchfully around him.

"Well, here I be," he croaked. "Ho, you Darby, fetch me a bottle o' rum. Yarely, lad!"

Darby skipped away on his errand, white-cheeked and shaking.

Nobody spoke, and Flint laughed—oh, dreadfully!

"Ye ain't glad to welcome your skipper back, eh? How'd ye make out, Bill?"

Bones had shouldered a path through the clustering ranks, but even he was speechless before Flint's ghastly figure.

"We—we—we're all right," he stuttered finally.

Silver, only, seemed unimpressed.

"Ye were seven as went ashore, cap'n," he said apologetically, "and one to return aboard."

Flint laughed that dreadful laugh a second time.

"Aye, there's six stayed ashore, Silver; six tall fellows. Six, says you, and seven's lucky. Aye, lucky! Main lucky! And Allardyce says he's safe wi' six! Ho, ho, ho!"

"Where—where—are they?" questioned Bones.

"Ashore, I told ye, Bill. All safe ashore."

"Dead?" pressed Bones.

"Aye, dead as Harry Morgan—or Avery."

Darby dived through the jam with an open bottle of rum, and Flint stretched out both arms and tossed men right and left to make way for the lad.

"Rum!" he exclaimed. "That's what I need. Rum—and plenty of it!"

He bent back his head, put the bottle to his lips and drank—and drank. You could hear the gurgle of it as it trickled down his gullet.

"Aaaa-aah!" he breathed. "That was rare stuff. Get me another, Darby."

He tossed the bottle overboard, and started to sing a stave of that savage sea-song which was the chief delight of the crew:

> "Tom Avery died of a cutlass slash—
> Yo-ho-ho and a bottle o' rum!
> Mounseer Tessin felt the galleys' lash—
> Yo-ho-ho, and a bottle o' rum!

"But the treasure," spoke up Silver. "What'd ye do wi' it, cap'n?"

Flint eyed him for as long as 'twould take to count twenty. And I am bound to say Silver met his eye unflinchingly.

"Why, 'tis safe, John," answered Flint in the horribly soft tones he had employed with Allardyce. "All tucked where it'll stay safe."

"Aye, but where?" persisted Silver.

Flint's blue, mottled visage became convulsed with a passion words can not describe.

"Where?" he mouthed. "Aye, where? Ask on, man! Or seek it, if ye wish. Aye, go ashore. Lay off those ropes," he shouted to the men at the falls to which his gig was hitched. "There's a boat," he went on. "There's tools on the island. Ye can have food and rum. Go ashore if ye like, and stay—any o' ye! Search for the treasure till —— opens wide for ye. But as for the ship, she'll beat up for more, by thunder!"

He waited a moment, but no man accepted his challenge. Silver, indeed, stumped deliberately out of the crowd, with a far-away look

in his eyes that were as bright and hard as a pair of polished buttons.
"That's well," said Flint. "The course is so'west by south, Bill. We're
for the Dead Man's Chest. All sail, and a lookout in every top!"

CHAPTER XXII

"FETCH AFT THE RUM, DARBY McGRAW!"

MURRAY had predicted that the looting of the *Santissima Trinidad*
would send the frigates to sea from Santo Domingo, St. Pierre, the
Havana and Kingston, and the adventures of the *Walrus* furnished
ample confirmation of his words. Six days' sail to the southward we
raised the tops'ls of a lofty stranger whom the lookouts identified as
a King's ship.

Flint, summoned from his perpetual debauch in the main cabin,
agreed with them and ordered the helm put over. The *Walrus* headed
west, and the stranger followed her. She clung to us through the day
and night, and in the morning our glasses revealed the ominous belt
of gunports of a sixty-gun razee. But like all English second-rates, she
was clumsy in the water; and Flint was a good seaman, if nothing else.
He contrived to keep beyond cannonshot and during the second
night shifted his course cleverly and gave our pursuer the slip.

Yet he dared not turn back immediately, and we held on northeast
into the track of the Spanish *flotas,* passing four ships westbound in
the three days we continued upon this course. On the fourth day Flint
deemed himself safe from the razee, the *Walrus* went about and he
resumed his solitary rum-swigging in the cabin, drinking bottle after
bottle the day long, cursing and singing and shouting his bloody tales
and chanteys to an invisible audience that sat or fought with him.

For us three prisoners the *Walrus* was a floating bedlam. Moira
might not stir from her stateroom unless it be at night when Flint
occasionally slept and the most of the crew were carousing in the
fo'c'sle; but she never complained of the confinement that washed

the color from her cheeks, and retained her buoyant spirits despite the hideous danger which shadowed her every hour.

Without Darby she would have been in even worse case. 'Twas he spied out the moments she could venture abroad and thrust himself dauntlessly betwixt her and any threats. He carried her such food as she would eat and often did the same for us, for Flint was become subject to seizures of ungovernable ferocity, in the grip of which he distrusted all aboard the ship saving Bill Bones and Darby, and was in terror of unseen presences that lurked about the cabin's corners and mowed at him from the stern windows.

In these seizures he would take his pistols and shoot in every direction, regardless of who might be present, or with his hanger he would hack at the walls and pursue imaginary enemies along the companionway. But for Darby he would have slain Ben Gunn, and he did actually cut down one unfortunate fellow who goggled at him as he stamped out upon the deck, foaming and mouthing defiance of the ghosts that tormented him.

Darby alone could handle him. Bones he trusted, but would brook no interference from; Darby, however, could talk to him freely and sometimes curb his violence, providing rum was forthcoming whenever he demanded it.

In the latitude of the Windward Passage a Spanish lineship and two frigates blundered upon us unexpectedly out of a bank of mist. There was naught to do but run, and again Flint rallied to the emergency. That day we held our own; but in the night a moderate gale blew up, and the seventy-four was able to carry canvas that would have ripped the masts from the *Walrus*.

At dawn she opened with her chase-guns, and for five glasses Flint must jockey his ship to dodge the eighteen-pounder shot. Then the wind moderated, and as we hoisted sail after sail we commenced to draw away from the big Spaniard. She was a lubberly craft, and her captain was no man to develop her possibilities—as her gunners were unable to get upon a bouncing target in those slashing head seas. The frigates even yet, I think, might have overhauled us, but they were afraid to close and engage by themselves.

In the night Flint attempted to escape his pursuers as he had the King's ship by heading west toward the empty gulf of the Atlantic.

But the Spaniards were prepared for this maneuver. They had spread out to cover a wide area of sea, with the result that we passed almost under the bows of one of the frigates, and the flashes of her guns warned her consorts where we were.

Undismayed, Flint varied the trick the next night, lying to in that dark hour which comes before moonrise, and they passed us without suspecting the ruse. By morning we were leagues away on our back-track, and Flint boasted of his luck until he became maudlin, sprawling upon the cabin-table in a mess of broken meats and glasses that must have sickened any sensible man.

He had a sorry awakening from his fool's dream two days later when a stately French forty-four showed herself at our heels. Ah, she was a greyhound! Every foot of her hull was molded for speed, and her rakish spars were clothed with a sail area that drove her a good three leagues to the glass. Bones, with Darby to aid him, pulled Flint away from the cabin-table and threw buckets of sea-water over him to unlock the fetters the rum had fastened upon his brain. And he staggered on deck, cursing like a fiend, to squint his bloodshot eyes over the stern rail. In a moment he was cold sober.

"Gut me, 'tis a Frenchy! We're his meat, mates. But we'll sell for our own price, eh? Pipe all hands to quarters, Bill. Cast loose and provide."

There was muttering amongst the crew. This was what Allardyce had foretold, and the survivors of his group of protestants were not slow to exploit the opportunity. But the majority of the men went to the guns as doggedly determined as Flint.

"Fight, ye dogs!" he bade them from the poop, swaying his mottled blue jowl from side to side. "'Tis a noose or the galleys for ye the one way, and Davy Jones' locker the other. Betwixt the two ye may win free if ye fight. But wi'out fighting ye are ruined men."

The Frenchman disdained to use his chase-guns, so confident was he of bringing us to action at broadside range; but all the forenoon the breeze dwindled, and at midday both ships were caught in a dead calm. The frigate put out her boats, and so did we, and at once the advantage shifted in our favor. For 'twas one thing to tow a great forty-four, loaded with vast weight of metal, men and stores, and entirely a different task to tow the *Walrus,* of two-thirds the bulk and practically unladen below the gundeck. Moreover, the French sailors were in no wise so hardy or so desperate as the pirates, who knew that their chances of life were in proportion to the distance they extended betwixt the two vessels.

Flint swaggered around the fo'c'sle, swearing and urging on the men in the boats like the spectator of a horse-race who has staked more than he can afford upon the issue.

"We'll make it, —— me," he would say. "My luck's with us, I tell ye all. Here, Darby, jump on to the bulwarks and let 'em see your red head. Mark him, men! There's luck for ye. There don't live the man can stop me whilst the lad's with us."

And he would brandish his hanger at the towering sails of the frigate, lying slack against the yards, just out of cannonshot, and burst into the wildest imprecations and challenges.

"No Frenchman'll pull down John Flint! Aye, —— —— me for a —— —— —— if he will! I tell ye I ha' luck. Look to what I ha' done. There were three after us but two days since, and we lost 'em as we'll lose yon fellow."

His promises were justified amazingly. In the course of the afternoon we gained a hard-won league; and that night under cloak of darkness we stole silently north before a freshening wind, which by morning was a tempest. The French frigate disappeared, making the best of the heavy weather, and the *Walrus* was blown north and west for five days, past the latitude of Spyglass Island, past the scattered rocks and cays of the Bahamas, past the Floridas. Impossible now to watch for the tall spars of fighting-ships—as impossible as it would have been to fight them or for them to fight us, with the gray waves toppling mainyard high and the gunports buried half the time.

Flint had only dead reckoning to go by, for low-hung clouds and black banks of rain obscured sun and stars. Literally we did not know where we were, and our lookouts were peering through the scud for a landfall in the Bermoothes the morning the storm flailed itself to pieces.

It was this morning that the fever first appeared in our midst. I can still see the look, half-doubt, half-misgiving, in Silver's face as he heaved himself aft by one of the life-lines which grilled the maindeck and hailed Flint on the poop.

"There's ten lads groanin' in their hammocks, cap'n."

"Take your crutch to 'em," snapped Flint.

"Them lads is sick," answered Silver. "Bellyaches and headaches a-twistin' 'em in knots."

"They're soldierin' so as not to have to go aloft," returned Flint. "But if you're afraid of 'em, I'm not."

The first of the sick men he prodded with his hanger already was dead, and he hastened back to the cabin and fortified himself anew with rum. I heard him mumbling to Bones as he entered the companionway:

"It's main queer, Bill. I don't like it. Maybe my luck ain't good against sickness."

"Maybe," answered Bones. "What ha' ye done wi' the map?"

Flint's teeth gritted together.

"If I thought ye—"

"Belay there, John. I'm only thinkin' as if ye was sick some o' them swabs for'ard might try and come by it."

"Don't ye worry about that," advised Flint grimly. "It's safe—and it will stay safe."

A second man died the next day, and there were eighteen sick instead of ten. A panic possessed the crew, and Silver mustered a fo'c'sle council of frightened pirates, who whispered and nudged each other as they gazed awestruck at Flint's congested visage atop of the barrel which was his official throne. Thorough scoundrels themselves, they accorded him the sincere respect which was the due of one who utterly surpassed them in wickedness. He was "a rare 'un," "a main desperate rogue," "lead and steel was same as bread and meat to him."

"What'll ye have?" he growled.

"Well, 'tis this way, cap'n," Silver broached diplomatically. "The crew feels as the fever comes from the ship bein' foul and so long at sea—"

"We ain't been long at sea."

"Maybe not so long from the Rendeyvoo, but we ain't careened or cleaned ship this year."

"Whose fault is that?"

"It ain't nobody's fault. But it do seem as if we'd oughter run into some likely port where we could get sweet water and greens and check the fever before it runs through the crew."

"There's a many ports we could make," commented Flint sarcastically.

"We could allus head up for the island," interposed a man.

"So's ye could go for to dig up the treasure we just stowed away," snorted Flint. "Not if I know it!"

"There ain't been talk o' the island," said Silver hastily. "But what would ye say to the Bermoothes?"

"Too many reefs to pile ourselves on—and Hamilton is a port o' call for the King's ships."

"Them's the very words I said myself!" exclaimed Silver. "And what would ye say to Savannah, cap'n, which same is a quiet spot and has no garrison, seein' as Georgy is the newest o' all the colonies in Ameriky?"

Flint reached down to the deck beside him and lifted a bottle of rum to his mouth, going through the usual performance of draining it at one colossal gulp to the considerable admiration of the crew.

"Aaa-aah," he muttered, wiping his lips with the back of his hand. "Savannah, eh? That might do. But mind ye, men, I'll ha' no talk o' disbandment there or elsewhere. We'll stop by to clean up the fever and water, and when that's done we'll square off south and collect what's comin' to us on the Dead Man's Chest. I'm a man o' my word!"

Silver made quick assent.

"Fairly put. And the while we're lyin' off Savannah the frigates will be a-wearin' themselves out on false scents. It works both ways, cap'n."

"It'll work my way," rapped Flint.

He slid off the barrel, balanced dizzily for a moment and walked into the companionway under the poop.

"Darby McGraw!" he called harshly. "Ho, Darby, fetch aft the rum."

That night he had another of his fits, declaring that Andrew Murray was come aboard to slay him. He chased Bones from the cabin, hanger in hand, and was for setting upon the watch on deck when Darby restrained him with a bottle of rum, asserting it to contain Murray's heart's blood. Flint tossed it off with howls of infernal glee and retired to snore on the cabin floor, twitching and foaming at the mouth in his slumber like one possessed. The next day as we rolled in the oily swell under a torrid sun with the pitch pricking up in bubbles from the seams, the fever laid its hot hand upon him.

"Don't ye look at me that way, Gonzalez," he would scream. "Here, Bill, what kind o' shipmate are you to be lettin' old Ross in here wi' his bloody throat?"

And then he would turn pious.

"Ah, now, mother, ye'd not ha' me bide home all my days like a baby, would ye? Look at these gold jos. Ain't they pretty? I'll wager ye ain't got a friend as has a son can fetch her stuff the like o' that! No, no; don't ye ask no questions. Oh, dear Christ, what a pain I got! God, God, don't ye let me go this way. I'll build a chapel home to Tewkesbury when I find Murray's cache. A million and a half pounds, God; aye, that and more—and just you 'n' me to share it, wi' some for Bill Bones and Darby, as is a good lad and lucky."

He babbled childishly of his luck.

"Ye wouldn't break my luck, God! Oh, Ye wouldn't! There never was none like John Flint to rove the seas, John Flint as outwitted old Murray and was the end of him."

The droning voice would ramble on day and night, with intervals of exhausted sleep, punctuated by awful, explosive screams:

"Ho, Darby! Darby McGraw! Fetch aft the rum, Darby!"

And again:

"I'm a-burnin' in my guts, Darby. Ye wouldn't leave me to burn. Fetch me a noggin o' rum!"

Other times he would sing, and always the one song that had been my introduction to his company:

> "Bellamy's hangin' all dried and brown—
> Yo-ho-ho, and a bottle o' rum!
> A-rattlin' his chains by Kingston town—
> Yo-ho-ho, and a bottle o' rum!"

But words can not describe the horrors of the week which succeeded. For five days men died at the rate of three a day. Then the disease seemed to diminish in virulence, and although we had as many as seventy sick at once, practically all survived. As a rule, men who were stricken either perished within twenty-four hours or else made a slow recovery. Flint was one of the few exceptions, and I can only suppose that in his case the illness resolved itself into a battle betwixt a naturally sinewy frame and the weaknesses developed by the strong liquors with which it had been saturated.

That we three and Darby were untouched I attribute as much as anything to the measures which Peter took. He brewed a drastic purgative of rum, molasses and gunpowder, and he was insistent that Darby should procure a large earthen crock to contain boiled water which we kept in Moira's stateroom. Bones, Silver, Pew and those others of the crew who escaped the infection did so simply because of their physical vigor or perhaps because they were so accustomed to living in filth that the exaggerated conditions aboard the *Walrus* might not harm them.

A week from the day we steered westward we sighted the mouth of a broad river, crossed a bar at high tide and bore upstream between low, sandy shores overgrown with pine forests. On the verge of evening we rounded a point of land and dropped our anchor opposite a little, log-built town perched on a sandy bluff.

A huddle of merchant shipping eyed askance the splintered sides and serried ports of the *Walrus,* and there was a general tendency to slacken anchor-cables and allow us ample room. Ashore men scurried to and fro; several small cannon were run out upon the platform of the stockade, and the British flag was displayed.

Peter and I had seized the opportunity of the semidarkness to escort Moira to the rail for a view of our new surroundings, and we were staring hungrily at this outpost of civilization when the *thud-thud* of Silver's crutch sounded on the deck behind us.

"Ye might think from them goin's-on ashore as there was a mighty treasure in Savannah," he observed; "but bless ye, there ain't enough worth the takin' in that town to pay for the gunpowder to blow down the stockade."

I assented, and Flint's voice came faintly through the twilight:

"Fifteen men on the Dead Man's Chest—
Yo-ho-ho, and a—

"Ho, Darby! Darby McGraw! Fetch aft the rum, Darby McGraw!"
"He's main bad, Flint is."
Silver thrust a thumb over his shoulder.
"Won't hardly last till mornin', Bill says."
"Oh, poor soul!" exclaimed Moira. "And him with so much wicked-

ness to answer for! I am thinking he will have a great need of prayers, so if you will be after taking me below, Bob—"

"Bide a moment, mistress," interrupted Silver. "Ha' ye seen aught o' the map, Master Ormerod?"

"No," I answered briefly. "And I'll not be involved in your quarrels aboard this hell-ship."

"Easy, easy," he admonished me. "Rough words won't further ye, my gentleman. Here's me as will be glad to stand your friend, and you know best whether you need a friend. Figger it out for yourselves. Flint's as good as dead. Who comes a'ter him—me or Bill Bones? Which o' us would ye plump for? Bill, he's a desp'rate villain—and has his fish-eyes on the maid here.

"Long John, he wants treasure and a clean path home. I'm none o' your rum-swiggers and tavern-brawlers, gentlemen. I ha' had eddication, and I aims to get more. Give me a million and a half pounds to divvy, and I'll sack the old *Walrus* and ride to Parlyment in my coach, I will."

"What has that to do with us?" I demanded.

He winked.

"What has it to do with you, says you? Ah, what! Why, just this. I'm your friend. You stand by me and I'll stand by you. There'll be a 'lection of a cap'n, and if I knows this crew, him as has the treasure-map will come out on top. You get me the map, and I'll put you ashore."

Flint called out again suddenly in a frenzy of fear:

"Bill! Where's Bill Bones? Stand afore me, Bill. There's them here I can't face."

The guttural mutter of Bones' voice answered the plea. Silver cocked his head on one side, hand cupped to ear, listening eagerly. But the words were impossible to distinguish.

"No, no, not yet, Bill," wailed Flint. "I ain't a-goin' to die. Where's Darby? Here, lad, you come and sit by me. You're my luck, Darby. I can't die with you by me."

Bones spoke again, and with an oath Silver cuddled his crutch in his armpit and hopped over the deck to the companionway.

"We better go," said Peter. "Ja, we take der little gal to her room, Bob. I don't like this."

Silver reached the door of Flint's stateroom as we stepped inside

the companionway. We could see him distinctly in the light of the
fading sunset glow which came through the stern-windows. Ben Gunn
was crouching by the door, with his back toward us, hugging his arms
about himself and evidently eavesdropping upon what went on in
the stateroom. As we watched, Silver swung his right arm and dealt
Gunn a blow which knocked him head over heels into the main
cabin. The steward emitted one agonized howl and scuttled under the
cabin table. Silver wrenched open the stateroom door and poked his
head inside.

"Well, well, if this ain't a touchin' picter!" he remarked. "Bill, I see
you're doin' the kind and dootiful by our lamented skipper. But anybody as knowed ye would expect it of ye. Is that the treasure-map?"

"What are ye goin' to do about it?" snarled Bones by way of answer.

Silver backed into the companionway, as if in mute obedience to
a leveled weapon.

"Do?" he repeated. "That depends, Bill. We'll see what the crew has
to say."

"Aye, that we will," retorted Bones, and his voice vibrated with
undisguised triumph. "Who's to come a'ter ye, cap'n?" he added.

"I ain't goin' to die, Bill," came Flint's mournful wail. "Where's the
rum, Darby? I'm a-burnin' wi' thirst."

"Who's to come a'ter ye, John?" pressed Bones remorselessly.

Silver indulged in a mocking laugh.

"Aye, he knows what to answer!"

And Flint echoed him gaspingly:

"Bill's mate. He—has—map."

"Satisfied?" jeered Bones.

"I be, Bill," Silver assured him. "But we'll put it to the crew first, all
fair and reg'lar. And whatever they say, Bill, you remember I'll be
watchin' ye. Don't try any tricks wi' that map. I'm ready for ye, and
if ye start tricks we'll put the Black Spot on ye."

"To —— wi' you and your Black Spot!" roared Bones. "Get out o'
here afore I take my knife to ye."

Silver stumped toward us, his face distorted with rage.

"He has it," he rasped. "—— him for the shifty scoundrel he is!
Well, the next move is for ye to plot, Master Ormerod."

"I see it not," I said coldly.

"Wait till he thinks o' the maid here," replied the one-legged man and hopped out on deck.

From Flint's stateroom Darby's voice rose in protest.

"Take your hand off me, ye—Ah, if he wants the rum do be lettin' him have it! Sure, what will it matther—"

"'Tain't no use wastin' good rum on a dead man," said Bones, chuckling thickly.

There was a gurgle of liquor, and Flint moaned:

"Where's my rum? Fetch aft the rum, Darby McGraw!"

"Ah, ye black-hearted wretch!" shrilled Darby. "May the banshees whistle for ye, and—I'll not! Beware do ye touch me, I say, or I'll—"

The door of the stateroom crashed open again, and Darby was bundled out into the companionway.

"'Tis bad luck, and not good, I'll wish on ye!" he screamed.

Bones' ugly face was projected from the doorway long enough to squirt a stream of tobacco-juice at the boy.

"Be off with ye, ye red-haired rat," he growled. "You and your luck! Aye, 'tis fine luck ye brought to John Flint, wi' the rattles in his throat."

"Darby McGraw!" wailed Flint. "Ho, Darby! Fetch aft the rum, McGraw!"

The stateroom door slammed shut on the dying man's plaint, and Darby stood for an instant shaking his fist at its panels.

"May the priest fall dead that would be sayin' mass for your soul!" he cursed. "May him that offers ye bite or sup put the bitter poison in it! May ye never know sleep that will rest ye or kindness that— Ah, but what will be the use of it all? For there will be nothing but just the fires of hell to punish one that's as bad as you."

He turned wearily and saw me, and the tears trickled down his freckled cheeks.

"Oh, Master Bob, I doubt me the cap'n dead or close to it, and Bones he—he—drove me forth, for—for fear I'd spy on him, says he— and him wi' the treasure-map he blanhandered from Flint in his weakness! By the Rock o' Cashel, I'm finished wi' pirates. They're a poor lot. Leave us go home."

"If we only could, Darby!" I said.

He dashed a grimy paw across his eyes and gave me one of his shrewd looks.

"Troth, Master Bob, I'm thinkin' we're none of us like to live else," he answered.

CHAPTER XXIII

CAP'N BILL BONES

CLUMP-clump-clump went the heavy sea-boots up and down the echoing length of the companionway, and the mutter of voices beat an accompaniment to them.

"Aye, there he lies."

"—— me, was there ever such a mug?"

"Ah, but ye'd oughter ha' seed him afore Long John put the pennies to his eyes!"

"'Tain't right to put pennies to John Flint's eyes, him as handled onzas like other fellers does fardin's."

"Are ye daft, mate? Ye'd never put gold in a dead man's shroud!"

"Mebbe not! Mebbe not! Not to be sewed up, no."

"Ah, what's it matter? He's dead. The river'll have him—"

The clumping became a measured tramp as four tall seamen carried out the canvas cylinder that had been John Flint. A babble of grief from Darby broke the silence. We could hear him even where we three were huddled in Moira's stateroom, biding what the future held for us.

"Glory be to God, and him gone overside in all his sin! Och, St. Bridget and St. Patrick and Blessed Veronica and Holy Mark, do ye intercede for him! Let ye cry upon the Virgin to be speakin' for him in the heavenly courts. Oh, whirra, whirra, whirra, evil he was, and good in his way, and there's none by to give him the chance of purgatory!"

A roar from Bones.

"Stow that guff! Here, a pair o' ye strangle the mick if he'll not hush."

Darby whimpered and was still.

"Down-stream," continued Bones. "Here, to la'b'd. Ease him up. Where's that shot? Is it fast? Let him go, mates!"

A splash.

"And now who'll say as Bill Bones is not cap'n o' the *Walrus?*" demanded Bones, gruffly menacing.

Peter touched my arm, pushing open Moira's door very gently.

"Ye'll not be leaving me?" she breathed.

"Neen," he denied. "But we better hear what they do."

Bones was talking again as we stole into the deserted companionway. He sat on the barrel which Flint had been used to occupy. A battle lanthorn hung over his head, and the pale yellow light showed him to be nigh as drunk as his dead commander.

"—and to —— wi' luck! He was a good pal, Flint was; but he thought too much o' luck. I'm a seaman, I am. Give me sun and stars, and I'll steer ye a course. Give me sight o' tops'ls, and I'll fetch ye 'longside o' a prize. I'm no man for fuss, I'm not. Ye can ha' all the rum ye want, so be ye sail the ship and fight her.

"Now, what ha' ye to say? Speak up, any o' you swabs as is for trouble!"

Long John Silver spoke from the shadows, his words flowing smoothly with an insinuating, oily inflection.

"We better make it all reg'lar, Bill. You're mate, and you say as how Flint give you the treasure-map and says you was to be cap'n a'ter him; but reg'lar's reg'lar, and it don't do no harm to—"

Bones pulled a stiff, crackling sheet of map-paper from his breast, and waved it in the air.

"Here's the map," he declared. "Long John there was a'ter it, but Flint give it to me, as he says."

"Sure I says it, Bill," proceeded Silver, undisturbed. "But what I says, too, is as we'd oughter have a 'lection as the Articles provide."

A murmur of assent greeted this declaration. Bones scowled.

"'Tain't necessary," he returned. "I'm mate, and I'm the only real navigator ye got. But go ahead and 'lect whoever ye please—only remember I got the treasure-map."

"Yes, you got the treasure-map, Bill," agreed Silver, and his voice somehow became more hateful than ever. "But we don't allow as it's yours, ye know. You're what the lawyer sharks calls a trustee. You keeps it for the rest o' us, and we—" he chuckled venomously—"why, we keeps our eyes on you, Bill."

Bones swore.

"Get on wi' the 'lection," he adjured the crew. "Who's to be cap'n? Speak up and name some one!"

A dozen sycophants shouted "Bones," with a vim which inspired him with sweating vanity, and several called out: "Silver!" and "Long John!"

"Anybody else?" challenged Bones.

Nobody answered.

"Well, Long John," he leered, "it seems like 'twas you 'n' me. The Articles says them what votes for one feller goes to one side, and them what votes for t'other goes opposite. So, seein' as you're on the la'b'd side, I'll say them as votes for you goes la'b'd and them as votes for me goes sta'b'd."

"Suits me," grunted Silver.

There was a subdued rustling and patter of feet as the men divided, and the lanthorn-light revealed two unequal groups on either side of the mizzen, with Bones sitting on his barrel between them. Probably three-fifths of the crew had voted for him.

"Well, Long John," he said without trying to repress the triumph in his tones, "d'ye want to tell over the vote?"

"No," replied Silver briefly. "You win."

Bones rubbed his hands gleefully.

"Ah, I win, do I?"

"I said yes."

The opposing factions regarded each other like packs of wolves preparing to dispute the carcass of a fresh-killed moose. I suspected for an instant that they would fight, but I misjudged Silver's self-control. Galled he might be, but be did not permit the sting to his pride to influence his policy.

"You win, Bill," he repeated, "and I'm the first to wish ye joy o' it. And seein' as you're dooly elected, s'pose you tell us what your plans are for the ship?"

"Plans?" answered Bones warily. "What plans might ye mean?"

"Are ye for liftin' the treasure on the two islands or beatin' up for more?"

Bones reflected. He was not nearly so clever as Silver, and I imagine he knew it. He feared a trap, but study as he might he could not detect any pitfall behind the innocent question.

"I'll be guided by the crew," he announced triumphantly. "You're gentlemen adventurers, all o' ye. Name your wishes!"

This time the crew looked instinctively to Silver for a lead.

"We got plenty o' treasure in them island caches," he replied tentatively. "Speakin' for myself, I'm for collectin' what we got, takin' three or four ships and dividin' up for different countries, accordin' to what men seek. There's enough waitin' for our spades to make us all comf'table for life, and them lads as wants to go on the Account again can easy do it. Turn over the *Walrus* to 'em if they fancy it. I don't care. But some o' us ha' had enough o' the sea, and we'll try our ease ashore."

A shout of approval capped this speech. There was not a man but was lured by the prospect of thousands of pounds to spend on the right side of the gallows. And like all sailors after a series of hard voyages, they never wanted to see a ship again—or so they thought.

Bones was enthusiastic for Silver's plan as any.

"Aye, aye," he applauded. "Long John has the right idea. We'll water tomorrow, and then we'll try for the Dead Man's Chest."

And he began to shout drunkenly the song that Flint had died singing:

"Fifteen men on the Dead Man's Chest—
    Yo-ho-ho, and a bottle o' rum!
Drink and the devil had done for the rest—
    Yo-ho-ho, and a bottle o' rum!"

Other men joined in, and as if by magic pannikins of rum appeared. Bones drank several whilst we watched.

"You drink wi' me, bullies!" he hailed his supporters. "An easy skipper is Bill Bones. Rum for all, and to ——— wi' discipline!"

They howled joyfully over this, and what I had expected to provide a free fight seemed about to develop into nothing worse than such an orgy of intoxication as occurred almost every night aboard the *Walrus*. But it did not suit Silver's plans to have all restraint cast off at that point. He stumped forward into the circle of lant-horn light, with Pew, Black Dog, Darby and a dozen others at his back.

"Belay, mates," he cried. "We got a vast task to settle here. Time to carouse afterward."

"There's no time for drinkin' like the time ye ha' the liquor at your elbow," retorted Bones.

"And them's true words," assented Silver heartily. "And 'tis plain to be seen as you're a skipper the lads'll all be blithe for, Bill. But I was just figgerin' as we none o' us has ever asked the pris'ners how long 'twill take to dig up that treasure o' Murray's. So I makes bold to suggest we have 'em up here and put 'em through their paces. 'Tain't no ways right as pris'ners should be as close-mouthed as Flint let 'em be. He was a good messmate, Flint was, but I allus thought them swabs pulled the wool a mite over his eyes, blow me if I didn't."

I could see Bones slowly run his tongue over his lips, blinking his eyes the while. He liked this idea. So did the crew. They were in the humor for baiting whoever were at their mercy.

"Have 'em out," ruled Bones. "Long John's right."

"Aye, have 'em out," yelled the crew. "Make 'em dance!"

Silver's hard, polished-agate eyes glinted around the circle of savage faces and came to rest upon Bones' sodden visage.

"Run aft, Darby, there's the sweet lad," he said, "and bring us the pris'ners."

"Not—not—her!" answered Darby haltingly.

"Yes, *her*," replied Silver with a slight emphasis.

And one of his hands reached out, and his strong fingers tweaked the Irish boy's ear. Darby yelped.

"O' course, you bring her," Silver continued. "Why's she too good to tell us what she knows, mates? Just because she had Andrew Murray's favor, I wonder!"

"Not—"

Darby started to protest again, but Silver cut him off with a word that dripped chill ferocity.

"Skip!"

"Fetch up the wench, boy," growled Bones, "or I'll give ye a taste o' Murray's triangles."

"Fetch her up!" howled the crew in rabid chorus. "Let's ha' a look at the wench!"

Darby started toward us with the tears running down his cheeks. We could see him picking his way slowly through the crowd. A man kicked him as we watched. Poor Darby! He had been Flint's favorite, and there are always men in any crew to hate the captain's pet.

I looked at Peter, and he met my gaze with dumb foreboding.

"We might take to the water," I said.

Moira spoke behind us.

"You will do no such thing," she answered. "Nor will I. We are not yet in such evil case."

"You don't know—"

"They would surely overtake us," she argued. "No, no, Bob; we must wait and pick a better time if we can."

"Ja," approved Peter. "Dot's right. I t'ink—"

He hesitated.

"Silver will be nursing some hidden plan," supplemented Moira.

"Ja," he said. "How didt you know?"

"I guessed," she said. "Glory, I will have been listening behind ye this quarter-glass, for I had a feeling in me there was new wickedness astir. But here's Darby, and for his sake we'd best be going quickly."

Darby fronted us with a gulp.

"Silver bade me—"

Moira slipped between Peter and me and dropped her hand on his shoulder.

"Don't ye be taking heed to what they say," she comforted him. "Faith, 'tis you are the grand knight, Darby lad, and I am that proud o' ye I could be giving ye a bit of a kerchief or gaudy ribbon to wear in your hat—only that ye will have no hat and me neither ribbon nor kerchief! But let's be after trying what the rogues want with us."

And out she marched at the boy's side before one or the other of us could step ahead.

The ranks of pirates parted to admit our procession, and we threaded the shadows to the edge of the central pool of light where Silver leaned upon his crutch. He moved aside to make room for us, and I found myself at his right hand. Perhaps fifteen feet away Bones sat on his barrel, his coarse face flushed and shiny, his cruel eyes devouring Moira's lissome grace. The scores of others were just so many vague blurs to me, but Moira frowned about her with a kind of high pride that turned the boldest stare. Peter looked stolidly over the heads of the throng. It was his way when he fronted danger; behind their mask of fat his little eyes were darting daggerwise from face to face, probing, guessing, estimating.

Silver spoke first.

"Well, here they be, Bill."

Bones' tongue traveled the circuit of his lips twice before he replied; he did not once take his gaze from Moira.

"A proper wench, ain't ye?" he fawned.

"Do ye tell me so!" she exclaimed.

And the pirates screeched with laughter.

"Lusty, ye are," sneered Bones. "Ye need tamin', and I ha' a hankerin' to take ye in hand."

"'Twould take ten of your like," retorted Moira, nose in air.

Silver interposed in the midst of a second burst of laughter. I had to admire the scoundrel's deftness. He contrived to appear to be coming to the rescue of Bones in such a way as to rouse all the man's resentment against the cause of the implied humiliation.

"Sure, mistress," said Long John very respectfully, "what the cap'n would know is how long it should take to shift the treasure Cap'n Murray had ye bury on the Dead Man's Chest?"

Moira's nose remained in air.

"If ye were not afraid of the hard work it would maybe take ye as much as the half of a watch," she answered.

He addressed me with equal respect, requiring confirmation of what she had said. I gave it, as did Peter.

"And is it far from the shore?" he asked her then.

"Some would say yes, and some might call it over near," she flashed.

At that Bones slid off his barrel.

"Tamin' is what I said ye needed, and tamin' is what ye'll get, my girl," he announced. "Leave the rest to me, Silver. I'll take her aft and soon find out all she knows."

"There's Rule Four, Bill," said Silver quickly.

"Blow Rule Four! Murray and Flint wrote them blasted Articles, and they're both dead. Why should we, as are free gentlemen adventurers, have any tomfool rules like we was a King's ship? I'll take the lass and chuck five hundred pounds o' my share o' the treasure into the common fund in pay for her. —— me, lads, d'ye grudge your cap'n a little fun?"

Men shouted, "Yes," and, "No," but nobody was inclined to interfere.

"Come on, my pretty," he invited Moira.

She met his hot eyes with level scorn.

"Do ye put your finger on me, I'll either be the death of you or myself," she warned him.

He laughed uncertainly and started toward her, and as I lifted my foot to step between them the hilt of a knife was thrust into my right hand.

"Go to it," Silver's voice bade me. "Tell him ye'll fight for her."

I finished my step automatically and found myself a pace inside the pool of light surrounding Bones' barrel. Bones himself had come to a halt and was examining me with some evidence of disconcertion.

"He says he'll fight ye for her, Bill," Silver called officiously over my shoulder, and as Bones discharged a streak of curses, he muttered in my ear:

"Put your mark on her. That's old buccaneer law."

And as I still hesitated, scarce understanding him and unwilling to remove my eyes from Bones, who was drawing his own knife:

"Go on, ye fool! Anywhere! A cross on her hand'll do—wi'your knife!"

Moira heard him and grasped his meaning. She shot her left hand under my arm.

"God be good to ye, Bob," she whispered. "Sure, I'm yours."

And with the point of Silver's knife I traced a crimson cross upon her palm, certes, the oddest betrothal any couple ever had.

"Mistress O'Donnell is pledged to me," I called as loudly as I could. "Further, we had the word of Captain Flint that no harm should be done to her or any of us."

"Flint's word was no better'n mine," grinned Bones. "'Twas only as Flint had no use for women, but I'm different, and first, I'm goin' to ha' ye caught and flogged, Buckskin, and then I'll cut your ears off for a keepsake like."

He waved his arm carelessly.

"Pull him down, mates. I can't be bothered fightin' a pris'ner."

Several of his cronies made to obey this command; but Silver, Black Dog and a number of others set up a protest.

"Give the Buckskin a fair show," they shouted. "He's put his mark on her. Took her himself, he did, when Murray carried the *Santissima Trinidad.*"

Bones' friends hung back. From the rear ranks of the circle came advice and opinions of all shades. But Silver's faction must have been primed for the incident, for they worked up such a furor in my support that they swayed the general opinion by sheer volume of noise. Silver even raised Moira's hand with the bloody cross upon it and held it up for those behind to see.

"Fair play for all," proclaimed his stentorian voice. "The Buckskin was one o' Murray's crew, and he took the girl in fair fight. He's put his mark on her, and if he wants to fight for her he can, pris'ner or no pris'ner."

Bones observed the mounting turmoil with an obvious mingling of emotions. He realized he had been tricked, but he did not yet see how it had been done or comprehend the ulterior purpose of Silver's strategy. To do him justice, I do not believe that he feared me or doubted his ability to kill me in a knife-fight, for I had never had occasion to exhibit my skill with the knife before the pirates. He simply knew that he had been lured into a position where he must fight personally to maintain his authority over the crew, and the initial flare of his hatred was naturally directed against me. But he did not forget Silver.

"I'll mind this," he flung at the one-legged man as he crouched forward to meet me, knife poised across his chest and left arm extended to clutch at my knife-wrist or parry a stab from the side.

"'Tain't my doin's, Bill, if ye will ha' the girl," remonstrated Silver. "I warned ye o' Rule Four. And the cap'n's all the same as any other in a question o' honor."

"That's right," shouted a score of throats. "Cap'n's got to meet anybody."

"I'll meet some others a'ter I finish this swab," gritted Bones.

I circled away from him, gaging the effect of the swaying lanthorn-light upon the deck shadows and the feel of the pitchy planks underfoot.

"Stand to it, ——— ye," he snarled. "Don't let him break from the ring, mates. I want his heart for that wench to chew on—and mind the fat Dutchman doesn't jump on my back. He's a bad 'un, he is."

Silver was prompt to summon half a dozen men to block off Peter, who, having seen me use the scalping-knife of the frontier since childhood, was not in any way concerned as to what I should be able to do against a half-drunken sailor whose one idea of knife-fighting was to grab his opponent's wrist at the same time the opponent grabbed his, and then strain and heave until one of the pair tore loose and struck.

"Don't ye worry, Bill," counseled the one-legged man soothingly. "We won't let the Dutchman nor nobody else harm ye. Just you hop in and gut the Buckskin—if ye can."

"If I can!" hissed Bones. "Watch me!"

He dropped to all fours and bounded into the air in a clumsy fashion—not at all as an Iroquois warrior would have done it, hurtling like a projectile, with his whole body behind the knife. I stepped to the left and stabbed down, aiming to drive inside the collar-bone. But the light or something fooled me, and my blade slashed his cheek from eye to mouth, a great searing cut that laid open the whole side of his face.

He bellowed with surprise, and I was put out myself, for I had thought to finish him. Not a man moved for two or three breaths in the circle around us, for none had expected to see the fight terminated so quickly. Moira told me afterward that it was comical to see how Silver's jaw gaped.

Bones staggered back, the spurting blood blinding him so that he had to feel his way. I followed him slowly, half-prepared for a ruse, and he must have heard me, for he called out:

"Don't let him slay me, mates! I can't see, and he's a-comin' a'ter me!"

At this a dozen pirates jolted in between us, cursing and threatening me, and I gave ground toward where my friends were standing with Silver. The one-legged man hopped out to meet me. But I had scant satisfaction from him. He snatched the knife from my hand and, bending low, spat at me with a scorn words can not possibly convey:

"Ye bungler! As good as blind, and ye didn't do for him!"

And he swung by me on his crutch, hallooing to his friends:

"They're after Black Dog yon! Lay into the dirty swabs, mates!"

Knives were out all over the deck, and men were slashing and stabbing at one another. Bones was swallowed up in the mass of frantic humanity that milled around the restricted space between the butt of the mizzen and the rise of the poop.

A man plucked at my sleeve, and I spun about defensively to confront Peter.

"Where's Moira?" I panted.

"Darby took her. He has a plan for us to get free. Hurry, Bob! We got a goodt chance, *ja*. This is what Silver worked for, to hafe you kill Bones or set der crew against him."

I noticed that Peter steered me for'ard where the deck was deserted; but I asked no questions, for Silver's voice spurred me on.

"Lay aft, lads," he was shouting. "We'll show 'em what! We won't let no perishin' fool like Bill Bones go for to hold out that treasure-map on us. Couldn't even handle the Buckskin, he couldn't!"

Moira hailed us from the shelter of the capstan.

"Will it be you, Bob? Oh, thank God, thank God!"

"And your hand?" I stammered.

She pressed it to my lips.

"There!" said she. "If you will be so chary of other places."

I strove to redress my fault, and she lay for one precious moment in my arms.

"Are you sure ye will have meant it?" she asked shyly.

"Meant it! Since the morning I heard the lilt of your voice in—"

A low whistle came from over the side to larboard.

"'Tis Darby!" she cried. "He slid down the anchor-cable to get at one of the boats they will have lowered by the side ladder for the water-party was going ashore, and didn't."

Peter beckoned urgently from the rail.

"We don't talk," he ordered grimly. "We go."

There was a coil of spare cable handy, and we dropped it overside, sliding one by one into the jolly-boat which Darby held steady beneath the heft of the bowsprit. The *Walrus* had swung with the tide until her stern was toward the town, and Darby and I took the

oars and rowed quietly along the mass of the pirate's hull in the direction of the scattered lights that represented Savannah. How beautiful
they seemed to us, those tiny glimmers of rush-lights and lanthorns
in a clearing in the wilderness! They spelled safety, perhaps home.

But we were none too sure of ourselves yet.The big vessel loomed
over us, her gunports like a row of gouging tusks, her spars and rigging a monstrous net poised for casting. Her decks seethed with lawless men, fighting and running, with harsh outcries and the clashing
of steel and an occasional pistol-shot.

We passed the cluster of boats moored by the side ladder, unwilling to risk the time it would take to cut them adrift. We passed the
poop, where a particularly savage fray was going on. Men were battering at the door to the cabin companionway and one called to "roll
up a chase-gun, and give the ———— ————a round-shot in his belly."

We rowed on under the *Walrus'* stern, and there we came upon
an amazing spectacle.

A longboat was always towed astern for the greater convenience
in case there was a sudden necessity for its use at sea.This boat had
been drawn beneath the stern windows, from which a man was lowering a heavy box or chest, which a second man was receiving into
its bow.The man in the longboat heard the rattle of our oars and gave
us one lightning glance before he slashed at the mooring-rope and
leaped to his own oars.The tide carried him immediately behind us,
and I had a vision of a bloody face wrapped in an old shirt. If he
knew who we were he gave no sign. He huddled on to a thwart and
pulled downstream with the tide.

But the man in the stern windows was not so reticent. He leaned
far out, wringing his hands and clamoring to be saved:

"Oh, Master Bones, ye wouldn't go for to leave poor Ben Gunn as
stood by ye stanch to the end, and held the cabin door the while ye
shot the bolt. Ah, and them ———— villains are a-hammerin' it this
moment. Don't 'ee go, and leave me like this! They'll keelhaul me,
they will. They'll trice me to the cat."

"Back oars, Darby," I said. "We can't leave the poor fellow."

"And him with Bones!" protested Darby.

"'Twas not his fault."

We rowed under the stern, and I called up to the steward—

"Jump into the water and we'll pick you up, Ben."

"Who're you?" he answered shakily.

"'Tis Master Ormerod."

I could hear the blows on the door at the end of the companion-way.

"Hasten, man! We can't wait for ever."

"And ye won't put me in a livery-shuit?" he pressed.

"Not I."

He jumped without a word, and we hauled him, dripping, into our midst.

CHAPTER XXIV

HOME

A CHORUS of yelping certified to the invasion of the main cabin, but its note of triumph was changed to consternation as Silver's blood-hounds discovered that their bird had flown.

"Gone!"

"The —— knave's scooped us!"

"Boats, lads; boats!"

And presently the *click-clock* of oars behind us caused Darby and me to redouble our labors. We drove ashore several rods down-stream from the town on the shallow bluff, and we dared not wait to seek shelter within its log walls. Truth to tell, we doubted now that the town itself spelled safety for us. The *Walrus'* carronades would make short work of such defenses as Savannah had to boast.

So we pelted up the bluff by a sandy path that debouched upon the cleared fields outside the stockade, urged on by that persistent oar-rattle and the shouts the pirates exchanged betwixt their several boats. Whether they were following us we could not discover, for the night was black as a cellar-vault; but we left nothing to chance, and ran hot-foot through the plantations of the citizens, overhearing, as we passed, the excited comments of the men on the firing-platforms of the stockade, who evidently anticipated an attack from their ugly visitor in the river. We never tarried for breath until we had gained the verge of the forest.

Peter was now in his element. He could find his way about a strange countryside by day or night as easily as a sailor could navigate the trackless wastes of the sea, and he led us in a beeline north and east in the general direction of the outlying settlements which intervened betwixt Savannah and the Carolinas. An hour or so after dawn we emerged upon a village in a clearing, whose inhabitants eyed us dubiously until Darby produced one of the golden doubloons from the store he had acquired during his reign as Flint's favorite.

These people had never before seen gold, and for a doubloon and an onza they sold us an old but serviceable musket with bullet-pouch, powder-horn and store of ammunition, and deerskin garments for all of us save Ben Gunn, who stoutly refused to don what he regarded as only another kind of a "livery-shuit." They also sold us a small quantity of salt and flour, and put us on the trail to Charleston in the Carolinas.

Of our journey thither I can say only that it was such an Odyssey as the frontier-dwellers of our provinces have long been accustomed to. To Peter and me its perils of forest and stream, red savages, and wild beasts, were far less formidable than those of the sea, and Moira and Darby thrived upon the experience—so much so that when at last, brier-torn and footsore, we entered Charleston's sedate streets and found awaiting us an ample choice of packetships to the north we four were unanimous for continuing our journey by land.

"Neen," said Peter. "I don't ever go to der sea again, Bob."

"Ah, who would be fool enough in his ignorance to be wandherin' wet and bedraggled on the salt waves of the sea when he might venture the forests and be shootin' at the red deer and the bears and the catamounts and it may be an Injun, if he was in the full tide o' his luck?" snorted Darby.

"I seem to remember one was all for the sea, and would wave the skull and crossbones in anybody's face," I jeered.

"Troth, and I knew less then than I do now," he replied unblushingly.

"Them pirates was enough to break the heart of Pontius Pilate. Barrin' Flint, there wasn't a one of them would be able to hold his own against such as us."

"Silver might—"

"He was a clever one, Long John; but he'll be in throuble, you see if he's not," insisted Darby. "Too graspin' he is by half."

"I care not how much trouble he is in," I said. "I want never to see him or any of his crew again."

Moira, sitting beside me on the settle of the tavern-porch, twined her arm in mine with a slight shudder.

"Never again!" she cried. "And if it will be the same to you, Bob, we'll stay off of the sea. I like fine the clutch of the earth on my feet and the whispering of the trees. Men may be cruel on the land, but faith, they're never so cruel as the cruelest of the seafarers. And all my days when I hear the rumble of the surf and the suck of the tide running out I'll be thinking of himself that lies so far and lone under the Spyglass—and of Master Murray, God rest his poor bones, and many another. The sea had them all! Ah, Holy Virgin, what a hunger it has for men!"

But Peter shook his head solemnly.

"*Neen,*" he said. "Der sea did not take them all. They died from der greed dot cankered in their hearts. I do not like der sea, but der sea is der same as der landt. It works *Gott*'s will."

We were silent for a space, looking out upon the busy life about us, the negroes in their bright bandanna headdresses, the planters passing on half-thoroughbreds, the decent townsfolk in hodden-gray.

"And you, Ben Gunn?" I said to the steward who sat across the porch from us. "Will you come north with us? My father—"

He jumped up, writhing and twisting in an excess of embarrassment, aye, and with something of fear in his face.

"'Twas yourself was promisin' me I'd not ha' to wear a livery-shuit," he protested. "And before that ye said as how ye'd find me a berth as a real, tarry sailor-man, a-pullin' on ropes and standin' tricks at the wheel. Yes, ye did, Master Ormerod; and I believed ye, I did—though there's a many think naught o' foolin' poor Ben Gunn."

"I'll not fool you, Ben," I answered. "If you would go to sea, to sea shall you go."

And on the morrow I found him a berth upon a Barbados packet, cautioning him to employ discretion in discussing his past life, lest he be handed over to the Admiralty officials as a former pirate. He was our last link with the infamous company that had owned the joint rule of my great-uncle and John Flint, and what became of him or of the remnants of Flint's crew aboard the *Walrus* I do not know to this day. But from the fact that the *Walrus* was never reported again I have suspected that she must either have been wrecked or voluntarily abandoned by her people. She left Savannah within twenty-four hours of our landing there—so much I discovered by correspondence with a merchant of that town.

Did she put back to the Rendezvous and ransack the island's surface for the treasure Flint had buried? Or did she try for the gold we concealed on the Dead Man's Chest? Hopeless ventures, either of the two! As well search for a certain grain of corn in a heaping bin.

And what happened to Bill Bones? Did he elude the pursuit of his deserted comrades and seek an opportunity to lift Flint's treasure for himself? I'll swear that was his intent from the first—precisely as I'll take oath that had Silver been first to get his hands upon Flint's map he would have plotted so that only he and a small circle of his immediate familiars should have shared in the prize. Ruthless scoundrels, one and all! But perhaps Bones never won clear. Perhaps Silver fastened upon his trail and pursued him with that fantastic vengeance they called the Black Spot. I have often wondered what it might be.

As to the treasure, they are welcome to it or any part of it if they can find it. Moira and I talked over the desirability of notifying her Jacobite friends of the hoard that was buried on the Dead Man's Chest, and for a time she leaned toward this course; but after she had dwelt a while in the Hanoverian prosperity of New York she revolted against the idea of taking any step which would embroil the peace of the realm, and any lingering doubts in her mind were dissipated by the titanic conflict of the Seven Years' War, with its world-wide convulsion of nations that set armies marching to battle all the way from the parched plains of India to the forests of our wilderness country.

"Here is no time to think of Hanoverian or Jacobite," said she. "We will all be English together."

"Der Irish, too?" asked Peter gravely.

"Troth, the Irish will be the best English!" she cried. "Unless it be the Dutch."

But I am galloping ahead of my story. Drop back across the years—'tis no more of an effort than it was for us to slide down the cable over the bow of the *Walrus* that night off Savannah—to the settle on the porch of the tavern in Charleston. Ben Gunn was disposed of; our plans were made for the northward journey along the seaboard. All that remained to be done was to come by a priest to wed Moira and me; and that, it seemed, was impossible short of Baltimore, in Maryland. Yet at the last our luck held, for the day we were to start turned stormy and we delayed our departure; and that afternoon a French West Indiaman put into the harbor under stress of the weather. Among her company was a kindly Franciscan, and he readily agreed to perform the ceremony.

For the rest, we rode into New York about four of the clock on the afternoon of April the 24th, in the year 1755. My father was in the counting-room of our house in Pearl Street, and he came to the door at the sound of the horses' hoofs on the cobbles. The sun was sloping out of the west full into his eyes; and for the time that it took me to dismount and swing Moira down from her saddle he stood dazed, fearful lest the dazzling light was playing tricks with him.

"Is it truly you, Robert?" he cried. "But it must be, for there are Peter and Darby."

"Yes, father," I answered. "And I have brought home another."

He opened his arms with an eager smile.

"There's room here for two of you, boy. Certes, you have but followed in my footsteps and fetched home a wife from your adventures."

"She is the little Irish maid I—"

"Whoever she is, she's more than welcome. But come in, come in, the pair of you. Safe and well—and with a wife! Robert, I can scarce credit it. After a whole year! Peter, God bless you! I knew with you he'd come to no harm. Ah, Darby, you have more sense in that red noddle of yours than when you left here; and if you stuck by Master Robert y'are forgiven. What a tale you'll all have to tell!"

That night as I lay in the upper room I had occupied since childhood I was aroused by a distant clatter and jangling which became louder and louder. At the corner it broke off with a heavy clang, and a pompous voice proclaimed:

"Past twelve o'clock of a fine, bright night, and Master Robert Ormerod is home from his captivity amongst the West Injin pirates. God save the King and the worshipful magistrates of New York!"

'Twas Diggory the watchman; and, listening to him, I recalled how Silver had cozened him the night I was kidnaped, and thereat I fell a-chuckling until Moira stirred sleepily and complained—

"'Tis an ill thing if ye'll not sleep the first night we will be in your own home, Bob."

"No, no, sweetheart," I said. "I was but thinking what an odd bundle of accident is this life we live. For if that fellow braying upon the corner had not been a stupid fool I should never have seen you after I took you to the Whale's Head."

"Do you think so!" she retorted. "Then 'tis you will be the fool, for if Captain Murray had not carried you after me I should have contrived to return to New York, though it kept me treading the highways and byways of the world come fifty years. Now get you to sleep! I am none of your wives to encourage a husband in loose fancies and romantical longings. Your wandering days are by and done with, and the sooner you square your back on them the better will I be pleased. I'll not let you forth again, and of that you may be prime confident!"

So I turned over and went to sleep.

CLASSICS OF NAUTICAL FICTION

"Marryat has the power to set us in the midst of ships and men and sea and sky all vivid, credible, authentic."
—Virginia Woolf

". . . [Marryat's] greatness is undeniable"
—Joseph Conrad

"This was Marryat's navy, his world, and no one brings it to us with greater authenticity."
—Alexander Kent

"When all your Patrick O'Brians are out, recommend Marryat."
—*Library Journal*

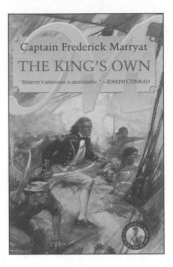

THE KING'S OWN
By Captain Frederick Marryat
352 Pages
$15.95, trade paperback
ISBN: 0-935526-56-0

WILLIAM SEYMOUR grows up on shipboard in the Royal Navy, after his father is hanged during the Mutiny at the Nore (1797). Later, our young hero is impressed into the crew of a daring smuggler. This amusing and exciting novel blends in the classic true tale of an English captain who deliberately lost his frigate on a lee shore, in order to wreck a French line-of-battle ship.

Available at your favorite bookstore, or call toll-free:
1-888-BOOKS-11 (1-888-266-5711).
Or visit the McBooks Press website
http://www.McBooks.com

More classic sea stories (including three other books by Captain Frederick Marryat) are available in the McBooks Press Classics of Nautical Fiction Series. To request a complimentary catalog, call 1-888-BOOKS-11.